"Pleasure to meet a fellow jazz enthusiast."

She shifts the hair away from her face again, her slender claws brushing the strands aside as her yellow eyes remain focused on me. I know for a fact I've got a stupid grin on my face, but I hope to high heaven that my dumb caveman cheeks ain't glowing. My ex-wife always teased me about blushing; it was one of a hundred things that gradually turned from a cute jab to a searing critique as our marriage fell apart.

All the same, I feel a twinge in my heart. I've got no earthly clue why; this is a velociraptor broad. I mean—she's pretty, as far as dinosaurs go, but—nah. That shit doesn't happen. Species stick to their lanes, even today. I think I'm just happy that I actually met someone else who enjoys the same music I do. A dinosaur, even...

A dinosaur that enjoys jazz, music that most dinosaurs rebuke as muddy, pointless noise made by neanderthals banging objects together and blowing into hunks of metal and wood.

She pauses for a moment to think before opening her mouth to speak again.

I'd have loved to have heard what she was gonna say next, if it weren't for the gunshots that interrupted her.

Books by JT Kamp

THAT OLD YORK TONE
Kind of Blue

Kind of Blue

Book One of That Old York Tone

—

JT Kamp

This book is a work of fiction. Names, characters, places, and incidents are the product of the author's imagination or are used fictitiously. Any resemblance to actual events, locales, or persons, living or dead, is coincidental.

Copyright © 2025 by JT Kamp

Cover Illustration and Design by HOc2pus
Cover Layout by Ryanon Ryker

No part of this book may be reproduced, or stored in a retrieval system, or transmitted in any form or by any means, electronic, mechanical, photocopying, recording, or otherwise (other than for review purposes), without express written permission of the publisher.

First Edition: March 2025

ISBN-13: 9798313580791

For Rachel M.

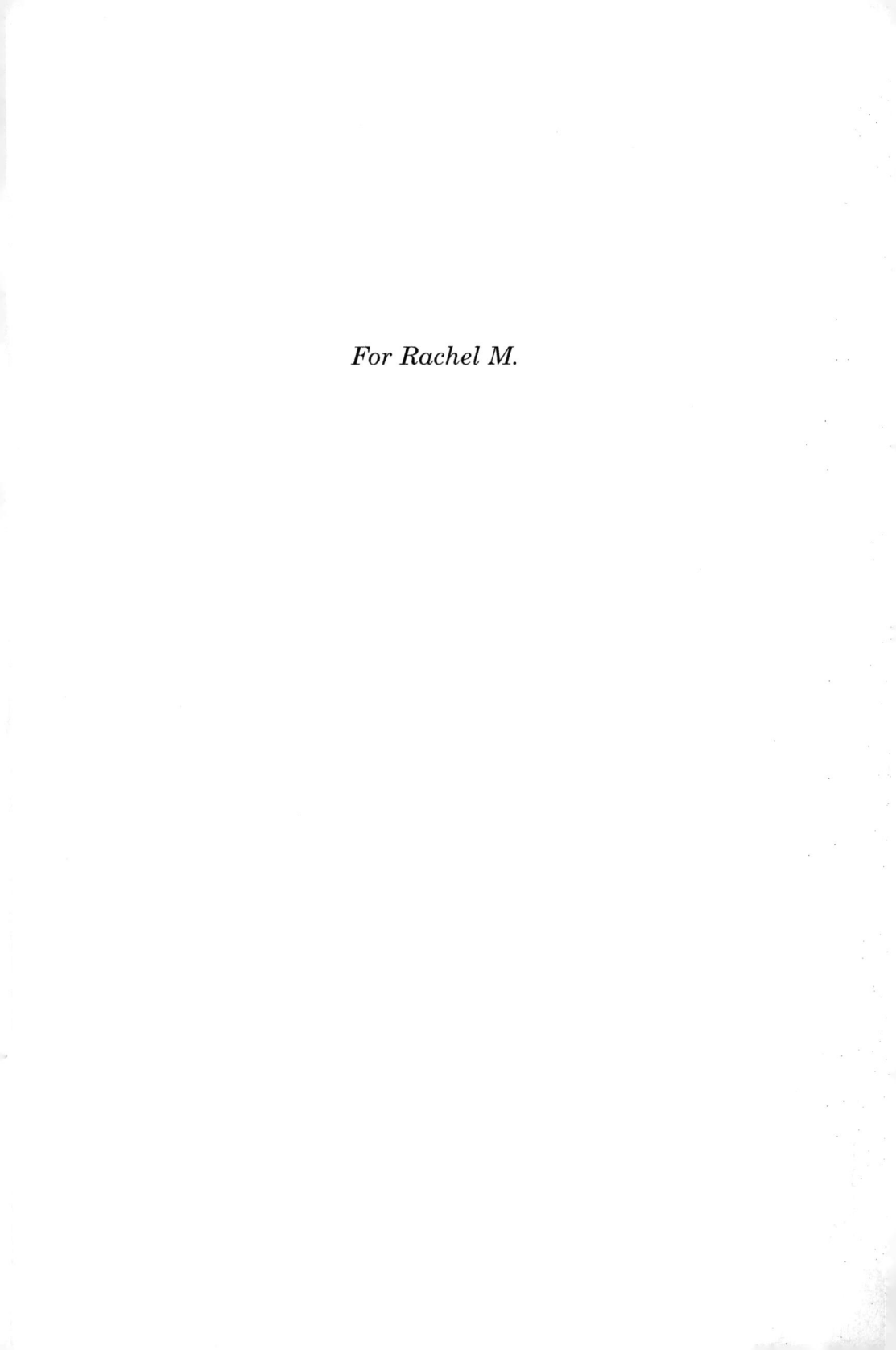

Chapter One: Samuel

"—onna be another hot one out there, so be sure to throw an extra ice pack into your lunch pail, fellas! It's 6:00 AM, and that means it's time for living legend Miles Cratis and his smokin' hot single, 'So What'."

The slow piano and double bass intro doesn't quite knock the weariness away from my eyelids. However, when the trumpet kicks into motion, the lingering hold of sleep is scattered to the wind by its piercing, perfectly timed notes. Sitting up from my prone position, the sheet draped over my mattress rises with me, affixed to the skin on my back with a thin adhesive layer of sweat. That radio jockey was right about two things: Miles Cratis is a living legend... and it's another damn hot one today.

Swinging my legs over the side of the twin-sized bed, I roll my neck and stretch my back, hearing a few more pops and cracks than I'd like to. I don't exactly *feel* old, but that rotten bastard Father Time keeps marching forward, dragging my ass along with him. But twenty-five ain't that old, right? I mean, Miles Cratis was twenty-five when he released his first record, so I still got time to get my act together.

My head rocks in rhythm with the song, one I've heard a

hundred times now but still haven't gotten sick of. This radio alarm clock is one of the best investments I've ever made; I'd give anything in the world to be able to wake up to music like this. O'course, I try not to think about the fact that I practically *did* give up everything else for this clock. The house, the car, the record player... hell, the only other thing worth a damn I got to keep from the divorce was—

"Woof!"

My eyes shift down to the shaggy carpet staring back up at me, his beady black eyes barely visible past the strands of curled white fur that hang over his head. His long tongue dangles out of his panting mouth as he looks to me expectantly.

"Good morning to you, too, Saxon. But what did I tell you about that barkin' shit? The neighbors are already pissy enough with how big your ass is, we don't need no more complaints to the landlord, ya hear me?"

Saxon lets out a quieter "Boof" in acknowledgment.

"That's better. Let's get you some water, ya lunk."

He rises to all fours and follows me across the meager abode to the kitchen. "Luxury Apartments", my ass. The only thing luxurious about this hole is the fact that the morning sun doesn't nail me in the eyes through my blindless window, and that's only because of that skyscraper they finished putting up across the street.

Old York City. "A City on the Rise", they call it. Sure. Rising rent prices. Rising crime rates. Rising drug abuse. About the only thing that ain't rising around here is job security, and if I don't have my ass in Mr. Fontana's office at 7:00 AM sharp, I'll be looking for a new job at 7:01.

I let the stress of my tenuous employment situation drain away just as smoothly as Cratis's trumpeting melts into John Coalmane's sultry sax. My head unconsciously bobs along to the tune as I twist the kitchen faucet's knob, filling the large bowl lying in the sink with water. Once it's topped off, I set it on the wooden floor atop its discolored circular groove. Saxon instantly sets to work on improving his art installation by clumsily lapping water into his mouth, launching just as much liquid out of the bowl in his thirsty dervish. Ah well, fuck my security deposit.

The cupboard door suspended above the sink creaks open and I grab another two bowls. In one, I dump a heaping helping of dog kibbles from a box adorned with a smiling face not unlike that of my oaf of a roommate. In the other, I pour a similar serving of human kibbles. The cereal box features a small boy wielding a spoon, the child's gormless grin an almost perfect mirror of the dog food mascot's dopey canine mouth.

I throw the refrigerator door open, feeling a blessed blast of cold air roll over my sweat-soaked form. I know the power company advises you to not use your fridge to cool your home, but when you're in a little shithole like mine without an air conditioner, you're tempted to tell the power company to piss off. I reluctantly close the fridge, milk bottle in hand, and return to the two bowls.

Uhh... Which one was the cereal, again?

Damn it. I've made this mistake before, and I'm not about to do it again. They need to make this shit look a little different. I pluck a morsel from one of the two identical bowls and gingerly place it in my mouth.

That's fuckin' dog food.

I spit the partially chewed chunk of meat byproduct and sawdust into the sink before placing the bowl containing Saxon's feast in front of him. He scarfs it down before I even finish putting the cap back on the milk bottle after dousing my own breakfast. He eagerly follows me the two steps it takes to get from the kitchen counter to the tiny one-chair table stuffed into the corner, staring up at me and panting as I begin shoveling my slightly less disgusting breakfast into my face.

I feel a little bad for the poor guy. I'm at work for ten hours a day and asleep for another seven, so I don't exactly have a lot of time to take care of him. Plus, with this heat and his shaggy mane I'm sure he's hotter than a witch in Salem. I should bring him into a pet groomer, but money's been so tight recently. I could just take a pair of scissors to him, I suppose. Can't do any worse on him than I do on myself.

Setting both our empty bowls in the sink, I top off Saxon's water once more before making my way into the bathroom. I don't need to let the shower heat up today, I'm jumping in while it's ice cold. I'd much prefer my testicles shriveling up to literally melting off my body in this God-forsaken heat. I lather myself up, washing away a day's worth of sweat and grime. My work isn't particularly dirty, but lumping crates and boxes off of trucks can build up a layer of yuck. I really should shower before I go to bed so I don't make my sheets gross. Well. With this weather, I'll be sweating through the whole night anyway, so what's the difference?

I run my shampoo-laden fingers through my mop of brown hair. A haircut would probably help me feel better in this heat, and I certainly don't want to come across as one of those beatniks, but I just like the feeling of it being a few fingers longer than average. My ex-wife never let me grow it out; nagged me relentlessly if it was even a quarter inch past her preferred length. Fucking control freak. Thank God I got out of that mess of a relationship, even if I did lose my early twenties in the process. Double thank God we didn't have any kids together.

The arid heat once again makes itself apparent as I shut off the water and step out of the shower. I barely begin toweling off before—

"Boof."

"Yeah, yeah. I know you gotta take a dump, gimme a

minute." I slap some deodorant under my arms and brush my teeth, still listening to the jazz resonating from the bedside radio. "So What" ended a few minutes ago; now they're playing something by Charlie Larker. One of his tracks from several years ago, before he died. I missed the radio jockey saying the name on account of being in the shower, but I recognize the tune. I wouldn't call myself a jazz whiz by any means, but I know enough to tell a Yardbird from a Duke.

Unfortunately, I can't spend any more time listening or else I'll be late for work, and late for work means finding new work. I throw on a pair of clothes, tame my hair with a quick pass of a comb, and make my way out of the apartment with an eager sheepdog in tow. The fourth floor means we've got a handful of steps to descend; I've trained Saxon pretty well to follow me down the stairs so he doesn't go barreling through at full speed and knock Mr. Garbowitz on his ass. I happen to like the old codger, and I'd hate to see him break his neck on account of my dumb dog.

Once I throw open the front door of the apartment building, however, Saxon is a blur of white, launching past me and toward his favorite patch of grass to pop a squat and do his dirty work. I take the opportunity to collect the paper from the front stoop. It's not technically my subscription to the newspaper, but if I carry it up to Mr. Garbowitz's door for him he doesn't mind if I read it for a couple minutes in the morning. Leaning against the handrail next to the steps, I unfold the paper and give it a quick scan:

The Old York Times
Monday, August 24th, 201M1959 BC

"8 Prisoners Killed by Fire At Crowded Jail in Old Jersey"—Sheesh, that sucks. Downers on the first page.

"*Steel Industry Wants U.S. to Act if Impasse Persists*"—I thought about working toward becoming a steel worker, but so many of those guys in this area end up getting saddled with building those skyscrapers, and I am *not* good with heights. Wonder what this "impasse" is?

"*Plan to Put Man Into Space Lags*"—Heh. Good fuckin' luck. It'll probably be 201M2000 BC before we get a man on the moon.

"*G.O.P. For Delay On Civil Rights*"—Civil Rights, huh—

"Get the *fuck* out of my way, *skinnie!*" The slur tumbling past an all-too familiar muzzle startles me out of my headline-skimming daze. Instinctively, I push myself as far to the side of the staircase as I can, bending backward over the railing as the hulking form of the voice's owner shoves past me. He turns toward me three steps below where I stand, which puts us at eye level with one another.

I avert my eyes, dodging away from his imposing glare. "S-sorry, Roger. I didn't see ya."

He snorts, his impressively long blood red tail flicking back and forth as he leers at me. "People got places to be. You're holding me up, you spear-chucking shit."

I still don't meet his gaze, only registering the crimson of his eyes through my peripheral vision. "I-I was just heading to work myself, Roger. I didn't mean t—"

"What kind of place would employ a skinnie like you? It ain't a place I'm interested in patronizing." I blink, unsure if he's sincerely asking me to tell him where I work. I don't want to start trouble with this guy, but I also don't want him knowing that kind of information. Last thing I need is him trying to come around and tell my boss that I shouldn't be employed there just because I'm a human.

Mercifully, Roger gets distracted by Saxon staring up at him, happily panting as he sits on the sidewalk. He glances from my dog to the fresh-squeezed present he left on the grass. His head whips back around to me, the pronounced ridges above his allosaurus eyes angling down sharply. His diamond-shaped pupils contract in fury and his razor-toothed scowl forces me to shrink back further. "Are you gonna clean up after your *fuckin'* dog or what, you disgusting troglodyte?! It's not enough that I have to hear that fuckin' thing stomping around at all hours, I gotta look at its shit, too?!"

"I—sorry! Yeah! I'll get it!" I sidle past him, being careful to not come into contact with any part of his scaled body lest he view that as an act of aggression and rip my head clean off my shoulders. I quickly pull one of the small bags from my pocket and scoop up Saxon's leavings. As I toss the bag in the nearby garbage can and stand upright again, Roger is an arm's length away, his towering height even more apparent as he looms over me. He utilizes the closed distance to jab a sharp claw into my chest.

"You keep that mongrel under control or I'll have the landlord kick your ass to the curb. You got that, you skinnie prick?!"

I look away again. "Y-yeah. Sorry, Roger. I'll do better with him." I glance down at Saxon who continues to look up at me with a slack-tongue smile on his face. Thank God he doesn't view my downstairs neighbor as a threat; if he started growling at Roger it'd likely be the last thing the big walking carpet did before ascending to doggie heaven. And you can bet your ass the police wouldn't spend very long looking into the matter.

With a triumphant smirk, Roger finally removes his finger from my chest and stomps down the sidewalk away from me, jamming his hands into his pockets as he goes. I let out a sigh of relief before starting the usual fare of internally beating myself up for being such a pussy. If I had more of a backbone I wouldn't stand for being treated like this. I mean, yeah, things still aren't easy for us humans and cro magnons, but they're a hell of a lot better than they were thirty years ago. Still, most dinosaurs view us as second class citizens. Old York is one of the most progressive places in the country, and even here the prejudice is inescapable.

And what would standing up to Roger and his barrage of derogatory slurs even do? Probably earn me an early grave. Dinosaurs are fuckin' terrifying with how strong they are—it's a big reason why they were so much higher on the pecking order than us skinbags for so long. Sure, humans and cro magnons came up with tools a little earlier, but it's because we don't have built-in spears and cudgels on our fingers and tails like most of those scaled bastards got.

I look down at Saxon once more, realizing I'm running low on time. With a flick of my head I gesture for him to follow me back upstairs, and he obeys. My apartment is sandwiched between two other similarly sized buildings, sharing walls on all sides with the behemoth of a structure taking up this city block. An apartment amidst apartments, a building amidst buildings, somewhere in the labyrinthine expanse of Brachlyn. And I'm one guy out of over eight million humans and dinosaurs that call this place home.

On the second floor landing, I toss the newspaper onto the doormat in front of Mr. Garbowitz's apartment. It's still early, and since he's retired he likes to sleep in 'til about eight. Like Roger, Mr. Garbowitz is a dinosaur, though he's an old gallimimus fella instead of an allosaurus jackass. Unlike Roger, Mr. Garbowitz is a pretty nice guy. Despite being older, he doesn't treat me like a piece of shit just because I'm a different species. Even invites me over for dinner once every few weeks. Granted, I'm polite to him and bring him his papers, and given his age and reduced mobility, I think he's just happy to have a friend.

I finish the trek upstairs, passing Roger's third floor door on the way up. I really have tried my best to be nice to the guy, but he just hates me outright. Only thing I can do is keep my head down around him and not cause trouble.

Arriving at my fourth floor home, I swing the door open to let Saxon back in the apartment. Before I can head out, however, I realize I left the radio on. As much as I like the local jazz station's tunes, Saxon is pretty indifferent to them, so it'd be wasted electricity to play it for him all day while I'm at work. I have to cut John Coalmane's "Blue Train" a little short; no disrespect, but duty calls. With a quick scruff of Saxon's head which he reciprocates by flopping his heavy tail back and forth, I throw on my flat cap, lock up and head out.

The walk isn't a long one, though the heat tries its damnedest to ruin the trip. I lost the car in the divorce and sure as hell can't afford one now, so my two legs do my commuting for me. I might look into getting a bicycle, especially if I ever have to work farther away than I am right now. Even if I were to get a car at some point, these roads aren't gonna get any more lanes than they got; it's not quite to the point of standstill jams, but you hear more and more complaining car horns every day.

I pass by a handful of street facing shops on the way to work: an ice cream parlor, a corner market, a pharmacy. There's even a record shop that I stare longingly into on days when I'm not in as much of a hurry. No time to daydream about starting my record collection again. I do make a quick stop at the produce stand and toss the lady working it a nickel for a juicy red apple. Only eating cereal for breakfast isn't great for me, so I do my doctor proud and chomp on the tasty fruit as I complete my journey, throwing the core into a garbage can outside my place of employment.

Sal's Butcher and Grocery. A pretty sizable establishment that brings in several trucks worth of meat and other goods every day to cater to its clientèle. The place opens at five in the morning and usually has a gaggle of women waiting as they unlock the front door, but since the trucks don't start showing up 'til about seven thirty I don't have to be in until seven. I'm not too keen on moving through the crowd inside the shop proper, so I make my way through the alley and in the back door next to the loading dock.

Of course, given the heat, maybe a stroll through the air-conditioned store might have been nice. There ain't any cool air back here, except for inside of Mr. Fontana's office, and you usually only get to go in there when it's your first day on the job, or your last day on the job. I step up to the time card puncher on the wall outside of the office and withdraw the slender brown sheet of cardstock with my name on it. I slide it into the grooved slot above the small clock and pull the lever on the side of the device, the familiar *kerchunk* adorning my time card with a punch and a stamp of my clock-in time: 6:58 AM. Cut it pretty close today, but we're still—

"*Samuel!* Get in my office *now!*"

Fuck. What did I do? I'm on time! I push my time card back into its home and cautiously open the door to Sal Fontana's office. He watches me as I maneuver into his chambers, the large glass windows facing the loading dock giving him perfect line of sight to everyone who works the back of the house. The parasaurolophus's elongated curved crest parts the black hair atop his head; his viridian scales rise from the seat behind his impressive desk, the lengthy tail protruding from his backside pushing the chair away with the movement.

I quickly snatch the cap from my head in a show of respect and pacifism. I gulp before speaking. "Y-yes, sir, Mr. Fontana?"

He doesn't reply immediately, choosing instead to narrow his sharp emerald eyes as he seems to size me up. I really need this job. If I did something bad enough to get fired, I've got no clue what it was. I have to fight against my knees to keep them from knocking into one another.

Finally, after a moment of consideration, he speaks up. "How long have you been working for me now, Mr. Lawson?"

Mr. Lawson? I don't think he's ever addressed me by my last name before. "Uh... just about nine months now, sir."

"And in all that time, you've never taken a sick day and never clocked in late. You even stayed after your shift a handful of times to help with other tasks, is that right?"

Despite the cool air flowing into the enclosed space from the window-mounted air conditioner, I still feel beads of sweat accumulating on my brow. "Th-that's right, sir. I always work hard, sir."

He narrows his eyes at me again. Mr. Fontana has never come across as an overly anti-human guy, but he's got no qualms kicking me or my kind to the curb if we put even a single toe out of line. Dinosaur employees usually get second chances; we don't. He considers for another moment before exhaling from his slitted nostrils. The edges of his beak-like snout lift as a faint smile graces his lips. "Good. I'm glad to hear that. You're doing well so far."

I didn't realize I was holding my breath, but I let go of it all the same. "Th-thank you, sir!"

The smile instantly falls from his face as he takes on a down-to-business tone. "I need you to do something for me today. It's not a hard task, but it is very important that it is done correctly. Do you understand me?"

I blink before nodding enthusiastically. "Yes, sir! Whatever you need!"

He gestures for me to come around to the side of his desk. I do so cautiously, being careful to not crowd his space. He pulls open a desk drawer, revealing a plain white envelope containing... I'm not sure what. Whatever it is, there's a lot of it. On the front of the envelope is a single word, scrawled in Mr. Fontana's distinctive handwriting: "Dues".

"In a few hours, a couple of guys are gonna come around looking for this. I need you to give it to them. Do not take it out of this office before they get here. Do not look inside of it.

Your job is to hand them this envelope and that's it. You got it?"

"Yeah, I got it. Seems easy enough." I pause for a moment. "Um... you won't be here when they come in?"

He lowers his head at me. "If I was, I wouldn't need to ask you to do this, now would I?"

"S-sorry..."

Another exhalation from his nostrils. "I'd prefer that I was here, but my wife's aunt died. Need to be at the funeral in a few hours."

I think for a moment. There's a few front of house managers, but they almost never come out back to do anything besides grab stuff to restock their shelves. And we really don't have a loading dock supervisor at the moment, aside from Sal himself. Despite coming to the realization that I'm the most tenured employee on the dock, I can't help but ask the question: "You sure I'm the right man to do this for ya?"

Mr. Fontana narrows his eyes at me again. "Less so now that you just asked that."

Stupid. Why'd I say a stupid shit thing like that? "No—I mean—is, uh... is there someone else—"

"I'm giving you a shot here, Samuel. Do this right and I might look into promoting you to supervisor. Screw it up and your ass is gone." His tone darkens in his last sentence. I really shouldn't screw this up.

"How will I know who to look out for?"

Mr. Fontana rolls his eyes. "Aside from the fact that they'll be the guys asking for my union dues?"

Ah. I got it now. These guys are gonna be with the Herdsters, that labor union that pretty much every shop in the neighborhood is associated with. There's been a few other unions that tried to muscle in over the past year, but those efforts usually fizzle out. Not sure why they never seem to catch wind. Well, doesn't really matter to me. Those organizations are almost exclusively for dinosaurs anyway.

He gestures with his head toward the loading dock. "Don't let me keep you. Get to work."

I snap out of my haze. "Y-yes, sir! I won't let you down, Mr. Fontana!" He gives me one final reaffirming nod as I exit his office. Closing the door behind myself, I let out a decompressing breath. Not only do I still have my job, I have a chance to make my boss proud and maybe even get a promotion. I *definitely* shouldn't screw this up.

Placing my cap back on my head, I cross the loading bay toward the large sliding dock doors. The first truck of the morning is still a few minutes away, but we got plenty to do before it gets here: move empty crates, sort out the staging area, and make sure everything's as ready as it can be when the deliveries arrive. If there's one thing delivery drivers hate, it's wasted time, so we do everything in our power to make our side of things as smooth as possible.

"Sammy! Everything okay, buddy?" A familiar voice calls to me from the other side of the loading dock. I look up from the handful of crates in my arms to the concerned frown of one of my coworkers, another human like myself. He pushes his thick-rimmed glasses up his nose as he looks past me toward Mr. Fontana's office. "You ain't in trouble, are ya?"

"Nah, Bernie. I'm good. Just got assigned a special project for later is all." Bernie is a pretty swell guy. Only started here about two months ago, but he's a hard worker despite his age. He hasn't told me outright but I think he's pushing fifty.

He lets out a sigh of relief. "Oh, thank goodness. I was worried, after what happened with Max last week..." Max was an example of the short rope we are extended, and what happens when you step off the edge of the hangman's platform.

I shrug. "Told him he needed to get his ass here on time.

But nah, I'm good. Come on, let's get this shit moved over so we don't hold up the produce delivery."

Around ten, Mr. Fontana puts on his trilby and exits his office, keys in hand. He'd normally lock the door; instead, he glances my way. When I make eye contact with him, he taps his wristwatch and nods at me. I nod back to him, fully aware of the task assigned. I've been thinking about little else for the past few hours. In fact, I take special care to never remove my attention from his unlocked office door unless I absolutely have to. Unless a poltergeist makes its way in through the air vents and whisks that envelope away, it's not going anywhere until those labor union fellas get here.

At about half past twelve, me and the other guys working the loading dock take our lunch break. It's well timed between a few trucks so nobody's waiting on us to eat and get back to work. Some of the guys pack their own lunches, but I usually go across the street to the sandwich shop with Bernie and get a cold cut. Today, however, I can't let that office out of eyeshot, so I hand Bernie a quarter and ask him to grab me a turkey on rye with no tomatoes. He agrees and starts to set off to retrieve our lunches.

Just as Bernie reaches for the handle of the back door it swings open, nearly knocking him on his ass. He stumbles backward, his mouth hanging open in preparation to shout at the reckless clown who just burst through the threshold. However, he can't find his words as the color drains from his face. His eyes move up—*far* up the towering form standing before him. The rest of the boys in the loading dock similarly shut up as they stare at the figure striding with purpose toward Mr. Fontana's office.

The behemoth of a stegosaurus stands at nearly seven feet tall, his midnight blue scales bulging as they desperately try to adhere to his muscles. His plated tail swings back and forth defiantly, the four jagged barbs at its end threatening to perforate anyone who comes too close. He wears a black sports jacket over his pressed white shirt; in combination with his well-tailored slacks and mirror-polished shoes, he gives off the air of a dinosaur who owns whatever room he's standing in.

After surveying the room, his focus comes to rest on me, the person closest to the office. He speaks in a cold, gruff voice. "Where's Sal Fontana?"

"H-he's not here. C-can I help you with—"

In two rapid strides of his long legs, the stegosaurus crosses the space between us. He literally overshadows me, coming between the light fixture hanging from the ceiling and myself. He glares down at me with a level of intensity that nearly makes me stumble backward.

His words are deliberate and carry a condescending tone, as though he's speaking to a small child. "Can you go *get* him for me?"

I am petrified. "H-he's n-not in the s-store. A-are you—"

He slowly brings his sharpened beak only a few inches away from my face. It's quite a lean, considering our height disparity; his lips curl back. "I am here for his dues. And you're telling me he's not here?"

I notice a small golden pin affixed to the lapel of his sports jacket; it bears the insignia of the International Brotherhood of Herdsters. If I had any doubt in my mind as to who this man was, it's gone now. I muster up what little courage I have left to reply. "I c-can get that for you!"

It seems he didn't expect this response, leaning back as a look of puzzlement and disgust washes over him. I take the opportunity to zip over to the office, throwing open the door and moving to the desk drawer containing the envelope. Sure enough, it's still where Mr. Fontana left it. I withdraw it, feeling the weight of what has to be a small stack of bills, and turn back to the entrance of the office. The Herdster man now stands at the door, his massive form blocking the opening entirely. If the need to escape suddenly arose, my only option would be diving through one of the windows.

"Mr. F-Fontana asked me to g-give this to you! Here!" I extend the envelope to the hulking stegosaurus. He scrutinizes me for another moment as he seems to contemplate whether to accept the envelope or twist my head around a hundred and eighty degrees. Mercifully, he settles on the former, snatching the dues from my hand with another sneer.

He extends a blunt finger in my direction before he speaks. "You tell Sal that the next time we come by to collect, it's *him* here, not some skinnie *fuck*." Before I lower my eyes in placation, they rest for a moment on a leather shape dangling between his suit jacket and overshirt. A leather shape that seems to hold another, more lethal shape.

My eyes dart down to the floor. "Y-yes, sir. S-sorry, sir."

With a final growl, he spins on his heel and strides toward the exit. As he throws it open, I notice another dinosaur standing outside; he turns to acknowledge the stegosaurus, but before any of their words can be worked out, the door slams shut behind them. The echoing sound of metal against metal is followed by that of my knees hitting the wooden office floor beneath me. The other guys quickly dash over to check on me, Bernie pushing his way to the front of the small crowd.

"Holy shit! Sammy, are you okay?! What was that?!"

I have to catch my breath before I can reply. "Remember that special project I mentioned? That was it."

"Raptor Jesus, that was intense. I thought he was gonna kill you!"

"I'll be honest, I kinda thought that, too."

Bernie helps me get back up to my feet. "Well, if you don't have to stick around anymore, you wanna run across the street for that sandwich with me?"

With a weak smile, I turn my palm upward. "Actually, if

you don't mind, I'll just ask for my quarter back. I lost my appetite."

The excitement of our close encounter with a massive, intimidating dinosaur wears off just around the time the next delivery truck backs itself up to our loading dock. I feed off of the adrenaline from my confrontation for a while, but the fact I skipped lunch catches up to me before too long. I fight off the growling of my stomach by humming some of my favorite jazz tunes to myself as I work. We're not allowed to have a radio in the loading dock, and even if we did, me and the other four guys who work back here would have to agree on what to listen to. Sure, we could take turns or something, but I'm content to just listen to the jukebox in my brain.

Some time in the afternoon, Mr. Fontana rolls back in. He immediately approaches me, asking if everything went well. I tell him that there were no problems, but opt to not relay the parting comments of the labor union representative. He gives me a clap on the shoulder before heading back into his office. I hope he meant what he said about a promotion; I could certainly use the extra money, but I won't press him on the matter.

We wrap up at about five, using brooms to push the collected dust and debris from the day's work out of the loading dock and onto the concrete below. With a stretch and a roll of my shoulders, I set the push broom in its corner and head over to my time card. As I punch out for the day, I glance through the window of Mr. Fontana's office. Scribbling away at some paperwork, he doesn't notice my look. Well. Like I said, I won't be pushy. If the gears are turning in that direction, that's good enough for me.

Offering the other fellas a farewell, I start making my way home. The heat was brutal today, but seems to have broken ever so slightly as the sun lowers in the sky. It won't be nightfall 'til well past eight, but any respite from the scorching fireball is welcomed at this point.

With my hands stuffed into my pockets, my head lowered and my stomach still doing its own musical number, I distract myself as best I can with another tune. I can always count on Miles Cratis to come through for me when I'm feeling down. The gentle, rhythmic tapping of the drums and cymbals, the fresh sound of the tickled ivories, the back and forth of Cratis's jaw-dropping trumpeting and the accompanying alto and tenor saxophones. It all fuses together into a jam session full of beauty and hope. The sound of our time. The sound of humanity.

I stop myself. For some reason, something about my humming sounded a bit off for a second. Like it wasn't just me doing it.

I glance over my shoulder. Nothing but a dark alleyway there.

I glance over my other shoulder. Nothing but a bus stop bench there. Except...

A slender shape is seated on this particular bus stop bench. Her hands are planted on the elongated seat on either side of her. The well-groomed claws attached to her fingers barely touch an upright paper bag filled with groceries. She wears a formal-looking business dress, neither revealing nor eye-catching. Its modest blue color is a few shades darker than the light blue of her scales. Her feathered tail, only a slight bit darker than the rest of her, sways back and forth as the foot attached to the leg crossed on top of the other bobs in a steady rhythm.

I listen closely.

She's humming, too.

In fact, she's humming the same tune I was. I take a step closer, circling a little to see if she was purposefully trying to join in with me or if it was pure coincidence. She doesn't seem to take note of me, her closed eyelids allowing her mind to focus only on the song in her head.

I cautiously take one step closer and clear my throat before speaking up. "Excuse me, miss?" Her humming abruptly stops and her eyes shoot open as her head spins in my direction. I hold out my hands apologetically. "I-I'm sorry, I didn't mean to startle you."

With a talon, she pushes some of her short blue hair away from her eyes. It doesn't go any lower than her shoulder, a professional look for a working woman like herself, no doubt. When her eyes meet mine, I realize they're about the only part of her that isn't some shade of blue. Instead, I'm met with bright, piercing yellow orbs of light. The sunlight seems to dance across them, her diamond pupils shifting as she evaluates me.

After a moment, her posture relaxes. "It's fine. I was in my own head for a second. What did you need?"

I scratch the back of my neck. I realize the absurdity of my next question, but can't come up with a better way to ask it. "Erm—uhh, well, I was just walkin' by, and it—well…" I straighten up and manage to spit the thought out. "Were you humming 'So What'? By Miles Cratis?"

Her eyes widen and she leans away from me a little, clearly taken aback by my question. After a moment, her tail flicks and a faint smile appears on her lips. "Why, yes. I was."

I can't help but grin back. "I thought so! I—well, sorry for the out of nowhere interruption, but I was humming it too as I was walkin' by!"

She raises an eyebrow at me as she maintains her smile. "Is that so? A fan of his work, are you?"

I nod enthusiastically, taking a small step closer to her. "Yes, ma'am! I love his music. Real genius on the horn, total revolutionary."

She shifts her posture to turn a little more in my direction, lessening the profile of her snout. "You can say that again. His new record is breathtaking."

I awkwardly chuckle. "Well, I mostly hear him on the

radio. No shortage of his stuff on the local jazz channel, though."

She lets out a gentle hum. "Pleasure to meet a fellow jazz enthusiast."

She shifts the hair away from her face again, her slender claws brushing the strands aside as her yellow eyes remain focused on me. I know for a fact I've got a stupid grin on my face, but I hope to high heaven that my dumb caveman cheeks ain't glowing. My ex-wife always teased me about blushing; it was one of a hundred things that gradually turned from a cute jab to a searing critique as our marriage fell apart.

All the same, I feel a twinge in my heart. I've got no earthly clue why; this is a velociraptor broad. I mean—she's pretty, as far as dinosaurs go, but—nah. That shit doesn't happen. Species stick to their lanes, even today. I think I'm just happy that I actually met someone else who enjoys the same music I do. A dinosaur, even...

A dinosaur that enjoys jazz, music that most dinosaurs rebuke as muddy, pointless noise made by neanderthals banging objects together and blowing into hunks of metal and wood.

She pauses for a moment to think before opening her mouth to speak again.

I'd have loved to have heard what she was gonna say next, if it weren't for the gunshots that interrupted her.

Chapter Two: Aubrey

"—all for today's smooth as silk traffic report. Anyway, it's gonna be another hot one out there, so be sure to throw an extra ice pack into your lunch pail, fellas! It's 6:00 AM, and that means it's time for living legend Miles Cratis and his smokin' hot single, 'So What'."

The dulcet tones of the piano and bass intro to one of my favorite songs washes away my slumber. Without realizing it, my tail begins twitching in time with the beat. A smile spreads across my snout as I lift my head from the pillow, but...

Bringing a hand up to my cheek, I feel the wet remnants of tears. God damn it. I had that dream again. It doesn't happen every night, but when it does, there's always waterworks.

Pull yourself together. It was just a dream. I'm not gonna ruminate on this. Not again.

I throw my legs over the side of the mattress, focusing instead on the sultry saxophone and torrid trumpet emanating from my clock radio. Miles Cratis. What an artist. And I heard he's in town, too. I'd love to see him play in person. I tap my foot in rhythm with his pitch-perfect trumpeting, feeling a flutter in my stomach with each rise and fall of the notes. Those humans really know how to work magic with their instruments.

I try to pull myself up to my feet, but my right knee locks up and buckles under the pressure, bringing my ass back down on the edge of the bed. Fucking thing. I start extending and retracting my leg to work the kink out of my muscle. I've been keeping up with my exercises every night, so why the hell is this thing still giving me grief? Am I doing something wrong, or is my doctor just an idiot?

After a minute of repeating the motion, I make a second attempt to stand up. This time, my knee cooperates and doesn't give out underneath me. I don't let the annoyance get to me, choosing to focus on the music again as I take care of my morning rituals. My one-bedroom apartment isn't anything to take pride in, but it gets the job done. I could go with a cheaper one and save a bit more money, but I'm not too hard-up for cash these days. Certainly think I could be making more, though... and doing more.

I turn on the shower, giving it a few moments to warm up. It's definitely another hot day today, but my air conditioner is doing the Lord's work. Granted, I've never minded the heat all that much, but a lot of my coworkers have been complaining, especially the fellas out running the beat. I tuck my hair into a shower cap before stepping into the porcelain basin, being sure to leave my tail hanging out on the other side of the curtain. I wash my hair and tail every few days, and today isn't one of those days. I'm happy to have the extra twenty minutes to myself on mornings when I don't have to deal with cleaning and drying all the hair and feathers.

Sufficiently cleansed, I cautiously climb out of the shower, taking care to not set off my trick knee again. It must be the heat that's getting to it. I'll just be careful with my movements today and I'll be good as new tomorrow. My usual morning evaluation in the mirror goes the same as it always does; I frown as I observe the two scrawny legs, the nearly visible rib cage and the pathetic A-cup breasts that make up the sorry excuse for a woman looking back at me. Not that I'm in the market for a man after... after everything that...

That was nearly eight months ago. I can't keep living in that shadow. I *can't*.

My arms involuntarily wrap around my stomach and I nearly double over as the emotions try to claw their way to the surface again.

Fight it. You're already over this. It's in the past and you're stronger than it. You have to be stronger.

My ears register the sound still resonating from my radio. It takes a moment for the music to become recognizable past the rapid beating of my heart and my labored breathing.

Charlie Larker. "Blues for Alice". 201M1951 BC. One of the finest examples of Bird Blues around, by the late Yardbird himself. I have the track on vinyl and put it on from time to time. It's not my favorite Larker standard, but it's a damn good one. The sound of his sax pushes the dreadful feeling in my gut back below the surface, calming me down enough to release my grip on my body and continue my morning prep in a more relaxed state of mind.

Gently bobbing my head along with the beat, I finish up my daily beautification, if you can call it that. I don't spend very long on makeup; the guys at the station give me shit for it, but I don't care. I'm there to do a job, not turn heads. I make my way over to my small bedside closet and withdraw a blue work dress. Nothing fancy. Practical, comfortable and professional; just the way I want it to be.

As I finish getting dressed and give myself one more review in the mirror, I glance around my apartment. Besides the music, there's no other sound here. It's... a bit lonely, to be honest.

Maybe I should get a pet. But what would I get? I sure

as hell don't want to be a cat lady. Twenty-four is way too early to give up and turn into an old maid. O'course, ain't that what I'm on the way to doing?

No. Shut up. You're fine. Just get through the week, like you always do. And, hell. It's Monday. I can make my usual request. I've been putting up excellent numbers, he can't keep stonewalling me forever.

Shutting off the radio, I give the apartment one last visual sweep before heading out, being sure to lock the door behind myself. It's not a rough neighborhood, but I've got quite a record collection I'd be really pissed to lose. At least I'm on the second story so some asshole kids jimmying open the window and crawling in ain't an option, but I still rest easier knowing my place is locked up.

Maybe a dog, then? It'd be a burglar deterrent, at least. I'd have to train the little furball, but it might be nice to have a friend, even one that can't communicate with anything beyond a wagging tail and an occasional bark.

I'll think about it more later.

The summer heat rolls over me in a thick wave the moment I push open the front door of the apartment building. Climate control is both a blessing and a curse; you love it when you're encircled by it, and you desperately miss it when you're not. It's not too long of a walk to the bus stop, and I time my mornings pretty well so I don't spend very long waiting. That is, so long as the line is running on time.

Thankfully, that is the case today as the green and white chariot pulls up only about a minute later. The ride is around ten minutes, give or take based on stops we make. I've come to recognize most of the other passengers on the morning route, but I haven't gotten to know any names. I don't enjoy talking to strangers much, being content to just spend the ride in my own head, listening to my internal record player.

On the platter now is another Miles Cratis standard, "Milestones", its upbeat and rhythmic flow perfectly matching the hustle and bustle of the Old York morning commute. My fingers tap on my knee in tandem with the horn and sax as they spar with one another, not quite dueling but not quite relinquishing authority over the song either. I've listened to the track so many times that it plays perfectly in my internal ear.

After a moment, I realize my eyes are closed. Got carried away by the melody. Not that I distrust anyone on the bus, but it's not wise to be completely unaware of your surroundings whenever you're in a city like this. As I regain focus of the cramped world around me, I spot a human gentleman seated across from me. He's one I've seen frequently; though it's not quite every day, most days he's on this same line with me in the morning. A real fidgety individual, seems like he can never get comfortable, always wringing his hands or trying to keep his restless leg from bouncing too furiously. His thick bottlecap-lensed glasses magnify his nervous eyes.

I can't exactly blame the fella. He's a scrawny little guy, and the bus has a fair number of dinosaurs on it. I've heard a few dinos mutter slurs his way under their breath over the weeks. Personally, I'm not keen on the idea of viewing humans as a subservient species. Things were different a lot of years ago. Humans are people just like we are, capable of just as great of things. Jazz wouldn't be what it is without the contribution of humans, after all. Hell, it probably wouldn't even exist.

Today, though... something's off about him. He seems more nervous than usual. What would normally just be mousy behavior comes off as downright petrified as he keeps shooting glances all around the bus, seeming to anticipate an attack at any moment. Sweat is pouring from underneath his pinstripe cap, more than just this heat would be responsible for. His arms are wrapped tightly around a briefcase I'm not used to seeing him carry. I wonder what's got him so flustered?

His eyes meet mine and linger for a moment before he offers a meek smile and turns his gaze downward. It doesn't rest on the bus floor for long, however, as he resumes his search for whatever assailant he fears. I just shrug and go back to my internal music. None of my business.

A few minutes later, we arrive at my stop. I give the coke-bottle human one more glance before I depart; he wipes a tremendous amount of sweat from his brow with a handkerchief and seems to mutter something under his breath, taking careful note of everyone who gets on the bus. I may not know the guy beyond recognizing him from these morning commutes, but I certainly hope he gets through whatever's got him so terrified.

Stepping down from the small set of stairs that direct me to the sidewalk, I gaze up at the structure before me. Its impressive architecture is only partly responsible for the respect it commands over Brachlyn Avenue and the nearly nine square miles of its jurisdiction. The letters emblazoned around our state crest make up for the rest of its grandeur:

Old York City Police Department
63rd Precinct

My little home away from home. My place of business. And a place where I want to do so much more. I know for a fact that I can be more good to Brachlyn on these streets than behind a desk pushing paperwork every day. But there's only one person who stands between me and that dream. And his office is my first stop, just as it is every Monday morning.

I push open the massive wooden doors atop the stone steps leading up to the building's face. Within, a spacious lobby holds a reception desk and an oak staircase leading to its second floor. All the trappings of a police station you'd imagine from a wild west movie are hidden from sight, the various holding cells concealed in the station's sublevels. Here, it's calming decor, wood trim paneling and pleasant atmosphere that greets those who use the building's primary entrance.

I've got my destination set. I make a right down a short hall and locate the most official looking office in the building. As I gently swing open its door, the burly brown pterodactyl seated behind the intimidatingly sized desk does not lift his gaze from the paperwork spread out before him. Without making eye contact with me, he mutters, "Yes, Carter. What is it?"

I stand up straight and look toward him with as much confidence as I can muster, my tail twitching due to the nervousness I always feel when I ask the same question. "Captain Aaron, I'd like to request entry to the Police Academy."

He lets out a sigh and raises his eyes to meet mine, his two leathery wings seeming to sag in annoyance. "We've been over this a hundred times."

I pause a moment before speaking. "Then let this be a hundred and one, sir."

He shakes his head. "No, Carter. That's still the answer."

"But, sir—"

He abruptly cuts me off. His voice is stern and holds absolute authority. "You are a clerk, and a damn good one at that. I know how much you want to move up, but it's just not possible."

I won't give up that easily. "Sir, just last year they started allowing women to—"

"I know what they started doing. Some other precincts already have lady officers, and that's fine by me. I'm sure we'll have some here, too, eventually. But you won't be one of them."

I foolishly ask the question, but I already know the answer he's going to give me. "Why not?"

His eyes flick down to my right knee, then back up to me. His expression is both weary and sympathetic. "I don't know how many times I need to tell you this. You're a good clerk, and you may have even been a good policewoman. But with that knee... you wouldn't even make it a week through the Academy."

I have to bite my lip to keep tears from forming in my eyes. "It's getting better, sir. I'm doing exercises."

He shakes his head again, seeing right through my lie. "A beat cop who can't keep up with culprits can't serve our city. You might have a chance in some backwater town where the worst crimes being committed are chicken theft and disorderly conduct. Out here, I need people who are at their best." He places his hands on his hips and looks down his sharpened beak at me with regret. "I'm sorry, Aubrey."

He doesn't use my first name often. When he does, it stings like hell. One of the only other times he had done so was shortly after my accident. He visited me in the hospital. Even brought flowers. It was a kind gesture of him, considering I was only working at the precinct for about a month at that time. I was practically catatonic, conscious and aware but unable to speak to or acknowledge those around me. When he sat next to me and put a hand on my shoulder, he used my first name:

"I'm terribly sorry this happened to you, Aubrey. Truly sorry. I can't even imagine."

I quickly lower my head, pushing the thoughts of that experience as far down as they will go. I mutter the words, but my voice cracks as I speak. "Thank you, sir." I barely see the captain's remorseful look past my clouded vision; I manage to make it out of his office and a few steps down the hall before the tears start falling.

Fucking... not now. Not in the office. I dart into the

nearby women's bathroom. It's empty, not a surprise given that there's only a few other women who work in this building, all of whom perform clerical duties like I do. I snatch several paper towels from the dispenser and dry the tears from my face, taking care to not ruin the small bit of makeup I applied.

I don't cry when the captain tells me "no"; it's a weekly occurrence, only causing me to steel my resolve and work even harder toward next week. But today, I blame the dream I had. Dredging up old memories. Terrible memories.

I have to be stronger than my past.

Composing myself with one final look-over in the mirror hanging over the sink, I exit the bathroom and make my way up to the second floor. As I head toward my desk, I spot a couple of large white boxes on a nearby table. Stereotypical, given the locale, but...

Screw it. I didn't have breakfast today, and I could go for a little pick-me-up. I throw open the box scrawled with an uppercase "E" and withdraw a tasty-looking doughnut. Herbivores don't exactly agree with eggs, so the other box contains doughnuts prepared without. Being a carnivore, I much prefer the taste of those made with unborn chicken.

I munch on the sweet fried round, already feeling my woes dissolve in its sugary bliss, and make my way toward the desk adorned with my name placard. A small stack of paperwork already waits for me, and the pile won't stop growing throughout the course of the day. My duties involve processing these tedious forms, tickets for minor violations mostly. Checking them for accuracy, making sure the cop who filled it out in the first place did what he needed to do, and stuffing envelopes with reminders of varying severity for tickets that have gone unpaid. All in a day's work for a woman who's apparently not fit to do anything but this menial and repetitive task.

Thankfully, they let me keep a small radio by my desk.

So long as I don't have the volume cranked loud enough to bother anyone else, I'm allowed to listen to whatever I want. The dial never moves from the local jazz station. The music helps me get through the day, transforming tedious busywork into melodic therapy. Regardless of how sloppy the forms I'm passed are, I never get frustrated when I've got my friends on the other side of the radio waves keeping me company.

"—over there's the break room, and this is where most of the paper pushin' gets done. Speaking of..." The voice is that of Officer Duffy, a seasoned cop who's been working this precinct for over ten years. His slicked-back hair makes way for the two pronounced ridges on the top of his dilophosaurus head. He gestures in my direction. "This here's Aubrey. She'll handle processing your ticket and citation paperwork as you bring it to her."

The dinosaur he speaks to is a younger guy, one I don't recognize. Must be his first day at the precinct, if not his first day as a cop. I feel a twinge of jealousy as he glances at me, quickly covering it up with my reply to Duffy's introduction. "Aubrey Carter. And I'll process your paperwork if you bring it to me filled out proper-like. I ain't gonna do your job for ya." I extend a hand to the rookie, a spinosaurus with massive, rigid extensions of vertebrae that form his namesake spine. The tailor must have had a hell of a go with his uniform to accommodate that particular protrusion.

He accepts my handshake, offering a sideways smile. "Officer Preston." He holds my grip for a moment, glancing down at the nameplate on my desk. "Aubrey', huh? Ain't that a fella's name?"

I withdraw my hand from his. "It isn't, no. Not exclusively, at least."

His grin widens, exposing sharpened teeth within his elongated snout. I don't like the sense I get from this guy. "But all the Aubrey's I met have been fellas." He scans me up and down; I involuntarily recoil away from him. His sneer turns downright menacing in response. "You one of them bull dykes or what?"

My mouth falls open in shock, but before I can reply Duffy claps the back of his hand across Preston's chest. "Enough of that, you numbskull. Aubrey is a fine worker. Don't give her shit on your first day. Come on, I'll show you the garage next." Duffy starts to lead Preston away as the spinosaurus's eyes linger on me a moment longer to gauge my reaction. He seems happy with the one he got and, with a chuckle, follows his tour guide down the stairs.

I slump back in my chair. Are you kidding me? A bull dyke?! The fucking nerve of that sleazeball. And Duffy didn't even correct him. Granted, me and Duffy aren't best buds but he fucking knows I ain't a lesbian. I was married, for Christ's sake. I—

My heartbeat begins to accelerate and the pain in my stomach makes itself apparent once more. Phantoms rattle their chains inside my mind and body yet again. I nearly keel over from the wave of despair that lashes out at me.

The sounds of horns playing in perfect rhythm with one another backed by a gentle piano, smooth bassline and light drum and cymbal taps break me free from the dreadful memories trying once more to worm their way forward. "Doxy". Sonny Rawlind. 201M1954 BC, originally recorded with Miles Cratis. It's sometimes mistakenly credited to Cratis for composing it, but it's a Rawlind track all the way. I have two versions of it on vinyl, and both sing the sweet song of what's possible when two of the greatest jazz minds put their skills to work on the same track.

I slowly straighten up, remaining conscious of my breathing as I go. It was a close call, but I'm good now. I can't keep having these fits, though. This just won't do if I'm trying to prove to the captain that I'm ready to move up. He thinks my knee is the problem, but if I freeze up every time my past knocks on my door I'm really gonna be useless.

I keep my head down and make it through the rest of the workday. The music helps keep my mind off things. A lot of the fellas around the station think I'm antisocial. A few tried being friendly; one even asked me out. I don't really try to be closed off. I just find myself not interested in their conversation, not interested in opening up to them. Nobody ever compliments my music, either. They just make snide remarks about it or tell me to turn off the racket. Usual shit.

Just another day blending into another day. A cycle that'll keep going until I pull myself out of it with effort. I'll prove my worth. I'll get this knee fixed up and I'll achieve what I know I can achieve.

As the hands of the clock nearly complete their journey toward punch out time, a familiar burly pterodactyl man wanders over by my desk. I glance up from the last bit of paperwork I'm processing to meet Captain Aaron's focus. He looks down at me with a stern gaze. He's a tough man to get an emotional read on, but I can't help but sense a twinge of sympathy in his eyes.

He opens his mouth to say something, stops, considers for a moment, then plops two slender pieces of cardstock on the desk between us. "Fella dropped these off at our station. Not sure why, his nightclub isn't in our jurisdiction. Might have just been trying to curry some favor with the OYPD all around town, I don't know. I was gonna toss them, but..." He glances at the radio next to me, quietly emanating one of the last songs it'll sing before I shut it off for the day and head home. "Well. You're the only one in the office with a taste for that sort of music. I figured, why let them go to waste?"

I cock my head at the captain before looking down at the items he placed on my desk. As the words printed on the slender slips register in my mind, my eyes widen and my breath hitches in my throat.

Birdland Nightclub presents
Miles Cratis
Tuesday, August 25th, 201M1959 BC
8:00 PM
Admit One

My gaze shoots back up to the pterodactyl. "Holy sh—" I cut myself off, seeing his eyes narrow. He's a pretty staunchly Catholic guy and doesn't abide cursing in his presence. I feel my cheeks redden as I try to recover. "Sir! Are—are you sure I can have these?!"

He shrugs. "It's this or the trash for them. Yours if you like." His teeth barely make themselves visible as the edges of his beak lift. "Have a good evening, Carter."

I can't stop the smile that tugs at my lips. "Y-you too, sir!" As he takes his leave, I pick up the tickets with shaking hands. Holy shit. *Holy shit.* I can't believe it. These things are like platinum, those shows have been sold out for months before they even started. And I'm holding two tickets in my hands.

Two tickets…

I feel a twinge of regret, knowing I've got nobody to invite. My family's all out of state, and I really don't have any close friends to speak of. I get along okay with a few of my neighbors, but nobody who would understand an opportunity like this. Sure, I might get someone to agree to come, but they'd probably be bored the whole time. And that'd be too disrespectful to Miles Cratis to bring someone who won't appreciate his craft the way it needs to be appreciated.

No. I'll go by myself. I take one of the two tickets and motion toward the trash can next to my desk.

I can't do it. I can't throw something like this out…

Alright. I'll keep it. Maybe on the way into the club there will be some poor soul at the door begging to be let in, and I can make their night. That'd be a lark. But one thing is for certain: I'm going. I wouldn't pass up an opportunity like this for the world.

With renewed vigor, I gather my things and clock out for the day. The music follows me even after I shut off the radio, a venerable cacophony of exuberant instruments blaring in my head as my own excitement for tomorrow plasters a stupid smile on my face. In a brief moment of clarity as I exit the station, I remember that I need to stop at the grocery store. Ran out of some necessities, and a gal's gotta eat.

I don't even try to keep my tail in check as I stroll down the sidewalk toward Sal's Butcher and Grocery; it sways back and forth, coming close to clipping other folks traveling the other direction. It's a metronome of my own delight, keeping rhythm with Miles Cratis's personal performance for only me.

The grocery store is packed, as usual. Mothers and wives hurriedly fill their baskets and trolleys with the finest groceries around. A slew of herbivores seem to be battling over the best quality vegetables on display. The employees wrangle the store as best they can, filling empty slots in shelves and checking out increasingly irate customers as quickly as possible. I even spot a man or two, lost and confused in the chaos that is quite possibly the best grocery store in the city.

I deftly dodge a pair of pachycephalosaurus who are practically colliding their hardened heads against one another as they argue over ownership of a particularly juicy head of lettuce. One of the advantages of being a carnivore in this world is that some sections of the grocery store are less traveled and less brutal. I step up to the butcher's counter and order a pound of ground beef. I think a hamburger sounds fine for dinner tonight.

Rounding out my short trip, I pick out a package of buns, a shiny tomato and a head of lettuce, opting to select from the less contentious portion of the display. Lettuce is lettuce,

I'm not about to get in a fist fight over produce like some of these ladies. I bring my small selection of goods to the checkout line, and a few minutes later and a couple dollars in my purse lighter I'm on my way home.

Stepping back into the slightly cooler but still hot early evening air, I can focus on my internal jazz again. The radio inside the grocery store was playing some crappy pop music, favored tunes of the placid masses. You don't have to think too hard when you hear the same boring four-chord structure over and over. I much prefer the complexity and bravery of jazz. They experiment. They have fun. Not everything works, but when it does, it's truly remarkable.

The bus stop is only a minute away from the storefront. My timing is less on point in the evening, so I sometimes have to wait a little while for a bus. Still beats hoofing it the three miles away I live, especially on days when my knee is being a little prick. It's felt pretty good since this morning, but my rejection by Captain Aaron keeps it in the forefront of my mind. I've gotta do something about it. Maybe ice it in the evenings, or try some different exercises. I need to fix this so that I can go into the Academy. I know it's a silly pipe dream, but I haven't wanted anything more than to be a police officer since I was a little girl. I was laughed at in the schoolyard, being told that girls can't be cops, but now that the times are changing my dream might be attainable, if I can just get past this stupid handicap.

I take a seat on the bus stop bench, setting the paper bag of groceries at my side. Nobody else is waiting for a ride; if someone does show up, I can move the bag to give them a spot to sit, but for right now it's me and the summer air. I remember the tickets in my purse and smile again as Miles starts playing his horn for me. "So What", one of his newest songs and an absolutely beautiful composition. It woke me up this morning, and now it finds its way into my mind again.

I can't help but close my eyes, relax in the calm moment, and softly hum along with his genius.

"Excuse me, miss?"

My eyelids fly open as I turn to focus on the source of the sudden, interrupting voice. A few feet away, a human stares at me, his cheeks instantly brightening as he holds up his hands in an apologetic gesture. "I-I'm sorry, I didn't mean to startle you."

I push some of the hair away from my eyes. I keep it short, but it still likes to intrude from time to time, especially when I spin my head like I did to see who was addressing me. The fella is pretty normal looking for a human: tanned skin, brown hair that's a little longer than average but nowhere near long enough to make me question his gender, and dirtied work clothes. Must be getting off his shift as a… well, whatever it is he does that builds up a layer of grime like that. Still, he doesn't come across as a slob as he politely stands before me and awaits my response.

I realize I'm still pretty tensed up from being startled. I loosen my shoulders and feel my tail feathers unbristle themselves. "It's fine. I was in my own head for a second. What did you need?"

He brings a hand to the back of his neck and scratches, glancing away nervously. His bright cheeks light up even further. "Erm—uhh, well, I was just walkin' by, and it—well…" His eyes meet mine again as he seems to steel his resolve. "Were you humming 'So What'? By Miles Cratis?"

What the—how did he know? Was I really humming that loudly? And—well, Miles Cratis is a popular jazz musician, but I don't know that I've ever met anyone who would recognize his work that quickly, and especially by way of my butchered humming. I love the sounds of jazz but I know for a fact I don't replicate it well with my voice. What's with this guy?

All the same, I can't help but feel a smile tug at the sides of my mouth as I offer him a reply. "Why, yes. I was."

His posture immediately loosens as he returns my smile. "I thought so! I—well, sorry for the out of nowhere interruption, but I was humming it too as I was walkin' by!"

My eyebrow lifts in his direction. "Is that so? A fan of his work, are you?"

He nods his head and takes a step closer. I don't register the gesture as being threatening or flirtatious. In fact, I don't even know this guy's name and I somehow feel relaxed around him. He speaks through a widening smile. "Yes, ma'am! I love his music. Real genius on the horn, total revolutionary."

I rotate a bit more in his direction, my crossed legs remaining so as I return a bit of his enthusiasm. "You can say that again. His new record is breathtaking."

He lets out a chuckle. "Well, I mostly hear him on the radio. No shortage of his stuff on the local jazz channel, though."

I can't help but release a soft hum. Between his reddened cheeks and his awkward manner, he's kinda…

What the hell is getting into me? I try to wrap up the conversation politely, the bus should be here any minute. "Pleasure to meet a fellow jazz enthusiast."

My hair intrudes on my eyes again; I brush it away and attempt to give him a courteous smile and nod, hoping the gesture will illustrate to this fellow that our social transaction is concluded, but I can't manage to find the expression. My eyes linger on him for a moment longer than I intend them to. His cheeks are absolutely burning red. Doesn't come across to me as a shy sort, but maybe one who doesn't interact with dinosaurs the most gracefully. Of course, it's hard for humans to interact with us when there's still so much societal pressure to navigate, but…

Something about him is different. Who is this guy that

just randomly stopped and questioned me on my humming? He was able to pick out Miles Cratis's tune from my tone-deaf rendition. He must be a jazz fan with a keen ear to be capable of such a feat.

His eyes remain locked to mine, their gentle blue offering a reflection of my own. Human eyes are smaller and house a round, black pupil whereas dinosaurs have diamond-shaped pupils that are often similarly colored to our irises. Many dinosaurs find human eyes to be boring and lifeless, not communicating as thoroughly as the eyes of our own species. But I don't agree with that sentiment. Instead, I find myself examining this man's eyes closely.

They seem kind.

A kind-looking human who likes jazz.

My mind wanders to the spare ticket that my purse holds. Would it be too brazen of me to ask him to join me? That would seem like I was asking him on a date, wouldn't it? And I don't want…

Or do I?

I open my mouth to reply, but my words are cut off before they even form by a loud, echoing pop. It's shortly followed by a second, then three more in rapid succession.

Gunshots. And they're not far away.

My head whips around to the nearby alley. Those shots were only a block away, maybe less, and this will be a direct route to the scene.

The man who was just smiling and blushing at me a moment ago is jolted by the sound, flinching before spinning in the same direction as me. "Holy fuckin' shit, was that gunshots?!"

I'm on my feet. Cop or no, I'm not standing by if someone just got shot. My tail knocks the paper bag to the ground as I take off, scattering my groceries across the concrete. I don't take a second look at them as I tear down the alleyway in the direction of the sound.

Footsteps behind me. This human is following me, running a few feet behind. Why?

"Are you fuckin' crazy, lady?! Usually you go in the *opposite* direction of gunshots!"

There's no time to explain everything to him, so I lie instead. "I'm a cop!"

"Holy shit, really?! Well, then, go get the bastard!" Though he's given me his blessing, he still runs after me.

I glance over my shoulder in irritation. "This is dangerous, you shouldn't be—"

He suddenly stops as we round the alley corner, his eyes widening immensely as he looks past me. I follow suit, spinning to see what he sees.

Propped against the brick exterior of one of the buildings forming the edge of this alleyway, a man struggles to breathe as he claws at several perforations in his chest and stomach. A slicked vertical trail of blood on the wall behind him denotes where he slid down to his seated position, and the gurgling from his throat indicates how much time he has left if he doesn't get help.

My eyes launch upward and away from the wounded human, the new perspective of the rounded corner offering only the faintest glimpse of someone fleeing. The tip of a tail is all I see, attached to a dinosaur that sprints around the corner of an adjacent alley across the street.

The shooter.

My feet launch me in the direction of the fleeing form as I shout over my shoulder. "Get him help! I'm going after the suspect!"

No response. There's no time to check on the jazz enthusiast who followed me to the scene of a crime; I've got more pressing matters to attend to. Namely, proving my worth and catching this culprit who just attempted murder. I charge across the street, hearing the screeching brakes and blaring horn of a delivery truck as I make the dangerous maneuver. No time to apologize.

I make it across the street and into the escape alley. I'm close. If I can just get around that corner I can ID the suspect and—

Crack!

No. No, no, fuck no, not now.

My hands shoot in front of me to break the fall as best I can as my knee seizes up, instantly halting my sprint and sending me hurtling to the paved ground in the alleyway. Several jagged pieces of gravel embed themselves into my palms and elbows, the searing ache and burgeoning blood rivulets causing me to grit my teeth. I didn't get around the corner, but if I can at least see...

I start crawling on my elbows, pulling my worthless leg behind me as intense pain fires from my right knee. Fucking thing. Fucking piece of shit. I can't miss this chance. I can't—

Just as I arrive at the corner, heaving myself as far forward as I can in one final lunge, the telltale sound of screeching tires informs me that I'm too late. They escaped. Their getaway ride was stationed a block away, and they only had to outrun an enfeebled and crippled woman pretending to be a cop to get away with shooting a man in broad daylight. God damn it. God damn this fucking knee. God damn this worthless woman.

I bring my fist down on the concrete below me, flecking blood from my palms across the ground with the motion. No tears fall; only bitterness and hatred reside in my mind now.

The captain was right. I can't be a cop.

Slowly, I place a hand on the brick wall next to me and try to swing my right leg around to unlock my knee. The motion is painful, both due to my bloodied palm and the angle I have to wrench my leg to bring it in front of my seated posture. My dress is absolutely ruined, scraped and ripped beyond recognition between my tumble and subsequent army crawl. Bracing myself, I put my hands on either side of my knee and pop the joint, feeling both screaming pain and relief in one motion. My leg can move properly again but feels tremendously weak due to the strain.

Using the wall for further leverage, I pull myself up to my feet, being careful to put as little weight on my right leg as I can manage. Thankfully, my tail helps to counterbalance my stance, so unless my knee seizes again the odds of me taking another tumble are low. In embarrassment and dejection, I limp back to the scene of the crime, hearing the sound of an approaching siren as I arrive next to the man I left behind in my pursuit.

He's as white as a ghost. I don't see any vomit on his shirt or on the ground, but I worry that a stiff breeze might knock him over. He stares past the individual who was shot toward a small indentation on the adjacent alley wall. The crevice holds several garbage bags of unknown age, many of which are split open with trash strewn about, likely the doing of rats. I doubt the locale holds any significance; the jazz enthusiast seems to be staring into space.

As I arrive at his side, I place a hand on his shoulder, both to get his attention and to steady my own balance as my knee continues to threaten me with immobilization. He barely reacts. Before I can say anything to him, my eyes rest on the victim. His arms hang limply at his sides, and his neck no longer holds the weight of his head. I don't consider myself squeamish, but I still gasp, not at the revelation that this body no longer houses a soul, but as the characteristics of this man register with me.

Large, coke-bottle lenses dangle at the end of his nose, magnifying his now-lifeless eyes just as much as they always did. A pinstripe cap lays on the ground next to the human, aiding in collecting some of the blood that escaped onto the concrete. His frozen expression of terror offers a conclusion to what had him so frightened this morning.

I never even got to ask him his name.

I turn back to the human standing next to me. His face is one of shock, his eyes wide and his mouth frozen partially agape. I don't blame him. Seeing one of your own kind gunned down like this… it's a lot for him to take in, I'm sure.

The sound of squealing tires and squad car doors being thrown open clue me in as to what's about to happen. I get the man's attention by gently squeezing his shoulder, he turns my way, still not blinking and still managing his breathing as best he can. I offer him a comforting smile. "The cops are here. They're gonna ask you a bunch of questions, but don't panic, alright?" He gives me a meek nod, his face still ghostly white.

Though it's a tall order with a dead body only a few feet away from us, I do my best to lift the heavy air hanging over the alley. "I'm Aubrey Carter. I never got your name, fellow jazz enthusiast."

His color returns ever so slightly. "Samuel. Samuel Lawson."

Chapter Three: Pierce

"—find yourself out in Cavemanhattan, watch out for a jam around 52nd and Broadway. Old York jazz seems to attract all sorts of cool cats, even during the morning commute. That's all for today's smooth as silk traffic report. Anyway, it's gonna be another hot one out there, so be sure to throw an extra ice pack into your lunch pail, fellas! It's 6:00 AM, and that means it's time for living legend Miles Cratis and his smokin' hot single, 'So What'."

The sound of what I assume to be a combination of plates being smashed on the ground and a cat being strangled resonates through the thin wall of our bedroom. I grunt, trying to roll over and tune out the racket to get a few more minutes of sleep, but the cacophony will not halt its invasion of my ear canal. With a huff, I throw the blanket off of my once cozy form and roll out of the bed I so desperately wish I could have spent a few more minutes enjoying.

I don't take any time to stretch or scratch my ass. I immediately stomp into the hallway and to the closed door concealing the hideous screeching, bringing a fist to it several times in rapid succession.

"*Russell!* Turn that shit down in *my* house!"

A scramble on the other side of the door is followed

swiftly by blessed relief for my irritated eardrums, then by the door being thrown open. My frazzled son stands before me, about a foot and a half shorter than I am but with some growing still left to do. He speaks in a cracking, pubescent voice. "S-sorry, dad! I thought you were still asleep."

I blow a puff of air from my nostrils as I look down at him. *"Was.* Not exactly the alarm clock I hoped for. What the hell are you even listening to in here? If you wanna hear jackhammers on concrete I can take you over to that construction they're doing on Stegen Island."

Russell glances at the radio, a newer adornment for his bedroom. He asked for it for his birthday last week. Damn thing wasn't cheap, but money's pretty good right now. I didn't mind springing for it, but if he's gonna be listening to crap like that...

"I-it's called jazz. It—"

I growl. "I know what *jazz* is. Pointless garbage noise made by skinnie mongrels. If that racket is going to be my wake-up call every morning, I'll—"

"Pierce Signorelli, you leave that boy alone and come get some breakfast!" I glance toward the voice of my wife that just carried itself up the staircase, then back at Russell. He continues looking up at me with his dark blue eyes, his even darker blue plated tail swaying slowly as he waits for dismissal from my scolding. Spitting image of his old man.

It was an annoying way to wake up, but now that the noise is turned off I'm not mad anymore. I give the boy a wink and a grin. "C'mon, son. Let's go get some grub."

He happily returns the smile. "Sure thing, pop!"

I speak over my shoulder as I start heading down the stairs. "Go ahead and get your sister up. Lazy girl's probably still in dreamland. Don't let her roll over and fall asleep again, either."

Russell knows the drill. I hear him cross the hall to his little sister's room and open the door, speaking quietly in order to gently wake her up. He's a good kid. They're both good kids.

I duck under the ceiling lip as I reach the bottom of the stairs. We purchased a house with nice high ceilings to accommodate my height, but there's still a couple spots where I can brain myself if I'm not careful. Turning the corner toward the kitchen, I see my beautiful stegosaurus wife hard at work doing what she does best: keeping the home. The smell of sizzling mixed greens on the stovetop makes my stomach growl instantly. Carnivores like to tease us herbies sometimes about not having access to the same flavor profiles they got. Dumbasses, they just need to marry a damn good cook like I did.

I cross the kitchen in two steps, bringing my head next to that of my wife so she can give me my morning kiss. Bianca obliges, a glowing smile on her snout as she does so. "Morning, Pierce. Not being too hard on Russell this morning, are you?"

I give an innocent shrug. "I just wanted him to turn down that radio was all. Trash can lids being banged together isn't my style. Now, if he was tuned in to a station playing some Bing Clawsby I wouldn't have had reason to bemoan him!"

Bianca giggles. "That boy might be growing up to look just like you, but that doesn't mean he has to like the same music as you!"

I let out a sigh. She's right, of course. That said, I wouldn't mind if he was listening to music made by upstanding *dinosaurs*. But that wretched jazz shit? Purely the product of skinnies. Filthy subspecies. If I tried to list out every single problem that's been caused by their kind, I'd be at it for a week.

Well. I don't need to start my day off bad. I've got my wife, my two beautiful children, a spacious home, and a solid paying job. They aren't taking those from me, and if they tried I could tear them apart with my bare hands. Thank you Raptor Jesus for letting me be born into this body. Fellas around the office always complain about the fact that they gotta work so hard at the gym to even come close. For me? I hardly exercise save for the hoofing I do during my errands. There's a reason why us dinosaurs were the superior race for so long.

Why we still are, far as I'm concerned.

I take a seat in the chair at the head of the table, its large frame capable of supporting all six foot eleven inches of my height and three hundred eighty pounds of my dense bone and muscle. The grooves carved into its sides give my tail somewhere to go when I sit, though my plates do still get caught on occasion. I've taken the chair a few feet toward the living room with me a few times after supper. Always makes the kids giggle and the wife scold me for being clumsy about it.

As I pick up the morning paper set next to my place, I notice the scales around my knuckles are healing up pretty well. A bit of red is still visible under the midnight blue of my hand, standing out due to the disparity in hue. Bianca never asks me how I get the cuts, bruises and broken knuckle scales I occasionally come home with. She knows my work is heavy work sometimes. She just helps me put some alcohol on the wounds and bandage them up if needed. Even discreetly threw out a couple changes of my clothes that were too tattered and bloodied to be washed. And it usually wasn't my blood that stained 'em.

Damn good woman.

Just about the time the kids make their way downstairs, four plates of succulent cooked greens are set on the table, one at each place. Russell excitedly plops into his chair and begins digging in while Angela more sluggishly finds her own place, yawning and wiping the residual sleep from her eyes.

Girl's only nine years old but acts like she's always in need of a nap.

I glance at my son and daughter from over the newspaper. "You two forget to say something to your mother?"

Russell hastily swallows his mouthful of food before turning to Bianca. "Good morning, mom. Thanks for breakfast!"

Angela yawns again before speaking quietly. "G'mornin'." Maybe we need to push her bedtime up.

Bianca smiles at our children as she takes her own seat. "Good morning, you two! Dig in while it's warm!"

The four of us enjoy a peaceful breakfast together, Russell excitedly telling me what he plans to do with one of the last free days of his summer break. School will be starting up again in a couple weeks, so he's getting in as much play time with his friends as he can in the meantime. With his build, I'm hoping he'll try out for the football team once he's eligible. He'd be a monster of a linebacker.

Angela has friends, too, but seems to prefer being with her mother, shadowing Bianca as she does her daily tasks and errands. Bianca dotes on both the kids, which is her God-given right to do since she's the one that gave birth to them. Angela is certainly more attached to her mother than me, but that doesn't upset me. I'm here to provide for the family and be a father; if Angela wants to grow up to be a woman like her mother, she'll have to learn everything she can from her.

Bianca glances my way. "So, Pierce. What's on your work schedule for today?"

The front of the newspaper informs me that it's August 24th, which means it's close to month end. "If I had to guess, I'll probably be playing the part of errand boy today, collecting dues from some of the places in town."

"Think you'll be home in time for supper?"

"Probably, unless something keeps me late. I'll let you know when my shift is done, as usual."

She gives me a smile and we finish up our breakfast. As Bianca clears the table and washes the dishes, the kids make their way to the living room to stare at the television for a while. Russell mentioned playing with some friends, so I imagine Bianca will drop him off somewhere, then attend to her errands with Angela in tow. We've got two cars so it's no trouble for us to do things like that. I head back upstairs, take care of my morning preparations, and get myself dressed.

Despite not having the highest post at the Local 237, I was always taught to dress for the job you want. The job I want isn't the one I've got right now. Even though I have some family connections, it seems like the higher-ups are dragging their feet in regards to putting me in a more comfortable position, still having me do things like run errands and handle messy jobs. I know I'm good at what I do now, but I don't want to be stuck in the same place forever.

I button up my pressed white shirt before affixing the slim necktie under its collar. I sling the leather straps of my shoulder holster over my arms and tuck the snub nose .38 Smith & Wesson into its concealed home. I've had this particular pistol for a few weeks now. They only ever last until they get used. The black sports coat completes my preferred look, and I head out.

I slide behind the steering wheel of my jet black Cadillac DeVille. Brand new model, just came out this year. As much as I want to move up in the business, the money I make now is good enough for me to afford a few luxuries like this. It drives like a dream. There's plenty of room for my bulk, a comfortable groove in the seat for my tail to rest, and four doors to accommodate when I have to play chauffeur. I love the car almost as much as I love my own children.

My house is in a quiet suburb on the outskirts of Old York City. The city keeps expanding, and someday it might overwhelm even where I've planted my roots; for now, the neighborhood grants serene escape from the chaos of downtown. The trade-off is that it's about twenty minutes away from the office, but that doesn't bother me. I like the peace and quiet of the drive. Don't have to listen to motormouth fellas who think they've got a lot to say. I'm not exactly a silent guy myself, but I understand that there's a time to talk, and a time to shut your trap and use your ears.

I bring my car around the back of the impressively sized building from which I do most of my daylight-hours operation. Standing at five stories, it isn't the tallest building in eyeshot but for where it rests in Cavemanhattan it commands respect. The seal emblazoning its front entrance features two pack mules flanking a wagon wheel engraved with our letters. It's one everyone knows, for better or worse. Sure, our organization has gotten in a little hot water over the years, but we still do what needs doing, and we provide a valuable service to millions of hard-working dinosaurs across the country. It's somewhere I'm proud as hell to work:

The International Brotherhood of Herdsters
Local 237

Most folks use the front entrance. That's where you'll find pristine offices filled with women processing the mountains of paperwork that come in every day, and men who will shake your hand and hear your case when a labor lawsuit arises. It's the part of the business that keeps us running, keeps hard-working fellas safe from abusive bosses and unfair work environments.

I use the back entrance. Not that I have anything against the front entrance, I just got no business up with the pencil pushers and hand shakers. My business is conducted around town for the most part, and what I need to do in the office takes place behind closed doors or, more often, not in the Herdsters building at all. If we're discussing heavy work, it's not being done here. Too many chances for unwelcome ears, especially given the government's hard-on for us over the past few years.

"Pierce, how ya doin' this fine Monday mornin'?" The familiar voice that greets me as I push open the sublevel door attached to the underground garage is that of a diplodocus with a wide smile to match the stubby fingers he holds toward me me in greeting. His brownish color accentuates the tweed of his own sports jacket. He's a little more casually dressed than I am, but professional enough to put on the right appearance for who we'll be interacting with today. His lengthy neck technically lets him beat me in the height department, but if we were measuring based on shoulders I'd have him by at least a foot.

I shake his proffered hand. "I'm not too bad, Marty. Yourself?"

"Ya know, can't complain. The wife, though... *phew*. You wasn't kiddin' when you said the month leading up to our kid bein' born was gonna be *rough*."

I chuckle, knowing all too well how ornery the women can get as they near that special day. I dealt with it twice already, and, God willing, that'll be the only two times. I love my kids and wouldn't be upset if a third made its way into my life, but we certainly aren't *trying* for it. I imparted some of my fatherly wisdom to first-time father-to-be Marty a few months back. Hopefully he remembered the part about being patient with your wife and getting her however much ice cream she wants.

Marty and I exchange a little small talk as we make our way further into the building. The basement level is a bit more spartan than upstairs, with less decoration and more unmarked doors, most of which lead to rooms with filing cabinets stuffed full of paperwork. The door we pass through, however, brings us into a simple room with a wooden conference table flanked by a dozen or so chairs. This morning, two of the chairs are occupied.

The first is filled by the form of the dinosaur I expected to see in here: Charles Rossi. Very professional fella, he doesn't go by Charlie or Chuck. One of the guys tried calling him Charlie once when we was at the bar after work. Ended up getting a bottle broken over his idiot skull. Had to tip the taxi driver pretty good after he bled all over the back seat on the way to the hospital. Charles is a professional guy unless you fuck around with things you aren't supposed to fuck around with.

The gray-colored triceratops looks up at Marty and I as we enter, flashing his flat herbivore teeth in our direction. Despite the chiseled appearance brought on by several menacing scars across his snout and surrounding the base of his foremost horn, he has a pleasant way about him when he's in a good mood. Must be in a good mood today. "Morning, gentlemen. How are the two of you doing?"

Marty speaks up. "Doin' well, Mr. Rossi. Wife's only about a month away from her due date."

Charles's smile widens. "That's wonderful to hear, Martin. I hope she's not too much trouble for you."

"Oh, no. Not at all. Well... she can be a little grouchy, but she's doing all that heavy lifting so I don't mind."

Charles turns my way, expecting a similar response to his original inquiry, but I don't offer it. Instead, my eyes are affixed to the second figure filling another of the dozen chairs in this room. A weasel of a human looks back at me from behind ridiculously thick lenses, his unsettling eyes magnified to twice their normal size. He nervously fidgets with the cap clasped in both his hands, its pinstripe pattern doing little to distract from how ugly he is even when he wears it pulled down tight.

I grit my teeth and scowl. Eggsy. What a fuckin' stupid name. Not that the name would work well even for a dinosaur, considering we don't lay eggs, but a fuckin' *skinnie?* When I was a child, some kids in my neighborhood convinced me that skinnies lay eggs, and I believed them. It'd suit their kind. They certainly got the mental capacity of birds, so it just made sense. Of course, I know he uses the nickname because his actual name is Egbert. Fuckin' ridiculous, and now he's sitting in this conference room.

Why is he sitting in this conference room? I turn my eyes to Charles, wordlessly asking the question with my disgusted look.

He answers it. "Egbert is going to be joining the two of you today for dues collection in northeastern Brachlyn. Make sure you don't let McIntyre push off payment again, either. He's a month behind as—"

"Excuse me, Mr. Rossi. But *why* is this skinnie joining us?"

Eggsy lowers his eyes, quaking feverishly with sweat pouring from his sickening troglodyte brow. Charles, on the other hand, merely cocks his head at me. "Because I said so. Egbert is working his way up the organization and has proven himself very loyal. You'll be training him today."

I can't help but clench my fists. How dare you. How dare you tell me to take this fucking skinnie with us on our dues pick-ups. The fucking nerve of—

Suddenly, a thought occurs to me. He just said "training". As in, Eggsy is learning this job. Maybe they're expecting a vacancy in the position soon. Hell, I've been busting my ass long enough, I deserve something bigger than running errands. Besides, how many times have I said that even a monkey could do this fuckin' job? And now I'm being asked to train a *monkey* how to do it.

My fingers uncurl and I take a slow, steadying breath. I'm unhappy about this arrangement, but if it means I'll be training my replacement, so be it. My eyes shift back over to Eggsy. He still doesn't meet my gaze, a common supplication tactic for his cowardly kind. Glancing back at Charles, I nod. "Not a problem, boss."

"Excellent! Well, good luck with the rounds. Give me a phone call when you're at the end of your route, I'll let you know where you can drop everything off."

I turn to the door, meeting Marty's eyes as I do so. He peers at me with concern; he's worked with me for a couple years now, and knows all too well my disdain for humans. He's got a softer heart than me. Unfortunately, that softer heart means he's a bit more susceptible to the manipulation of these lower species.

As I exit the room and start heading toward my car, I hear the scramble of Eggsy darting behind us, keeping several feet away as we head back out to the parking garage. He holds a hand on his cap, preventing it from flying off his head since he has to hustle to keep up with our longer strides. Yet another evolutionary pratfall that proves his kind should still be serving us. In his other hand, he clutches the handle of a black briefcase that swings back and forth.

Arriving next to my Cadillac, I spin around to face Eggsy. He screeches to a halt, stepping back a pace as to not be too close, and averts his eyes. I extend my pointer finger at him and speak slowly and deliberately. I've found this tactic in combination with using small, uncomplicated words to be the best way to get your point across when dealing with their kind.

"Listen up and listen well, skinnie. You will be doing what we tell you to do today. You will keep your mouth shut unless we speak to you. You will listen, and you will *hopefully* learn a thing or two. You got that?"

His knees practically knock together. "Y-y-yes, sir, Mr. Signorelli, s-sir!"

"And if you put *one* scratch on my car, I will fuckin' *behead* you."

He gulps and frantically nods in acknowledgment, nearly setting his cap loose from its tenuous hold atop his greasy, disgusting hair. With a final puff of air from my nostrils, I gesture with my head for him to get into the back seat.

I'm gonna have to steam clean the whole car after this.

We follow a standard schedule as it gets to the end of the month, taking care of dues collection by neighborhood, a few blocks at a time. Each stop can take anywhere from a couple minutes to a half hour, depending on how chatty the owner of each establishment happens to be. Sometimes that's small talk, and sometimes that's us listening to excuses about how they came up short this month or how their guys are moaning about switching to another labor union. During the day, I just listen. I don't thump skulls or break bones. That's left for the higher-ups to decide on before anything of that magnitude goes down. After all, we're the face of the Herdsters. Can't be going around plugging guys in broad daylight just because they missed a few months of dues.

Today, we've got about twenty stops to make. It shouldn't take us longer than the business day, but we'll have to do a little driving. We've got a lot of clients in Brachlyn, and they're a bit spread out. Our first stop is a liquor store that specializes in fancy wines. "The Vineyard", it's called. I like stopping here first because the owner's a nice fella, never gives us trouble, and always breaks out a bottle to send Marty and I away with a glass of delicious, top quality wine in our stomachs.

As we pull up to the well-dressed building tucked between a few other storefronts facing the road, I suddenly remember the quivering lump of skin in the backseat. I put the car in park and rotate as far as I can to bring Eggsy into view. He sits in the center of the backseat, hands tucked between his knees, with his black briefcase cradled between his arms and his stomach. He jolts away from me as I turn toward him, perhaps anticipating the back of my hand. As fun as it'd be to rough him up, I should at least try to keep things professional.

"You're staying in the car. Marty and I will be back in a few minutes. Don't touch anything."

Eggsy seems to open his mouth to protest, but quickly closes it. Smart move. Instead, he sheepishly nods before withdrawing his handkerchief and wiping some of the ceaseless moisture from his brow. I know it's a hot day today, but Raptor Christ he's gonna really sick up my backseat with his everflowing sweat.

I can't dwell on it. I'll just get angrier the more I think about it. Instead, I shut off the car and hoist myself out of the driver's seat. Marty follows suit on the opposite side of the vehicle, craning his neck around to arch his eyebrows at me. I know the look. He's gonna grouse at me. As we make our way to the front door of the wine shop, he makes good on my supposition. "Pierce, you sure we shouldn't be bringing him in with us?"

I roll my eyes. "Yes, I'm sure. It's bad enough he's here at all, but I'm tolerating it because it might mean I'm not gonna be at this menial busywork for much longer."

Marty furrows his brow for a moment before realization sets in. He knows I'm not thrilled about performing this tedium; he and I have had plenty of time to chat during the course of our workdays together. He glances over his shoulder at the car. "You think they're fixing up Eggsy to take your place?"

"Charles did say we're 'training' him. What else would that mean?"

"Well, if that *is* the case, then he really should be coming in with us, shouldn't he? He'll have to learn how to handle the clientèle when they, ya know… try to get one over on us."

I chuckle. "And you think that petrified weasel of a skinnie is gonna be able to manage our almost entirely dinosaur patronage? Fuckin' doubt that. You'd better harden up a bit, Marty. I think you'll be the new smiling muscle for these transactions moving forward."

Marty gives a nervous chuckle in reply. He's not a weakling by any means; bastard's got a right hook that'll ring your bell for a week. That said, he tries to be diplomatic past the point when diplomacy should have ended. We don't rough people up during the day, but we do sometimes have to harshly remind them where they stand.

Pushing open the door to The Vineyard, we are immediately greeted by the beaming smile of Marcel Sauveterre, a lime green iguanodon with a pot belly and an accent nearly as incomprehensible as his last name. He tried guiding me through pronouncing it once. I gave up after about twelve attempts. However, his pleasant demeanor more than makes up for the difficulty I sometimes have understanding him.

He instantly uncorks a bottle as we enter. *"Bienvenue, mes amis!* It is another *journée chaude,* no?"

I return his smile but scratch my head in the process. Journey what now? Marty seemed to pick up on the context. "You can say that again, Marcel. I'm already down a pound and a half just by sweatin'!"

Marcel lets out a hearty laugh as he pours three glasses of the freshly opened wine. He joins us in our morning taste, rattling off the name of a village somewhere on the other side of the world that I've never been to and will never go to. Damn delicious wine, though. I might not appreciate the history or craftsmanship behind it, but I sure as hell know a good taste when it hits my tongue.

As he makes a little more partially cryptic small talk with us, Marcel slides a white envelope toward us. Marty gives a nod and plucks it off the counter. Another minute later, we finish our drinks and bid the wine salesman a pleasant day.

Back at the car, I notice Eggsy in the same place, briefcase in the same position, with his eyes focused on nothing in particular. Half the time I don't even think thoughts go through the thick skulls of those apes, and moments like this prove my theory. As I open the driver's side door, however, his head jerks in my direction. He decides to speak up. "D-did everything g-go well?"

I don't say anything, but Marty, ever the polite one, answers. "Yep. This place is run by a fella named Marcel. Real nice guy, can't make out a damn word he says. Always on time with his dues, though, so it's a pleasant first stop."

Eggsy smiles at Marty, clearly happy that he's being treated as less of a burden by him than by me. Nothing I can do about it; I've discussed the topic at great length with Marty in the past, but he seems convinced that skinnies "aren't all bad". Fool thoughts like that will get you shot in the back of the head someday.

As I ignite the engine and start moving us toward our next few stops, Marty glances down at the briefcase that the skinnie in my backseat is clutching. He looks down at the envelope in his hands, then back at the case. "Hey, Eggsy, why don't you hand that up here?"

Eggsy blinks. Before he can respond, I make an inquiry. "Marty, what on God's green earth would you want that skinnie's wretched luggage for?"

Marty shrugs. "I'm guessing he brought it to help carry the dues. Hell, I been saying we should bring one, but we always just stuff everything in your glove box. By the end of the day there's six envelopes that can't fit in there." He looks toward Eggsy again. "That *is* why you brought it, isn't it?"

Eggsy excitedly nods. "Y-yeah! Yeah! I figured, ya know, we could use somethin' to carry the dues. I figured you guys woulda had one, but, ya know, just in case, I could help out and show that I'm ready to—"

"For fuck's sake. Give Marty the fuckin' case already. I'm gettin' a headache listening to you yap."

Eggsy casts his eyes downward again before holding the briefcase out to Marty. My dinosaur cohort accepts it, flicks open its clasp and opens it up in his lap. The gaudy green felt lining of its interior informs me of two things: one, the case is indeed empty, and two, Eggsy has fuckin' terrible taste in accessories.

Marty drops the envelope into the case, clicks it shut and attempts to tuck it into the floor by his leg. This takes some effort on his part; for as roomy as my car is, we are both large dinosaurs who have to make some sacrifices with comfort when it comes to travel. One of those sacrifices is having very little extra space when transporting ourselves via means besides our own two legs. He seems to find a spot for the case, though he wears a bit of a sour expression, possibly due to being jabbed in the leg by one of its corners.

His inconvenience doesn't last for very long since our next few stops are only about a minute away. The following several hours go by with little issue. I still don't allow Eggsy to join us, demanding that he wait in the car while me, Marty and Eggsy's briefcase do the rounds. If I'm gonna be training this guy, it'll be my way, and I am not going to tolerate walking into these establishments with a skinnie in tow. I've got some god damn pride.

Around twelve thirty, we pull up to another stop on our list. I slam my car door a little more fiercely than I meant to, immediately regretting the action as I hear the lowered window loudly rattling inside of it. That would have been a real fucking mess if I just shattered the glass inside of the door. Thankfully, I dodged a disaster. Not thankfully, I'm still in a rotten mood.

The place we just came from is one of the few "businesses" we service that's run by a skinnie. Some fuckin' produce stand down the street. Place reeks of rotten fruit and disgusting flesh bags. It makes my skin crawl to go in there, but they pay up every month so we gotta collect.

That is, they *usually* pay up every month. This time, the owner was sniveling and mewling about coming up short. Begged us for some leniency. We don't rough people up during the working day, but I never wanted to backhand a piece of trash skinnie more in my life. Instead, I was professional about it.

I'll wait for the order from upstairs to take care of the trash.

Using the fantasy of executing that little shit to cheer me up a bit, I head around to the back entrance of Sal's Butcher and Grocery. I know where Sal's office is, having been here a handful of times already, and it's easier to just use the back door. Less ornery dames slapping the cabbage out of each other's hands to deal with. Plus, Sal is a pretty stand-up guy. It's another one of the easier stops of the day.

At the steps leading up to the door stationed next to the loading dock, I tell Marty to wait for me. He does so, briefcase in hand as he withdraws his pack of smokes. He knows I don't like him smoking in my car, so he uses these opportunities to get his nicotine fix. I jog up the small set of stairs and throw open the door.

A skinnie in overalls and glasses nearly as thick as Eggsy's stumbles backward from the swinging metal barrier. Whether he was about to leave or was just standing there like the braindead mongrel he is... well, that's anyone's guess. Glancing around, I see several more skinnies staring up at me, jaws slacked and eyes devoid of thought. Warehouse workers. Physical labor is about the best thing they're suited for. Shame we have to pay them now.

I stride across the internal portion of the loading dock

toward Sal's office, leaning my head to peer through its large glass windows and hopefully flag down the parasaurolophus so I can collect his dues and be on my way. However, I do not see him. Instead, yet another skinnie stands near the office, gazing up at me like a toddler mesmerized by a balloon salesman.

Apparently I have to interact with these troglodytes. I speak slowly and with authority. "Where's Sal Fontana?"

"H-he's not here. C-can I help you with—"

In two steps I'm across the space, staring down at the lump of worthless skin in front of me. I grit my teeth and he stumbles backward. "Can you go *get* him for me?"

"H-he's n-not in the s-store. A-are you—"

I'm surprised the beast can even form sentences. Feeling the sickening disdain spreading across my face, I lower myself closer to the skinnie and address him as I would a preschooler. "I am here for his dues. And you're telling me he's not here?"

He is petrified beyond words for a moment, lowering his head in cowardice. They come to rest on the Herdsters pin on my jacket before widening. His eyes shoot back up to meet mine again. "I c-can get that for you!"

He can *what?* Before I can process his rambling, he darts into Sal's office and pulls open a drawer of Sal's desk. I feel my plates stand on end as I stride over to the door. If this skinnie draws iron on me, he'll be losing that gunfight in a sore way. However, he doesn't lift a pistol from the drawer; rather, he fishes out an envelope with the word "Dues" scrawled across its front.

"Mr. F-Fontana asked me to g-give this to you! Here!" He holds a quaking hand containing the envelope in my direction. I will admit, I'm a bit shocked by the development. Did Sal really entrust a *skinnie,* of all people, to handle this for him? Wouldn't he be worried about the dishonest fuck running off with the money, or, more likely, failing to remember where it was? The fuckin' things can't even tie their shoes most days.

I just don't understand other dinosaurs sometimes. Begrudgingly, I snatch the envelope from his hand, taking a quick glance inside of it to ensure it's full of the owed money and not folded up tissue paper. The cash is all there. Looking back down toward the human, his messy and unkempt brown hair doing little to contain the sweat atop his head or shield his nauseatingly reddened cheeks, I jab a stern finger in his direction.

"You tell Sal that the next time we come by to collect, it's *him* here, not some skinnie *fuck.*"

He rapidly looks downward, adequately intimidated. "Y-yes, sir. S-sorry, sir."

I let out an audible grumble. While I'm not pleased I had to deal with even more skinnies, at least these ones weren't completely retarded. My business here concluded, I turn and head to the exit. As I throw it open and step outside, Marty's head cranes around to me. He drops his cigarette to the ground and stomps it out. "Everything go okay in there?"

I hand him the envelope which he stuffs into the briefcase as we both make our way back toward the car. "If I never have to see another god damn skinnie in my life, it'll be too soon." Of course, Raptor Jesus is fickle and immediately blesses me with the sight of Eggsy, still seated in the backseat of the car, just as sweaty and nervous as ever.

But... something makes me pause. Something about the encounter I just had. I climb behind the steering wheel again and start the engine, mulling over the skinnie in Sal's and how quickly he fetched that envelope. Sal, someone I know to be a pretty reasonable guy despite employing those apes, actually *trusted* one of 'em enough to hand off his dues. And the skinnie actually did it.

I glance in my rearview mirror at Eggsy. He peers out the window, watching the cars pass by in the other direction.

Though it looks to me like his head is empty of thoughts, he *is* working his way up in the Herdsters. Enough for Charles to assign the little shit some work that requires a lot of trust.

Huh. Maybe...

Nah, I'm not gonna think about it too hard.

The rest of the day goes by without a hitch. At some point in the afternoon Marty finally gets fed up with trying to find a compromise between the sharp edges of the briefcase and his thighs, so he tosses the case in the empty space of the backseat next to Eggsy. At first I glare daggers at him, wordlessly emphasizing that I wouldn't trust a skinnie with a fuckin' nickel, but Eggsy doesn't do anything with the case. He barely even acknowledges it, going back to looking out the window or occasionally making small talk with Marty.

That twinge in the back of my head again.

Maybe I am being too hard on the little fucker. He's been pretty kosher all day, despite the usual nervous behavior and profuse sweating. He's done what I told him, and he hasn't put a toe out of line. He even waited in the car while Marty and I got lunch, despite Marty inviting him. Said he wasn't hungry. When we came back, I'd have expected him to have wandered out of the car, milling about and fanning himself off with his cap, but he was right where we left him, patiently waiting.

Hmm. Well, granted, I'm not gonna change my perception on skinnies due to the good behavior of one. But Eggsy might not be such a waste of space as the rest of them.

As the small hand on my wrist watch reaches the five, I park the car about fifty feet away from a payphone. Closest spot I could find. The briefcase, laying on the seat next to Eggsy, is packed full of almost two dozen envelopes stuffed with cash. It was a long day with a few minor hiccups, but nothing that needed any drastic action. All that's left is to give Charles a call to let him know we're done, get our meet-up location and make our deposit.

Lifting the handset from its cradle, I slide a dime into the slot next to it before punching in the familiar numbers for the Herdsters office. Once connected to the receptionist, they transfer me to Charles's desk. He answers as punctually as he always does: exactly two rings, then a click followed by his voice.

"Charles Rossi speaking."

"Hey, Charles. It's Pierce. We're all done for the day."

The sound of him passing his own handset from one hand to the other is followed by his response. *"Excellent. How did it go?"*

I shrug unconsciously, knowing the gesture doesn't communicate itself through the phone lines. "Pretty good, all things considered. Did have a problem with the produce stand on 43rd. Owner thinks they don't have to pay on time."

Silence for a moment as I hear Charles rustling some papers. *"Hm. Seems they've got a pretty good payment record. When did they say they can settle up?"*

"She said next week, but I ain't—"

"We'll give them a week. No reason to break eggs if they haven't gone rotten yet." I let out an irritated huff a little too loudly. *"What was that?"*

"Nothing, sir. No problem."

"Very good. Meet me at Santiago's in a half hour. After that, you'll be all done for the day." He pauses. *"Of course, you'd be welcome to stay for a few drinks."*

I chuckle. "Not tonight, sir. Wife is expecting me home for supper. Speaking of, I need to give her a call real quick before I head your way. I'll see you in a bit, Mr. Rossi."

"Very good. See you soon."

I place the handset back on its metal holster, hearing the telltale sound of my dime settling in with all the others. Waiting a moment, I lift the receiver again, deposit another coin, and tap the only numbers more familiar to me than those of my office.

"Hello?"

"Hey there, beautiful."

She giggles. *"Well, if it isn't my darling husband. How was your day?"*

"Long, but almost done. I'll be on my way home after making a quick stop."

"Mmhmm. And how many drinks will this quick stop involve?"

"Hey! I told you I'd be home for supper, so I'm gonna be home for supper! I even told my boss 'no' when he mentioned the prospect of drinks."

"Oh, my! And you're trying to move up in the business? I don't think you'll go anywhere if you turn down Charles Rossi when he's offering to socialize with you."

This woman. I sigh, rotating in the phone booth. "You know, Bianca, here I thought I was being a good husband and prioritizing my wife's delicious supper over…" I trail off.

After a moment, Bianca notices. *"Pierce? Are you still there?"*

I narrow my eyes, peering back toward my car. It remains parked where it was, with Marty lazily resting his chin on his hand, eyes half closed. But…

The back seat is empty.

Where is Eggsy?

Where the *fuck* is Eggsy?!

I instantly drop the phone, its metal cord emitting a sharp *snap* as it hits the bottom of its reach, momentum sending the device clattering against the glass walls surrounding me. I only barely hear the voice of my wife as I slam open the door of the booth, nearly ripping it off its hinges before I barrel down the street toward my car.

I arrive in only a few seconds, roaring as I come to a stop. "Marty! Where is Eggsy?!"

Marty only partially opens his eyes before addressing me through the rolled down windows. "He said he was hungry.

Said there was a hot dog stand behind us he wanted to hit."

My head snaps left and right, looking for any hot dog stalls in sight. There are none. Already knowing what I'm about to not see resting in my backseat, I push my head through the open rear window.

"The fuckin' briefcase is *gone!* He fuckin' *took it!*"

Only now do Marty's eyes shoot open. His head instantly whips around, scanning every part of the backseat, including the floor, before throwing open the passenger door and stumbling out of the vehicle. "Holy shit. *Holy shit!* Oh my God, what the *fuck?!*"

As much as I want to box this idiot's ears, there's no time. We have to find that lying piece of shit skinnie, and *now*. I charge down the street in the direction our car does not face, scanning every place I can for any sign of the little shit. Marty follows close behind, worthless apologies tumbling from his lips. He can apologize to me after we wring this puke's neck and recover our money.

I can't fuckin' believe it. Just when I was thinking even one skinnie might not be that bad, they prove my disdain right yet again.

Two dinosaurs walking in the opposite direction complain as I shove past them. I don't stick around to hear exactly what rude words they spew at me. Bigger fish to fry. Just as I pass by an alleyway, frantically surveying the other side of the street for the freakishly thick glasses and pinstripe cap, Marty shouts at me. "Pierce! The alley! There's the case!"

Spinning around, I dart into the alley that Marty's long neck is already surveying. Sure enough, a black briefcase lined with nauseating green felt lies discarded on the ground, its contents and its owner nowhere to be seen. I only spend a second scanning the concrete for any evidence of the envelopes before throwing myself toward the other end of the alley. It bends, which means it might—

I turn the corner, spotting the back of a sweat-drenched skinnie in the alley opposite the street. Not a second later, a large truck pulls to a stop between us, blocking my view. I barrel out of the alley and dart around the back of the truck, not bothering to look both ways. My blood's too boiled for a stray bumper to do anything but piss me off more. I make it to the other side and rush into the alley.

At that moment, Eggsy spins around and collides with me, letting out a cowardly shriek. My hands instantly close around his head and I toss him like a rag doll into the wall next to us. The sickening slap of his skull hitting brick brings his screaming to a rapid stop. He probably ain't dead yet, but his bell is definitely rung.

I shout at the crumpled heap of worthless skin in front of me. "Where's the fuckin' money, Eggsy?!"

He doesn't reply, trying to pull himself off the ground. His legs wobble underneath him and he falls back to his knees again. Not that escape is an option anymore; Marty stands at the entrance of the alley from which we entered, panting due to being a bit out of shape and because of his smoking habit. I feel fit as a fiddle, full of adrenaline and ready to break this fuckin' skinnie's neck.

I repeat my question, slower and more clearly so that his addled mind can process my words. *"Where* is the *money,* you skinnie piece of *shit?"*

Eggsy pulls himself from his daze and onto his feet, glaring up at me with newfound hatred in his eyes. "I don't have it, you meteor-dodging fuck. It ain't here." Gone is the nervous exterior; either it was all a ruse, or he's come to accept his fate.

I stare down at him for a moment before throwing open his coat and rapidly patting him down. If there are any envelopes stuffed into his pants, I'll be ripping more than just the money away from his groin. He slaps at me, but it is a fruitless gesture. I am the stronger race.

Standing up straight again and still empty handed of the money, I move a rung up the ladder of *how fucking serious I am right now,* drawing the .38 from my shoulder holster and pointing it directly at Eggsy's heart. He flinches in response, but still stands defiant against me. Marty, on the other hand, immediately whips his head around, making sure no bystanders observe the unfolding scene before scolding me in a whisper. *"Pierce, are you nuts? Put that away, we need to bring him back in. Charles will know what to do!"*

I coolly repeat my question a third time. "The money, Eggsy. Where did you hide it?"

Eggsy glares at me, a strange combination of foolhardy bravery and undeserved confidence in his eyes. "You're not gonna shoot me in public, you club-toed sack of scales. How am I gonna show you where it's at if I'm dead?"

I glance around the alleyway. It's an absolute rat-nest paradise, packed with trash and filth. Fitting place for a skinnie to die, if you ask me. I look back at Eggsy and shrug. "It'll take a while, but we'll find it. I don't think your services will be needed."

Marty's eyes widen. "Pierce, we need to—"

He doesn't finish the sentence. The only sound any of us hear for a moment is that of the tinnitus ringing in our ears. Eggsy looks surprised. It doesn't seem like he felt the lead pass through his torso and embed itself in the brick wall behind him. He glances down at the slowly spreading red spot on his white dress shirt before looking back up at me in disbelief.

One isn't enough for the skinnie fuck, so I release another from the gun's chamber. Then three more in rapid succession, each bullet pushing him further backward until he collides with the wall and slides downward. He keeps staring up at me, unable to speak through the blood that begins seeping from his mouth but communicating his intense hatred of me all the same. His pained expression conveys his absolute shock at his bluff being called by the smoking end of my snub-nosed companion. His quivering eyes make known the utter betrayal he feels in this moment.

The feeling is mutual.

A second or two goes by before I can hear Marty's voice past the ringing in my ears. "Pierce! What the *fuck* did you do?! We have to go! *Now!*"

I calmly turn his direction, a serene smile resting on my lips. And here I thought it was gonna be a bad day. Nothing quite like executing a skinnie to turn a frown upside down. But Marty is right. His panicked look communicates the urgency of our situation, and we both charge across the street and into the adjacent alley.

A few bystanders peer our way, but nobody points or screams. Nobody calls our names after us. It's just another day in Old York for them. Someone got greased in an alley, someone who probably deserved it or maybe didn't. The cops would show up soon, putting up their tape and waving people along, giving themselves something to do. The ambulance would arrive, identify that the skinnie is, in fact, dead, and stuff Eggsy into a black bag to be carted off to some furnace. Burned and sent to hell... a fitting end for a cowardly traitor like him.

We throw ourselves into my car; my foot's on the gas before the engine even finishes spinning up. Not a moment too soon, either, as the approaching sirens herald the arrival of those boys in blue. Once again out of breath, Marty stammers. "Raptor Jesus fuck, Pierce. You-you fuckin' killed him. You shot him in broad daylight. Are you out of your fuckin' mind?!"

I shrug. "He betrayed us. Stole Herdster money. He got what was comin' to him."

Marty's tone reveals the anger boiling inside of him. "That wasn't your call to make and you know it. We should have dragged him back to the car and taken him to Charles."

I wave a hand in his direction. "Ahh, pomp and circumstance. You know Eggsy was gonna end up on the wet side of a pier for this stunt, even if he handed the money back to us."

"That *wasn't* your call to *make.*"

I glance at him, not taking my eyes off the road for too long. I know he's got a softer heart than me, but I honestly can't tell why he's making such a big stink about this. He ain't the one that pulled the trigger, I am. "Well, what's done is done. We'll go to Charles and let him know what happened. I'm sure he'll understand."

Marty shakes his head at me in disbelief before slumping back in his chair and crossing his arms. He doesn't speak to me again, but he knows we have a new stop to make on the way to Santiago's.

I pull the car up to the small iron bridge that connects part of Stegen Island to one of its several adjoined man-made "islands", a platform littered with cranes and industrial equipment designed for loading and unloading cargo ships. This particular dock doesn't see much use anymore as it's been outclassed by several other larger and more modernized operations. Rather than tear this one apart, it's been mostly abandoned save for the occasional need to load a ship that couldn't fit into the other overcrowded bays.

I'm not here to load, however. I'm here to unload. Stepping up to the edge of the bridge, I glance around, making sure no kids on bicycles or nosy old women out for an evening stroll are looking my way. Confirming that the coast is clear, I toss my .38 revolver into the bay. Twenty feet below, a small *kerplunk* is followed by the metal sinking to the bottom of the sea, joining what is almost certainly several hundred of its retired brothers. I've made my fair share of contributions here, but I'm not the only fella who likes to send spent pieces to the pasture off of this particular bridge.

Looking up toward the ocean, the setting sun at my back paints the water in a majestic tapestry of orange and blue. I breathe deeply through my nostrils, the scent of salt and brine adding a sense of nostalgia to the moment. The sound of the waves lapping at the steel beams below me whisper words I do not understand, but they speak to me all the same.

I wonder what Bianca is making for dinner tonight.

Chapter Four: Samuel

"Holy fuckin' shit, was that gunshots?!" I whip around, peering cautiously toward the sequence of loud pops that just rang out. The primal part of my brain forces me to hunch over, ready to tear off in the opposite direction the moment I see a gun come into view. I ain't about to fuck around with—

A clatter startles me a second time and I spin to face the sudden racket. The velociraptor lady's grocery bag is strewn on the ground, a package of hamburger buns bouncing a few inches away. I think her tail swept em' off the bench, and now she's on her feet and darting *toward* the gunshots?!

My rationality tells me to let this broad charge headfirst to her suicide all by herself. Every iota of my survival instinct screams at me to put as much distance between myself and the nearby danger that's made itself known as humanly possible. But for some reason, I don't. Instead, my legs carry me in the same direction as this blue-tinted dinosaur woman.

Despite my body refusing to obey its intrinsic drive to protect my own life, my throat manages to vocalize disagreement. "Are you fuckin' crazy, lady?! Usually you go in the *opposite* direction of gunshots!"

She continues charging forward. "I'm a cop!"

"Holy shit, really?! Well, then, go get the bastard!" I

didn't realize this lady was a cop. She's in pretty normal work attire, but maybe that's her "after shift" change of clothes? Or before shift, even? I don't know a thing about this woman. That said, hopefully she'll know how to defuse this situation.

She turns her head to me as I run after her. "This is dangerous, you shouldn't be—"

My sudden stop causes her to pause and face forward again. We've arrived at the scene of the shooting, and—it's a human. A human fella got shot. He sits propped against the brick wall of the alleyway across from us, clutching his chest and trying to prevent as much blood from leaking out of his torso as he can. He's already as white as a ghost, and tries gurgling something at us but can't form the words past the fluid clogging his throat.

The raptor immediately darts further down the alley, shouting at me as she approaches its bend. "Get him help! I'm going after the suspect!"

I try to acknowledge her orders, but nothing comes out. Much like this poor guy, I find myself unable to form a sentence. Instead I slowly step toward him, frantically scanning my brain for any sort of help I can offer. Do I apply pressure? Do I make a tourniquet? Do I get this guy a hot dog and a beer so he can enjoy something before he fuckin' dies? I don't know what to do. I glance around, but nobody else is here. Nobody else investigated the gunshots. Nobody is calling for help.

It's just me and this dying stranger. I can only stare down at him in disbelief and shock. I feel awful for being unable to help him in some way, but… I'm just an average guy. I'm not a doctor, a combat medic or a priest. I don't have any morphine to give him or absolution to offer him. All I can do is watch him struggle to cling to the last few moments of life he's got left.

With what I'm sure is immeasurable difficulty, the man limply waves me closer. I oblige his request, stepping toward him and kneeling down next to his resting place, my leg coming dangerously close to the pool of blood collecting underneath his legs. He doesn't try speaking, already realizing the futility of his attempts. Instead, he points a single finger toward a small crevice in the alleyway. It's an odd junction between two buildings, not quite an alley of its own due to abruptly ending in the supporting wall of one of the adjacent structures, and only receding into the edge of the alley by about six feet. Partially split open garbage bags are packed into the strange divot, their contents strewn and obliterated by weather and wildlife.

I look back to him, perplexed by his gesture, but he adamantly points toward the space, his quaking finger calling out not the trash in the alcove, but something else.

An odd slurry of both shock and curiosity causes my legs to carry me toward the grotto. I know I should be running for help, or cradling this man while he breathes his last, but the look of hopeless sincerity in his eyes forces me to follow his guidance. Traveling about thirty feet down the alley to the crevice, I peer deeper into it. If it's something buried in this trash heap, I'll be here for a while trying to find whatever it is, but…

I cautiously climb over the garbage, my legs sinking into God knows what beneath me, wrapped within decayed garbage bags. The smell is musty and ancient, but thankfully nothing explodes and coats my clothes with rotten filth. I have to turn sideways to squeeze into the opening; a larger form would have zero chance of fitting into this claustrophobia made manifest. I turn once more to look toward my guide; he still clings to life, continuing to point, nodding encouragement in my direction.

Turning back, I shuffle another few feet into the passage. I feel movement by my work boots—rats making a break for it, I'd imagine. Thank God I ain't squeamish about the little pests. I do my best to scan the area for anything that would be so important to this guy that he'd ask me to retrieve it for him, or maybe he's—

A particular brick set into the wall catches my attention. From a distance, nothing about it seemed peculiar, but now that I'm only a few inches away from it...

I reach out and poke at it. It doesn't budge. I slide my fingers into the tiny spaces on either side of the stone and try pulling.

Ah. That did it. The brick slides loose, revealing a small opening. Inside is a pile of envelopes, some white and some brown, hastily jammed into the hiding spot. Many are bent and some have started coming open. I reach into the hole in the wall, drawing out one in particular near the front of the pile that catches my attention.

On the face of the envelope rests a single word, scrawled in thick, black lines. The handwriting is unmistakably that of my boss, Sal Fontana.

"Dues".

It takes a moment for me to register that my mouth hangs slack open as I stare at the word. I slowly lift my eyes to look at the roughly two dozen other envelopes, all similarly stuffed with assorted bills. My hand quakes as I pull open the paper flap and peer inside. Twenties and fifties. Probably close to a hundred bills. My brow furrows as I do some quick math. This has gotta be close to two thousand bucks, if not more. And there's so many more envelopes, equally stuffed with—

The sound of an approaching siren snaps me out of the moment. My head whips toward the alley, then back at the stash. In a panic, I cram the envelope back into the hole and replace the brick, careful to set it as neatly flush against the wall as it was before. I scramble out of the trash pile, stumbling a bit as a bag catches around my ankle. I kick some of the strewn garbage back into the alcove after I exit, trying to make it look less apparent that someone was rooting around in there. Stepping back and staring at the literal trove I was just shown, I can't help but whistle.

"Holy shit, man. I don't know if you put that there or if you found a fuckin' treasure map, but that is some serious…"

I turn back to the man as I speak. He no longer holds his finger pointing toward a stockpile of more money than I've ever seen before in my life. Instead, his arm rests on the ground, partially helping to prop his lifeless torso in its seated final pose. The eyes that only moments ago desperately clung to the spark of his soul now stare purposelessly at the concrete below him.

I find myself unable to move. All I can do is stand and stare. As the reality of what I'm looking at sets in, a place deep in my stomach tries to churn, insisting that I vomit. The fact that I skipped lunch turns the reaction into nothing more than a dry heave, but I feel the color drain from my skin all the same.

As I straighten up from my doubled over position and wipe nothing but a little drool from my chin, I force myself to look at the dead man again. Who was this guy? What was his name? What did he do to deserve getting shot in the middle of the day?

Did it have something to do with that money? It… had to have, right?

I absent-mindedly stare at the hiding spot as a hand comes to rest on my shoulder. I feel like I should be on high fuckin' alert right now, but I barely even flinch. I turn to acknowledge who it is. The raptor lady again. She seems to be favoring one leg, and her pretty dress is all sorts of fucked up now. Whether she took a nasty tumble or got into a fist fight with a pile of gravel, she looks worse for wear. She stares down at the man, a sort of sad look in her eyes. She did say she's a cop, so she's probably seen a body before. In this city, unless she just started yesterday, there's no way she hasn't.

The sirens have arrived, joined by the sounds of car doors being thrown open and orders being barked. The woman squeezes my shoulder lightly before speaking. "The cops are here. They're gonna ask you a bunch of questions, but don't panic, alright?" Christ. I'm standing over a dead body with a cop next to me. I hope that's enough of an alibi for them to not shoot me to death right here and now.

Her eyes meet mine, their yellow hue glistening in the traces of light that make their way past the buildings surrounding us. For some reason, in those eyes, I'm able to find a little bit of calmness. She gives me a gentle smile. "I'm Aubrey Carter. I never got your name, fellow jazz enthusiast."

I do my best to return her gesture. "Samuel. Samuel Lawson."

Before she can say another word, the wind is knocked out of me as a fuckin' freight train slams into me and crushes me into the concrete below. A chorus of shouts for me to "get on the ground" and "stop resisting" join the angels that sing sweetly within my thoroughly rung bell. Somewhere through the thick haze, I hear the protestations of...

Aubrey. She said her name was Aubrey.

That's a really pretty name. I like it.

A pair of greenish hands roughly pulls me up to my feet, only partially helping to stabilize the spinning world around me. The speed lever on the phonograph in my head slowly ratchets up, the noise around me becoming clearer and more understandable as my brain stops sliding around in my skull.

"—just said, you fuckin' knuckleheads! He was with *me!* He ain't a suspect!" Aubrey seems pissed. That's nice of her. I attempt to focus on her but there's about three or four half-transparent Aubreys sorta rotating around one another. I think I need to sit down.

I try to bring my hands up to wipe some of the stars away from my eyes, but they don't budge from behind my back. It takes a moment to process the metal restraints fastening my wrists together and the absolute vice grip of fingers and claws that hold my arm in place.

The voice attached to the claws speaks gruffly toward Aubrey. "You're tellin' me this skinnie was just standin' around and didn't have nothin' to do with another skinnie gettin' shot in an alleyway?"

Aubrey sounds completely incensed now. "First off, cut the shit with callin' him that word. He's an innocent bystander that just saw another human die. Second, yes, I am sayin' that. He was talkin' to me at the bus stop and we both heard the gunshots. I almost caught up to the shoo—" She cuts herself off, hesitating before finishing her sentence more quietly than she began it. "—the suspect."

A moment of silence, then laughter. Uproarious laughter from the cop holding my arm as well as the other two who are standing nearby. "You—*hahaha!* You actually *chased* someone? No wonder your clothes are completely fucked! Miss Carter, desk jockey tryin' to play cops and robbers! Hey, how's that bum knee of yours workin' out for ya?"

Aubrey lowers her gaze to the ground, her cheeks brightening in embarrassment. Her tail wraps around her stomach and she cradles its feathered tip in her hands.

So she's not a cop?

Suddenly, her eyes widen. She lets her tail fall back to its resting position before refocusing on the guy holding my arm in defiance. "I didn't get a good look at the suspect, but I saw a tail. The suspect was a dinosaur, not a human."

Though his laughter has stopped, my captor still speaks in an overly condescending tone. "Well, *that* helps us narrow it down, don't it? Why don't you leave the police work to actual cops, you daffy broad? Speaking of—" He roughly spins me around to face him. The green twin ridges on the dilophosaurus's head push aside the neatly trimmed black hair that makes itself visible under the sides of his uniquely shaped police cap. "We got some questions for you. You're comin' back to the station."

All I can do is nod in acknowledgment. As he shoves me in the direction of the squad cars, three more pull up to join the two that had already parked. Officers begin piling out of them, shooing away rubber-necking pedestrians who are suddenly interested in the scene now that there's a police presence. One cop pulls a strand of yellow tape across the entrance of the alley that reads "Crime Scene—Do Not Cross".

Another dinosaur, a spinosaurus fella with a frilled and jagged spine splitting his back in two, throws open the back door of the police car and shoots me a wicked-looking grin past his long, narrow snout. The few times I've seen a guy get arrested, they at least help him into the backseat, being careful that the arrestee doesn't hit his head on the way in. I guess I didn't warrant such care; the big dilophosaurus bastard chucks me into the car like a bag of golf clubs. A few moments later, all three of us are on our way to the station.

I've never been arrested before. The neighbors called 'em on me and my ex a few times when our fights turned into a competition of who can toss more of the other person's shit out the bedroom window. This is my first time being in irons and getting hauled in, though. I've got no clue what's gonna happen. For all I know, they could toss me in a cell and let me rot. If I don't get out before my shift tomorrow, I'm losing my job for sure. Raptor Christ, what do I do? What am I—

I try to shake off the paranoia. I didn't do anything wrong. I think back to Aubrey's words. Don't panic. Just answer their questions honestly. I'll be okay.

The chair nearly comes out from underneath me as I'm forcefully tossed onto it by the surly dilophosaurus. My hands are still bound behind my back as I glance around the room, seeing only a small table and a few chairs illuminated by a single flickering bulb. An interrogation room. I remember seeing 'em on that TV show, TrawlNet. When a suspect is brought in here, they don't leave without having confessed to their crimes, and it usually happens before the next commercial break, too.

As my eyes come to focus on the dinosaur that's been man-handling me so far, I catch the name on his badge: "Duffy". The other guy with him, the spinosaurus, wears the name "Preston" on his chest. Unlike Duffy, Preston's badge practically sparkles, as if the thing was just minted yesterday.

Preston's diamond eyes flash at me before he turns to Duffy. "So, what do we get to do now? Rough him up a bit? We need to get him to talk, right?" His hand slides across the nightstick that hangs at his hip in a grotesquely sensual manner. If this guy has his way, I'm fuckin' dead.

Duffy shakes his head at the spinosaurus. "Don't be an idiot, Preston. We only do that if he doesn't cooperate with us." He turns my way, a sly grin tugging at the sides of his snout. "You *are* gonna cooperate with us, ain't ya?"

In the back of my mind, I want to make a snarky remark about how it seems to be in my best interest, considering my hands are still shackled behind my back and I'm in a room with two stacks of muscles who could easily kick the shit out of me. I opt instead for a simple reply. "Y-yeah, of course."

Preston leans against the wall next to the door and crosses his arms, clicking his tongue against the roof of his mouth in clear disapproval of my willingness to cooperate. Duffy grabs one of the other chairs and takes a seat across from me. He scans me up and down before he begins his interrogation. "So, what exactly was a skinnie like you doin' standing over a dead body?"

I do my best to steel my resolve against his probing gaze. I'm innocent, I just have to convince these guys of it. "I was on my way home from work. I heard the gunshots while I was near the alley where it connects to 46th Street."

"So you just happened to be walkin' by when a man got shot dead, is that right?"

"Yeah, that's right."

Preston snorts. Duffy merely rolls his eyes. "Well, forgive me for finding that a little hard to believe. Because, you see, most people go in the opposite direction of gunshots. That is, unless they're soldiers." He crosses his arms. "You a soldier, skinnie?"

I avert my focus to the floor. "No, sir."

"Then let me repeat my question. Why were you standin' over that dead body?"

These guys are trying to get into my head. I didn't do anything wrong. I just need to be honest. "I had stopped to talk to that velociraptor woman. Aubrey, she said her name was. At the bus stop. Few seconds later, the gunshots were goin' off."

At this, Preston leans closer, a wicked sneer revealing his lethal-looking teeth. "And what, exactly, would compel a skinnie like you to talk to a bull dyke like her?"

Bull d—a *lesbian?* I didn't get that impression from her. A pit forms in my stomach upon hearing the news, but I do my best to shake off the feeling. "She was hummin' a jazz tune that I know. I recognized it, and stopped to mention it."

At this, Duffy lets out a long breath through pursed muzzle and crosses his arms. He turns to Preston. "Well, *that* much checks out. That loopy dame never has her station set to anything but that fuckin' mess of noise."

Without thinking, I blurt out the words. "It's not fuckin' noise, it's *music.*"

Both sets of eyes across the room lock back onto me. I sincerely wish they had cuffed my ankles together, too, because it would have prevented me from so thoroughly inserting my boot into my own mouth. I feel my cheeks flush red as Duffy stands. "Then again, I don't know that I'm buyin' the story. You skinnies are always shootin' each other without reason. Dunno why you'd just stand there instead of runnin' away, but hey. Made our jobs easier, didn't it?"

Preston chuckles in response. I balk. "I-I don't have a gun!"

Duffy shrugs. "Awful lot of garbage in that alleyway, lots of places you coulda dumped a piece. We'll have to dig around for a while, but when it turns up, your goose will be well and truly fucked."

My gut churns. The alley. The money. If they go searching top to bottom, they could easily find it. And if they do—

Preston leans forward. "If you just confess to doin' it, this would all go a lot easier for ya."

I try to bring a hand up to wipe the moisture that's accumulating on my brow, but the handcuffs make this a difficult prospect. Raptor Christ, between the heat and the pressure, I'm sweating like a whore in church. What the hell do I have to say to prove to these two that I'm innocent?! "Y-you guys heard Aubrey! She's a—she works for the police, doesn't she? You said yourself that she's a desk jockey."

Duffy frowns. "Yeah, she is. She ain't a fuckin' cop though."

"But she still works for you. Why would she lie about me to you?"

This causes him to pause. He glances down, running his thumb and forefinger across the bottom of his snout in contemplation. Before he can come up with an answer, however, Preston provides one. "It wouldn't surprise me if a bitch that likes horrible skinnie music would try to protect a skinnie. Allegiance is a funny thing, ain't it?"

Duffy glances over at Preston, taking his words into consideration. Though he doesn't seem fully convinced, he shrugs. "Well, I don't think we're gonna get any further today. I say we let you stew in a cell for a few days. See if it jogs your memory at all."

No! I can't—I'll get fired! I can't lose my job! I try to open my mouth to vocalize these points in protest, but no words come out. Preston steps across the room and rips me out of the chair, nearly dislocating my arm in the process. Duffy opens the door and begins moving into the hallway, only to be interrupted by a stern, authoritative voice.

"What is the meaning of this?!" On the other side of the portal, I can barely make out the features of a brown, leathery wing and the tip of a beak. A pterodactyl, I think. Preston's grip on my arm tightens so hard I can feel the blood flow to my hand ceasing.

Duffy stutters. "C-Captain?! We were just—"

A trace of an orange crest that grants the hallway occupant an additional eight inches of height comes into view for only a moment. The so-called "captain" glances past Duffy in my direction, then back to the officer. "Uncuff him this instant."

"But sir! We have reason to believe this skinnie was involved—"

The pterodactyl's words are icy. "Don't you *dare* use that kind of language in my precinct, do you hear me? You speak that foulness around me again, you'll be washing every cruiser in the garage for a *month*." Duffy doesn't reply. "Carter filled me in on what happened. Cut him loose, and pray he doesn't file a complaint. If he does, it's going in *both* of your records."

Begrudgingly, Duffy turns toward me and Preston. The look in his eyes is one of pure hatred. He nods, causing Preston to violently grab the iron links around my wrists and slide a small key into each, unlocking and removing the restraints in the process. My hands now unbound, I bring them in front of my body, gently rubbing the sore skin where the metal had been cutting off my circulation.

The pterodactyl is already out of sight. Duffy takes a wide step in my direction and jabs a claw within an inch of my nose. "If you file a fuckin' complaint, I will hunt you down and toss you off a rooftop. You *got that?*"

"Y-yeah. I got it."

He glares at me a moment longer before storming out of the room. Preston pushes me through the door, then down the hallway toward a staircase. When the shoving stops, I turn to inquire as to my next action, but all he does is shoot me one last cruel, toothy smile before disappearing from eyesight.

I guess this is where I'm supposed to go, and I'm not staying here a second longer than I need to. Thank God for divine interventions. I thought I was gonna be spending the next few days in a cell for some shit I didn't even do.

But why did the police captain suddenly come to my rescue? He said it was someone named... Carter?

Just as my mind puts two and two together, I arrive at the top of the stairs. In the lobby of the police station, seated on one of the benches near the entrance, is the same blue velociraptor woman I met earlier. The grocery bag that had been perched next to her at the bus stop once again rests by her side, though the bag has a noticeable rip in it that allows some of the groceries to peek out of their small brown prison.

Aubrey.

Aubrey Carter. That's right, Carter was her last name. She stuck up for me to the police captain and got my ass bailed out. Her head turns my direction just as I come into view; she springs to her feet, still seeming to favor her left leg as she offers me an apologetic smile. "Samuel! Raptor Jesus, you're alright! I'm sorry they did this to you!"

I shrug and smirk as I approach, afforded an air of unearned confidence now that I'm not sweating my balls off and shackled in the dark dungeon. "Hey, it's no problem. They just questioned me was all. Besides, I had some good advice going into it. Thank you for that."

She blinks, confused for a moment as to what I meant

before smiling again. She has a really nice smile. "Oh, that. I'm glad you were able to keep your cool."

"Dunno about all that. Honestly, I got you to thank for putting in a good word for me with that pissed off pterodactyl fella."

"That *pterodactyl fella* is Captain Aaron. He's a good man. Wouldn't have let that happen to you if he knew what was going on right away. It's..." She trails off for a moment, glancing around to see if anyone is nearby and listening. Noting that the coast is clear, she leans a little closer and speaks quietly. "It can be rough around here. Some of the officers can be assholes."

I chuckle, quickly cutting myself off when I notice the look she shoots me. "Tryin' to keep the sentiment on the down-low, sure, sure. I just—well, I got first hand experience with that now is all. Present company excluded, o'course."

At this, Aubrey turns her eyes downward and lets out a sigh. Her tail twitches, bringing its tip up toward her front, seeming to beg to be held by her. She doesn't accept its request, instead fastening her gaze to mine again. "I'm sorry about lying to you about being a cop. I shouldn't have done that."

My hand moves to the back of my neck. "Well, you weren't being *entirely* dishonest with it. You do work *for* the police, right?"

"Yeah, but I do clerical work. I'm trying to become a police officer."

"Ahh, I heard about that. They're letting women into those police programs now, aren't they? Think I read about it in the paper, some precincts here in Old York are already getting lady officers." I scrunch my nose. "What are they gonna be called? Policewomen?"

"I suppose so. But, still. I shouldn't have lied to you. I might have put you in danger. That's not what a cop is supposed to do." Her tail beckons her to cradle it again, and this time she obliges, putting her hands around its feathered end and holding it in embarrassment.

I do my best to shrug it off. "Hey, don't sweat it, Aubrey. You were trying to do the right thing. Cop or not, that's admirable. Besides, you had me there with you!" I pause. "Not that I woulda been any good, mind you. But, hey. I'm great at providing moral support."

This finally gets her to laugh, causing her posture to relax and her tail to return to its place behind her. Her smile is bright and her laugh is enchanting. "You are an odd one, Samuel Lawson! But thank you for the moral support!"

I can't help but chuckle along. "Happy to be of service!" I glance down at her dirtied dress and bloodied knees. "Though I wish I coulda been of more help, by the looks of it. You alright?"

She brushes some of the hair from her face. "Mmhmm, no big deal. It's just a dress. I took a bad fall while pursuing the suspect." I glance down at her shoes, noticing she's not wearing heels so I'm unsure what might have caused her to take a dive. The cops at the scene of the crime said something about... her leg? Her knee? I can barely remember; hope to God I didn't get a concussion from that tackle I took. She opens her mouth as if to say something, but stops with a shake of her head. "I'm fine. But thank you for asking."

The air hangs idle between us for a moment. Aubrey holds fast to my eyes with her own, their yellow glimmer swirling with consideration. I've got no clue what she's thinking right now, but I silently curse myself for not being more charming than I am. Instead, I awkwardly stuff my hands into my pockets and glance past her toward the exit. "Well, I guess since I'm not behind bars, I can head ho—"

"Samuel." She cuts me off, but doesn't provide a reason why. Instead, she seems to wrestle with her own mind for a moment, her eyes darting left and right as she witnesses some sort of internal melee occurring. All I can do is cock my head, unsure as to what else she needs.

After a moment, she takes a deep, resolute breath, nods to herself, and pulls the small purse she has tucked under her arm around to her front. It's not one of those purses that's packed with everything and the kitchen sink like you see some women walkin' around with. Instead, it looks to only have her bare essentials, though I can't see inside of it from where I'm at. Her hand comes to rest inside the purse, and after one more moment of what looks to be decisive encouragement, she withdraws what she was searching for.

Thus far, she's come across as a pretty clear-spoken woman, but for the first time I hear her stumble over her words. "You—I mean, *I* got these tickets. I got two of 'em, and—I was just—mind you, it's not a date or nothin', but I—*here.*" She jams one of the two tickets into my hands with a huff, clearly not satisfied with her delivery. Her cheeks glow red. What on earth?

My mind trails off as I read the ticket. Birdland Nightclub presents...

"Holy fuckin' shit!" I exclaim much louder than I intended to, immediately receiving a scornful look and a sharp *shushing* from Aubrey. I recoil at my foolish outburst as I glance around, realizing that... oh, there's almost nobody else here in the lobby. Only a single, tired-looking receptionist who glances my way with annoyance before returning to her crossword puzzle. All the same, I turn back to Aubrey in embarrassment. "S-sorry! I just—*holy shit.* Miles Cratis? Live?!"

She nods, giving me a small glimpse of her sharp but nicely kept teeth by way of a beaming smile. "Uh huh! I just about had the same reaction when the captain gave these to me! Someone from the nightclub dropped 'em off here at the station, and nobody else wanted 'em!"

I glance down at the ticket again, then back up to the woman who just...

My expression causes her to clue into my train of thought. She repeats her sentiment from before. "N-not like a date or nothin'! I just had an extra is all. And you're a jazz enthusiast, too, so I thought, as a 'thank you' for helpin' me earlier..." She averts her eyes as her cheeks redden further.

I offer her an awkward, dejected smile. "Yeah. I didn't think it'd be a date. Makes sense."

This causes her to furrow her brow toward me. "What do you mean by that?"

"Uhh—the officers who were interrogating me—they told me that you..." I desperately hope for her to cut me off, realizing what I'm trying to say without actually saying it out loud, but she doesn't. Instead, she patiently awaits my words. I scratch the back of my neck as I glance around before speaking in a whisper. *"Y'know, prefer the company of ladies or wh—"*

"Son of a *bitch!*" This time it's Aubrey's turn to provide a poorly volumed outburst, once again earning the two of us an ire-filled look from the otherwise disinterested receptionist. Aubrey puts her hands to her hips in a show of equal parts defiance and irritation. "I'm not a god damn lesbian!"

I stumble over my words, the boot I've once again inserted into my mouth making it difficult to speak. "Oh—OH! Oh, geez. I'm—I'm sorry, I didn't—"

She rolls her eyes and lets out another irritated huff before glancing at me apologetically. "N-no, that... wasn't directed at you. It's those stupid fuckin' knuckleheads. I mean, Duffy knows I wa—" She quickly cuts herself off, her eyes widening before she glances down again. I notice her fingers clench into fists as she seems to wage another internal conflict with herself.

I don't know what that was about, but I gotta cut the tension somehow. I glance at the ticket again. "Are you sure you're okay with me taggin' along? You could probably get a fair chunk of change if you scalped this to some sucker standing around outside the venue tomorrow night."

She shakes off the temporary turmoil that overtook her and looks back up at me. "Like I said. It's my way of saying 'thanks', and... also an apology for how you were treated by those idiots."

I can't help but smile. "In that case, yeah! I'd be honored! Thank you!"

She returns the smile. "See you tomorrow night at eight o'clock then."

I interject as she turns to leave. "Um! Should we exchange phone numbers? Ya know, just in case somethin' comes up?"

She raises an eyebrow at me. Real smooth, dumbass. She just got done sayin' it ain't a date and here I go, tryin' to get her number. As I open my mouth to apologize and take back my stupid request, she steps across the lobby toward the receptionist's desk. A moment later, she returns with a pen and a sheet of paper that she tears in half before scribbling several digits upon one of the two halves. She hands it to me, along with the pen and the other unmarked half of the paper. With an embarrassed grin, I do the same.

I'm sure I'm blushing like a god damn idiot right now, but I just got her number. I got Aubrey's number. Hot damn.

After she returns the pen to the eternally grumpy receptionist, she bids me adieu once more. "Until tomorrow night. I'm looking forward to the show."

"M-me too! See you then! Have a good night, Aubrey!"

"You too, Samuel."

In a repeat of my previous interruption of her departure, I get one last word in. "My friends call me 'Sammy'."

She pauses, turns my way once more with arched eyebrows and a playful grin on her lips. "'Sammy' it is, then."

I don't interrupt a third time, allowing her to gather her half-torn grocery bag and make her way out of the police station lobby. I can only stand in place and watch as she goes, mesmerized by the gentle sway of the blue feathered tail attached to her... attached to her really nice...

I'm staring like a fuckin' creep. But I'll be damned if that ain't a great sight to take in.

Okay, cool down, Sammy. She said it ain't a date. It's just friends. She's just going out with me to a jazz club to see one of the greatest living jazz musicians in the world.

No big deal. You got this.

Shaking off my daze, I finally make my way out of the lobby, the lowered early evening sun still heating the street with its oppressive ultraviolet rays. I barely notice. Though the police station is about three quarters of a mile out of the way from where I need to go to get home, I stroll down the street as though I don't have a single care in the world. In one hand, I hold a ticket to see Miles Cratis in person in one of the hottest nightclubs in the entire city. In the other, the phone number of a beautiful velociraptor woman.

Aubrey. Her subtle curves find their way into my imagination again, causing a stupid grin to spread across my face and other parts of me located a little farther south to tingle a little bit. I can't say I've ever looked at a dinosaur woman and thought to myself, 'Wow, I'd like to bring her back home', but I suppose there's a first time for everything, right?

O'course, I got no clue how she feels about me. She did emphasize several times that this isn't a date. And, I mean, she's a dinosaur and I'm a human. You just don't see that sort of thing happening almost ever. I think I remember a story about a dinosaur and a human getting married years ago here in Old York, but in a lot of other places in the country it's completely illegal for the species to even be together with one another, let alone get married.

It's a big part of the Civil Rights movement. Not just

letting people be with who they want to be with, but humans being treated equally in courts, in other legal matters and—well, everywhere, really. An end to segregation and discrimination. Even though Old York is pretty progressive, there's loads of places where humans are still second-class citizens. Hell, I still feel that way here most days and we're supposedly ahead of the curve.

With that all in mind, I just don't know if Aubrey would see me in that way. Yeah, she smiled at me and was nice enough to invite me to this show with her, but that doesn't mean she likes me. She's probably just being polite. I try to shake away the thought of her smile, but it keeps finding its way back into my mind. The image of her gently brushing the hair away from her eyes makes my heart flutter.

Geez. I think I might have really fallen for—

I come to an abrupt stop, having finally registered the space around me enough to tell how far my trip home has brought me. About eighty feet ahead of me, a police car remains parked next to the alley from which I was so violently plucked, along with an ambulance that wasn't there when I left. Two paramedics move an elongated metal stretcher with wheels toward the back of the vehicle, lifting the yellow tape as they pass underneath it. Their cargo rests inside of a sealed black bag upon the stretcher, as still and lifeless as he was when I left him.

Poor bastard. I was the last person he saw in this world, and I didn't even know his name. He just—

My eyes widen. *The money.* That stash he pointed out to me. I got so swept up with getting hauled into the station and then talking to Aubrey that it completely slipped my mind. Did the cops find it? They must have if they were investigating the crime scene, right? They... wouldn't know that I knew about it, would they?

I stand around with the gaggle of other people who observe the body being loaded into the back of the ambulance, a combination of gasps and tisks escaping some of the onlookers. Neither the paramedics nor the police pay us any mind as they climb into their vehicles and depart; I purposefully keep my cap pulled a bit lower to prevent the officers from recognizing me. Neither Duffy nor Preston are here, but I'm sure these cops were around when I got tossed into the back of the squad car.

The excitement having concluded, the rest of the pedestrians all shuffle away, exchanging a few speculative words as they depart. I, on the other hand, cautiously move up to the edge of the alley. I dare not move past the tape, despite the police presence being currently absent. Instead, I squint my eyes toward the crevice containing the treasure this man most likely died over.

It appears undisturbed. The trash is just as piled into the alcove as I had left it. It doesn't even look like anyone tried to root around in the garbage. Of course, if the cops were unaware of any sort of hidden stash, why would they? They'd just do their investigation, clean up the scene and collect the body.

A chill fires through my spine. I might legitimately be the only person who knows where this money is hidden. Considering the perforations that adorned the man who pointed it out to me, I'm probably not the only person who knows the money exists. That said, *why* would they have killed the guy if they knew *where* the money was? This guy might not have avoided his fate, but that pile of cash definitely wouldn't still be there.

Raptor Christ. What do I do? Do I go to the cops? After how they just treated me, how would they react if I waltzed back in there and said, "Hey, you know that dead guy you just picked up and accused me of killin'? Yeah, I know about a mountain of money right next to where he died!" Probably not a smart move.

Do I... tell Aubrey? She ain't a cop, but she seems

trustworthy. I mean, so far, at least. I barely know her. How would *she* react if I told her about this buried treasure at the crime scene?

No. I shouldn't do anything right now. I know where it is. If I come back here in a couple days after the crime scene tape's been removed and there's no more eyes on this place, I can check it out then. If the money's gone by that point, so be it. I don't even know what the hell I'd do with that kind of cash.

I could start my record collection again, that's for damn sure.

Either way, there's nothing to be done about it now. I'll just forget about it and focus on tomorrow night.

Tomorrow night with Aubrey, watching Miles Cratis play his greatest songs for us…

But that's tomorrow. Tonight, I got a dog back home that probably has to take a wicked shit.

Chapter Five: Aubrey

Tap, tap.
Tap, tap.
Hmm.
Tap, tap.
Tap, tap.
What is that?
Tap, tap.
Tap, tap.
Sounds like a drum beat. But a fast one. Something with that cool tempo that makes you want to move your feet...
Tap, tap.
Tap, tap.
I wonder if it's "Nica's Dream" by Horace Bronze. 201M1956 BC. Certainly got the tempo for it, but seems to be lacking the wonderful bass line and horn work.
Tap, tap.
Tap, tap.
No, it's something else. it almost reminds me of Art Drakey's "Moanin'", an instant classic from him and his Jazz Couriers that came out at the beginning of this year. If it is, it's bein' played in double time because this beat is maddeningly fast.

Tap, tap.
Tap, thump.
It's not a drum at all.
I bring a hand to my chest, feeling the reverberations of the heightened pace of my heart.
Thump, thump.
Thump, thump.
I glance forward. It's him. Samuel. Standing against the darkness surrounding me.
Thump, thump.
Thump, thump.
Sammy. His kind smile urges me to step toward him.
I begin to do so, but realize there's no place for my foot to go.
I look down. A staircase.
Thump, thump.
Thump, thump.
The voice I always dread draws close.
Thump, thump—
Thump—thump—
I try to spin around, but it's too late.
Thump—thu—

—

With a gasp, I fling the blanket off of myself and rapidly sit up. My hands tightly grip my midsection as I double over, sucking in air to try to steady my heartbeat. My tail quivers as it wraps around me, squeezing me in an unconscious hug. I try to draw my legs toward myself, but my right knee is locked up. I let out a sob, unable to work the kink out of it because of my hunched posture and occupied hands.
That god damn dream again. Why, of all days—
His smile appears past the blackened cloud in my mind.
Sammy.

My breathing slows and my grip loosens, but my heartbeat doesn't steady itself, now compelled to its accelerated rhythm by a different emotion. It's the same way I felt yesterday when I was trying to decide whether to give him one of my tickets. It's the same way I felt when he asked for my number. When I felt his eyes linger on me as I departed the station and headed home.

This feeling in my chest, caused by his kind eyes and his warm smile.

I glance at the clock radio next to me. About forty-five minutes before I would have woken up for my shift. I roll my eyes and slump back onto the bed, the muscles around my right knee loosening with my posture shift. There's no use in trying to go back to sleep now. Not with the way I'm feeling.

His smile returns to my imagination again.

Get a grip on yourself, Aubrey. It's not a date. You told him as much.

But did he buy it?

I bury my face in my hands as I try to conceal my own stupid grin, feeling the heat emanating from my reddened cheeks. Raptor Christ, I feel like a fuckin' school girl. What's getting into me? He's a human, for goodness sake. Forget about his warm smile, or his kind eyes, or his handsome features. He's a...

No. It's nothing. He's just a nice fella that had to go through some shit because of me. If he hadn't stopped to talk to me, he wouldn't have gone to that crime scene. He wouldn't have been arrested and questioned by those assholes at the station. He wouldn't be going to this show tonight with me.

He wouldn't have been in my dream. The only bright spot amidst the darkness of that hell I keep reliving. Most mornings I wake up with tears staining my cheeks. Today, though—yes, my heart was going a mile a minute, but was it because of the dream, or...?

I shake away the notions and force myself to sit up again, my locked knee straining itself once more. My escapades yesterday didn't help it any; I fully expected it to be an asshole to me this morning after my plunge in the alley. Quietly cursing the bungled heap of cartilage under my knee cap, I slowly massage the sides of the joint to work the kink out. Eventually, I'm able to retract my leg properly, its looming tenderness warning me that I'd better be careful with it today unless I want to taste concrete again.

I cautiously climb out of bed, favoring my other leg more heavily with my tail adding a little extra acrobatic balance to my slow gait. It's a curious thing that humans don't have the extra appendage; I've often found myself wondering how they manage without one. My mind wanders back to Sammy again, somewhat to my dismay as my tail begins neglecting its balancing duty in favor of happily swaying back and forth.

This is gonna be a hell of a long day. I already know it.

I spend some extra time on my morning shower and preparation, both because of the additional minutes afforded me by my nightmare and because of the butterflies in my stomach. The show's not until eight o'clock which means I'll have time to swing home and freshen up. All the same, I'm filled with the desire to make myself pretty, a desire I haven't had in a very long time.

It's not a date, but I still want to look nice. I'm gonna be in public, and I'm gonna be at a Miles Cratis concert.

And Sammy is gonna be there.

I let out an irritated huff due to my reddening cheeks making the application of my blush makeup more difficult than it should have been. The brush clatters on the bathroom counter as I stomp back to the bedroom to turn on the clock radio. It's still ten minutes before my alarm would have turned on the tunes naturally, but I need to distract myself.

As the radio crackles to life and begins intercepting the invisible sound waves and translating them for my ears to register, my breath catches in my throat. It's "Nica's Dream". One of the songs I thought about during my dream due to the rapid drumming of my own heart. The trumpet and tenor sax playfully weave around one another with the backing of Horace's beautiful piano riffs. My tail sways in time with the uptempo beat as Sammy's smiling face lights up my imagination yet again.

Apparently there's nothing for it. Only thing to do is get myself ready and get my ass into the station so that my daily mountain of paperwork can keep me sufficiently distracted. I finish my morning prep and make my way to the bus stop, doing my best to think about anything but the date I have toni—

It's not a date. *It's not a date.*

Aboard the familiar green and white vessel, distraction comes to me in about the most unpleasant way possible. I stare across the aisle of the bus at a vacant seat, one that was occupied just yesterday by the gentleman who died in that alley. The skittish, panicked man whose killer I was unable to identify due to my piece of shit knee. I lower my gaze, feeling as though I failed the stranger. I might not have been able to save his life, but I could have at least ID'd the one responsible for his death. Give him a little justice, let his spirit be at peace.

I just have to leave it to the professionals. I hope they're taking the case seriously and not just writing it off as a random homicide that'll go cold and get shoved into a filing cabinet somewhere. I know this city has a reputation, but a person doesn't just get gunned down in broad daylight for no reason, especially not a human getting murdered by a dinosaur.

I climb the staircase leading up to the police station's impressive front doors, lavishly crafted oak slabs beneath the state crest that hangs above the threshold. There are side entrances that staff and officers frequently use, but I enjoy utilizing the main entrance. The building almost feels alive when you see it from this perspective, hosting a long and storied history of keeping a small piece of the largest city in our nation safe.

"Aubrey." The receptionist's voice catches my attention. I turn her way, noticing the mostly blank crossword puzzle on the desk in front of her. Understandably, she has a job to do so she ticks in a few boxes whenever the opportunity presents itself. I tried offering her an answer once and she injected ice into my veins with the stare she gave me in reply. Guess she likes doing 'em herself, without any help.

"Good morning, Ruth. What do you need?"

Her focus moves from my approach back down to her crossword puzzle. "Captain Aaron asked to see you."

My stomach drops. I don't offer further reply besides turning toward my fate and swallowing hard. I already know why I'm being called upon, but I had hoped it wouldn't happen the moment I stepped foot in the building. My discussion with the captain was a brief one yesterday; I only told him that Samuel was guilty of nothing, and I was dismissed after that since he had to deal with everything else, including the two officers who were unlawfully detaining an innocent bystander. I figured I'd be questioned today, but it's still a tough way to start my morning.

The walk to his office is a physically short distance but emotionally long journey. His door is ajar, allowing me to squeeze through the opening to the space on the other side. He looks up from the paperwork on his desk to meet my eyes, wordlessly conveying that I should close the door behind myself; I do so. Taking a seat across from him, I try to greet him with pleasantry before the reprimand I expect. "Good morning, Captain Aaron."

He lets out a small grunt in acknowledgment. If I was in a *lot* of trouble, he wouldn't have even done that. I only got in a lot of trouble once, and that was when I mailed a reminder of unpaid parking tickets to the wrong person. It was an honest mistake, I didn't realize who it was since Ragnar is such a common last name among dinosaurs. This didn't appease Captain Aaron who chewed me out as fiercely as he got chewed out by Mayor Robert Ragnar for my blunder. As I learned that day, we don't ticket the mayor. Ever.

The pterodactyl before me folds his hands on his desk and leans forward. He doesn't look happy, but doesn't speak as harshly as I would have expected. "Can you please explain to me in more detail what happened yesterday?" I glance down, my tail slowly gliding across the floor, twitching in anticipation as it yearns to be cradled in my hands. "You told me that the human we brought in wasn't the shooter, and I appreciate that. But what I'm hazy on is why *you* were there. Why were you battered and bloodied, standing next to a deceased individual with a human bystander?"

I unconsciously rub the palms of my hands. They're still scraped up from yesterday, not enough to need bandages but the broken scales sting a bit. "I was at the bus stop when the gunshots went off. I heard five shots, two at first, then three in rapid succession. Sa—The human who was with me—had stopped to talk with me at the bus stop a couple minutes before the shots."

Captain Aaron flips over a few sheets of paper and uncaps his pen, beginning to jot down notes. As the trails of ink begin drying, he glances up at me again, clearly not content with where my explanation ended thus far. I sigh before continuing, realizing what I have to confess. "I went toward the gunshots. I—"

"You were trying to be a *cop*."

I hesitate before responding. "Yes, sir."

The fingers of his free hand close around the bridge of his beak in irritation. "After the discussion we had yesterday morning, the same discussion we have *every week?*" My only reply is to lower my head. "You work for the police department, and you're an employee of the city, but that doesn't mean you should try to be a hero in situations like this. You should have called us. We could have been there even sooner if we got a call from someone we knew and *trusted* instead of a random panicked citizen."

I'm not certain he meant it that way, but his emphasis stings like a parent saying they aren't sure that they can trust you anymore after you get caught in a lie. Captain Aaron seems to notice my emotional downturn, clearing his throat before speaking again. "What happened next?"

I still don't meet his eyes, doing everything in my power to keep my tail from climbing into my arms. "When we came across the body, I saw the suspect fleeing across the street. They darted around the corner of the alley across from me before I could get a solid look at them, but it was a dinosaur of some sort. I saw the tip of their tail."

He scribbles more notes. "Can you tell what kind of dinosaur it was, or the color?"

I shake my head. "It seemed like a longer tail, so probably not a pterodactyl. Too big to be a compsognathus, too. But that's all I could really tell you. It was too dark to make out the color. Might have been a dark blue, or dark green. I'm not certain."

"Notice any plates, feathers, anything like that?"

I shake my head again. "I'm sorry, no." His pen continues moving across the paper. "I tried to pursue. I wanted to get a visual ID on the suspect, but my knee locked up. I wasn't able to see them in time. I heard their car peel out before I could crawl around the corner of the alley."

He sighs as he finishes his notes, setting his pen down and meeting my eyes again. He doesn't have to say anything at all for me to understand his thoughts. He just told me yesterday that my bad knee would prevent me from entering the academy, and now the harsh truth of my disability stares me in the face just as clearly as Captain Aaron's disappointed gaze. I do my best to fight back the tears that threaten to spill forth, biting my lip and embedding my claws into my bruised palms.

Graciously, the captain rises from his desk and turns away from me, clasping his wrist underneath the joints where his wings meet his back. He stares out the window of his office; I use the opportunity to wipe my eyes with my sleeves, doing everything in my power to keep from audibly sniffling.

His words fill the silence. "I'm not going to formally reprimand you. This all technically took place while you were off the clock, and despite your reckless behavior, you didn't do anything to impede police work. The suspect would have fled either way." He turns to me once more, wearing a smile. "At least we know it was a dinosaur that fled the scene, thanks to you. It might not be much, but it's better than nothing."

His small olive branch of praise is a kind gesture, but I know what still needs to be said. "I'm sorry for being reckless, sir. I should have used my head. If the suspect was still by the victim, I could have put myself at risk, or the human who was with me." I lower my head again. "I don't need to have gone to the academy to know that a proper police officer wouldn't put people in danger needlessly."

He closes his eyes and nods, approving of my self-reflection. "You're a bright young woman and you've got a lot of guts." He meets my eyes again, offering an almost fatherly look. "You'd have made a fine police officer, if fate had dealt you a different hand. As it stands, I'm glad to have you here with us."

"Thank you, sir."

As he retakes his seat, he adds the afterthought, "Oh, you might want to steer clear of Duffy and Preston at shift change. I put them both on night duty for the little stunt they pulled with that human fellow. Neither of them are too happy with you right now, I'm afraid."

That makes sense. Even if Captain Aaron hadn't told them outright that it was my word that got Sammy cut loose, they'd be smart enough to put two and two together. I'm just glad they didn't hurt him, or keep him locked up for longer than they did. Otherwise, I wouldn't have been able to ask him to the show tonight.

My sit-down with the captain had distracted me from Sammy for a while, but now he's front and center in my imagination again, smiling his gentle smile at me, filling my stomach with butterflies. Tonight is gonna be great, I just know—

The captain glances up at me from his paperwork, raising an eyebrow to wordlessly question why I'm still in his office. Oops, guess I spaced out for a second. He clarifies his position on the matter. "Dismissed, Carter."

"O-oh! Sorry! Thank you, sir." I hurriedly shuffle out of the room and upstairs to my own desk, feeling the heat radiating from my flushed cheeks. I hope I wasn't blushing like a moron in there. The fifteen minutes I spent with him has given the accumulating paperwork on my desk a head start for the day, and I quickly set to work on processing the forms and fulfilling my responsibilities. I need the distraction to keep my mind from wandering as capriciously as it's been doing all morning. In a rare show of self-control, I even stop myself from turning on my radio, worrying that the familiar jazz tunes will make my thoughts return to the show tonight, and to...

Paperwork. Focus on paperwork, Aubrey.

I stay a little past my normal clock-out time to ensure that I'm caught up with everything I needed to get done for the day. I occasionally glance around, keeping an eye out for Duffy or Preston, but neither of them make their presence known. I'll take a little good luck. Though I doubt either of them would do anything too outrageous, I don't need to get an earful from them on how they think I'm responsible for the shit hours they gotta work. Hell, I'd say it to their faces: they were way out of line with how they treated Sammy. Maybe the cooler evening air will help simmer their hot heads a little bit.

The bus ride home feels like it takes an eternity. It doesn't have any more stops than average, but each minute that passes is agony as my heart threatens to beat its way out of my chest. I fidget with my purse, pushing my keys and lip balm around absent-mindedly to do *something* besides think about tonight. I desperately wish I had gum, but I keep forgetting to pick up another pack. I chew it rarely, never having had an oral fixation, but it's still nice to freshen your breath when it's needed, or chomp on it when you desperately seek distraction.

It'll be fine. Everything will be fine tonight. I'm going to enjoy the music, and I'm sure Sammy will have a nice time, too. That is, unless I make an ass of myself or say something boneheaded. Shit, I don't even know what to talk about with him. He likes jazz, obviously, but is he as much of a jazz hound as I am? Is he gonna be turned off if I start spewing factoids about when a song was released, or how many pressings the album had? I'm like a damned encyclopedia with this useless information.

What if he thinks I'm a loon? A dizzy dame who spends more time with her snout in a book about music theory than cooking or cleaning? I mean, I'm no slob and I'm an *okay* cook, but what is he gonna think about me as a woman?

What would any man? After...

My fingers tighten into fists. No, Aubrey. You're not doing that to yourself. Not now, not so close to tonight. I'm not going to ruin the evening for myself, or for Sammy.

I'm lurched out of my malaise by the bus coming to a stop, realizing just in time that it's *my* stop. I dart through the doors before the driver pulls them shut, earning an irritated look from the punctual dinosaur. Taking a quick breath to steady myself, I travel the few blocks it takes me to arrive home.

The blissful AC of my apartment offers escape from the sweltering outdoor air. With all the excitement going on in my head, I had barely registered the oppressive heat that only grows more cruel with each passing day. Back in June, the papers said that records were being broken; seventy-year highs were outdone by fractions of a degree. It's not getting to be quite that hot yet, but it's damn close. Only when the sun goes down does the temperature become tolerable. And the sun should be going down right around the time the show starts tonight.

I focus on throwing together my supper quickly instead of the goosebumps that crawl across my arms. Leftover hamburger from last night, a quick dinner that won't bog me down too much. Though, I wonder if Sammy is going to eat before the show. My eyes dart over to my purse that rests on the kitchen table. His phone number is in there. I could give him a quick call, see if he wants to get some food, too—

No, no, no. It's not a date! I shake my head and go back to my meal preparation. I'm sure he can get something for himself before the show. I glance at the clock as the patty within the stovetop pan sizzles and pops. Almost six. I'll eat, get myself freshened up, and be out the door by seven. I don't want to be late, I wouldn't miss tonight for the world.

A hamburger in the stomach heavier and a fresh application of makeup later, I give myself one final review in the mirror. I don't have much in terms of fancy clothes, but this particular dress is special to me. Its vibrant color perfectly matches my eyes, the golden yellow hue offering stark contrast to the blue of my scales and feathers. Though it's a few years old and maybe not the hot style anymore, it still looks great on me. I only wear it on special occasions when I want to look my best, and I haven't had a good reason to bring it out of the closet in a lot of months.

I roll my shoulders a bit, ensuring the portrait collar rests in an even spot on my frame. The white lace accents on the collar lend the otherwise simple dress a certain air of beauty that I really love. I twist my hips a little and tug at the pleats of the skirt, finding the correct spot for the dress to rest on my meager curves. When my eyes meet their reflection in the mirror, taking in the full scope of my transformation, a smile forms at the sides of my mouth.

I look really nice.

I shake off the momentary pride and glance at the clock. A little after seven. I shouldn't have a problem catching a bus to Birdland jazz club; it's on 52nd and Broadway, over in Cavemanhattan. With my purse in hand, ticket secured within, I make my way down to the street.

The evening air has begun predictably cooling, albeit ever so slightly. I'll have no need for a jacket even after the sun sets, it'll stay above seventy all night. Arriving at the bus stop, I take a seat upon the familiar bench, glancing down the road to see if my ride is already approaching. Only cars zip by, so I return to my as-of-late favorite pastime: worrying immensely about the night ahead.

I do hope I haven't overdone it with my look. I mean, I wanted to dress up anyway because—well, it's Birdland. *The* Birdland. You don't just waltz into the single hottest jazz club this side of Old Orleans without paying it the proper respect.

But what if I make Sammy uncomfortable? He might not have dressed up himself, and if I drastically outclass him in the fashion department, will that make him unhappy?

I bring an irritated hand to my forehead. Knock it off, you fuckin' school girl. Everything will be fine! As soon as I step off the bus and see him waiting outside the club, all this worry and panic is just gonna melt away. You're a strong gal, Aubrey. You've got this.

Speaking of the bus, I try to spot an incoming shuttle, but still don't catch sight of one. It's been a few minutes, at least—

My heart stops in my chest. Is the bus even still running this late? I know *some* buses keep going, but how many shut down their routes at the end of the work day?! Is this one of them?! I spring to my feet, craning my neck to try to catch sight of the familiar green and white vehicle, but see no form of public transportation.

Shit. How long do I wait? How long has it already been? I can't risk being late! Not tonight! Stupid, why didn't you check the bus schedule earlier? I weigh my options, cursing the fact that I don't own a wristwatch to tell the time easily. With a groan, I begin briskly making my way in the direction of downtown. It's way too far to go on foot, but the closer I get to the center of the city, the quicker I'll see a taxi I can flag down.

Thankfully, I didn't wear heels. Given my bad knee, heeled shoes are a terrible idea regardless of the occasion. I was blessed with decent height for a velociraptor so I don't feel the need to compensate in that particular area. Even with my comfortable footwear, I don't dare move at anything faster than a quick walk. I can't risk another fall, not in this dress. Not tonight.

After about ten minutes of travel, I finally spot the familiar black and yellow checkers of a vacant cab. I flag it down and climb into the back seat. The driver, a sallow-eyed gallimimus with a cigarette hanging out of his mouth, cranes his neck around to size me up. His eyes roam up and down my dress before meeting my stern look. He speaks in a grizzled tone. "Where to, lady?"

"52nd and Broadway, and make it fast, please."

He emits a raspy chuckle. "Yeah, sure thing. Hope ya don't got plans."

I raise an eyebrow. "What do you mean?"

"Traffic's a nightmare aroun' there at dis time o' day. Well, *any* time o' day, 'cept the asscrack o' three AM, maybe!" He slaps the small ticker box hanging from his dash, causing the numbers indicating the fare to spin down to their initial position of twenty-five cents. As soon as he takes off, the numbers slowly begin ticking up every few blocks in increments of five.

I stare out the window, cursing my bad luck and even worse planning. Even if I *had* gotten to a bus, it couldn't have gotten through traffic any better than a cab could have. You idiot, Aubrey. Why didn't you leave earlier? Sure, there's "fashionably late", but this is Miles Cratis. You don't show up late for Miles Cratis! You don't show up late for your first date wi—

I let out a sigh, already exhausted with having to correct myself so many times. All I can do is watch as the buildings soar by, their proximity to one another tightening just as much as their height grows. Block by block, the city becomes more imposing, neon lights bathing the streets in their multichromatic hues.

We slow to a crawl around 40th and Broadway. Still twelve blocks away from the club. I peer past the cabbie and his fare box that currently reads eighty cents. Nothing but brake lights and the occasional blaring car horn ahead of us for the foreseeable future. I let out a defeated sigh before pulling a dollar out of my purse and handing it to the driver. As he accepts it, I ask, "Do you have the time, by chance?"

He brings his left wrist into view, scanning the device upon it before replying. "About 7:52." I climb out of the taxi, earning a half-hearted "Thanks" on my way toward the sidewalk. Twelve blocks in eight minutes, with a shit knee. Even if I jogged, that'd be cutting it close, and I can't risk jogging. I just have to do my best and get there as quickly as my legs can carry me.

The sidewalks are bustling with life and energy. Even on a weekday night, hundreds of people come and go, making their way into and out of the numerous shops, restaurants and places of entertainment. Despite its name, Cavemanhattan is host to more than just humans; dinosaurs of all shapes, sizes and colors explore everything the city has to offer alongside the cavemen and cro magnons that, less than a hundred years ago, involuntarily served dinokind in many parts of the country. Even today, even in this metropolis I call home, if you look close enough you can still see signs of prejudice and lingering malice toward the humans.

At least we're making progress. I wish it was more, but it's something.

Several minutes go by before I lay eyes on the silhouette of the sidewalk-overhanging canopy. Bold letters emblazon each of its three visible sides: "Birdland". Above it hangs another banner with even larger letters that reads: "This Week Only: Miles Cratis". My heart skips a beat as I grow closer, knowing that in just a few short minutes I'll be able to see, in person, one of the greatest living jazz musicians on the planet.

It's still a couple blocks away, but I begin to make out the shapes of people standing around the entrance. Several dozen, maybe even a hundred. Whether they're in line with tickets in hand, or part of the sorry collection that didn't get a ticket and now mill about in hopes that a seat may randomly open up, I can't be sure. But I'm positive that Sammy is among the crowd. He didn't strike me as the type to be late, even fashionably so.

My knee sings a song of its own as I get within a block of the club. Though I didn't run, my quickened pace has irritated the already annoyed tendons, and while I don't sense a lock-up approaching, it's warning me that it isn't afraid to employ that tactic again if I push it. I pray that the tenuous peace I've achieved with it holds out for the night.

Finally arriving at the edge of the small crowd, I begin my search for Sammy. Almost everyone gathered around is human; I only spot one other dinosaur, a stocky but well-dressed dimetrodon who mills about with the others that await admittance, being careful not to strike anyone with his sizable frilled spine as he observes the crowd. Another jazz enthusiast who appreciates the music despite the stereotypes, I hope. I move my gaze further around, craning my neck to see if he might be—

"Hey, there you are!" The voice makes me jump and I spin around to face its owner. He holds up his hands in an apologetic gesture. "Whoah, sorry about that! Didn't mean to startle ya." He offers me an embarrassed grin as he nervously scratches the back of his neck. The moment I lay eyes on his smile, I feel my heart try to beat its way out of my chest.

I can't tell if I'm blushing like an idiot, but I have to try to keep cool. I clear my throat as I tilt my head up a little and employ what little gravitas I can fake. "It's not polite to sneak up on a woman, you know!" Try as I might, I can't keep the sides of my own lips from moving upward, betraying my incensed tone.

Sammy leans into the bit with me, doffing his cap as he offers an overly corny bow and an even more corny and foppish accent. "Well, I am so immensely sorry, milady! It shan't happen again!"

I can't help but let out a laugh, one that he joins me in as he retakes his upright stance and puts his hat back on. I wasn't sure how he was going to dress for the night, but I am impressed by what I see. The light gray button-up shirt is the only non-black article of clothing he wears, with his suit jacket, slacks and mirror-polished shoes all lending themselves to a cool yet mysterious look. He wears a bowler hat in place of the flat cap he had on when I met him yesterday, as black as the rest of his outerwear and offering a wonderfully formal-yet-informal feel to his wardrobe.

It seems that he's been eyeing up my outfit at the same time I was examining him. He lets out a short whistle. "Wow, Aubrey. You look—well, you look great!"

Now I know I'm blushing. I flick my eyes to the side. "Th-thank you, Sammy. You look nice, too."

A wide grin overtakes him that causes my heart to skip a beat again. He scratches the back of his neck. "Heh, thanks. I never been to a place like this before, so I wasn't sure how nice I should dress up. Hope I didn't overdo it, or *under*-do it." He glances around at the crowd, nervously sliding a hand across the front of his shirt where a tie would be hanging if he was wearing one.

I smile at his display, but it fades quickly as I realize I still owe him an apology. "Um—I'm really sorry about keeping you waiting. I don't like being late for things, especially something like this, but traffic was a nightmare."

Sammy peeks over his shoulder toward the road. Sure enough, many of the cars that had been stationed there at the beginning of our conversation remain where they are, the occasional horn offering its contribution to the soundscape of the city. "Yeah, it wasn't much better for me. I had to bail outta my cab about ten blocks away and hustle my ass over here. I was worried *I* was gonna be late!" His eyes meet mine again. "S'no problem, anyways! See, they ain't even started lettin' folks in ye—"

As he gestures toward the front door, the burly cro magnon man who stands security unhooks the red velvet rope that hangs in front of the entrance and begins ushering people in. Another human, less muscular and more feminine, accepts tickets being presented to her. Sammy grins. "Whoops. Guess they made a liar outta me."

I giggle as I reach for my purse and withdraw my token of admittance. "Shall we?"

Sammy fishes the ticket I gave him yesterday out of a jacket pocket. "After you!"

We step into the line as folks are slowly ushered into the building. The club doesn't always have advanced ticket entry, but they have to implement the policy every now and again. For a big act like Miles Cratis, you bet your bottom dollar it'll be a pre-booked show. Hell, if these tickets hadn't showed up at the station like they did, I wouldn't be here right now.

It turns out, not everyone in line is as lucky as I was. A few disgruntled people are turned away at the door, with one particular man beginning to shout vulgarities at the bouncer. His tirade includes shaking fists and embarrassing posturing against the unfazed cro magnon. All the same, the "gentleman" feels the need to make a show of his machismo that honestly appears like nothing more than a tantrum.

Sammy steps a little ahead of me, positioning himself between the belligerent fella and myself. He doesn't say anything, instead keeping an eye on the man as we get closer to the front of the line. However, before we step past the rescinded velvet rope, a final string of curse words sees the irate buffoon away from the entrance and down the sidewalk, stuffing his hands into his pockets and drooping his shoulders dejectedly. Sammy replies to the scene by turning back to me and flicking his eyebrows. "Good thing we got our tickets in advance, huh?"

I smile and nod, feeling myself blush again as he looks ahead toward the ticket collector. He put himself between me and that potential danger. Well, as dangerous as that inconsolable toddler was, at least, but he still looked out for my safety. And he didn't do it consciously, either. I might have been insulted if he did; I'm a capable woman, I can take care of myself. Sammy just sorta did it. Almost...

instinctively. The butterflies in my stomach nearly lift me off the ground.

I glance around, frantically trying to find something to take my mind off of the rapid beating of my heart. Noticing the name of the club suspended over the front door we have nearly arrived at, I stammer out the first thing that pops into my head. "S-so, Sammy! Do you know why they call it Birdland?"

He faces me again with his intensely handsome smile before pondering the question for a moment. "Hmm. Does it got somethin' to do with Charlie Larker?"

"That's right! He went by 'Bird' which was a shortening of his nickname 'Yardbird', and he helped open the club up in December of 201M1949 BC! Though, to be truthful, it was him lending his name to the club more so than doing any real business! Besides, he's a musician, not a jazz club operator. He's performed here a few times, but a lot less than you'd expect considering it's… it's his name above the door and all…" I start to trail off. "Aw, geez, I'm sorry. I'm rambling on about nothin'."

Sammy's grin only widens. "Are you kidding? You're a regular Farmer's Almanac, but for, like, jazz factoids. It's pretty cute, actually!"

Ohmygodohmygodohmygod—

The ticket collector clearing her throat distracts Sammy away from my meltdown. "Oh, we're up! Got your ticket, Aubrey?"

I extend a shaking hand toward the usher. She lifts an eyebrow at me as she accepts my ticket and rips it in half. I'm unsure if her reaction is because I'm a velociraptor or because of the beet red glow of my otherwise blue cheeks. I only barely catch her informing Sammy and I that our table number is fourteen. The squealing voice echoing in my head nearly drowns out all other sound:

He said I'm cute. Oh my God, he said I'm cute!

My internal breakdown is interrupted as we pass through the doors to the club. The exterior of the building is deceptively plain compared to the lavish interior. The main hall is spacious and elegant, with intricately detailed half-pillars lining the walls. The ceiling, a few feet higher up than an average enclosure but not quite of grand concert hall scale, is coated with purple velvet to reduce echo and maximize the auditory experience for the audience in addition to adding an almost regal feel to the space.

Dozens of tables surround a beautifully intimate stage, one where you could literally reach out and touch the musicians upon it. Of course, such an action would cost you your admittance as the nearby security staff would rapidly bounce you into the alley. A luxurious bar offers all sorts of drinks; several members of the waitstaff already mingle amidst the occupied tables, delivering any sort of inebriant one could imagine to the gathering, thirsty patrons.

My mouth hangs open as I drink in the sight before me, hearing Sammy echo my amazement with another whistle. "Okay, maybe I *did* underdress. This place is incredible!"

I giggle and step closer to him. "Quit your fretting! Come on, let's go find our table."

We work our way through the smattering of tables encircling the stage, briefly passing through a small open section directly in front of it. Our assigned seating is adorned by a white card with the number fourteen scrawled upon it, resting next to a vase containing a few roses. Sammy rapidly moves behind the chair I was about to sit in, politely pulling it out for me. I give him a smile and a nod as I take my seat, allowing him to nudge it under my posterior before he circles to his own spot.

He's a gentleman, too.

I'm given no time to heed the squealing of my inner voice as a waitress approaches our table. An older human woman in a modest purple and black dress, she speaks in a tone I recognize as she nervously sizes me up. "G-good evening! Can I get you *two* something to drink?"

I try my best to apologetically smile at her. She's someone who has dealt with dinosaurs treating her badly, and worries that I'll do the same. I want to assuage her fears, but before I can say anything Sammy throws an arm over the back of his chair, craning his neck to stare at the collection of bottles behind the bar. "Hmm... you got a good spiced rum?"

The waitress offers him a polite nod before turning back to me. "A-and for you, ma'am?"

I hesitate, not having given the question any thought prior to now. Not wishing to make the poor woman more uncomfortable than she already is, I merely echo Sammy's order. "I'll take the same, thank you."

With a slight bow of her head, the waitress scurries away as quickly as she can without being rude. I watch her go, feeling regretful that I'm causing her such discomfort. Sammy doesn't let me wallow in my emotions for very long. "You a rum gal? I woulda expected you to go for the wine, or somethin', I dunno, more lady-like?"

I raise an eyebrow. "More lady-like, you say?"

His cheeks redden. "Um—well, I mean—not sayin' that in a *bad* way—I just figured—"

My giggling clues him in on my intentions. "You're an easy one to tease, you know that?" His nose scrunches in reply, but he still smiles before I continue. "Honestly, I'm not much of a drinker. Never got a taste for the stuff."

He nods thoughtfully. "Same, actually. I mean, I won't say 'no' to the occasional drink on a special night like tonight, but I don't keep anythin' stocked in my apartment."

Before I can speak up again, the waitress returns with two glasses of bronze-colored liquid, gently placing a cocktail napkin in front of each of us before setting the glasses upon them. She steps back before asking neither Sammy or I in particular, "Sixty cents, please."

Phew. That's pricey for two glasses of rum. I mean, it's a higher-class establishment, but still. I reach for my purse, but Sammy holds up his outstretched palm to stop me as he withdraws his wallet. A dollar bill passes from his hand to hers; before she can rummage for the change, Sammy coolly adds, "Keep it."

Her eyes light up at his generosity and she fervently thanks him before heading off to take another table's order. His only reply is to hold a small, gentle smile as he takes a sip of his drink while glancing around the establishment. Patrons continue filing in; the tables are all nearly full now, with the sounds of small talk and placed orders encircling us on every side.

A thought emerges. It begins gnawing at me, tiny and pestering at first, but rapidly growing in size and volume. I take in the crowd around me. Sideways glances and nervous halts in conversation occur as my eyes pass over the human patrons. I spot the dimetrodon from earlier, seated at a table by himself in the corner, seeming to pay no mind to the humans around him who steal wary looks in his direction.

We are the anomalies here. We are the odd ones out. Two dinosaurs amidst a sea of humans who tiptoe around us, offering timid smiles and wide berths.

I suddenly feel like I don't belong here.

"Everything okay, Aubrey? You ain't touched your drink yet." Sammy's gentle voice momentarily breaks me out of the intrusive thoughts. I turn my attention to him, meeting his blue eyes. I want so desperately to wave the sentiment off, act like nothing's bothering me at all and have a pleasant evening of jazz and Sammy's company. I want to compliment his generosity with the waitress, offering him praise for being such a gentleman so far, despite this not being a date.

I want to say so many things, something, *anything* but what comes tumbling out of my lips:

"Why aren't you afraid of me?"

Sammy's only reply is to blink in confusion. I continue in a hushed tone, having to release eye contact with him to avoid breaking down into a sobbing mess. "Everyone is staring at me. Everyone is afraid of me. The waitress could barely look me in the eyes, she was terrified. I don't belong here. This is a human club, with human music. So—why? Why are you treating me like nothing's wrong?"

I finally manage to lift my head again. I expect the worst: a scowl, an annoyed eye roll, or worse—the fear that so many other humans show me. But he offers none of those things. Instead, he only smiles at me. "Should I be?"

His question catches me off guard. "What?"

"Should I be afraid of you?"

My eyes widen. "No! Of course not!"

He offers a shrug. "Well, then, there's no problem, right?"

I'm flabbergasted, unable to find a reply.

He doesn't let the air hang dead between us for long before he lowers his own gaze and lets out a half-hearted chuckle. "Heh. To be totally honest, I'm not sure where I got the stones to approach you yesterday about the tune you were hummin'. That really isn't like me. I'm usually a pretty nervous guy, especially around—" He swirls his hands in an all-encompassing gesture. "—well, around dinosaurs like yourself. I've had my fair share of bad run-ins." He meets my eyes again. "But you seemed different. On that bus stop bench. You seemed… lonely. Like you needed someone to just say 'hello'. Someone to share a small laugh with, or just get a quick compliment from." His eyes take in the room surrounding us. "I certainly didn't expect it'd end up with me being here." He smiles at me once more. "That said, I'm glad I did stop to say 'hello' to you. And not just because of this show you invited me to!"

My mind spins. His sentiments swirl around me, drowning out the gnawing self-consciousness. But another half-cocked thought escapes my mouth. "If you hadn't stopped yesterday, you wouldn't have had to see that body. And the way those officers treated you…"

He waves a hand dismissively. "More excitement than I normally experience on a Monday night, that's for sure. But I don't regret a thing. Sure, it was a pain getting manhandled by those cops, and I def—" He trails off, his eyes glazing over for a moment as though he just recalled something. I cock my head inquisitively, but he quickly shakes away whatever distracted him. "It's certainly a hell of a way to meet someone. But I'm glad I met you, Aubrey. I mean that. Don't let the way these other folks are looking at ya make you uncomfortable. I'm happy to be here with you."

I bite my lip as I do my best to keep the tears from escaping my eyes. "Th-thank you, Sammy. I'm glad to be here with you, too. Thank you for being such a gentleman." I reach across the table and place a hand on top of his.

He glances down at it before his eyes shoot back up to mine, his cheeks brightening rapidly. "U-uh! Thanks! You too! W-wait, I mean—uhh—"

My giggle shatters the malaise-filled cloud that I had cast over the table, with Sammy's laughter soon joining mine. I feel like a total idiot for being such a sourpuss on what's supposed to be a nice night of jazz and pleasant company, but his measured and meaningful words lifted the weight from my shoulders.

He is a real catch.

We spend the next several minutes making small talk, sharing with one another details about ourselves and our lives. My eyes widen as he informs me that he currently works for Sal's Butcher and Grocery, the very same one I frequent on my way home from work. I question why I'd never seen him before until he reveals that he works in the dock, loading and unloading trucks every day. If he was a checkout person or bagboy I'd have recognized him, but that single concrete wall at the back of the store kept us from ever meeting before yesterday.

He mentions living in an apartment not far from the grocery store, and his dog named Saxon who he describes as "a big lovable lunk". Though he doesn't outright say that he's single, he doesn't make mention of a roommate, girlfriend or wife, causing me to silently cheer in my head. He does remark about some buddies with whom he plays a weekly poker game. He's modest about himself, but I get the feeling that he's not a bad card player based on what I've gleaned about him so far.

Though he shares plenty with me about himself, he offers me even more opportunity to talk about my life and career. I first fill him in on my profession, apologizing again for having lied about being a full-fledged police officer when I'm just a clerical worker. He waves it off, commending me for being gutsy enough to charge headfirst toward a crime scene in pursuit of justice.

I similarly bring up my living situation, emphasizing that I don't have any pets but leaving the specifics of my love life up to speculation. As the topic crosses my mind, I feel the specter of my past poke at my subconscious, but quickly push it aside. Instead, I smile as I watch the gears turn in Sammy's head, wondering if he's trying to solve the same riddle that he presented to me. I round out my brief introduction by mentioning my own social circle. Though I don't have anyone I can really call my "friends", I do participate in a book club with a few pleasant women. They're a little annoyed that I keep recommending jazz memoirs when it's my month to suggest a book, but they can deal with it. My turn, my pick.

Throughout all of our talk, Sammy is attentive and positive. He engages in our conversation, asking questions and making corny little jokes when he gets the chance. I don't get the impression that he's *trying* to be charming, but he's doing a damn good job of it so far. I just hope that I'm not putting him off. I already have to make up for that stupid outburst.

Before we can continue, a figure makes his way onto the stage, earning a brief round of applause from the rapidly shushing crowd. Sammy offers me a smile as he turns toward the front of the house, but his expression is outdone by the wide grin that overtakes me. I know who this man on stage is. Sammy cocks a questioning eyebrow at me; I respond by nodding my head toward the fellow in the spotlight.

Though he is undoubtedly a human, the positively diminutive figure seems to share more in common with a compsognathus than a cro magnon. He has no tail or elongated snout, but I'd be surprised if he broke four feet even, and that's including the tall captain's hat that he wears. He quickly rotates the microphone stand's height adjuster, an audible *clang* echoing out as it falls to its lowest setting, one that still requires the lilliputian fellow to stand on tip-toes to reach it. His voice is understandably higher pitched, but he speaks with bravado:

"Ladies and gentlemen, welcome to the one and only Birdland Nightclub!" He nods as cheers and applause ring out from the crowd. "I am your host, Pee Wee Minkette, and I gotta tell ya, folks. We have an absolutely astounding show for you tonight! Of course, I know you're all here to see the legendary Miles Cratis Quintet—" Another round of applause expectedly interrupts him. "—But first! We've got a bunch of cool cats who want to serenade you with their locally brewed jams. Give it up for the Brett Boner Four!"

Pee Wee Minkette strides down the small staircase to a mix of applause and confused looks as four gentlemen take to the stage. Their expressions are equal parts nervousness and annoyance as the frontman cradles his trombone in one arm while pulling the mic stand back up to an average person's height. He clears his throat before addressing the crowd. "Uh, hi. We're actually the Brett *Horner* Four. Anyway, I hope you're all having a good night tonight! This first one is called—"

I don't catch the name of the song. My fit of snickering overwhelms me to the point where I can hardly breathe. I do my best to stifle the laughter, but like a joke that gets stuck in your head in the middle of a church sermon, the attempts to bottle it up only make it worse. Thankfully, the band either doesn't notice or they decide to not challenge the velociraptor woman having a conniption at table fourteen as they begin their first tune.

I catch sight of Sammy grinning at me, both delighted and perplexed at my uncontrollable laughter. I wave a hand in front of my face, trying desperately to cool myself down. Sucking in several deep breaths to return to a somewhat composed state, I manage to eke out an answer to Sammy's unasked question, speaking in a hushed tone between occasional giggles so as to not interrupt the local band any worse than I already have.

"H-he—*haha*—Pee Wee Minkette—he's such a little *bastard! Heehee!*"

Sammy's grin widens but he still doesn't get the whole picture. "What do you mean? What did he do? I mean, it sounded like he didn't say that band's name right—"

"*That's just it!* He does that shit on *purpose!* I heard rumors that he purposely mispronounces the names of bands that don't tip him, and I betcha that's *exactly* what happened!"

Now it's Sammy's turn to chuckle quietly to himself. "What a little prick!"

The two of us quietly continue laughing through the band's first song, one or the other of us kicking the fit back into gear with a sideways glance or an utterance of the word "boner". We're acting like teenagers, totally immature and certainly inappropriate for a venue like this, but I don't care. I haven't laughed like this in ages, and I get to share this moment with Sammy.

By the end of the Brett Boner Four's first tune we've managed to compose ourselves. I earn myself a few leers from the patrons seated around us, but my eyes are only for the man positioned next to me right now. He's handsome, he's charming, he's a gentleman and I laugh with him harder than I've laughed in as long as I can remember. At this moment, I'm entirely smitten.

As the frontman introduces the next song and they begin playing, the actual quality of their music registers with me. It's upbeat and exciting. Not exactly expert level stuff, nowhere near the talent that we should expect to see later, but it's certainly good for a local band, and getting to play here is probably a big break for them. I even find myself tapping my foot along with their song, enjoying the composition almost as much as the company.

A handful of people from nearby tables begin filing out of their seats and into the empty space in front of the stage, swept up by the energizing tempo of the song as they start dancing with one another. Their gyrations are subtle but fun, with rotating hips and bobbing knees punctuating the smiles and laughter of each dancer and their partner. The band takes note, suddenly putting a bit more gusto into their own performance to encourage the spontaneous movement that's broken out. It fills me with a twinge of regret that I can't—

I suddenly see Sammy rise from his seat and extend a hand to me, a wide smile on his face as he beckons me toward him.

Oh no.

My mouth hangs open for a moment before I shake my head. I try to speak up, but he beckons me again. "Come on, Aubrey! It'll be fun!"

I feel my cheeks begin to burn. I avert my eyes. "I—I can't, Sammy."

"There's no reason to be shy! Come on!"

"Sammy, no. I can't."

He doesn't relent, stepping closer to me. "Oh, don't be like that! You'll be great at—"

I sharply cut him off, my eyes flaring at him. "No!"

His smile instantly falls away and he withdraws his hand. I cover my face in embarrassment as he shifts back to his seat next to me. He speaks in a dejected tone. "I'm sorry. I didn't mean to pressure you."

I lower my hands before replying. "No... no, I'm sorry. I didn't mean to snap at you. It's just—I *literally* can't dance. I have a bad knee."

His eyes go out of focus for a second as he seems to scan his memories before they shoot wide open. "Oh my God! I—oh shit, the cops said that, didn't they?! I'm so sorry, I forgot!"

I shake my head. "You didn't do anything wrong, Sammy."

He turns away from me, scowling at himself. "Gah. I'm so fuckin' stupid, why didn't I remember that?" He remains rigid for a few moments, not speaking aloud but almost certainly beating himself up internally.

I slowly reach my hand across the table and place it on his arm. Thankfully, he doesn't recoil away from me, instead looking up at me with remorse. "Well, you *had* just been tackled to the ground by those cops. I'm surprised you remembered your name after that!" I offer him a smile which he only reciprocates with a slight puff of air from his nostrils. "Plus, those same cops called me a lesbian, remember? And *that* was bullshit. They just... happened to be right about my knee."

His frustration finally cracks as he returns my smile, though it's sullied with regret. "Still. I'm sorry for pressuring ya like that. I got swept up. Thought it'd be fun to dance. I just—"

"You didn't know. It's okay."

With a sigh, he nods to me. We both turn our attention back to the band, their upbeat song offering an awkward backdrop to the sudden shift in mood. I sip at my drink as I silently curse myself for making such a fucking mess of this night. I was late, I had an emotional outburst of self-consciousness, and now I snapped at Sammy when he was just trying to have a fun dance with me.

I'm blowing it. He's not gonna want to see me again after this. I know it's not a date, but I was hoping...

The band finishes their song, earning another round of applause from both the audience and the tuckered out dancers. After reminding us of their actual name and excusing themselves from the stage, Pee Wee Minkette finds his way in front of the audience again, dropping the mic stand to his height in similar fashion to before.

"Hey, those kids were great! Lookin' forward to hearing more from them in the future! But now, the moment I know you've all been waiting for! One of the biggest names in jazz today, hot off the release of their newest, hottest record, *Kind of Blue,* let's give it up for the Miles Cratis Quintet!"

There's no mispronunciation of the headliner's name, and Pee Wee even takes the time to adjust the microphone back up to its original height. As he shuffles off the stage, the air in the room instantly shifts. Uproarious applause and cheers ring out as the legend himself steps onto the stage, followed closely by his four other men. In his hands he holds a trumpet, the instrument that skyrocketed him to fame and fortune. He pauses for a moment to glance around the audience, but says nothing. Instead, he turns to his bandmates, mutters something, then faces us once more with a calculating look.

From the first notes tapped out on the piano by Bill Ephans in unison with the double bass strings plucked by Paul Chainers, I know the song. A chill fires up my tail and through my spine as everything else melts away. The first track on Side One of their record, the same tune I woke up to yesterday, the same one I was humming when Sammy approached me:

"So What".

The entire crowd is deathly silent, holding their breath and straining to hear every note. A few moments later, Jimmy Dobb's gentle drumming joins the fray, offering a smooth as silk backdrop to the instrumental fusion. Shortly thereafter, John Coalmane's tenor sax speaks up, breathing fresh soul into the already sweltering symphony.

And at long last, Miles Cratis brings the trumpet to his lips, inhaling deeply before he adds his first notes to the mix. It is perfect. Absolutely beautiful. Mesmerizing. Everything I had ever heard through my record player or my radio could not have prepared me for the real deal. My ears yearn to take in every sound, every playful weave of these five musicians and the culmination of all of their skills in a single, masterful song.

For nine and a half minutes, the world melts away. Every single thing that has ever troubled me fades into oblivion as I'm left only with the music of a jazz genius. My eyes close, shutting out all sensations but the sounds in the air around me. For a moment, I even forget where I am, so wholly absorbed by the melodious marriage of strings and brass that I could have been floating through space and been none the wiser.

One of the most unfortunate certainties of the world is that "all good things must come to an end". For a moment's breath upon the song's conclusion, pure, unbroken silence fills the space. It is rapidly shattered by the thunderous applause and awe-filled cheers of the crowd, my own joining them as I smile uncontrollably. Miles Cratis replies in the way I expected: a simple, small bow, immediately followed by turning to his bandmates and muttering something else. A moment later, their next song begins, "Freddy Freeloader", the very next track on the same album. It's their newest record and a huge hit, so it's no surprise they'd be playing their fresh creations right off the bat. Though I hope we get to hear some of his earlier tunes tonight, too.

As they spin their magic on stage for a second time, a factoid pops into my brain. Though Bill Ephans is playing the piano with them tonight, it was technically Wynton Kawly who performed on the piano for the recorded version of "Freddy Freeloader". I turn to Sammy, anxious to share this with him before I stop myself.

He doesn't notice me, instead focusing on the stage. He doesn't look upset—far from it, in fact, as his finger taps on the table in time with the percussion. But he's listening to the music. He's not interested in my useless trivia right now.

He's not interested in me.

I turn back to the stage, still listening to the beautiful tapestry being woven by Miles Cratis and his companions, but a cold, empty gap opens up in my heart. I keep replaying the foolish mistakes I'd made throughout the night, uttering internal blasphemies that I dare not repeat out loud.

I'm not gonna let this ruin my night. I wanted to hear Miles Cratis play, and I'm hearing him play right now.

So why does it hurt so badly?

My head sinks. I hope and pray that it looks like I'm absorbed by the music, but right now I feel lower than low. I fucked up the one glimmer of light that had shone on me in so many months, casting away the kind and gentle human with my self-loathing and bitterness. After tonight, I'll go back to being alone again.

As the song comes to a close, another round of applause and cheers fills the room, but this time I don't join in. I'm too wrapped up in my own resentment to even move. I expect to hear another lull followed by another song that I'm not going to be able to enjoy as much as I want to, but instead I hear a voice that I'd not heard as of yet resonate through the stage's microphone. His words are scratchy and gravelly, as though he has sandpaper wrapped around his vocal cords. However, his tone is calm and reserved.

"Thank'y all for comin' out tonight. This next one, feel free t'dance if y'want. 'Blue in Green'."

Another moment later, the piano and double bass begin the hauntingly beautiful and melodic opening to the third track on their same album. I absolutely adore this song, but feel the swelling anger and sadness as that word reverberates around in my head.

Dance. If only I could, Miles. I want so badly to be able to. I want to hold Sammy in my arms. I want to feel his hands on my hips as we gently rock back and forth. I want…

I glance up. Several people have taken up Miles's offer and have moved into the center of the room, but their dancing is not frenetic or energized. Instead, it is slow and intimate, with partners graciously swaying with one another in time with the soulful song.

I turn to Sammy again. Though his focus is still on the stage, he notices my look this time and meets my gaze. He subtly raises an eyebrow as though to wordlessly ask if everything is okay, but shifts to a look of confusion as I rise from my seat. Stepping around the table, I extend a hand to him, averting my eyes as the rattling of my nerves causes my voice to crack.

"I'd like to dance… if you'll have me."

Sammy quickly rises to his feet, but doesn't accept my hand. "A-are you sure? Your—I mean, can you—"

"This is slow enough that I can handle it."

The shock on his face is replaced by a resolute nod, causing my stomach to turn over on itself. My hand quivers as he accepts it, and he slowly leads me to the dance floor. We find a small spot for ourselves before he turns to face me. His eyes nervously dart down before meeting mine again. I know he's trying to be polite, but right now I just want to be in his arms. I want to know that I haven't squandered my chance. I want to know if he feels the same way about me that I do about him.

I step closer to him, waiting for him to make the first touch.

He gingerly places his hands just above my hips on either side of my frame. I reciprocate by draping my arms over his shoulders, bringing our bodies nearly into contact with one another as we begin gently swaying with the song. My tail slowly wraps itself behind him, startling him as the unfamiliar feathered appendage comes into contact with his back. The thing has a mind of its own most of the time, but this is a conscious effort, both to keep it out of the way of other dancers and to allow it to share in the moment.

He glances from the end of my tail back up to me. My snout is inches away from his reddened face, both of us rocking in time with the song. He does not smile and he does not speak, instead wearing an intense expression as though he's lost in thought. However, his eyes do not wander, focusing only on mine. Wholly absorbed in my gaze, just as much as I am absorbed in his.

For the second time tonight, the world around me melts away. The beauty of Miles Cratis's music fills my ears, but this time I do not drift alone in the soundscape. I am joined by a man who holds me in his arms. A man who approached me randomly at a bus stop to compliment my humming, only to run with me toward a crime scene and get arrested for his troubles. A man who, despite my unacceptable behavior tonight, has still accepted my dance.

Sammy.

Too soon, the song comes to a close. It's such a beautiful

track on the record and a perfect way to close out Side One. As the crowd applauds the band, Sammy and I remain in one another's arms for a moment before he smiles at me. "Th-thank you for the dance, Aubrey."

I return his smile and take a small step back, removing my hands from his shoulders. "Thank you, Samuel. You're a very good dancer."

He blushes again, scratching the back of his neck. "Aw, I don't think I'm anythin' special."

I disagree.

As we make our way back to our seats, Miles Cratis approaches the microphone once more. "Thank'y. We're gonn' take a short break, then we got some more songs for ya." He offers another quick nod to the applause of the crowd before setting his trumpet down and heading over toward the bar. I notice him approach a blonde woman and begin chatting with her; perhaps a lucky gal that caught his eye, who knows?

I turn my attention back to Sammy who gulps down the last little bit of rum that had melded with the remaining ice in his glass. He sets it back on the table, tapping his finger on its rim as he seems to contemplate something. After a moment he finds some words, though they're not particularly eloquent ones. "Aubrey. Would—uhh—I mean, is there— umm... *shit.*"

I extend him a patient smile. "Take your time."

He sighs. "Ah, geez. I'm not great with words is all. Doesn't help when my nerves are all rattled. I'm tryin' to find the right way to ask this."

My heart nearly flutters out of my throat, but I somehow keep my composure as I coolly respond. "What do you want to ask?"

He looks up at me again, his eyes suddenly filled with resolve. He takes several deep breaths before speaking. "I know you said this isn't a date. But... *could* it be?"

I have no earthly clue how I keep myself from fainting, let alone how I manage to eke out my smarmy reply. "Could it be what, Sammy?"

"Oh, come on! Could it—could it be a *date?*"

The sides of my mouth lift in an uncontrollable, giddy smile. "I'd like that very much."

He lets out an immense sigh of relief. "Raptor Christ, why was that so damn hard? Sheesh! I feel like I'm a fuckin' teenager again or somethin'." I can't help but giggle, knowing the sentiment all too well after how I was feeling earlier today. However, his change in expression makes my laughter die down as he seems to dread what he prepares to say next. "Aubrey, I've really enjoyed tonight. A lot. And I'd love to go on another date with you—if you want to, of course. But…"

Out of the corner of my eye, I notice Miles Cratis leading that blonde woman out of the club. I refocus on Sammy as I lean forward. "But what?"

He turns his head away, wrestling with himself internally before steeling his nerve and meeting my eyes again. "Okay. Cards on the table. I don't like keeping shit like this inside, so I just gotta be forward with it. I'm a divorcee." I blink at him which he seems to interpret as judgment. "I'm sorry, that's just the truth. It was a couple years ago, she's outta the picture and, well, outta the state too. We was hitched over in Old Jersey, where I grew up. I moved out here after—well, after it all went down."

"I thought I heard an Old Jersey accent in there."

He smirks but presses on. "If that's not somethin' you wanna deal with, I just needed to get it out there right away, be upfront about it. I didn't want it to come jumping out of the closet like a boogeyman if things… I dunno, *progressed* with us."

I once again reach across the table and put my hands on top of his. I'm really getting used to the feeling of his hands in mine. "Sammy. That's not a problem. I—" My eyes involuntarily cast themselves downward. "I'm divorced, too."

Sammy balks at my statement. "Wait, seriously? But you're so young!"

I shoot his balk right back to him. "I'm twenty-four, whaddya mean 'I'm so young'?"

"I—well, I mean, you *are* a year younger than me."

I click my tongue at him. "You dope." This gets a chuckle out of him. As it dies down, I speak more seriously. "My situation wasn't so long ago. Less than a year. But he's... out of the picture, too." Though I'm also not interested in keeping secrets, I'm nowhere near prepared enough to tell him everything regarding that situation. Another time.

Sammy nods sympathetically. "A couple o' divorcées, lookin' to reenter the dating pool." His kind eyes linger on mine. "So, how about it? Could I ask you on another date? Ya know, a proper date. Dinner, maybe a movie or somethin' if you like that sorta thing?"

My cheeks glow even brighter red than his. "I'd love that, Sammy."

His smile widens immensely, but before he can speak again a commotion in the club distracts us both. A gaggle of people seem to be crowding around the entrance, trying to peer over the top of one another to see what's going on outside. From the muffled sounds beyond the door, I can only make out shouting.

Sammy rises to his feet, again taking a step forward to posture himself between myself and the crowd. However, before any sort of threat makes itself known, the sound of the microphone stand clattering to its lowered position startles us. Pee Wee Minkette is back, the two members of the Miles Cratis Quintet who are still on stage staring at him in confusion. His voice lacks the performative quality from before, now only carrying with it panic.

"L-ladies and g-gentlemen! There's been an *incident*. I'm sorry, but we have to cancel the rest of the show."

Now I'm on my feet, wide eyed and bewildered at what he just said. I hear Sammy mutter, "What the hell?" as dozens of other patrons around us echo the confused and angered sentiments. Pee Wee tries to raise his hands to quell the crowd, but realizes his efforts will be in vain unless he elaborates. As he wipes the sweat away from his brow with his handkerchief, he stammers out words that make my heart drop in my chest like a stone:

"Miles Cratis has been arrested."

Chapter Six: Pierce

    A thin tendril of smoke rises from the smothered tobacco in the ashtray, intertwining with crystals hanging from a chandelier above the table. The posh mahogany-colored leather lining of the booth crinkles and squeaks under my scales as I take a seat. The face of Charles Rossi is illuminated on the other side of the corner booth by the small lamp in the center of the round table between us. The match he strikes to light up a fresh cigar casts further shadows across his chiseled beak, scar-laden snout and triplicate horns.
    Marty does not join me at the executive booth, choosing instead to sit at the bar three empty table lengths away. Close enough that he can overhear us if he feels inclined to listen in, but given how he reacted in the car and the lack of words exchanged between us since I dumped my used piece in the bay, I don't think he'll be sticking his long neck out for me tonight. Not that I need him to, I've got this under control.
    Charles takes a long drag from his cigar as he sizes me up, keeping his steeled gaze locked firmly on my face. His bright purple eyes are his most chromatic element, seeming to clash violently with his gray scales. His diamond pupils flare ever so slightly as he begins piecing the situation

together. He is no idiot. The fact that Eggsy didn't enter the bar with us is more than enough for him to realize that shit went wrong.

Beyond the nearly imperceptible tell of his eyes, he doesn't react, wearing a cool, almost contemplative expression as he asks the question that probably doesn't need asking. "Where's Egbert?"

I fold my hands in front of me, putting as much of a matter-of-fact tone onto my words as I can. "We ran into some complications. Eggsy had to be retired."

One of Charles's eyelids twitches. "What do you mean, 'retired'?"

"He tried to steal Herdster money. All the money we collected today. We chased him down and... well, somethin' happened to him." From the corner of my vision, I notice Marty's tail snap back and forth angrily; though his eyes are elsewhere, he's acutely aware of our conversation.

The triceratops exhales a plume of smoke with his sigh before leaning forward. "This isn't the time for cute turns of phrase, Pierce. What did you do with Egbert?"

"I shot him."

A sickening silence hangs between us, causing me to fidget unconsciously. Sure, I wasn't anticipating Charles being thrilled with my decision to take matters into my own hands, but did he not hear me when I said Eggsy tried to rob us? I decide to fill the stale air by continuing. "We found the empty briefcase. He must have stashed—"

"You shot Egbert." His icy tone cuts me short.

"Yes. He stole—"

"Without my authorization."

I can't help but click my tongue against the roof of my mouth. "Charles, what difference does it make? He didn't give us back the money so I shot him. So what? He was just a fucking worthless, two-faced, lying prick of a skinnie."

I know I'm beginning to outwardly show my irritation,

but Charles remains as statuesque as he always does, cold and calculating to a fault. However, his words drip with callous authority. "The difference that it makes, Pierce, is that you acted without my permission. You knew that protocol was for you to come to me *first* before something like that was done, but you did it anyway."

I let out a sigh. "Yeah, I might have jumped the gun on the red tape a little, but he was gonna get done in anyway."

"That wasn't your call to make." Charles's frigid words seem to echo the same as Marty's from the car ride. "You know for a fact that you should have brought him back here, alive, so that we could deal with him professionally. But instead you gunned him down in the street?"

"It was an alleyway, actually." His eyes flare at me. I should probably tread a little more carefully with my words.

"And how many people saw you and Martin? Two dinosaurs fleeing a bullet-riddled corpse in an alleyway in broad daylight?"

I shake my head. "Nobody."

He leans back in disbelief. "Nobody. You sure of that?"

"We were gone before people could even poke their head around the corner of the alley. Marty can back me up on that." I jab a thumb in my partner's direction, but he doesn't turn to face us. Instead, I only see his tail flick again.

"And what about the money? You got that back, at least?"

I hesitate. "No. He didn't have it on him, and we had to run before I could find it."

Charles slowly brings a hand to his head, rubbing his temple with two fingers. He closes his eyes for a moment and exhales before looking back at me again. "Do you realize what a fucking mess you've made? You killed one of our employees in broad daylight. One of our few *human* employees. The cops are going to be able to ID him, you realize that? Tie him back to the Herdsters? With how many noses we already have sniffing around here, what the *fuck* do you think that's gonna do?"

I raise my hands defensively. "I dumped the piece in the bay. They've got nothing to tie it to us—"

"*If* he was gonna be done in, there were cleaner ways to do it. You lost the money, and you killed the one person who might have been able to get it back to us without having to scrounge several city blocks for every nook and cranny he coulda stuffed it into." His eyes ignite again. "You were completely out of line today. You already know that you walk on thin ice around here, and taking matters of this gravity into your own hands is wholly unprofessional and unacceptable." I try to open my mouth to reply, but he speaks with finality before I can utter a single word:

"Consider this strike two."

The plates on my back go completely rigid. My mouth hangs open, attempting to allow my windpipe and vocal cords the proper egress to protest, but nothing escapes. For several seconds, I don't even breathe as the weight of the situation begins crushing down on me. My heartbeat quickens and my pupils dilate. I suddenly find myself acutely aware of my surroundings, prepared to defend myself against attack from any angle. In an instant I'm on my feet next to the booth, still staring at Charles but locked in a defensive stance, my tail instinctively soaring back and forth behind me.

However, no attack comes. In stark contrast to my fight or flight response, Charles simply takes another puff of his cigar, staring at me with contempt as he exhales slowly. His lips curl as he speaks again. "Take tomorrow off. There'll be too much heat here anyways. I'll talk to some guys and get this mess sorted out."

He doesn't break eye contact with me, merely rolling the cigar around in his lips as he waits for my adrenaline to drop and my composure to return to me. It eventually does; as my instincts no longer scream at me to defend myself against a lurking predator, my tail slows and my limbs loosen. Taking in a shaky breath, all I can manage is a nod before I turn toward the exit.

Marty rises from his barstool and moves toward Charles as I pass him on my way to the door. He says nothing, nor does he offer a sympathetic look. He's still pissed at me, and based on the cold shoulder I guess he agrees with the judgment I received. I watch Marty sit across from Charles, sending a sharp look over his shoulder before turning to our boss to discuss who knows what.

A second strike.

I shudder as I push open the door leading to the evening air, and not due to coolness; the heat's barely letting up at all as the sun descends beyond the skyscrapers to the west. No, the chill I feel is entirely psychological. Unlike a batter swinging for the fences and coming up short a second time, this is a threat of an entirely different league.

This is my life. I get a third strike, and I'm out. Literally.

I shake my head, trying desperately to clear it of the swirling thoughts. Panic, rage, confusion, remorse—I just can't fathom what the fuck got me into this position. Sure, I mighta overstepped my bounds a little, but seriously? A second strike over a skinnie prick who stole our money? What the fuck woulda been done differently if I brought him in alive? Charles doesn't get his hands dirty often, but I wouldn't have been surprised if he gored Eggsy on the spot for that kind of stunt.

The walk to my car is a miserable one. As much as it hurts knowing that I managed to get myself in deep shit tonight, the haunting recollection of my "first strike" grows in the recesses of my mind. I do everything in my power to push the memories down, but they keep clawing their way back up, invasive and consuming. The same hatred that compelled me to do what I did back then starts causing my blood to boil all over again.

No. I have to get a grip. If I let my temper get the best of me now, it really will be the end of the road. I stop in the middle of the sidewalk, paying no heed to the passersby that have to adjust their course to avoid bumping into me. Closing my eyes, I take several slow, deep breaths, concentrating on the air passing through my nostrils before exiting past my snout. My balled fists gradually uncurl themselves long enough to fish the car keys out of my pocket. Sliding behind the driver's seat, I ignite the engine and make my way home.

I manage to suppress the encroaching dark thoughts, instead replacing them with an attempt to reason through the present situation. It's a bad spot. But not necessarily the end. After all, they didn't drag me out back of Santiago's right then and there, which they very well could have done if I was being offered an early retirement. Charles ain't happy with me, of course, and neither is Marty... but I'm not beat yet. Maybe I can still do some damage control here.

I shake my head. Nothing for it. Like Charles said, there'll be too much heat in that area to go fishing around for the money right now. But first chance I get, I gotta do what I can to make things right.

As I pull my Cadillac into the driveway in front of my home, I take a deep, steadying breath. It was a bad day, but there's no use worrying the missus about it right now. I'll be strong for the family, like a man oughta be. Even with my little personal pep talk, the walk from my car up to the front door is an abnormally long one. I take one more draw of fresh air before putting on my best after-work smile and opening the door.

"A little later than I expected!" My wife's voice calls from the kitchen. The smell of roasting vegetables wafts in my direction as Bianca strides toward me, wiping her hands with a towel before offering her usual hug and kiss on the cheek. Before I can even say one word, her smile falls away. "What's the matter?"

Damn. Either this woman's a bloodhound, or I did a shit job of concealing my emotions. I try to give an innocent smile. "It's nothing. How was your day, honey?"

Her suspended eyebrow doesn't relent. She scans me up and down, possibly looking for a physical clue as to my soured emotional state. I've got no blood on my clothes or bruises on my face, so she eventually lets out a small sigh, issuing a command instead of an answer to my question. "Dinner's just about ready. Call the kids into the dining room, please."

I try to assuage her concerns with another smile. "No problem, hon." Following one final sideways look, my beautiful but frustratingly astute wife moves back to the kitchen. I sigh, wishing that I had spent more time at the poker tables working on my bluffing face. Guess I'm just a lousy liar.

I do as Bianca asked, announcing dinnertime up the stairs and, hopefully, toward at least one of the kids. Unsurprisingly, Angela rounds the corner from the living room with the echoing sounds of some sort of Western playing on the television following closely behind her. I'm not keen on hearing more gunshots tonight, so I ask her to turn the TV off before joining us at the dinner table. She obeys, and with traces of Russell exiting his bedroom, I traverse the short distance from the entryway to the dining room.

Photographs line the walls of the short hallway, captured snapshots of happiness nestled safely behind glass and frame. Everything from family vacations to simple trips to the park, immortalized in suspended motion, smiles that will never falter or fade in that perfect instant. I linger for a moment, taking in the two dozen or so various scenes. Most feature our children at different ages and different levels of interest in the glinting lens pointed in their direction. To me, it's those pictures where they weren't even aware of the camera that make for the most cherished memories.

The scents of delectable fruits and roasted vegetables

snap me out of my nostalgic trance, beckoning me to my open seat at the head of the freshly set table. Bianca brings forth the final dish to complete the dinner spread, a steaming casserole of broccoli, carrots and cauliflower. I fight off the desire to jam the serving spoon straight into the tray, instead extending my hands to the son and daughter seated on my left and right. They take my hand in theirs, and as Bianca finds her seat and completes the circle, we bow our heads and say grace.

The conversation is pleasant, but stale. I don't mention my day, instead opting to listen to Russell regale us with the adventure he went on with his friends, a bike ride across the neighborhood culminating in a frenzied chase for frogs near the storm drains. Though I see Bianca's eyebrows raise disapprovingly, she doesn't scold our son; we both know he's smart enough to be safe, even when playing around spots like that. Angela's day requires much less verbosity as she proffers the usual less-than-five word answers to any inquiries about her time with her mother. I do hope that she'll come out of her shell and be a little less shy and withdrawn once she grows up.

Occasionally, Bianca steals glances at me. They strike me as less romantic and more inquisitive, as though she's waiting for me to offer up some explanation as to my mood upon my return home. When I don't give one, her expression shifts to worry. The kids don't notice it, haven't had a reason to yet, but I've known her long enough to tell when her gears are turning. I tap my fingers on the table's surface, considering my next move carefully.

I was told I can't come in tomorrow. And I sure as hell don't want to sit around the house moping about the sorry state of my professional life. My mind wanders once more to the smiling moments adorning the walls and shelves of our home. After a moment, as the children reach the last few forkfuls of their meals, I clear my throat.

"What do you kids say to a trip to the beach tomorrow?"

They both freeze in place, a piece of broccoli suspended in air on its journey toward Russell's mouth. Their wide eyes give way to wider smiles, and their stunned silence is replaced with enthusiastic cheering.

Despite her normally sleepy demeanor, Angela is the first to get a cohesive word out. "The beach! Wow! Can we get ice cream while we're there?!"

I nod with a smile. "Don't see why not."

Russell pipes up next. "Do you think I can invite Sebastian, too?"

"Sure, give him a phone call once we're done with supper."

The two of them bounce excitedly on their seats as they shovel the remainder of their food away. They clearly agree with my sudden suggestion, but Bianca scrutinizes me from across the table. She does not protest, having no reason to deflate the children by rebuffing my offer. Hell, she might even take a dip in the cool ocean water herself with how hot it's been these past several days. Still, this particular diversion tactic obviously won't work to quell her concern about me.

With dinner concluded and the table cleared, the excitement moves into the living room. The delighted chatter of Russell and Angela finally gives way to enthralled silence as another cool-handed lawman dispenses his own brand of justice on the outlaws and desperados of the wild west. While the make-believe gunfire emanating from its speakers rattled my nerves earlier, I find myself strangely calmed by the wooden acting and over-the-top stunt work on the television set this evening.

After a few hours of lazily staring at the glowing glass, the wife declares it bedtime for the household, earning protestation from the children. "Just one more episode," they whimper, but both know full well that bargaining of this nature will never work with their mother. She turns off the television to the sound of their groans and shoos them both upstairs. I give her a smile before following the kids to the second floor; with all the *excitement* of today, I'm ready to get some shut-eye myself.

I take a seat on the edge of our bed and peel the socks from my feet, flexing my tendons and wiggling my toes in response to the cool air that now has free access to those lowest digits. Before I can disrobe further, the bedroom door closes behind Bianca. She stands wordless and monolithic, awaiting the explanation she is owed. I don't meet her eyes, opting to let out a muted sigh as I gather my thoughts. I knew I wouldn't be able to end the night without spilling the beans, but somehow I didn't prepare for the moment of truth.

For only a second, the idea of trying to downplay the situation crosses my mind. I had already fibbed by telling Bianca nothing was wrong when I got home, and she didn't believe me then. Her posture and patience tell me that she won't believe it now, either. I only see one way to proceed.

"I shot a guy today. A *coworker,* I suppose. He worked for the Herdsters and he was assigned to help Marty and I with our pick-ups. He tried to steal the money we collected. We chased him down in an alley and I shot him."

Bianca doesn't react. She already knows the nature of my work and understands that sometimes a man has to do what he has to in order to provide for his family. She loves me and the kids too much to raise a fuss over me exercising the more harsh brand of justice that my organization has to enforce from time to time.

She also knows there's more to the story than what I'm letting on. Something as simple as what I've said so far wouldn't have me rattled like I am. She waits for me to continue.

I take a deep breath before doing so. "Charles wasn't happy about it. Said I was out of line taking matters into my own hands, said I should have brought the skinnie weasel to him." I run a trembling hand over my hair. "I got a second strike."

Only now does my wife make a noise, emitting a small gasp as a hand comes to her mouth. She understands as well as I do what this means. I finally find the strength to bring my eyes up to meet hers, doing everything in my power to keep my voice from quivering as I speak. "A second fucking strike, over a god damn skinnie. And I wouldn't have even gotten the first one if Francisco—if he—"

In two strides Bianca is across the room, wrapping her arms around my head and pulling me toward her bosom. I'm powerless to do anything but bite my lip as the memories surge over me, calling forth the same pain, fury and hopelessness I felt all those months ago. I sharply inhale, bringing in as much oxygen as I can past the fabric of Bianca's shirt. She responds by stroking the back of my head and shushing me, keeping me nestled between her breasts.

I hate showing weakness like this. But if it has to be done in front of anyone, the woman who pledged herself to me in marriage and brought our children into the world is an acceptable option.

Though it feels longer, it only takes me about half a minute to calm down and recompose myself. Bianca leans back to meet my eyes before speaking. "I'm sorry this happened to you, Pierce. You didn't deserve that first strike, and you sure as hell don't deserve this second one. The only thing you can do now is be as careful as you possibly can. Don't make waves. Don't do anything else that'll even make Charles look at you funny. Keep your head down and this'll blow over." She averts her gaze. "I don't want anything to happen to you. Me, the kids... *we* need you, Pierce."

Now it's her turn to fight back her emotions, but I don't waste a moment in coming to her aid. I'm on my feet in a flash, wrapping my arms around her and bringing her close as she shudders. "I'm not going anywhere." She grips the front of my shirt, squeezing herself into me to absorb my words and warmth. "I love you, Bee."

She meets my eyes again, blinking away the budding droplets. The nickname came about early in our courtship, originally being met with protestation. She was, after all, a proud woman with a respectable name, and the louse that had taken her on a couple dates hadn't earned the right to bestow a contemptible single-syllabic pet name to her. It took several more months and a drop to one knee with a diamond in hand for her to finally warm up to the idea of it.

"I love you, too." Her cheeks redden, betraying her next move as she brings her lips to my own. She's the woman who accepted an awkward teenager who got rejected in the draft for the second world war, watching as his older brother traveled over the ocean in a C-47 to never return home. She's the woman who accepted my hand in marriage, beauty beyond my comprehension enveloped in a radiant white dress. She's the woman who didn't bat an eye the first time I came home after killing a man, knowing that the world is full of bad people and believing that I'm one of the good ones worth loving.

I'll prove her right. I'll survive. For her, for the kids, for a world that deserves good people like us.

I'll survive.

—

"—so there he is, right, this big fucker of a baryonyx, staring down his fuckin' runway of a snout at me. Again he says, in his stupid Southie accent: *fork over yer lunch money or yer dead!*' O'course, I could barely hear the guy with how bad he rung my bell. There were about three of him spinnin' around one anotha when I tried to look up at his ugly mug." He shot his eyes in my direction before jabbing a thumb at me, his signature grin plastered on his face. "Then this beefy fucker's silhouette shows up behind the baryonyx prick. Casts a shadow over him like a fuckin' mountain range at sunset. The asshole bully barely has time to react before Pierce wraps his fuckin' hands around the guy's mouth and starts swinging him around like a baseball bat! And that's when I learned my big brother is Babe-fuckin'-Tooth!"

Franky's wild pantomiming of a batter swinging for the fences elicited another round of laughter from the enraptured crowd of coworkers and bar employees he had drawn. He was always a lot more talented than I was when it came to making folks laugh and feel comfortable. I still felt the need to critique his storytelling: "That baryonyx wasn't *that* big. Hence me being able to toss him around like a rag doll."

My baby brother shot me another toothy grin. "Hey, I'm the one telling the story here, Pierce! Besides, you should be flattered that I didn't include the part where his two goon buddies blackened your eye!"

"And I'm pretty sure I sent one of them to the hospital." More laughter ushered in more clinking glassware and more downed liquor. It was another enjoyable night after a successful day at the office, and I watched with pride as Franky began spinning another yarn to entertain everyone around us. He was doing good work, not that I was worried that he'd be a good worker. He was a brilliant fella, and charismatic as all get-out. I knew he'd fit right in with the Herdster team.

My smile faltered as I glanced over at Charles in his usual corner booth, chomping on the familiar cigar he always had between his lips after the work day was done. He was a professional man, and professional men save their vices for when they're off the clock. He didn't smile back at me, instead merely taking in the sight of our post-work carousing with the authority of a boss who only mingles with the peons from time to time. Again, he was a professional man.

Of course, things with Franky hadn't gone perfectly. There were a few shifts where he had to punch out early on account of being too hung over to operate properly. We managed to hand-wave it as a stomach bug or a nasty migraine, but I warned him with increasing severity that a new guy only gets so many sick days before the boss starts looking real close as to the reason for those absences. And Charles wasn't the kind of guy who would miss the signs of a young man with an alcohol problem for very long.

It had been a few weeks without incident. Franky was going on six months with the team, and was being assigned more responsibility. I just needed to be the big brother. I needed to ensure he didn't fuck up this opportunity.

"Pierce!" His voice brought me back to the moment and I turned his way in acknowledgment. "What was the name of that dish ma always used to make? You know the one, with the flatbread and caramelized onions?"

"*Flammekueche,* or *tarte flambée.* It was one of her best dishes."

One of the fellas behind the bar who normally works the kitchen piped up. "Ay, don't dat usually got bacon on it?"

Franky rolled his eyes at the tyrannosaurus. "Not everythin' has to have meat on it, ya fuckin' carnivore. Try eatin' a salad once in a while!" More laughter, including from the t-rex that was just chided by the young blowhard in control of the conversation. I had to hand it to him, those same words out of a less charming guy would have earned a punch in the snout, but somehow he managed to pull off these social interactions with aplomb.

He shot back the last swig of bourbon in his glass before tapping the rim and nodding at the bartender. However, I took a step forward and put my hand on his shoulder. "We should probably get rolling, buddy. Still gotta work tomorrow."

Now it was my turn to catch an eye-roll. "Whaddya mean, Pierce? The night's still young!"

The slight slur in his words told me I needed to remain resolute in my stance. "Let's call it a night. We gotta make up some time on our routes, so we'll have to be fresh come morning."

With an exaggerated sigh and a mighty slump of his shoulders, Franky relented. "Aaaalright. Well, fellas, my grouch-ass of a brother says the fun's done, so I guess I'll see you chuckefucks tomorrow!" A round of goodbyes saw him out of his seat and venturing into the cool night air with me. He nudged me with an elbow as he lit up a fresh cigarette tucked between his lips, knowing I wouldn't allow him to have one in my car. "I think they're finally starting to warm up to me a bit!"

I smirked. "Making friends wasn't ever gonna be a problem for you, Franky. Though, I did notice Charles lookin' our way with a bit of disapproval."

"Pfft. That old sobersides probably has a fourth horn growing right between his buttcheeks." His turn of phrase made me snort out a laugh that I quickly stifled as I shot a glance over my shoulder toward the door. Thankfully, Charles hadn't sprung into existence there.

"Are you fuckin' crazy? If there's anyone you don't joke about, it's Charles. He once—"

"Yeah, yeah. Broke a bottle over some bozo who called him Charlie. I heard the story, and I ain't afraid of that gray trike."

"If you were smart, you would be. At least enough to know you don't fuck with him like that."

He surrendered the point as he drew down the last of his cigarette before stamping it out. With a roar of the engine, we began the short trek back to his home.

Silence was rare between us, mostly due to Franky's efforts. He was a regular chatterbox, not just with guys pourin' him drinks but with me and our other siblings, too. He was the only one who could get ma to smile at Gabriel's funeral. O'course, nobody was in a smiling mood after the crate and folded flag showed up, but Franky's just the kind of guy who offers wit as his special form of comfort and love. That was a lot of years ago, though, and these days...

"Franky, you been by to see ma recently?" My words filled the void between us, earning a slow turn of my kid brother's head. He stared at me as though he didn't believe what came out of my mouth for a moment before turning back toward the window. I cleared my throat before continuing. "You brought up her *flammekueche* back at the bar, so I thought she mighta been on your mind." More quiet. "I thought it might be good for your wife to meet her before—"

"No."

I blinked in surprise at the curtness of his response. "No?"

"No. I ain't been by to see her."

"Why not? You know she's sick. She probably doesn't have much—"

"I said no. I don't want to see her."

I sighed. "Francisco, you—"

"What the *fuck* is your problem, Pierce?! I said no, why don't you fuckin' drop it?!" His eyes were ablaze, wordlessly threatening me to not push the subject.

I pushed the subject. "What the fuck is *your* problem, huh? Just because she's sick, you don't wanna see her? What kind of son are you?"

He began shouting. "I don't wanna *see* her because she don't even fuckin' *know* who I *am!* She lays there like a fuckin' vegetable, and when she does have her eyes open, she don't even *recognize me!* What fuckin' good is it gonna do for me to visit her, huh?! Wastin' my fuckin' time!"

"Raptor Christ, Franky. You're acting like she's already

dead. I'm not telling you to visit dad's gravestone, I'm telling you that you need—"

"Pull over the car."

I paused in disbelief. "What?"

"Pull over the car, *now*."

I slowed the car before bringing it to the side of the road. The moment the concrete below us wasn't soaring by at a high speed, Franky tossed open the door and stomped out of the vehicle. I threw the parking brake before climbing out myself, preparing to call after him over its roof. However, I stopped short and stared in disbelief at his destination.

He was heading straight toward a liquor store.

I groaned. "Are you fucking serious, Franky?"

He spun around, backpedaling as he spoke with an unfitting smile on his lips. "I ran outta some stuff at home! Gotta make a quick pit stop."

I was exasperated. "We have to *work* tomorrow."

A disingenuous chuckle. "Ahhh, it ain't for tonight. 'Sides, the missus wouldn't let me drink *this* late!" He winked before spinning on his heel again and strolling through the door as though he hadn't a care in the world.

A cocktail of frustration and disappointment swirled in my stomach. I tried to tell him in the past that his drinking is bordering on a problem, maybe even turning into one given his sick days and frequent hangovers. But I was only ever met with hand-waves and disregarding remarks. Franky knew what was best for Franky, of course. Why the fuck would his older brother or any of his other brothers and sisters know better than him, after all? Not like he was the youngest of seven, with his five living siblings all constantly worrying about his stupidity and recklessness with alcohol. Hell, he had his license revoked for driving under the influence, and ended up in the hospital on two separate occasions because of this bullshit. But no. A "pit stop" to the liquor store, past midnight, on a work night. *That's* the ticket, Franky.

I climbed back into the car dejectedly. Part of the reason I even got him this job was because I thought it might help clean him up. If nothing else, I'd have my eyes on him and could be an example for how to be a professional and not depend on bourbon and gin for emotional support. Hell, he had a kid on the way. Alcohol wasn't the answer to his problems. It wasn't the answer to the stress of life, nor to the pain of losing dad last year and with ma probably following him home soon.

Franky needs help. My baby brother needs help, and he needs it soon. Or else...

Or else...

A gentle hand pulls me from my slumber, and an angelic voice ushers my consciousness back to the realm of the living.

"Pierce, honey. Wake up. You promised the kids you'd take them to the beach, remember?"

I pull myself up on my elbows, giving Bianca the best attention I can in my groggy, half-asleep state. "Morning, Bee. I'll be out of bed in—" A yawn interrupts me. "—in a second."

She strokes my shoulder and plants a kiss on my cheek before stepping away. She's already out of bed and dressed, probably has breakfast cooking, too. As she takes a seat at her bureau to apply a bit more makeup, she steals a glance in my direction. Another smile betrays her feelings.

As a couple that have been married for thirteen years, opportunities to express our love to one another physically become much less commonplace. It's difficult to schedule intimacy when you've got a family, and age brings with it a bit more exhaustion and lowered libido from one or both members of the relationship.

But last night...

I can't help but return Bianca's smile as I recall the way she passionately kissed me, the way she finished peeling my work clothes away, the way she offered her love and her comfort and her body to me. We kept things quiet; you have to with two kids in the house only a door away, but our passion for one another blazed as fiercely as it did when we were first married. She sighed and gasped as I made love to her, and she whispered her love to me as we fell asleep in one another's arms.

Some of the fellas at the office complain about their wives not putting out anymore. I can't relate.

I slide myself out from under the sheets, feeling a few joints pop and muscles wrench as I do. As glad as I am that Bianca and I can still express our love to one another physically, it *does* take a bit of a toll on my thirty-six-year-old bones. With a stretch and a bend, I'm on my feet and on my way toward the master bathroom for my morning rituals.

The house is alight with joy and excitement; both Russell and Angela can barely contain their delighted laughter as they scramble about collecting their snorkels and beach balls. Even Bianca gets swept up in the mood, humming a tune to herself as she packs our picnic lunch. Before long, we gather everything we need for an enjoyable day at the beach, swimsuits included, and pile into my Cadillac.

The arid skies greet us once more as we collect our provisions from the parked car and travel to the beachfront. This particular location was about an hour drive, far enough from the city proper to not risk swimming into sewage or stepping on broken glass or spent pieces. Though, it appears we weren't the only family to have an idea like this today. Despite being a Tuesday, finding a blank patch of sand for us to set down our beach towels and parasol proves difficult.

Dozens of other families jockey for position, but before long we find an adequate spot for ourselves.

Glancing momentarily to Bianca and I for permission, our nod of approval sends both Russell and Angela soaring toward the water, with my eldest blowing air into a multicolored inflatable ball as he runs. His friend Sebastian wasn't available today, but he rapidly kicks up conversation with some other nearby boys around his age, utilizing the beach ball as an icebreaker. Angela squeals in delight as her feet make contact with the lapping waves of the ocean; she skitters to a halt before taking a deep breath and plunging herself into the water. Only her tail is visible as she scours the shallows for trinkets.

I wear a contented smile as I lean back in my folding chair, keeping a calm but vigilant eye on the kids. My attention is captured as Bianca hands me a cold can of soda. I graciously accept before pushing the claw of my thumb through its top. She plops down next to me atop a blanket with a beverage of her own, relaxing under the shade of our beach umbrella. After a moment, she speaks up.

"Will you be going back in to work tomorrow?"

I don't look her way, opting to keep watching the children play. "Yeah, I think so."

"What do you plan to do?"

My smile falters. "Well, you suggested last night that I keep my head down. That's probably a safe bet."

A small puff of air from her nostrils bids me to turn her direction. A notable frown rests on her lips. "I mean, what do you plan to do *after* that? How are you gonna proceed?"

I slide the tip of my claw around the rim of my soda can, eliciting a faint, tinny scraping noise as I think. I had given it some thought myself, but haven't been forced to articulate it until now. When my words come, they are clumsy. "I can't get a third strike. We both know that. But I—well, I can't just *quit*. I'm in too deep with the organization. Seen too much. I'll either retire an old man who's done everything he needed to for the Herdsters until my knees knock together and I can't chew my food... or I'll retire in a bodybag."

My choice of words was poor, causing Bianca to gasp before scowling at me. "You ain't retiring in no bodybag! I won't accept it."

I shrug. "Well, that leaves the former. I have to do my job, and I have to do it right. I can't slip up. Not again." An involuntary sigh escapes my lips.

"Pierce, what happened wasn't your fault. With your brother—with Francisco—that wasn't your fault. And what you did was completely justified. Charles should have known that you would do what you did. There was no other way around it. Him punishing you with a strike is outrageous, and this second strike is even more inconceivable. You don't deserve this treatment."

I remain silent for a moment, only turning to bring my watchful gaze upon the kids once more. Russell is surrounded by a trio of other dinosaur boys, waist deep in waves as they bounce the air-filled multichromatic sphere between themselves, punctuating each lunge and dive with laughter. Even Angela, shy and reserved, beams with pride at another young girl to whom she shows off her small handful of seashells.

Bianca rests a hand on my shoulder before continuing. "You've put in a lot of years with the Herdsters and you've been doing good work. Charles obviously doesn't see that." She gingerly squeezes her fingers, causing me to turn in her direction again. She meets my eyes with a level of sternness not typical for her. "You could do Charles's job better than he could."

I scoff. "Heh. Yeah. Way things are goin' for me, I doubt *that* promotion is coming any sooner than the next extinction event."

She doesn't reply, instead only holding her gaze. My

brow involuntarily furrows, but before my mouth can open to question her, Angela comes trotting in our direction, holding forth her chitinous bounty. Bianca turns to our daughter with a beaming smile, showering the little girl in praise. I join in on the adulation when she displays her treasures to me.

The rest of the day goes by quickly, with Bianca and I joining the kids in the water, enjoying its cool temperature amidst the sweltering sunbeams. Our lunch is refreshing and delicious, and, as Angela requested, we make a stop at the nearby ice cream stand for an afternoon treat. Around four o'clock, my announcement of the conclusion of today's festivities is met with protestation from both children. Their grumbling quickly turns to quiet breathing as they both sleep peacefully in the backseat of the car the entire way home.

The topic of Charles doesn't come up again for the rest of the day. At least, not out loud.

—

Marty waits for me in his usual spot, standing near the building's entrance nestled in the parking garage. His neck cranes to allow his eyes to meet mine as I pass through the metal door and into the building proper. Though he offers me a smile, it feels less genuine than normal.

"Morning, Pierce." We begin our short walk toward Charles's office.

"Heya Marty. How, uh—how'd things go yesterday?"

He shrugs. "Boring day. They had me hang around here in the office in case they needed me for anything. They didn't. Kicked the hell out of the paper's crossword puzzle, though."

I try to smile, but still feel a pit in my gut. The air needs clearing. "Look, Marty. I'm sorry I caused problems.

Especially for you. You didn't deserve trouble, not for my mistake."

He stops and turns to face me. At first, his raised eyebrow communicates apprehension toward my words. However, after analyzing me for a moment, he averts his gaze and sighs. "I told you it wasn't the right move."

"I know. I shoulda listened to you, and I'm sorry."

His eyes flick in my direction again. A small smile tugs at his lips. "I mean, I got in a lot less trouble than you did. But... thanks, Pierce." He taps my shoulder with his knuckles in a show of good faith. "Just be careful, buddy. From now on. You really gotta tow the line."

I nod.

His smile widens into the one I've known for the past few years, genuine and warm. "Believe it or not, I like workin' with ya. And I care about ya. Despite the humongous pain in the ass you are sometimes."

I can't help but chuckle. "Alright, you goose-necked bastard. Let's go. Getting all mushy on me and then insulting me like this."

He delivers a few more playful jabs at my ego that I take in stride as we make our way to our destination. Pushing open the door to Charles's chambers, we both quiet down as we step through the entryway and find our seats across from him. Our boss doesn't keep a standard office, instead preferring to utilize one of the sublevel conference rooms as a semi-permanent headquarters. A coworker once snickered to a few others in the office that Charles did this to sit behind a great big "desk", as a sort of intimidation tactic.

That coworker didn't work for us much longer.

The gray triceratops glances up from his paperwork to acknowledge the two of us as we take our seats across from him, separated by a massive expanse of oak. He sets his pen down and folds his hands on the table before speaking. "Good morning Martin. Pierce. You'll be handling the south side today, businesses around Pelagic Park. Start with a ten block radius, if you can get more done, wonderful."

He offers his typical smile and nods toward the door before returning to his pen. Marty shoots a sideways glance at me, silently acknowledging the curtness of our boss. With a nearly imperceptible shrug, he gingerly claps his hands to his knees and rises from his seat.

I linger for a moment, staring at Charles. He said nothing about yesterday or whether they had to do any work to clean up the "mess" that I made. He barely even acknowledged my existence, instead plastering on a sickening facade of apathy and ignorance.

He acts normal. As though he didn't effectively threaten my life just two nights prior.

My eye twitches and my lip curls, but I quickly stifle the emotions, choosing instead to join Marty in departure. Somewhere in the back of my mind, the phantom of Bianca's voice finds purchase:

"You could do Charles's job better than he could."

The day drags on at a sickening pace. We encounter no difficulties; the owners of the stores we visit are cordial and accommodating, producing their dues without hassle. Marty makes pleasant chatter in the car, and I respond as best as I'm able, but my mind continues to wander.

Why *aren't* I in a higher ranking position yet? If I was managing other Herdsters instead of doing this grunt footwork, I never would have had to do Eggsy in. Sure, I had originally thought he was being trained up to replace me, but even if that was the case he proved himself to be untrustworthy. What's to say someone else can't replace me? Someone that's actually as dependable as I am?

I deserve to be further along, further up the ladder. I've broken my back for the Herdsters, and what do I have to show for it? Two strikes. The threat that one more mistake will be the end of me. And that doesn't even have to be a *legitimate* fuck-up on my part, just something Charles decides is a big enough issue to send me to pasture. Am I gonna spend the rest of my days running errands for an ungrateful boss who holds my fate on a fragile string?

The wheels turn, but at a slow and calculating pace. Before anything else happens, I need to make up for the disaster that was two days ago. I need to prove not to Charles but to the Herdsters as a whole that I can be trusted to handle something as simple as collecting dues from the neighborhood.

Marty and I pull up outside of Santiago's around five forty-five. He begins climbing out of the car, but pauses when I don't turn off the engine. "You coming in, Pierce?"

I shake my head. "Not tonight, Marty. You go ahead and run the money in for Charles and give him our report. I need to take care of something."

Marty raises an eyebrow at me. "Anything you need help with?"

"No, I got it. You have a good night, I'll see you again tomorrow."

He nods before gripping the stuffed envelopes from within the dash and exiting the car. I watch him enter Santiago's. Not that I don't trust him; rather, I keep an eye on him to ensure an errant junkie doesn't leap out of an alley and try to stick him up. After he safely passes through the front door, I throw on my signal before performing a U-turn.

Fifteen minutes later, I find myself in front of the same alleyway that caused me so much trouble. The remnants of police tape lazily flutter in the near undetectable breeze, one which offers no comfort against the stagnant summer heat. I glance around, seeing signs of neither cop nor pedestrian. The scene where a man was shot dead, so quickly abandoned, a victim to the apathy of a city too gargantuan to worry about its citizens or their fates for more than twenty-four hours.

I don't need to crouch to get past the tape; it's already

split and mostly absent, so nothing prevents me from entering the alley. A blemished patch of discoloration in roughly the outline of a seated man is traced into the brick exterior of one of the walls. The same soiled silhouette runs down the pavement a short distance before ending abruptly. Looks like the city's cleanup crew went over it quickly with a hose, but anything more than a passing glance betrays the grisly aftermath still visible here.

My eyes begin scanning the piles of garbage. It appears largely undisturbed, though a few of the bags were likely picked through by the police for potential evidence. Neither Marty nor I left anything behind; one of the perks of using a revolver is not having to dig around for bullet casings, unless I get into a situation where I have to fire more than five shots. And in a situation like that, I doubt I'm too concerned about retrieving bullet casings.

My lip curls as I realize what I'm going to have to do. Eggsy hid the money, and he hid it somewhere very close to here. It could be in these piles of garbage next to him, or it could be stuffed into a sewer grate or drainage pipe. No matter how you slice it, I'm gonna have to get my hands dirty to find this—

Footsteps. My plates stand on end as the echoes approach from around the alley's bend, coming from the opposite direction of where I entered. I move as silently as I can to press my back against the wall, concealing myself from their peripheral vision long enough for me to figure out who the fuck this is. If it's some passerby taking a shortcut, I can just pretend I'm fishing for a pack of cigarettes I don't have on me. If it's a cop, I might have to jostle his noggin well enough that he doesn't remember me when he comes to. Either way, I didn't want company.

The footsteps grow louder. I do my best to look relaxed, but coil my muscles in case I need to lunge. After several agonizing seconds, the trespasser comes into view. A flat cap rests upon the head of a human, messy tufts of short brown hair poking from under its rim. His clothes are well worn but plain; blue collar rather than white, I don't figure this guy as a lost banker. He intently stares into the corner of the alley, toward an alcove packed full with trash, before seeming to remember that another entrance connects to this place. He peers over his shoulder and nearly flies out of his shoes when his eyes come to rest on me.

His blue eyes. Eyes that I've seen before. Only two days before, in fact.

The skinnie from Sal's Butcher and Grocery. The one that Sal Fontana himself entrusted with delivering me the envelope of Sal's dues.

A single stride is all it takes to close the distance between us. He stares up at me, wide-eyed and mouth agape, much like he did when I first "met" him. My words rumble past my snarling teeth.

"What the *fuck* are you doing here, skinnie?"

Chapter Seven: Samuel

Well, this is some rotten luck.

I desperately try to suck oxygen into my lungs as I crumple to the pavement, having all the wind violently expelled from my torso by the titanic fist that just got acquainted with my stomach. My insides make sounds they aren't supposed to make, crunches and gurgles informing me that my organs are reorganizing themselves. I attempt to move my limbs, but they involuntarily squeeze inward, trying desperately to protect what remains of my vital parts from further onslaught.

The irony of ending up on my ass in this exact same alleyway twice in the span of forty-eight hours isn't lost on me. Last time it was due to a well-executed tackle by a defensive line of police officers. As painful as that was, and as shitty as it was to get carted into the station after being tenderized, I'd honestly say I preferred that treatment. Despite how racist some cops can be, I didn't fear that my life might end at their hands. But now?

I probably won't be so fortunate.

The juggernaut of a stegosaurus looms over me, his face shrouded in black shadows as the waning sun sinks below the horizon of glass and steel at his back. His fist uncurls before he reaches down to seize the front of my shirt. With little effort, he hoists me into the air, narrowing his eyes as I keep gasping for air that just won't settle in my lungs. He brings my face inches away from his own before speaking.

"I said, what the fuck are you *doing* here, skinnie?" He sneers at me before releasing his grip, allowing me to crumple to my knees in my continuing pursuit of not suffocating. "I recognize you. You were there at Sal's. The mangy mutt that Sal asked to deliver his dues." He pauses. "Guess that means you probably recognize me, too. Hence your stunned silence."

He begins pacing the alley, not removing his eyes from me as my composure slowly returns and the horrifying pain in my abdomen is numbed by the adrenaline. He continues. "Of course, the real mystery here is why you'd come bumbling down this particular alleyway. You just unlucky? You live down the street and just happened to be taking a shortcut on your way home after work?" A click of his tongue foretells his disbelief of this posited scenario. "They say it's a small world, but it isn't that small. Nah, you were looking for something, and I think I have an idea of what it was."

I can finally speak, though my voice is cracked and my breathing is still labored. "I... I do live... near here... I was just... there's been a mistake—"

"Bullshit, skinnie. Don't fuckin' lie to me. Were you in cahoots with Eggsy the whole way? I bet he planned to pass the money off to you that night, you little scumbag." Eggsy? Was that the name of the man that died in this alley? A wicked grin spreads across the stegosaurus's snout. "Sorry for throwing a wrench into that plan of yours. Real shame what happened to Eggsy. You probably figured that out, though. Which means you waited for the heat to die down before coming back here to pick up his deposit, wherever it might be. Squirreled away in a bag of trash or a hole in the wall, probably." He stops pacing and bends down, cocking his head at me. "How close am I?"

I do my best to straighten myself out, still on my knees but hopefully looking less pathetic. "I don't know any 'Eggsy'. I'm telling you, I don't know anything about—"

My words trail off as the stegosaurus's hand moves to the revolver at his side. It slides free of its home before aiming directly at my head. My assailant's eyes seem to glaze over as he begins muttering. "I'm not even gonna bother asking again. I'm done dealing with fucking skinnies at this point. I'll find the money. Sure, I'll have to wait a week or so. Two hits in the same alley in as many days?" He chuckles. "The cops will be flabbergasted. But they'll move on. And when they do, I'll find the money."

He draws back the hammer of his pistol. I try to protest, but all that escapes is a rasping wheeze. My teeth clench together as my body instinctively prepares itself for the inevitable, horrific, conclusive pain that is about to be inflicted upon it.

Please. I'll tell you where the money is, just give me a chance to speak.

I don't want to die.

Not now.

Not when...

Aubrey...

—

"I'm t-terribly sorry, everyone. We'll give you *all* refunds. Please, just remain calm—" The microphone offered little benefit to the lilliputian man's voice. His words were drowned out by the thunderous racket that erupted from the crowd, a cacophony of confused jeers and enraged questioning.

Aubrey took a step back and gasped, bumping into me

with the movement. I placed my hands on her shoulders to steady her; she spun around in response. "Wh-what do they mean, 'arrested'? Who would have—" Her eyes shot wide, suddenly filled with anger. She began shoving her way through the rabble toward the entrance. I followed, not fully understanding her enraged response. I mean, I was pissed off that the show was canceled, too, but if Miles Cratis got arrested, what good could we do?

A tangle of bodies plugged the doorway, elbows and curses flying as the impatient crowd sought an answer to the most pressing question: *why* was Miles Cratis arrested? What could he have possibly done to lead to his detention and an interruption to this perfect night of performance?

Aubrey exercised no patience or delicacy in her march forward. Her eyes were ablaze and her teeth were brandished. Some patrons evacuated from her path upon seeing her; others had to be encouraged with a nudge or a shove, eliciting half-spoken curses until those that uttered them turn to see the hue of the person pushing past. As riled up as everyone was, nobody was going to argue with a pissed off velociraptor on the warpath.

With a bit of effort, we squeezed out of the claustrophobic, stuffed entryway and into the stifling late evening air. Though a gaggle of onlookers milled about, there was more room to maneuver here than there was inside; Aubrey rapidly shifted around the crowd to get as close to the pair of nearby squad cars as she could.

We only saw him for a brief moment. Handcuffed and with a partially dried rivulet of blood splayed across the side of his face, Miles Cratis was stuffed into the backseat of one of the cruisers. Aubrey's gasp quickly turned to a growl as she lunged forward. However, she didn't get within twenty feet of Cratis before a police officer extended his hand to rebuff her advance.

"Ma'am, please stay back," the officer commanded, but

Aubrey screamed past him toward the men closing the back door of the squad car.

"Duffy! Preston! What the *fuck* did you do?!"

The blue-clad dilophosaurus and spinosaurus turned to witness the infuriated velociraptor at the edge of the crowd. As they did I instantly sank backward, hoping to avoid their notice.

The same fucking guys that arrested me. The same ones that interrogated me back at the precinct. What the fuck were *they* doing here?!

In reply to Aubrey's fury, the pair only offered sneering grins as they climbed into the front seats of their vehicle. A few quick taps of their siren allowed them to perform a rapid U-turn and travel in the direction of the station from which they hailed. The station that wasn't even *close* to this nightclub. Hell, it was an entire borough away.

Aubrey took a step back, causing the blockading officer to lower his arm and move his attention elsewhere. I stood behind her for a moment, unsure of what to say. I glanced down; her fingers were curled into tight fists and her tail snapped to and fro.

She didn't hold the suspended position for long, spinning on her heel and stomping several yards away, only to turn about and stride back. She repeated this process a half dozen times, saying nothing but keeping her limbs tensed and her eyes focused on nothing in particular. Occasionally her lip curled as though she was about to blurt out a blasphemy, but each time it sank back down to a scowl before any utterance was made.

All I could do was watch as she processes her emotions. I wished I had a word of comfort I could offer, but I was still confused about the entire situation. Everything happened so fast, and nobody said why Miles Cratis was being arrested. I strained my ears for any insight offered by nearby gossip, but only caught wind of a few clues. The police stopped, an argument broke out, and the next thing anyone knew Miles was clobbered and in the back of the police car. None of it made any—

"Those damn crooked sons of bitches. Those god damn asshole sons of *bitches!*" Aubrey's pacing had stopped, being replaced with a string of expletives directed toward two individuals who were blocks away by then. "I swear to God I'll kick their asses. Both of 'em. I'll hospitalize those sons of bitches."

"Aubrey." I took a cautious step forward.

She didn't seem to hear me. "Why in God's name would they do this? Why are they being so *cruel?* Racist bastards, there was no reason for them to arrest Miles Cratis! I bet they came here just because they knew *I* was here! Those god damn pricks, they ruined *everything!* They ruined my date! They hurt Miles Cratis! Fucking *why?!*"

I gingerly moved a little closer. "Aubrey, listen. It'll be alright."

Her eyes were glued to the sidewalk. Tears rolled down her cheeks. Her fists trembled. "Why can't I have anything? Not even one god damn night of happiness?! *Why—*"

Aubrey gasped, interrupted by my next action.

I'll admit, this might not have been the smartest thing I'd ever done. After all, this was a furious velociraptor I was dealing with, complete with sharpened claws and eviscerating teeth. As an unqualified human, I didn't know what all a dinosaur's emotional breakdown involved or how best to treat it safely. As such, there was a non-zero chance that my jugular was about to get torn out, and if that happened there'd be no one to blame but the stupid caveman who approached an enraged predator. But I executed a hail mary. Nothing ventured, nothing gained.

I slid my arms around her shoulders and brought her body into contact with mine, my wrists passing one another as the encircling motion came to rest. Her already stiff posture practically went rigor mortis as she locked in place, her tail snapping to an almost perfect vertical angle. With our close proximity I could no longer see her face, and aside from her gasp of surprise I didn't hear her breathe.

If I was about to die, I might as well go for broke.

I rested my head against the side of hers, feeling her short blue hair rustle against my cheek. I gently squeezed her in my embrace before whispering to her. "It's okay. Everything's gonna be okay."

She finally released the breath that had caught in her throat, a shuddering, decompressing sigh entwined with a choked sob. Her posture slacked, the rigid tail behind her collapsing to the ground in a defeated *thud*. Her fingers uncurled before finding their way to my back, gripping tightly to my suit jacket. She nuzzled her snout into the crook of my shoulder, whimpering only one word.

"Sammy..."

I stroked the nape of her neck. This meeting-turned-date had been a roller coaster for both of us. What started friendly and amicable quickly turned sour when I opened my stupid mouth and asked a woman with a bad knee to a fuckin' swing dance. I embarrassed the hell out of myself and I thought that was gonna be the end of it. Sure, she said it was "okay" but I know all too well that it only takes one boneheaded fuck-up to turn a potential courtship into a "never speak to me again".

But she danced with me. Just when I was feeling like I'd blown my chance with this beautiful, strong-willed woman, she offered me her hand and led me to the dance floor for a slow enough song that her knee could handle. When her gentle hands came to rest on my shoulders, I felt like my heart was gonna fly out of my chest. And when her tail crept up on me like some sort of feathered commando, I just about yelped in surprise. But after the initial shock, the sensation provided by her alien appendage was comforting.

Even kinda sexy.

I felt my cheeks lighting up like they did back on the dance floor. I wished I could keep myself from blushing like an imbecile, but there was nothing for it. Instead, I tried to shift my focus back to the moment at hand. Feeling that her trembling has calmed and her breathing has steadied, I leaned back to meet Aubrey's eyes. The yellow orbs scintillated in the moonlight, shimmering with residual moisture. Again, the primal need inside of me to protect this woman who likely didn't need my protection in the slightest flared up; I gently ran my fingers across her cheek, brushing away the small streaks that marred her makeup. She responded by tilting her head into my hand, staring up at me as she awaited my words.

"I'm sorry that tonight has been rough on you, Aubrey. I wish that things had gone different. We could still be in that club, with Miles Cratis playing his heart out for nobody but the two of us. I might have even built up the courage to hold your hand while we listened." This elicited a small giggle from Aubrey. "I wish none of this bad shit happened, but I'm still thankful that you invited me out tonight. Some random guy who stopped and complimented your humming at a bus stop got to enjoy a wonderful evening with a kind, charming, beautiful woman. I'm glad I got to spend tonight with you."

She drew in a sharp breath, her own cheeks reddening at my remarks. Her eyes shifted back and forth, not settling on a specific place on which to focus. Her face was awash with emotions, none of which I could properly pin down. I mean, I *hoped* she felt a certain way, like how I felt about her in the moment, but her expressions weren't easy to read. I was left unsure on how to proceed, any building debonair momentum being lost to hesitation.

She filled in the blank for me in an instant, drawing her face to mine. Our lips connected, electric and exotic, thrilling and saccharine. It was a sensation completely foreign to me, yet perfectly familiar, both alarming and alluring. Though briefly caught off guard by her brazenness, I quickly became enthralled, returning her kiss with my own. The lingering tension in her body melted as she realized I reciprocated her emotion, a soft, solitary gasp escaping from between our joined lips.

Aubrey. You are everything I want in a woman.

Aubrey…

"Pierce!"

An unfamiliar voice causes my tightly squeezed eyes to shoot open, a brief flurry of spots and stars bombarding my vision. The barrel of the gun held mere inches away from my face rocks backward a fraction as its wielder snaps his head around to regard the person that interrupted him.

The midnight blue stegosaurus speaks in a growl. "Marty?! What are you doing here?!"

A brownish dinosaur halts his jog at the edge of the alley, his elongated neck bobbing as he catches his breath. I'm not sure if he's a brontosaurus or a diplodocus—I've never had a perfect eye for picking out similar dinosaur species from one another, but my guess is the latter. A smooth tail sways behind the fella apparently named Marty, and once his composure returns he stares daggers at both of us.

"Pierce, you idiot. You think you'll just drop me off and mysteriously say you gotta 'take care of something', expecting me *not* to know exactly where you're headed?" He focuses on me, then the gun that the stegosaurus he called Pierce points at my head. "The real question is, what the *fuck* is going on here?! Who the hell is this human?! And why do you got iron drawn on him?!"

Pierce lets out a sigh before flitting his eyebrows at me.

"Someone who happened to be in the wrong place at the wrong time. Isn't that right, skinnie?"

Marty's hissed words are sharp. *"Pierce!* Put that thing away, are you actually out of your fucking mind?! The cops were just here two days ago, what makes you think they won't be around the corner?!"

An eye roll from Pierce causes my heart to drop again. Every moment I think this long-necked angel has saved my life, I'm brought back to reality by the bullet that remains aimed directly at my head. "I'm tired, Marty. I'm tired of humans fucking things up for me, and I just want to feel a little better." His wicked gaze rests on me again. "One less skinnie in the world would help me feel a *lot* better, actually."

My voice suddenly returns to me, but my words tumble from my mouth before my brain can properly register whether it was the right move or not.

"I work at Sal's Butcher and Grocery! I'm the one that gave Pierce our dues!"

For an agonizing moment, the only sound is that of the rustling, broken police tape still affixed to the entryways of the alley. It seems the entire city fell to a hush, the typically ever-present din of electricity, engines, horns and sirens all but vanished in the sickening quiet.

Marty's jaw hangs open in befuddlement. His neck swings his head to look from my visage to that of my captor; Pierce wears a pronounced frown that borders on a snarl.

With a quick shake of his head to clear his confused expression, Marty speaks. "Wh—This guy works at *Sal's?* He gave you Sal's dues?" As he says this, the vague memory of the diplodocus's form creeps into my mind. He was standing outside the dock's man door. He must not have seen me, and I just barely saw him.

Pierce only shrugs in reply, forcing Marty to continue. "That means he knows who you are. Who we work for." Marty's face scrunches as he pieces the situation together.

"Does he know about the rest of the money? About Eggsy?"

The barrel of the gun shifts closer to my eyeline, causing me to flinch again. Pierce's words ooze with cruelty. "Good question. *Does* he know about the rest of the money?"

Despite my desperation, despite the gun pointed at my head, something keeps me from blurting out that I know where the money is and immediately taking them to it. With Pierce's clear hubris for humans and Marty's continued confusion, I get the distinct feeling that I wouldn't survive long after handing them their prize. After all, I'd just be a "loose end", someone who knows who they are and who they work for.

If I tell them, I'm dead. If I don't... I'm dead.

God, please throw me a bone here.

"We should bring him to Charles."

Only in response to these glorious, blessed words uttered by the diplodocus saint before me does the gun barrel descend to point at the concrete beneath us instead of at my skull. However, Pierce's anger only seems to be exacerbated. "What the *fuck* good is Charles gonna do in this situation, huh? What does he want with this literal nobody?"

Marty's expression hardens. "Pierce. We need to bring him in. Don't do this again."

Pierce's hands find his hips as he begins pacing, shaking his head and muttering under his breath. My mind unconsciously recollects Aubrey's similar show of emotional distress from yesterday, though the beautiful woman I comforted didn't have a cocked revolver in her hand. Besides that, I don't think there'll be any comforting of *this* dinosaur with a warm hug and kind words. Instead, Pierce shoots furious glances at me, wrestling with his own conscience on whether he's going to acquiesce to Marty's request or finish doing what he so transparently wants to do.

After an agonizing half a minute, his pacing concludes. He snarls before thumbing the hammer of his revolver and gently squeezing the trigger, allowing the hammer to slide back to its resting, less dangerous position. Absent is the crack of gunpowder and the blinding flash that I was certain would spell the end of Samuel Lawson. I let out a tremendous sigh as I slump forward, mentally and physically spent.

But my night isn't over yet. I may have earned a stay of execution, but that doesn't mean I'm out of the weeds. Not even close. Marty grabs me by the arm and hoists me to my feet as Pierce marches down the alleyway in the opposite direction from which I had entered. I curse myself and my blind stupidity for not being more cautious and scoping out every angle of this alley before I went blundering in toward the wealth it conceals. If I had, none of this would have happened. Stupid, stupid.

I'm escorted forcefully to a parked Cadillac DeVille, as black as night and a fitting ride for the dinosaur that woulda killed me were it not for some divine timing by his coworker. Pierce groans in my direction again. "It's not bad enough you're letting this skinnie prick live, now I have to have another one of these disease-bags in *my* back seat?"

Marty shrugs. "I took a cab here. Unless you want to foot the bill for another one to get back to Santiago's, yes. You'll just have to live with the *'disease-bag'* in your back seat." I sense both annoyance and sarcasm in Marty's voice. Though he's obviously not my friend, I get the feeling that he's not as intolerant of humans as his coworker.

With an annoyed grunt, Pierce climbs behind the steering wheel. Marty opens the back door and ushers me inside; while not quite a shove, he doesn't give me the option of anywhere else to go. The idea of bolting from the car crosses my mind, but the loaded and anxious revolver that still rests in Pierce's grip dashes the notion. As Marty slides into the front passenger seat, the engine roars to life and the tires beneath us carry me toward who knows what. My death? Probably.

Geez, what a fucking lousy way for things to go.

Reflected, waning light dances across the storefront windows that sail past us. Despite its scintillating beauty, my mind wanders to last night. To Aubrey. God, I wanna live so I can see her again. So I can hold her in my arms again. So I can kiss her again.

"Hey, you two. Move along."

We separated quickly, startled from the moment by the officer's stern command. He eyed both of us with contempt, clicking his tongue before climbing back into his cruiser. Though some percentage of the crowd had dispersed, others had shifted focus from the scene where Miles Cratis was arrested to the human and dinosaur that were now canoodling only a few yards away. Aubrey's face flushed bright red and her tail instantly retracted away from me, instead coiling tightly around her midsection. She hustled down the sidewalk, escaping the gawkers as rapidly as her legs would allow.

Of course, I followed closely behind. I was still enraptured. I wanted more of what we just had, even more than that. My primitive caveman brain was guiding me in that moment. Yes, I wanted her to be happy, and yes, I wanted to be supportive of her. But more than anything, I wanted her.

I wanted to be with Aubrey.

Almost in response to my unspoken words, she spun around to face me, well outside of both eye and earshot of the lingering onlookers. Her cheeks were still red, but her expression had become stern. "Sammy—" She stopped herself before clearing her throat. "Samuel. I had a nice time this evening, all things considered. But I have to go. If I get to the precinct, maybe I can help straighten out whatever happened with Miles Cratis." She hesitated, shifting her gaze downward. "Thank you for tonight. But... this should be goodbye."

My nose scrunched. "Goodbye? What do you mean, goodbye? I mean, could we do this again sometime?"

She shook her head. "You saw the way those people were looking at us. The way they whispered. The way they stared. That's—I don't want that for you."

I brought my hand to my chin, contemplating for a moment before replying. "As a matter of fact, I didn't really notice that at all."

She let out a huff. "Come on. Don't be dense. They were staring at us like we were a sideshow at the carnival!"

"I'm being serious. I mean, I know there were people there, and maybe they were lookin' at us, but I wasn't paying attention to them. I was only paying attention to you."

Again, her cheeks brightened but she tried to remain resolute. "Sammy, if this—if *we* continue on, that's gonna be our lives. Looks and stares and nasty comments behind our backs. People think this is *wrong*. That our kinds shouldn't be together. Like it's some sorta taboo." Her head sank as she convinced herself further. "People think that humans should be with humans, and dinosaurs should be with dinosaurs."

I scoffed. "Heh. Fuck 'em."

Aubrey was taken aback, lifting her head with a raised eyebrow.

I continued. "So what if they think it's wrong? You can't tell me that what we have isn't real. The way I feel about you is as real as the way I've ever felt about any human. Maybe even more so. Why do some rubber-necking yahoos have any right to tell us otherwise?" I shook my head. "I'm telling you right now, Aubrey. I'd be willing to weather that storm. I've already lived a life of nasty remarks being made at my expense just because of who I am. I've suffered prejudice and profiling. But I've always endured it. And—well, if I was with a gal like you, it'd make enduring any other hardships that much more worthwhile."

She glanced away again, biting her quivering lip. I stepped toward her, hoping she would mirror my movement, but she did not.

I let out a sigh. "That said, I don't want *you* to endure something you don't want to endure, either. You're probably right. People would look at us funny. And you'd probably catch the worst of it, choosing to be with a caveman like me. I can't imagine the type of shit they'll fling at you." I hesitated before completing the thought. "I don't want you to get hurt. Not on account of me. As much as I wanna be with you, I want you to be happy."

Her eyes shifted downward as she processed my words. After a moment, she gently stepped closer, closing the gap between us. She lifted her face to meet my gaze as a small smile spread across her lips.

"Fuck 'em."

I was now the one to take the initiative, leaning forward to kiss her. She reciprocated the gesture instantly, interlocking her hands around my waist to draw us closer together. Her tail performed the maneuver with which I was quickly growing accustomed, wrapping around my back in an additional layer of downy embrace. Our eyes closed as we explored uncharted territory with one another, basking in ambrosial sensations wholly new to us.

Too soon, she drew back from our tender kiss, gazing up at me with her beautiful yellow eyes. I still struggled to properly read her expressions, but my guess was that she was... hopeful.

She smiled. "You're a real catch, Sammy. You know that?"

My hand instinctively scratched the back of my neck in embarrassment. "Ahh, I'm nothin' special. But you? You are a woman worth asking out again. That is, unless you wanted to continue this date somewhere else?"

Her tone became indignant, though the lingering grin informed me of its intended playfulness. "Mr. Lawson! What sort of woman do you take me for?"

I quickly backpedaled, stumbling over my faux pas. "Oh! Oh, no! Not—I mean, not that I'm—I'd—I meant, like, for coffee or somethin'!"

She let out a giggle that turned to a sigh. "You are too easy to tease, you know that? But, no. Not tonight. I need to get to the station and see if there's anything I can do for Miles Cratis. It's likely the captain is gonna be called up based on the high profile of who they arrested. I just need to find out *why* it happened, and whether I can help him."

"Oh. Do you want me to come along? I could be, like, an extra witness?"

Aubrey shook her head. "I don't want to risk Duffy or Preston seeing you again. They'd likely arrest you on the spot just for showing your face there. Truthfully, I'm glad they didn't see you tonight." A look I interpreted as worry crossed her face. "I shouldn't have shouted at them. If they *were* here just because of me, I gave them all the gratification they wanted, and now they can spin a yarn about how it *wasn't* because of me that they arrested Miles."

I tightened my grip around her, stroking her back as I spoke. "You didn't do anything wrong. If those pricks had some sorta vendetta, then you take that info to your boss and let him handle it." I recalled what she had told me of the police captain over our drinks; from what she said, he seemed to be a level-headed and good-hearted person. "I'm sure everything will work out."

She nuzzled her snout into my neck again, causing a shiver of desire to fire up my spine. "Thank you."

After a moment, she took a step back. Her beautiful yellow dress sparkled in the moonlight, accentuating every subtle curve of her slender form. The primal part of me began rumbling in the back of my mind again, sparking the fire of my libido, but I quickly stamped out the growing embers. "Uh—so, maybe we could do another date, then?"

"I'd like that very much. Give me a call tomorrow night, okay?"

I stepped toward the curb, raising a hand to hail a cab for her. The light atop a yellow and black checkered vehicle flicked off as it pulled to the side of the road. In continuation of my dignified gentleman act, I fished a dollar out of my pocket and handed it to the driver before opening the back door for Aubrey. She blushed and smiled again before sliding into the back seat.

I bent over to speak. "I'll call you tomorrow night. Have a good evening, Aubrey."

She leaned up, planting a quick kiss on my cheek. "You, too, Sammy."

—

Give her a call. I was supposed to give Aubrey a call *tonight*. And now I'm being carted God knows where to have God knows what done to me, all because my stupid ass went trundling back into that alley.

I wish I had never seen that money. I certainly didn't want that Eggsy fella to die in that alley, but I find myself wishing he'd croaked before he pointed me toward his buried treasure. Hell, I'm a broke guy who's falling head over heels for a beautiful woman. That dollar I forked over to the cab driver stung as bad as the one I gave to the waitress at the jazz club. Raptor Jesus, a forty cent tip. I could practically feel my belt tightening with the gesture. And, sure, I felt cool and hip and generous in front of the pretty velociraptor sittin' next to me, but I don't exactly have a wallet stuffed full of bills to keep acting that suave all the time.

My mattress just never got comfortable last night. I tossed and turned, my thoughts flipping back and forth between how much I wanted to treat Aubrey to a fancy dinner at an upper-class place and which of my meager possessions I'd have to sell to afford such a night. As much as I loved my clock radio, I could probably get a few bucks for it at an electronics shop. Saxon, on the other hand—well, I loved the walking carpet, but I couldn't even get a nickel for the big lunk.

It wasn't until the morning sun was rising over the bay that my memory was jogged. With everything that happened last night, Aubrey was front and center in all of my thoughts. I kept recalling her laughter, and our dance, and our kiss. Well, *both* kisses. I was stumbling over my own emotions trying to figure out what I could do to afford taking her somewhere she deserved when I finally recalled that money. Life-changing money, tucked behind a brick in an alcove of a dingy alleyway where a guy got shot dead on its behalf.

If I was lucky, nobody else knew where that money was. If I was lucky, I'd be able to sneak in there after the cops lost interest in the scene, snatch those envelopes, and have more than enough to support myself and the woman who I wanted to be mine.

I wasn't lucky. Not by a longshot.

Why the fuck was I so stupid? Am I really gonna get done in over *money?* Aubrey didn't strike me as the kind of woman who would scram when she realized I barely had two pennies to rub together. Why was I so moronic that I'd risk my life for some stupid cash when I coulda just explained my situation and taken her out for a hamburger instead?

The car is deathly silent. We've been on the road for fifteen minutes now. I can't even tell which neighborhood we're in; none of the buildings are familiar to me. Neither of my captors speak, not to me and not to each other. Though I doubt idle chatter would put me much at ease right now, it doesn't feel any better to sit in awkward silence, left only to contemplate my mistakes and how much I want to see Aubrey again.

What am I gonna do? What should I say to this "Charles" guy? He's clearly the boss of these two, and Pierce didn't even want to bring me in at all. Part of me hopes that the introduction of another person might mean a little more reasonable treatment than a cocked gun pointed in my face, but then again, I don't know anything about the guy. These fellas are Herdsters, aren't they? Don't they have a half dozen offices with their shiny logo sprinkled around the city? They do fuckin' fundraisers for kids with leukemia. Am I really gonna get killed by union guys?

The building we pull up to isn't a union office. Instead, I see a small sign, only partially illuminated due to one of its bulbs being burned out. I squint to make out the name: Santiago's. Never heard of the place. As he shuts off the engine and exits the vehicle, I notice Pierce tuck the revolver back into its shoulder holster before tugging at the front of his suit jacket to conceal it properly.

Marty doesn't immediately exit the car, instead turning his elongated neck to face me. "We're taking you inside to our boss, Charles Rossi. To you, he's Mr. Rossi. You wanna have a shot at keeping your insides inside of you, I recommend you be respectful and *honest.*" He tilts his head downward to wordlessly ask whether or not I'm picking up what he's putting down. I nervously nod in understanding. With his own subtle nod of approval, he escorts me toward the establishment.

Marty takes the lead and Pierce brings up the rear, sandwiching me between the two of them as we pass through the entrance. Within, I see a cozy, albeit pretty empty, restaurant with a drink-lined bar affixed to one wall and several dining booths attached to the other. A smattering of tables fill the space between, but my eyes are drawn to a figure seated in the rear corner of the restaurant.

Lit cigar held between his lips, the gray triceratops peers down at a stack of papers in front of him. He glances up at the sound of the front door's jingling bell, narrowing his purple eyes as he takes in the sight of his two subordinates and their captive. At least, I assume as much. Not sure who else here would be this Mr. Rossi fella, considering the well-pressed suit and air of supreme authority emanating from him.

A sharp shove to my back pushes me forward, and I follow Marty through the spaces between the empty tables and to the edge of the triceratops's booth. He tilts his head forward, examining me past the pristine horn atop his scar-laden snout. Light dances across his frilled crest flanked by two additional horns, giving the already regal-seeming figure a sort of natural crown.

His voice is breathy and gruff, a clue as to how long he's enjoyed those cigars. "Who is this?"

Pierce growls through his teeth. "I caught him snooping around the alley where we think Eggsy hid the money. The one where... where I shot him." Mr. Rossi's eyebrows raise and he offers a small shrug, waiting for Pierce to clarify further. "He's a skinnie who works for Sal Fontana, at his grocery store. He handed me Sal's dues on Monday when I stopped by."

This seems to pique Mr. Rossi's interest. He turns to me. "Is this true?"

I gulp before responding, Marty's words from the car echoing in my head. "Y-yes, sir. Mr. Rossi, sir."

At this, a slight smile graces his stubby beak. "I see you already know my name, which puts me at a disadvantage, Mr...?"

"Lawson, sir. Samuel Lawson."

"I see. Mr. Lawson—ah, do you mind if I call you

'Samuel'?" I nod my head as agreeably as I can. "Samuel. Please, take a seat."

I quickly slide into the booth across from the well-dressed triceratops, fearing that Pierce would forcibly send me here if I didn't follow Mr. Rossi's command on the double. The stegosaurus remains standing, arms crossed and glaring down at me, as Marty swings a vacant chair away from one of the nearby tables to join us.

Mr. Rossi pushes the papers in front of him to the side before folding his hands on the table separating us. "So, Samuel. Can you explain to me why you were the one to give Pierce Sal's dues on Monday?"

I blink, trying to straighten the events out in my mind as best I can, straining to appear as honest as possible. "Sal—that is, my boss, Mr. Fontana, called me into his office that morning. Said he had to go to a funeral, that he wouldn't be around to give the unio—I mean, the Herdsters representatives the dues that he owed 'em. He asked me to handle it for him."

"And did you handle it for him?"

I glance toward Pierce who remains statuesque. "Y-yes, sir. I gave Pier—uhh—"

Pierce's voice rumbles. "Mr. Signorelli."

"I g-gave Mr. Signorelli the envelope, just as Mr. Fontana asked."

Mr. Rossi sizes me up. "Well, that is admirable considering your station. Did you know what was inside of that envelope?"

A stone forms in my throat. "I didn't, no. Not for sure, at least. It said 'Dues' on it, so I—"

"A lot of money. There was a lot of money inside of that envelope. And there was a lot of money in a *lot* of other envelopes that my associates here gathered throughout the course of that day. Money that has since been *misplaced.*" His words are deliberate and chilling. I feel outclassed, outmaneuvered, like I brought a stack of checkers to a chess match.

He leans forward before speaking again. "Now. What, exactly, were you doing in the alleyway where the only person who knew where that money ended up breathed his last?"

This is it. I either play dumb and get dragged out back to be fitted for a pair of cement shoes, or I fess up, and likely meet the same fate.

I want to cower. I want to beg for my life. I want to do anything to stave off the executioner. I'm scared beyond belief, only able to think about Aubrey and how much it'll hurt her if I vanish off the face of the earth. I want to be there for her. I want to call her, like I told her I would. I want to hold her in my arms again.

My back straightens, and my eyes lock with Mr. Rossi's. For an almost imperceptible moment, a flicker of surprise crosses his face, but he stalwarts himself just as quickly. I sense the stegosaurus to my right tensing up, ready to draw out his pistol and make good on what he wanted to do to me less than a half hour ago.

Unbelievably, I speak without stutter or falter. "I was in the alley the night Eggsy was shot dead. I didn't know his name then, and I didn't see anyone else but the fella bleeding out. With his dying breaths, he pointed toward an alcove in the alley. That's where he hid the money, and when I turned back to him, he was dead." I exhale slowly. "I know exactly where your money is, Mr. Rossi."

He blinks. I can't tell if my sudden surge of bravery surprised or merely annoyed him, but for a long moment he does not respond, instead lazily fingering the cigar between his teeth as he puffs away at it. He continues to scan my face, peering into my mind, my subconscious, my very soul as he searches for deceit or contradiction.

It's Pierce that finally breaks the silence. "I know what

alcove he's talking about, Charles. It's stuffed full of trash, and it'll be a tight fit for me, but I can find the money. I'll go right now, and take care of this one while I'm at it." He slaps down on my shoulder, digging his nails into my flesh and preparing to hoist me out of the booth when Mr. Rossi interrupts him with a raised hand.

"No. Instead, let's all take a ride, together." Pierce's grip loosens and his mouth hangs open. Mr. Rossi moves his gaze up toward the dark blue stegosaurus before raising an eyebrow. "What, am I not allowed to leave this bar? I'd like to see this thing through in person, considering the—" He turns to face me again. "—*investment* at stake."

I can hear Pierce's teeth grind together as he steps back. The faux leather of the booth seat squeaks underneath Mr. Rossi as he slides out and to his feet. He rolls his shoulders and straightens his back before gesturing for me to accompany him. I do so.

Back outside the establishment, Mr. Rossi slides a key into the driver's side door of a silver Buick Roadmaster, an absolute behemoth of a car. My awe of its luxurious, immaculate form turns into downright jealousy as the triceratops thumbs a control on his door, causing all three remaining locks to spring upright. Automatic locks; you only see that on the fanciest of automobiles. While I feel a bit stupid gawking at a car when I might not even be alive an hour from now, I still enter the vessel as gingerly as possible to avoid marring its beauty with my clumsiness.

Marty shifts into the back seat next to me, eyeing me suspiciously. The futility of an escape attempt is still present in my mind, considering Pierce is along for the ride as well, scowling in the front passenger seat. Despite the smoothness of the drive, the trip back to the alley feels somehow twice as long. At a certain point, Pierce begins offering directions to Mr. Rossi who, I assume, hadn't been to this crime scene himself yet. The severity of the situation weighs on me in an instant. All three of these men are aware that a murder took place where we're headed, and all three are completely fine with it.

I don't see myself surviving this.

I suddenly wish the car ride were even longer, desperately clinging to each second as though it'll be my last. The blue-tinted woman who charmed me and laughed at my stupid jokes and let me hold her and kiss her is at forefront of my mind.

Aubrey. If it means I can see Aubrey, even one more time, I'll do anything it takes to make it out of this alive.

My mind starts rolling through possibilities. I could always book it once we're in the alley and they're distracted by the alcove. That is, if Pierce isn't sinking his fingers into my shoulder blade again. Maybe I could make a play for Pierce's revolver and try to turn the tables on them... is what I would be saying if I was delusional enough to disregard my head being swiftly torn from my neck for such a maneuver.

We come to a stop about a block away from the alley. Pierce assists me out of the vehicle forcefully, keeping one hand tucked beneath his suit jacket. I know what it rests on. Marty's neck cranes around as he checks for anyone interested in three well dressed dinosaurs and a scruffy loading dock worker about to head into a darkened alley. Mr. Rossi, on the other hand, stretches his back and withdraws another cigar, performing a somewhat interesting stunt by using one of his razor sharp horns to clip its tip off. With the flick of a lighter, its freed end ignites and he puffs contentedly on the tobacco-laden wrapping.

The mostly set sun barely illuminates the alley's sheltered form. The sharp angles burst into shadows that continue sluggishly sliding across the opposing walls. Our focus comes to rest on the small alcove in the back of the alley, just as trash-stuffed and claustrophobia-inducing as it ever was. I briefly consider making a comment about Pierce not being able to fit in there, but do away with the thought. As much as I'd love to lighten the mood before my execution, for some reason I just don't have it in me right now.

The three dinosaurs turn their attention to me. I meet their gazes in turn, unsure what to do next, until Mr. Rossi instructs me. He gestures toward the alcove. "Well? You're the man of the hour. If you will, Samuel."

I take a deep breath. This is it. I'm gonna wade back into that trash pile, fish out their money, and earn a bullet to the head for my troubles. But, to my surprise, I don't feel panic. I don't weep or piss my pants like I feel I should in a situation like this. Instead, I simply do as I'm asked.

The heaped trash shifts under my weight, the homes of the same rats and insects I disturbed two nights ago brought to ruination all over again. Their scampers and scuttles send a chill up my spine, but nothing climbs into my boot or under the brims of my pant legs. I sidle carefully, reaching the end of the small cavern before glancing at the familiar loose brick. It appears undisturbed; pulling it away reveals the same plethora of cash-packed envelopes resting within the wall's hidden trove. A few bugs that had taken up residence in the space scurry away as I carefully remove the envelopes, being cautious to not tear them open with my movements and send money tumbling into the garbage bags below me.

Turning back to the trio of Herdsters, I see Marty's mouth hanging open. He quietly mutters, "Holy shit. He really did know where it was. He was tellin' the truth." Pierce is less impressed, instead choosing to caress the grip of his revolver with his thumb. It has exited its holster and now holds fast at his side, ready to swing in my direction at a moment's notice. Mr. Rossi rolls his cigar from one end of his mouth to the other, allowing plumes of smoke to pass through his teeth and rise to the heavens.

I step out of the alcove, shaking my ankles briefly to clear them of any rubbish that clings to my pant legs.

Envelopes clutched in both hands, I approach Mr. Rossi and offer the bounty to him. He accepts them, easily able to grip all two dozen or so in one of his colossal mitts. He says nothing, only narrowing his eyes as the gears in his overwhelming mind turn. Most likely thinking of the least messy way to dispose of me.

Even still, even facing down my inevitable destruction, I feel no fear in the moment. I lift my head and straighten out my back before speaking. "I did what you asked. You've got your money. Now that it's done, and my future's looking pretty uncertain, I'm not gonna beg for my life. Do what you gotta do."

A terrifying grin spreads across Pierce's lips as he anticipates the job about to be assigned to him. Marty averts his eyes, appearing almost remorseful. But Mr. Rossi...

He turns the envelopes over in his hand, skimming through them with a lazy nail until he settles on one. Withdrawing it, I can see it's the very same envelope I handed Pierce. The word "Dues" is still scrawled across its surface. Mr. Rossi calls attention to the same thing, almost as though reading my mind. "Sal's handwriting. I can always recognize it. When you're in the business as long as I have been, you make it your job to notice such things. A single person's handwriting, the order in which someone stuffs their bills of varying denominations into their dues envelopes, even the excuses that some will try to peddle more than once to weasel out of paying what they owe."

His eyes lift from the envelopes to me before he continues. "I'm willing to wager you recognize this handwriting, too. Which likely means you recognized it when you discovered this stash of envelopes. So, tell me, boy. If Pierce hadn't caught you tonight, if you had walked in here as you intended to and pulled these envelopes out of that hole in that wall... would you have returned this money to the Herdsters?"

I hold his gaze. His brilliant purple eyes are icy, analytical and inescapable. I'm not about to start lying now. Not when I'm a dead man anyway.

"No, I wouldn't have."

A sudden, almost deafening boom. I flinch, my mind clearly not processing the fact that I've just been shot in the head. The moment seems to suspend itself, a snapshot of time, unwavering and unrelenting. Perhaps this is what it means to die. Your brain just freeze-frames on your final moment and you stare at it for all eternity.

Except... motion slowly returns to the scene. As the ringing in my ears subsides and the dizziness that clouds my head clears, I realize that Mr. Rossi is laughing.

The humongous, intimidating triceratops in front of me is actually laughing. As though he was just told the best joke of his life. Each roil of his laughter rings louder than the one that came before, bursting forth like thunderclaps. I stand in utter shock as he uses his free hand to wipe the tears from his eyes, being joined in mutual perplexity by the other two dinosaurs standing next to us.

As his composure returns, he finally clears the air of our confusion. "Samuel Lawson, it has been a lot of years since I've come across anyone so bluntly honest as you. Truly, only a fool or a saint would be *that* transparently candid in such a situation as the one you're in. And, by my estimation, you are no fool."

My cheeks redden at the sudden compliment, though I'm not convinced that I'm not the biggest idiot to walk the earth.

Mr. Rossi almost beams down at me as he takes a deep breath, allowing more smoke to rise in the wake of his exhalation. He contemplates something before nodding. "You are an intriguing fellow, and one I'd like to have in my employ. What do you say to a job?"

Nah. At this point, I'm fully convinced that I'm lying dead on the pavement. This is some sorta delusion my brain cooked up as the searing lead tore its way through my gray matter. There's no way on God's green earth that this is real.

Pierce's holler echoes around the alley. *"What?!"*

Mr. Rossi ignores him, patiently awaiting my answer as his tongue bobs the cigar up and down. Almost as badly as when Pierce knocked the wind out of me, I find myself unable to form a coherent word. I've been blindsided by some things in my life, most recently Aubrey asking me to dance after rebuking my previous request to do so, but this is a whole 'nother level of *"what in the holy fuck is going on?"*

I finally manage to eke out a reply. "M-Mr. Rossi, sir—"

"Please, call me Charles."

"Ch-Charles, sir. I-I'm flattered by the offer. Truly, I am. But I got a job already, over at Sal's."

Charles's smile turns downward ever so slightly. "How much is Sal paying you over there?"

"Um—about sixty dollars a week, sir."

This earns a brief pause from the triceratops. "Hm. He really should pay his workers more than that. Anyway—" He peels open the envelope that Sal himself had stuffed with cash, withdraws four fifty-dollar bills, and offers them to me. "Consider it a sign-on bonus. And you can expect to earn that much every week. After you've proven yourself a loyal worker, that is."

My mind is spinning beyond belief. I feel like I could pass out at any given moment, but somehow my feet remain beneath me. I thought I was a dead man, and now I'm being offered a *job?!*

Panic finally begins to set in. Am I really cut out to work for these guys? Like, truthfully? From what I've seen, they're ruthless killers. Are they expecting me to start gunning down fellas in alleyways? The words tumble past my lips, malformed and wholly inadequate. "S-sir. I-I just don't know if I can—if I *could*—"

Charles sighs, partially withdrawing the proffered

money. "Well, we could explore the other options presented to us tonight."

In a flash, my mind clears. His intentions aren't hidden in the slightest. I'm accepting this job, or I'm dead. I snap to attention, as though facing down a drill sergeant. "I'll take the job, sir."

His beaming smile returns to him. "Wonderful! I'm glad to have you on the team, Samuel!" He shakes my hand, clapping the bills into my grip with the same motion. "We're Local 237, over in Cavemanhattan. Start time is 8:00 AM, don't be late!" He pauses. "Do you have your own car?"

"N-no, sir. Will I need one?"

"Perhaps, down the road, but we can get that sorted out for you when the time comes. Until then, I'd recommend picking up a transit map to plot out which buses you want to take. That is, unless you want to blow all that money on cab fare!" His tone is almost jovial, like an uncle who recognized you at a ball game. "We'll have you fill out some paperwork tomorrow and get you acquainted with our operation. I'm sure you'll be a wonderful fit!"

I rock back on my heels, still in complete disbelief at this turn of events. Sure, I might not have had much of a choice on the matter, but instead of a bodybag I was given a new job that'll pay me over three times what I was making at Sal's. I'll be able to provide for Aubrey with this kinda money.

I turn my attention from the bills in my palm up to Charles, but motion from the corner of my eye causes me to recoil. The midnight blue stegosaurus takes one enormous stride to come within arm's reach of me. I squeeze my eyelids shut in anticipation of being punched out by an incoming fist or punched out of the time clock of life, but neither comes. Instead, Pierce only gestures angrily toward me as he addresses his—I guess *our* boss.

"Are you out of your fuckin' mind?! You're actually giving

this skinnie money? The money *he* admitted he wasn't gonna return to us?!"

Charles turns his half-lidded eyes to his enraged employee. "Yes, Pierce. That's exactly what I'm doing."

Pierce balks. "I can't fuckin' believe this. We get rid of one dishonest, thieving skinnie, and you immediately go find another one. You must really enjoy your hand gettin' stung, cuz you keep jamming it into honeycombs full of backstabbing bees."

A click of his tongue expresses Charles's growing annoyance. "Your analogies leave a lot to be desired. Besides, it's because of *you* that we have a vacancy that needs filling." I feel a chill fire down my spine. I hadn't considered that I just got offered the job that was occupied by the fella I watched die only a few feet away from where we stand. Charles turns from Pierce to me as a grin spreads across his face. "In fact, I say we pick up right where we left off."

I don't understand his meaning, but the color in Pierce's scales seems to drain away.

Charles stamps out the small remaining butt of his cigar on the pavement before tucking his thumbs behind his belt and rocking his heels. "Once Samuel here gets processed and oriented, he'll be joining you and Martin on your rounds." He drinks in the sight of the stegosaurus's petrification. His smile shifts from amicable to sinister. "Do try to train him right this time. I'd *hate* to see a repeat of what happened with Egbert."

Chapter Eight: Aubrey

As the cab door latches shut and the vehicle merges back into traffic, I crane my neck to watch Sammy fade from sight. He doesn't take his eyes off of me until he can no longer see me beyond the tangle of steel and headlights that still clutter the street, even at this late hour. I bring a hand to my cheek, feeling the burning hot capillaries just beneath my scales. They betray my emotions, parading before an audience of none that my heart is racing, my mind is spinning, and my deepest, most private recesses are yearning. Longing for the embrace and passionate love of a man with piercing blue eyes and handsome tanned skin. A muted sigh escapes as Sammy's bravado replays, his lips dancing across the surface of mine in exploratory exultation. My imagination desperately clings to the moment like it's an enrapturing song on a record, and I refresh the needle to the most explosive and enthralling part over and over and—

"Where to, miss?"

I involuntarily let out a yip, startled from my fantasy by the only other living being in this vehicle. He scans me through the rearview mirror; my face flushes to twice the brightness it had previously exuded. "Ahh—um, the, uh—

Police Department. Precinct 63, over on Brachlyn Avenue, please."

He raises an eyebrow at me before offering a brief affirmative; I do my best to sink into the recess of the backseat out of embarrassment. Who knows what manner of lascivious expression I was wearing when the cabbie *poofed* into existence from nothingness and took note of me. My mind was most certainly elsewhere.

Graciously, the driver does not fill the silence with idle chatter. Some are regular motor mouths, prodding with questions and cracking jokes. Perhaps the faraway, lustful gaze he pulled me away from turned him off to the idea of getting chummy. Hell, he might think I'm a crazy person, asking to be brought to the Police Department at close to eleven in the evening. That said, I don't mind the silence. I'd rather be in my own head right now.

With Sammy.

The end of my tail rests in my lap, furtively twitching as its own primitive mind recalls the sensation of Sammy's back. The feathers bristle and quiver of their own accord, sending chills from the tip of the appendage to the nape of my neck. I've been apart from Sammy for all of two minutes and already long for his touch again. His gentle hands, his calming breath, his tender kiss...

I shake my head. Yes, the night went well, and yes, I'm glad it turned into a date, and yes, my heart is racing at the thought of being with him again. But there's more pressing matters that need my attention. My emotions shift from longing to frustration. I need to get into the station. I need to get in contact with the captain. I need to get this cleared up as soon as possible. The show was already ruined, but Miles Cratis doesn't deserve to rot in a cell because a couple racist assholes decided to arrest him.

As I mull over my plan of action, the cab slows to a halt in front of the police station. I begin digging in my purse, but the driver reminds me that the "gentleman" already paid for my ride. My face begins warming up again; I quickly thank the cabbie and exit the vehicle, hearing it zip down the road behind me as I gaze up at my moonlight-soaked destination.

The station's herculean presence over the road is imposing while the sun is out, but at night the building appears downright ominous. Sparse lighting tickles its emblem and the surrounding concrete festoons that rest above the main entrance. Despite looking at this building five days a week, my visitation occurs during the daylight hours. Now, it feels cold, almost otherworldly. Very few people consider a police station welcoming, but this haunting monolith rising from the hewn earth fills me with the desire to go in any direction but toward it.

I take a deep breath before marching up the stairs. The front entrance isn't locked; though most of the administrative personnel work the standard nine-to-five shift, policing a city like this is a twenty-four hour operation. Blue uniforms pass to and fro, some nursing cups of coffee, others hauling irate handcuffed individuals to the lower levels of the station for booking. I don't see Duffy or Preston anywhere, so I purposefully stride over to the front desk.

Unlike the humorless Ruth that works the same hours as me, the night shift desk corporal beams an enormous smile in my direction from beneath the mop of curly hair atop his rhinorex head. Somehow, he seems both younger than me and older than me at the same time. "Good evening, miss! How can I help you?"

I blink. "Umm—I need to speak to the captain. Can you call him?"

His smile does not falter, and his tone remains overly jovial. Whether it's this fella's default mood or a copious amount of caffeine in his system, I can't be certain. "Ma'am, we can't be calling on the police captain for every little thing!

I'm sure there's something I can help you with? Is this in regards to a violation of yours or someone you know?"

Oh. Of course. He doesn't know I work for the police department. I can't blame him, considering I don't know his name, either. With a click of my tongue, I fish around in my purse before withdrawing the identification card adorned with my name. "I work here, in clerical, but it's not about that. I need to speak to Captain Aaron regarding a man that was arrested tonight. It's urgent."

The young rhinorex's eyes light up. "Ohh! I see, Miss—" He leans in, squinting past the thin-rimmed silver glasses atop his curiously shaped snout to read the name on my ID. "—Carter! You can head on over to his office."

"Wait, he's in right now?"

"Mmhmm! Been here since I clocked in, as far as I know." I glance down from the receptionist's friendly gaze, perplexed by this news. He was here all of today's day shift, too. Shouldn't he have gone home by now?

The smiling framed portraits of police captains past watch me travel toward the office. I ignore their frozen stares, going over once more how I want to approach this situation. I have to convince the captain that Miles Cratis is innocent and shouldn't be detained here. I have to tell him about Duffy and Preston, how far out of their jurisdiction they had to go to have pulled something like this. How out of line they were. He has to be able to see that what they did was wrong. He'll be able to make this right.

The captain's office door is ajar, his signal that he's not on an important call or speaking privately with anyone. I gently rap my knuckles against the wood as I push the barrier open, peeking my head in with an awkward half-smile. Captain Aaron glances up from his paperwork before raising an eyebrow at me. "Carter? What are you doing here?"

I slip through the opening and close the door behind

myself. "I could ask you the same question, sir. You don't always work this late, do you?"

He looses a puff of air from his nostrils. "No. It's been—well, it's been a day." A scan of my outfit leads to another elevated brow. "What's the occasion?"

I glance down at myself, only now remembering the yellow dress. The captain's confusion isn't unwarranted; I don't dress like a slob for work, but this is an unusual level of accoutrement for me. "Oh! I went to that event that you gave me tickets for. The jazz club over in Cavemanhattan." He stares at me, wordlessly awaiting further explanation of my appearance in his office tonight. "The show was interrupted because Miles Cratis—the lead performer for the band—was... he was arrested."

Captain Aaron subtly shakes his head. "So why are you here, then? That's Cavemanhattan jurisdiction, probably Midtown North—"

"It was Duffy and Preston that arrested him. Miles Cratis stepped outside during a break and, next thing anyone knew, he was bloodied and in the back of those two's squad car."

His eyes glaze over for a moment before he lets out a sigh and pinches the bridge of his beak. His arms then cross themselves across his chest, one finger tapping his bicep.

I don't know what's going through his head, but I have to make sure he understands. "Like you said, that isn't our jurisdiction. They were—"

His eyes quickly refocus on me. *"Our* jurisdiction?"

Shit. "Your—I mean, this station's jurisdiction."

Another sigh. "I'll take care of it. Thank you, Carter."

I feel a thankful smile start to spread across my lips before it halts. He said he'd take care of it. The captain is an honest man, and if he says he'll do something, he'll do it.

So why do I feel unsatisfied by his answer?

He's already turned back to his paperwork, wearing an

expression of equal parts annoyance and exhaustion. I catch his attention again. "Sir. If I may ask, what are you going to do?"

He frowns. "I'll take care of it, Carter. Thank you for your help."

"But what about Miles Cratis?"

"I'm sure he's being booked right now."

"But he didn't do anything wrong! He doesn't deserve to be—"

"If he didn't do anything wrong, he'll likely be released in the morning."

My voice unwillingly takes on a pleading tone. "Sir! This is the same thing Duffy and Preston did with Samuel, arresting a human for no reason! You have to—"

His eyes flare at me and his voice sharpens. *"Carter.* You are dismissed."

My mouth hangs open in shock and defeat. Unable to overcome his steeled gaze, I sheepishly turn toward the door and slip back into the hall. My tail has coiled itself around my midsection again; I quickly push it down and back to its resting position. I hate that it does that, it makes me feel foolish and look weak. A weak woman who's not a real police officer, just some gabbing broad who needs to be put in her place.

Standing outside the captain's office, I try to force down the bubbling anger that rises in my stomach. The rage is sharpened, like darts being thrown at a board adorned with images of those deserving of ire. He should have shared my righteous zeal and stormed down to the booking room to free Miles Cratis. Duffy and Preston should be fired on the spot. My face is peppered with needle points, and my fingers tighten into fists.

The anger guides my feet deeper into the building. I make a beeline toward a rear access staircase leading to the lowest floor, less traveled and less conspicuous. The metal stairs reverberate under my soft-soled heels, but not loud enough to escape the mildewy concrete-encased column. At the bottom, a smattering of doors on either side of the off-brown hallway lead to storage areas and unused offices, and the end of the hall bends toward the holding and processing departments where detainees are carted in, ID'd if possible, and tossed into cells to await further action. Drunks are usually cut loose the following morning; more serious offenders inevitably get transferred elsewhere when the time comes.

As I stare down the hallway, blood still boiling, a sudden cold sweat breaks out on my forehead. What, exactly, am I going to do? I'm furious, yes, and filled with conviction, but what can I actually accomplish here? I can scream at Duffy and Preston about what fools they are, but all that will do is give them further reason to antagonize me. I have no authority to reprimand or fire them. I couldn't set Miles Cratis free without committing a felony in the process. Regardless of being employed by the city, I couldn't even write myself out of a parking ticket, let alone release a man from a holding cell.

Still convinced that I must do something but suddenly unsure of myself, I make a hasty decision and push through the door to the darkened locker room on my right. I'd only ever been in there once before, when I was shown the layout of the building during my orientation tour. It's used by officers to swap into their uniforms or back into their civilian clothes; since I'm not an officer, I have no need for the space. Besides that, I don't know that I'd care to change clothes in front of the leering eyes of men like Duffy or Preston, though if such a sacrifice meant I'd be a police officer...

I shake my head, clearing it of any unnecessary delusions of grandeur. The next shift change isn't for another several hours, so I assume the space will be unused. Even still, I peek about the blackened chamber cautiously, waiting for my eyes to adjust to the darkness, listening for any rustling clothes or clattering lockers of an officer who might be present even with the lights off. Some species of dinosaurs aren't bothered too much by the absence of light, after all. When I don't hear anything and my pupils have sufficiently dilated, I quietly move through the space toward its opposite end. Past the rows of lockers and wooden slats, I press my ear against another door, hearing the faint murmurs of voices on its other side. With utmost caution and delicacy, I crack open the threshold.

Beyond is a common room adjacent to booking, its handful of tables and chairs offering respite to an officer on break that doesn't want to trudge up to the second story, or space for the mundanity of paperwork that comes with arresting a person. Presently, a handful of men occupy the chairs; some cradle coffee mugs, others scrawl upon white sheets adorned with numerous clerical lines and checkboxes. Two of these men I recognize all too well, and one of them loudly chatters as his pen slides across another form.

"—more god damn paperwork. You guys actually take this shit seriously? I could probably just scribble punchlines from today's funny papers and I bet nobody would even notice." The spinosaurus's grating, callous voice makes my feathers stand on end.

Duffy lets out an annoyed grunt before replying. "Just fill it out proper. Those bitches in clerical *will* make you redo it, and redo it again after that if you keep fucking it up."

Preston's tail snaps against the floor behind his chair. "Feh. Didn't figure there'd be so much of this boring bullshit when I signed on."

"Welcome to the force, this is a good chunk of what we do." Duffy's voice is resigned and weary; whether due to the late hour of his new shift or his own apathy toward his job, I can't tell.

Preston sets his pen down before scratching the side of

his sharp snout. "Hey, Duffy. What were we puttin' as the reason for that skinnie's arrest? We should keep it, uh—constant, right?"

The dilophosaurus turns to his partner, squinting his eyes. *"Consistent* is the word you're looking for. And, yes. Our paperwork should be *consistent."* He rustles a few forms before withdrawing one. "I marked it down as 'loitering' and 'refusing to cooperate when questioned'. Should be good enough."

Preston frowns. "But what about me takin' my nightstick to his skull? Won't they question why I bloodied him up if that's all we're sayin' he did?"

Duffy shrugs. "Probably not. But, I suppose we could add 'battery' to the list. He was swingin' his hands around pretty aggressively. Good thing he wasn't holdin' a spear, otherwise we woulda had to escalate our response!" His chuckle is echoed by the spinosaurus next to him before they both return to their paperwork.

My teeth grind together and my breathing is labored. The reddened veins in my eyeballs intrude into my peripheral vision. I extend my claws as I fantasize kicking the door down, leaping across the room and tearing both of their heads from their bodies.

They made it up. They arrested Miles Cratis for no reason but the ones they conjured out of thin air. They injured him just because they *could*. Despicable monsters, unworthy of their badges.

Preston leans back in his seat and cracks his knuckles before throwing an arm over his chair to address another officer across the room. "Hey, Johnson. You think any more on what I mentioned about the Local 237?"

Johnson, a wide-eyed deinonychus officer with frilled elbows glances up from his lunch pail. "Uhh, not much. I mean, ain't we already with the PCA?"

The spinosaurus's grin spreads wider, his words slick

with a feigned tone of sincerity. "Oh, *naaah*. I'm not talking about us *switching* unions! It's more of a volunteer opportunity! We're looking for some able-bodied men to help with some fundraising, and sure, it's not the *station's* union but they got a good bunch of guys over there! Plus, it'd help to have some friendly faces in blue to show our support for the workin' fellas!"

As the other officer scratches his chin in contemplation, Preston rises from his seat and begins striding—*oh no.*

"I've got some paperwork in my locker, lemme grab you one of the pamphlets!"

I stumble backward as time slows to a crawl. He's only a few steps away from the door; escape isn't an option. If I tried sprinting for the other exit, even if my knee holds out, I wouldn't get out of Preston's line of sight in time. I briefly consider attacking him, given my continued blood boil, but I know it will lead to my firing and arrest, or worse.

There's only one option. I desperately throw open a locker to my side, praying that it's vacant.

It is.

I quickly shimmy into the tight space, fearing that even this will be accomplished too late, that the door will swing open and Preston's exclamation of surprise and anger will spell my capture and punishment. With a quick heave, I yank my tail into the frighteningly restrictive confinement and pull it closed as rapidly and noiselessly as possible. Not even a half second after it latches shut, light from the door I was peering through just a moment ago pours into the room.

"Tch. Where's that switch?" I hear Preston's hand clumsily slap at the wall until a soft click bathes the locker room in fluorescent light. Some of it slips past the three horizontal slits in my hiding spot; I lean back as far as possible, holding my breath and trying to steady the roaring beat of my heart. I'm certain that the spinosaurus's head is going to whip in my direction, his malevolent emerald eyes boring through the thin piece of metal that separates us.

Instead, he saunters down the row of lockers upon which my field of view rests. Near the end, he pulls open a hatch with his last name affixed at eye level. Preston rustles through his locker's contents when the sound of another door opening intrudes upon the room. This time, it was the entrance at the other end, the one I used a few minutes ago to sneak in here. Heavy footsteps stride in our direction, the echo of leathered heel on tile reverberating against the steel surroundings. A massive shape abruptly halts in front of my porthole, smothering me in blackness again.

"Oh, hey, capt—*grawwkmmmph!*" Preston's words are cut short as Captain Aaron crosses the space between them in two gargantuan steps before wrapping his hand around the spinosaurus's beak, twisting his head and slamming him against the nearby lockers. He struggles only momentarily and quite fruitlessly as the pterodactyl pins him in place, left only to peer at his captor with a wide, bewildered sideways eye. Fearful, sharp breaths escape Preston's muzzled teeth as the captain speaks.

"You imbecile. You worthless sack of garbage. Twice now. *Twice* in *two days* I get word that you are being a reckless *fool!*" His words are acrid and unnerving, carrying a level of anger I've never heard from the usually stern but kind leader. "Is this position not going to work for you? Did I make a mistake in bringing you into this department?!"

The questions seem rhetorical as the iron grip Captain Aaron holds around Preston's snout prevents him from replying. All the same, he tries to mumble out a muffled reply, still held at the mercy of his boss's imprisonment.

"You realize this position carries with it numerous responsibilities, do you not? It's not about being a cowboy and doing whatever the hell you feel like doing. That badge isn't carte blanche to make a mess of things and cause problems for me and everyone else around you. You are *serving* the city of Old York, first and foremost. You are expected to uphold the law and do the right thing when you wear that uniform. Do I make myself perfectly clear?"

He waits, not loosening the hold he has on Preston. A moment goes by before the entrapped spinosaurus lets out a muted affirmative.

Captain Aaron's posture straightens. He leers down at the chastised officer before speaking with finality. "If I hear even one more peep of you stepping out of line, I will not be as gentle as I've been tonight." With one final burst of air from his nostrils, the pterodactyl releases Preston who immediately gasps for air through his now freely open mouth. He slumps down, cowering away from the captain who spins on his heel and exits the locker room through the passage that leads to the common room. Though I can't make out the exact words he says, his muffled voice still resonates with fury. I can only guess that Duffy is receiving a verbal lashing, though seemingly without the manhandling that Preston just got.

I stare ahead at the now seated spinosaurus, perched on the thin wooden bench that slides down the center of the lockers. I expect to see his hands curl into balls, his tail thrash about and his teeth bare in fury. Instead, he sits motionless, arms slumped at his sides, staring at the tiled floor between his feet. He remains like this for several minutes. The voices from the adjacent room have dulled; whether the space is now vacant or merely filled with the same officers now keeping silent after the reprimand is unclear. Finally, Preston stands, meekly placing one foot before the other to exit the room, forgetting his original reason for being here as the paperwork he had mentioned to Johnson remains inside his locker.

My breath catches in my throat again and I remain as still and silent as possible, fearing he'll notice me as he walks directly toward me, but he does not. His jaw hangs ajar, and he mumbles something to himself as he turns toward the common room exit. I can't discern what he says, but it doesn't seem to be grumbles or blasphemies. Instead, he almost comes across as contemplative, a trait I wouldn't expect such a horrid man to possess.

He doesn't turn the light off before leaving the room. I wait another two minutes past his departure, listening intently for any voices or footsteps. I hear none. With a little trouble I manage to disengage the latch from the inside of the locker door. It swings open, allowing me to stumble out and breathe a sigh of relief. Just before I hustle out of this dangerous space, something catches the corner of my eye.

Preston's locker is still open. He mentioned paperwork about—what was it? Local 237? I tiptoe over and peer inside. Within rests a change of casual clothes befitting a fella like Preston, including a tacky red-checkered overshirt and well worn slacks. Below the hanging outfit, piled beneath several other manilla folders stuffed with paperwork, the corner of a brochure pokes out, resting on top of several duplicates. I grip the paper and slide it free, being careful to not shift the other items too noticeably. On the brochure's surface is an emblem with the heads of two mules jutting from the sides of a large, stylized wheel. Below it, the words:

> The International Brotherhood of Herdsters
> Old York, Local 237
> Information and Membership Opportunities

I stuff the pamphlet into my purse and hurry toward the exit closer to the less used staircase. After taking a moment to determine that the coast is clear, I slip into the hallway and back upstairs. I do not see Preston, Duffy or Captain Aaron on my way out of the precinct's front entrance. Only once the muggy evening air washes over me does my heartbeat start to slow. Sweat stains my yellow dress and my knee hollers at me, displeased with the extra stress I've caused it so late into the night.

A taxi cab coasts to a stop next to the sidewalk in response to my raised hand. I climb in, give the driver my destination, and proceed to slump back, relieved and exhausted. The ride is only a few minutes, and I consider staring out the window until I catch sight of my home and the bed it contains, but something about the interaction I just witnessed gnaws at my mind. I swing my purse around to my front and withdraw the hastily plunged folded paper.

On its surface, the same twin-mule-adorned logo stares back at me. I'd only heard about the Herdsters in passing, and never anything good. Sure, they put on big smiles for parades and local events that they sponsor, but their organization has been in the news on more than one occasion. It's usually a senator throwing accusations of corruption or treachery at the highest echelon members of the union, with some even being arrested. There's no definitive proof that the Herdsters are crooked to the bone, hence why they can still operate in the city. Even still, I'm more than a little wary of them.

I thumb the pamphlet open, staring at the lines of text with hazy eyes. Platitudes extolling the virtues of the union grace the fold-out's interior, testimonials of retained jobs and money saved by employers. I click my tongue, trying to piece everything together.

"Ya thinkin' o' joinin' da Herdstahs?" The cab driver's voice snaps me out of my lull. He gazes back at me through the rearview mirror, his thick accent second only to the thickness of the unibrow above his allosaurus eyes. "Dey a real good peoples, dey is!"

I blink, unsure of how the pale green saurian read my thoughts until I realize I'm holding the pamphlet's front toward his field of vision. "Oh. Umm—not exactly. I was just taking a look at this is all."

He doesn't seem to get the hint that I'm not in a chatty mood. "Dey's a good union! I was workin' fer a cab comp'ny, an' dey got bought out, an' I was gonna lose my job, but da Herdstahs helped me get dis job wit' dem! I owe dem bigtime fer helpin' me keep workin' an' doin' what I loves ta do!"

"So they hired you?"

"Nah, nah, dey was da union fer da otha cab comp'ny. Dey, uhh—" His colossal eyebrow furrows as he seems to struggle with the next word. "—*absorp'd* da one I was wit'! Real good guys, real good!"

"And have you ever been worried about the Herdsters doing anything shady?"

He glances over his shoulder at me for a brief moment. In it, I spot a genuine smile. "Nah! They good guys! Real helpin' an' kind! Mista' Rossi's a good man!"

I return his smile but don't ask anything further. The name 'Rossi' doesn't mean anything to me, but this cab driver's word about the Herdsters is all I have to go on right now. Despite coming across as a little simple, he expressed nothing but admiration for them. That said, he's only an employee of a company that uses the union, not directly employed by them. It'd make sense that he would be unaware of, or perhaps completely blind to, any sort of misdeeds they might be committing.

Before long the cab pulls over. I hand the driver several coins to cover my fare plus a small tip and bid him goodnight before entering my apartment building. My knee twinges several times on the flight of stairs, threatening to send me sprawling if I misstep even slightly. Thankfully, I make it to the top without incident and unlock the door to my apartment.

In a matter of seconds, my dress falls off of me in a heap and I collapse onto my bed. Even though I'm physically exhausted, my brain doesn't turn itself off quite yet. I think back to the precinct, to my sudden stint in espionage as I spied on conversations that weren't meant for my ears. A twinge of regret fires through me; I'm not a dishonest person, and I don't enjoy eavesdropping. I'm the only one to blame for having snooped on those two officers, and my actions led to me having to hide and, consequently, watch Captain Aaron reprimand Preston.

I understand that the captain is an intimidating guy, and he was rightfully pissed off, but why was Preston so rattled?

I think again of the brochure, filled with encouragement to join a labor union that competes with that of our precinct. Hell, our whole city. The Police Compassion Association, despite its corny name, has serviced all of the city's police officers and administrative employees for over fifty years. Preston told Johnson that he wasn't trying to get anyone to switch unions, but is that true? Is Preston working for the Herdsters and trying to sway members of the police force to call for a change? If so, how many other Prestons are there at other precincts in the city, or even in ours?

I shake my head, my hair tousling against the pillow beneath it. I don't know nearly enough about the Herdsters or Preston to start throwing around accusations. Sure, I despise the spinosaurus and want to see him gone, but I can't go to the captain with a hunch and a brochure I could have found anywhere. Hell, Preston could easily hand-wave the duplicates in his locker with the same innocent explanation he presented to Johnson, and then eyebrows would raise at me as to how I knew about the contents of a male officer's private storage space. I'm a woman, and I'm not a police officer. I have no business knowing what I know now.

A sigh escapes my lips. The heat is sufficiently combated by the air conditioner I've let run all day. I know the electric bill will be outrageous, but I need to escape the stifling air especially as my mind drifts again, moving itself further back in the evening. To the jazz club, to the performance of a lifetime that was cut short, and to the man who held me in his arms and kissed me. My face flushes and my heartbeat rises as I think about him, but I push the feelings down. It was a wonderful night and he was a gentleman, but *kissing* on the first date, especially when it wasn't even a date to begin with? What sort of woman will he think I am?

I'll just have to be a bit more stern with him. I enjoy being with him, and I'd be thrilled if this turned into a real relationship, but I'm not going to rush into things. I can't. I need to be sure. Sure that Sammy will treat me right. That he won't...

No. Don't think about it. Don't think about *him*. You're a strong woman. You've got good judgment now. That will never happen again.

I can tell that Sammy's not that sort of man. He's kind, and he's gentle. The way he comforted me when I was so angry, the way he held me until I stopped trembling, the way he returned my kiss. I can tell.

Sammy. Even if I'm gonna put my foot down and insist we take things at a respectful and patient pace...

I hope I dream about you tonight.

—

The hands of the clock had moved well past midnight, yet the spot next to me in bed was still empty. I rolled over again, unable to get comfortable. We were so close, and yet he kept doing this. I've reasoned with him, I've yelled at him, I've pleaded with him, but it was never anything more than a hand wave and a sarcastic remark.

The cruel thought pecked at the back of my mind like a caged raven searching its enclosure for a weak spot, desperately seeking escape. This man wasn't the same as when I married him. He was so charming back then, and funny. But now, he was hardly ever home. "Work", he said. Why would he have bothered to tell me what he does for a living? Why would he tell me anything? Just kept me in the dark, expecting me to keep my mouth shut and keep the home in order like a good, obedient wife.

I brought a palm to my forehead, wiping away the stress-induced sweat. I wanted to be a good wife to him. I *wanted* us to be happy together. But it seemed he only ever knew how to push me away.

The sound of the front door opening and then clumsily slamming shut informed me of what I already knew. I should have just pretended to be asleep, letting him stumble into the bedroom and collapse on the bed next to me. He wouldn't bother trying to get handsy. He hadn't done that for months. Despite everything, I still had needs and I still wanted his affection, but he wouldn't provide it anymore.

I heard him whistling, jovial and carefree. *Whistling.* My teeth grated together as his loud footfalls rose up the stairs.

I wasn't going to stand for this. He was going to get a piece of my mind.

I swung my legs out of bed and stood with a bit of a struggle, the weariness and anger combining in a vitriolic ichor in my mind. After crossing the space, I threw the bedroom door open, meeting his gaze as he reached the top of the staircase.

His form was... distorted. A shifting amalgamation of color and shape. I saw no eyes, no snout, no tail and no body. But I knew for a fact that this was my husband. The rancid smell of his evening hung heavy in the air; that was proof enough.

"Heeey, Aubie! How's my gal—"

"Don't you 'how's my gal' me, mister. Do you know what time it is?!"

A distended blob waved lazily in front of him. "Ohh, there ya go, bustin' my balls again. I was just—"

"I don't care. Enough is enough. You have responsibilities, to me and—"

His voice rose instantly. "Don't you fuckin' tell me what my responsibilities are! All you've ever been is a pain in my ass. All I want is to be left the fuck alone, but it's nag, nag, nag, on all ends. No slack at work, no slack at home. Why can't I just get some fuckin' peace and quiet?"

Despite the sudden sullen downturn in his tone, the tears in my eyes and the anger in my heart led me to step toward him. I pleaded and chastised equally. "This isn't who you are. I know you're a loving man who wants what's best for us! You have to get past this, you *have* to do better—"

In a flash, the chaotic void of darkness lunged forward. It grappled with the front of my nightgown and shook me violently. "Don't tell me what to do, you *bitch!*"

I couldn't scream. I could barely gasp. All that was left was the feeling of weightlessness, and then... darkness.

—

I lunge forward in my bed, sucking in air as quickly as my lungs will allow. My tail has coiled so tightly around me that it throbs, its circulation cut off by my positioning. I choke out sobs between my gasps, wiping the tears I already know are streaming down my cheeks away with my wrists.

God damn it. I just wanted one night without that dream. Why do I always wake up like this? Why can't I get over this fucking memory?

Almost in response, my knee aches unbearably. I pull my tail free from its pinned position, feeling the tingling sensation of blood returning to it, and proceed to rub my locked tendon in the usual morning ritual it requires.

Recurring nightmares. Sobbing mess in the morning.

Constantly fucked knee. How is Sammy going to tolerate a woman in this condition? How can he love someone as broken as I am? More tears well in my eyes as I keep massaging the sore joint; after a minute it finally loosens its death grip on the surrounding muscles and allows me the range of motion to shift my foot farther up the bed.

It's a work day, Aubrey. There's no time to feel bad for yourself. I glance at my alarm clock, realizing there's only another three minutes before it's going to sound. Instead of trying to doze off again, I spend the extra time continuing to massage my knee, gently extending and retracting it, being wary of any sudden knots or pangs so I can focus on those spots. After the excessive work I had it do yesterday, it can use a little TLC this morning.

"—seems those cats on Stegen Island can't catch a break with construction. Anyway, that'll do it for our traffic round-up. It's 6:00 AM, and another balmy Old York City day calls for the cool, cool sound of Dizzy Granitespie's 'Con Alma'."

My eyelids lower as the soothing Latin sound of Réne Hornendez's piano melds with the bebop tip-tap percussion work of Ralph Baranda. Dizzy Granitespie's trumpet joins them both soon enough; the music rocks back and forth as the key centers shift, seeming to emulate a lazy rowboat being bobbed in a gentle river. I feel foolish for claiming so many tracks by so many different musicians to be among my favorites, but I do love this song. *Afro*, the album to which this song belongs, has seen more than a little playtime on my record player.

The radio keeps me company as I handle my usual morning preparations. I notice the crumpled yellow dress in the same spot I left it last night. I'll have to get to the laundromat soon; that dress means too much for me to let it wrinkle and fade in a sloppy pile on the floor. Besides, Sammy said I looked beautiful in it. I'll absolutely wear it again, but *definitely* not for our next date. I don't want him to think I don't own any other clothes besides that old thing, despite how much I like it.

Of course, that's assuming we have another date. I asked him to call me tonight, but will he? I mean, I think everything went well. But with how I'm feeling right now, I don't even know that I deserve a man like him. I'd be such a burden to him. He deserves a woman who doesn't have all this baggage, who can actually traverse a flight of stairs without being worried her knee will give out.

At the office, I immediately check as to whether Miles Cratis was released. The dispatcher checks his logs with sleepy eyes before informing me that the human brought in last night was released this morning, about thirty minutes ago. I let out a sigh of relief, thankful that the captain kept his word and handled the situation properly. A sting of regret follows as I recall losing my temper with him. He was here late, he was probably tired, and I nagged him. I make a mental note to apologize to him when I get a chance.

Emotionally, my day is a roller coaster. I go from swooning over the prospect of another date with Sammy to feeling bad for wanting to be with him. I think about Preston's potential treachery, only to discourage myself with the knowledge that I don't have anything on him beyond a flimsy hunch. I ruminate over the time wasted filling out envelopes and licking stamps that could have been spent serving the community, unlike what those incompetent officers are capable of doing.

Mercifully, the day ends without incident. Duffy and Preston must still be on night shift. I had also tried casually strolling past the captain's office a few times, but it was always vacant with the light turned off and the blinds over his interior windows pulled shut. Considering how late he was here last night, he must have taken the day off.

I waste no time in getting home, anxiously boarding the earliest bus that's pointed in my apartment's direction. Once there, I plop myself down on one of the kitchen chairs, staring at the telephone resting on the table directly across from me. Sammy said that he usually gets off work around five o'clock and is home around six, so he could call any time!

After about fifteen minutes of staring at the phone with my hands in my lap, I realize how childish the gesture is. He'll call me when he calls. There's nothing that'll prevent me from picking up the phone so long as I'm home. I decide to thumb through my record collection, settling on Miles Cratis's *Milestones*. As much as I love his newest jams, his 201M1958 BC album is a tremendous entry to his catalog and an absolutely breathtaking work of art.

Setting the black grooved disk on the turntable, a flip of a switch sends it rotating methodically. I lower the needle to the very edge of the record; some folks like to skip around, but I find albums best when they're listened to in full. They tell stories that you won't hear if you only listen to that one hit from the radio and skip everything else.

Unlike the slow, sultry opening track of *Kind of Blue*, *Milestones* opens with a frenetic, frenzied tune called "Dr. Jekyll". I'd never read the namesake book featuring said character and his grisly counterpart Mr. Hyde, but if the tone of this perfectly blended cacophony is anything to go by, I'm sure the story is unnerving and enthralling. Still, I can't help but bob my head with the seemingly disjointed rhythm on display in Cratis's expertly crafted chaos.

Several seconds into the song, I realize the volume is a little loud. I'd probably still hear the phone, but just to be safe I adjust the dial down. I love my music, but I don't want to risk missing Sammy's call on account of an album I've listened to a few dozen times by this point.

My stomach angrily reminds me that it still exists with a loud, sustained gurgle that can be heard even over Miles Cratis and his quintet. I silently curse myself, realizing that I completely forgot to eat lunch today. And with how much of a rush I was in to get home, I don't exactly have a refrigerator bursting with food. I fish around in my cabinets before settling on a packet of saltine crackers. Not exactly nourishing and healthy, but they'll do in a pinch and I *won't* risk leaving to get food. Not when Sammy's phone call is so close.

The needle reaches the end of the first side of Milestones; I flip the record over and reset it to enjoy Side B. When that exhausts itself, I grab another album, Dizzy Granitespie's *Afro*. The track on the radio this morning got me in the mood to listen to it again. With the same motions as before, I set the record on the turntable and place the needle at its edge.

This repeats several more times, with a flipped vinyl being followed by a fresh one. By the end of the sixth, *The Genius of Charlie Larker, #5,* I finally glance at the digits next to my bed. Almost ten o'clock. Up until now, the music had been joined by my chewing of salted crackers, my pacing, my attempts and failures to read a lousy, boring suggestion from my book club, and even a stint of staring out the window, waiting for the music to swell as the phone rings like in one of those corny romance movies.

The phone never rang. My emotions had shifted from happiness to anxiety to discomfort to anger to renewed, blind hopefulness across the near four hours I've been sitting around waiting for this man to do what he said he'd do. Now, as I re-house the spent record in its sleeve, the only thing left in my heart is resentment and disappointment. As I sit on the edge of my bed, slowly pulling down my dress to shift into my pajamas, these emotions are replaced by one.

Emptiness.

He's decided that he doesn't want to see me again. And it's only fair. A woman like me doesn't deserve a man like Sammy. He could easily catch himself a gal with better looks, a healthier frame, a more radiant smile and no broken knees. I had hoped a fool's hope that things would work between us, but he's come to his senses. The kisses we shared last night were only because of the heat of the moment. They were only part of his attempt to console me as I lost my cool upon Miles Cratis's unjust arrest.

Heh. Ever the gentleman. He was looking out for my well-being, but it was just a gesture of kindness, not of love. I understand. I'm prepared to move on. Tomorrow will be a new day, perhaps with the sun shining a little less bright, but I'll survive. I've survived this long, and I'll—

Riiing. Riiing.

I spring from the mattress so quickly that I nearly trip and land on my face. Thankfully it's not due to my knee seizing up but only my own clumsiness as the tips of my claws catch on the rug next to my bed. My tail swings around violently to help me keep my balance; once both legs are firmly beneath me, I practically sprint across my apartment toward the receiver. It doesn't complete its third ring before I snatch the phone from its cradle and hold it to my ear.

"Hello?"

"Uhh—hey, Aubrey. This is Sam."

My cheeks are flushing uncontrollably. "Hi, Sammy. I—well, I was worried you weren't gonna call. It's already so late."

A pause. *"Yeah. I'm real sorry about that. I wanted to call you earlier, I really did, but... somethin' came up."*

It feels as though my heart drops into my stomach. Something came up? What does that mean? "Is everything okay?"

"Yeah, yeah. I'm fine now. I just..." More silence.

I can't stand the silence. I wish he'd just spit it out, whatever it was. If he's gonna rebuke me and say he never wants to see me again, he should just get it over with so I can be done with this emotional hell I'm in.

He finally speaks. *"I guess there's no easier way to put this. I got a new job."*

I'm confused beyond belief. Why would he have gotten a new job in the span of less than twenty-four hours since I last spoke with him? Wasn't he just telling me last night about how he enjoyed his loading dock gig? And, more importantly, why would this new job have prevented him from calling me a little sooner?

Instead of articulating any of these questions aloud, all I can manage is a simple: "What?"

"Yep. It was a bit of a surprise for me, to say the least. But I guess it was an opportunity I couldn't pass up. Or somethin'. To be honest, I'm still trying to wrap my head around it."

"Sammy, you're not making any sense. What is this job?"

"I'm working for the Herdsters now."

Chapter Nine: Pierce

"Unbelievable."

It must be the fifth time the word has tumbled past my gritted teeth. Of course, the target of my ire has been this little piss-stain of a skinnie, having showed up fifteen minutes before—ugh, before *our* shift started. He stood around the lobby like a lost child, too meek and afraid to ask anyone for direction until Charles, Marty and I approached him. Charles was all smiles and handshakes, and even Marty was cordial with the fucker. My fingers were clamped too tightly into fists to extend any pleasantries, and it was the first time that word slipped out today:

"Unbelievable."

Charles heard it. I made sure that Charles heard it, and his reply was to peek over his shoulder and shoot me a shit-eating grin. He knows what he's fucking doing. He's setting me up for failure. He's clamping the metaphorical manacle and lead ball around my ankle before pushing me off a bridge and watching me sink into the inky depths. He's trying to kill me without pointing a gun at the back of my head and pulling the trigger himself.

Coward.

That one I *didn't* say out loud. But I'm not standing for

this. My hands might be tied, but I'm not gonna let Charles Rossi get the better of me. My planning starts now. He's gonna be the one to take this fall, not me. And when he's lying in the gutter, grasping at my feet, begging me for help, I'm really gonna enjoy it when I get to tell him: "No."

Whether that's a metaphorical gutter or a literal one, guess we'll just have to wait and see what pans out.

Samuel Lawson. Even thinking his name makes me gag. Scrawny fucker, not as sweaty or twitchy as Eggsy but still looks like a stiff breeze would knock him over. His plain brown jacket and wrinkled tie seem to only offend me, since nobody else has said a damn thing about his appalling outfit. He comes across as less an employee of the Herdsters and more a grimy door to door salesman trying to peddle trashy kitchenware and cleaning supplies.

It's all grins and greetings from everyone else as the skinnie gets shown around our office, shaking hands and exchanging names with anyone Charles points him out to. He wears a nervous smile as the triceratops leads him deeper into the building before plopping him in a chair across from Irene, our personnel manager. The chubby compsognathus slides a stack of paperwork across her desk for the skinnie to fill out, usual employment rigmarole. I know Charles will be getting a copy of that paperwork later on to stuff into his own little dossier he has on each employee under his supervision. After all, information is power, and holding a man's address and social security number is pretty motivating if push comes to shove.

I attempt to excuse myself several times, not really having an interest in watching this troglodyte sign his name on two dozen different forms, but each time Charles asks me to do something for him. Fetch another form for our "new employee", get him a cup of coffee, check with his assistant to see if any phone calls have come in—I know exactly what he's doing. He's yanking my leash every time I try to make a break for it, and it's really pissing me off.

This goes on for the majority of the morning. How I kept my composure through it all and didn't just tear Charles's throat out is beyond my comprehension, but the time wasn't a complete waste. It gave me an opportunity to watch the triceratops I have every intention of supplanting in his natural habitat. Sure, I could easily walk up to him and tap his forehead with a .38 round, but all that'd earn me is a lead kiss of my own. I have to be smarter about it. If I'm gonna knock this honeycomb off the tree, I need to make sure I'm not gonna get stung.

I've worked with the Herdsters for almost ten years now. In the beginning I wasn't doing anything more than standing security at pickets or the occasional delivery. It wasn't until I was brought under Charles Rossi's wing that I started being asked to undertake heavier work. The kind where the deliverable is usually around two hundred pounds and turns from warm to cold real quick after the job's done.

With heavy work came heftier pay. I was able to afford our beautiful house, and both the cars. Bianca was able to quit her job and focus on keeping the home and the kids. I even started moving up the ranks, slowly but surely. Things were looking good for me.

And then... everything with Franky happened.

Ever since, I've been busted back down to errand boy and quick fixer, though they didn't dock my pay too badly. I'm still bringing in enough to keep Bianca happy and keep food on the table, but I've been here nearly *ten years*. Regardless of any alleged "mistakes" or "setbacks" or "troubles" that I may or may not have caused, I don't deserve to be treated like dirt and made to babysit a fucking skinnie.

Almost on cue, the skinnie gets a clap on the back from Charles as the last of his paperwork is completed. The entire morning is wasted with this latest acquisition, another worthless human who's going to be a pain in my ass at best and a backstabbing thief at worst. Charles turns to Marty and I with a grin; I know what's about to come, but dread it all the same.

"Well, Samuel. You're all set on the administrative side. I say it's high time for you to get out there on the streets and get some practical work under your belt. Pierce and Marty here will show you the ropes on how we do things!" His tongue slides back and forth behind his teeth as he stares directly at me, his disingenuous smile not faltering in the slightest. It takes every ounce of my composure to not lash him across the snout with my tail.

Marty breaks the tense moment of silence. "Not a problem at all, boss. We'll take him on our rounds."

Charles stuffs a hand into his pocket and withdraws a stack of bills. He hands the skinnie thirty bucks before patting his shoulder. "Why don't you fellas go get yourselves some lunch, and then take care of as much of the route as you can before all that beautiful, scalding sunlight outside dries up?"

The human looks at the money with saucepan eyes before turning back to Charles. "Um—I'll bring you back your change when we're done, Mr. Rossi!" Charles only shakes his head and gives a wink before striding away, humming to himself like he's the king of the world.

It feels like the vein in my neck is gonna burst. My claws dig into my palms. Charles gives this filthy human *two hundred dollars* as a "sign-on bonus" and now forks over another *thirty bucks* just for *lunch?!* After we nearly lost all those dues that we collected to Eggsy and his bullshit—is Charles actually mentally retarded or does he think that inconveniencing me is truly worth this much money?!

I'm at a loss for how I'll make it through the day without strangling this skinnie to death with my own two hands. If I do, it'll cost me my own life, but I just don't see how I'm gonna be able to keep from doing it. Charles is playing his cards perfectly to put me in the most infuriating, inescapable spot that he can.

I take a deep breath, thinking of Bianca and the kids and how much it would hurt them if I was given an early retirement. I repeat to myself several times: *it ain't worth throwing your life away over one worthless skinnie.*

"Pierce? You there, bud?" Marty's voice pulls me back to reality. "Guess lunch is on the boss today, so let's go get some grub. I'm starvin'!"

The skinnie takes a step forward, bills clenched in hand and dopey smile plastered on his face before he flinches away from my furious gaze. I snort before spinning on my heel, heading toward the parking garage and the long overdue escape from this place. The thorn in my side sheepishly follows behind Marty and myself, but at least I'm free of Charles's antagonizing bullshit for the time being.

Three of the doors belonging to my Cadillac click shut; I'm too angry to even bother getting more upset by another skinnie being in my vehicle in such a short amount of time. As we pull out of the parking garage, Marty glances between me and the intruder in my back seat. "So, where you fellas in the mood to go for lun—"

"Horatio's."

Marty's mouth hangs open. "H-Horatio's? That place is *top* top stuff! Heck, we're probably underdressed for—"

"We'll be fine." Despite my anger, I'm able to put on a half-smile. "Besides, boss is payin' for it, right?"

The only response Marty can muster is a shrug; the skinnie keeps his silence.

We arrive at the restaurant about five minutes later. A valet whisks my car away from the small pull-through lane in front of the building. At the entrance, twin marbled pillars are adorned with vines and flowers of every color. The lattice of chromatic vegetation weaves around each column before joining together at the center of the arch connecting the pillars. They flank an enormous oakwood door attended by an ankylosaurus gentleman in a fine white suit. He offers a subtle bow as he ushers us into the restaurant.

I'd been to Horatio's a few times before, but the splendor of its decor still gives me pause. Unlike the rainbow-infused archway, white and green seem to be the only colors on display inside. The walls function as trellises for exquisite and exotic plant life. Their leaves are disturbed only by the gentle overhead fans that cool the space. We're led to a round table dressed in an immaculate white cloth and already furnished with utensils and wine glasses.

As I expected, the heads of a few staff members turn our direction, likely due to the skinnie in our company. None of us are in our most formal clothing, but his shabby outfit is assuredly causing snouts to turn up. No matter, I'm gonna get a nice meal at his, and by proxy Charles's, expense.

A dapper stegosaurus strides over to us, placing menus at our places before asking what we'd like to drink. A tall glass of some of their finest wine sounds nice, so I order it. Marty raises an eyebrow at me before ordering the same. The skinnie asks for water. Typical. Maybe they'll bring it to him in a bowl so he can lap it up.

I chuckle as I watch the color drain from the human's face upon reading the menu. Marty notices, too, before speaking. "Sorry, Samuel. This here's an herbivore-exclusive restaurant. Ya won't find any burgers or chicken breasts on there. Though humans are omnivorous, so you're okay with that, right?"

The skinnie gulps. "Y-yeah. I'm okay with that." He isn't fretting over the lack of meat options. It's the price that's bothering him. And I intend to milk that for all it's worth.

The waiter returns with a bottle of wine, showcasing its name and vintage to us before gently pouring it into the glasses in front of Marty and I. Water from a pitcher finds its way into the skinnie's glass. Shame. As our server asks us for our lunch orders, I can't help but wear a smile of self-satisfaction. "I'll have the *Salade d'Eden Paradiso*. Extra fern leaves, extra ginkgo. Please and thank you."

The waiter offers a polite nod before turning to Marty whose mouth now hangs open in my direction. He shakes away the surprise before glancing back at his menu as though he's never seen it before in his life. "I'll get the Panthalassa, easy on the dressing, please."

The rest of the color has drained from the skinnie's face. "I-I'll just have the Caesar salad, sir. N-no tomatoes. Thank you."

With another reserved and gracious bow, our server disappears into the kitchen, clutching the menus he collected before departing. The little shit who gave me such a headache yesterday now stares at his hands in his lap. He might have ordered the cheapest item on the menu for himself, but that thirty bucks isn't gonna cover our food. Hell, my salad alone is gonna come to over fifteen smackers. He can dip into that "sign-on bonus" that Charles foolishly gave him to cover the excess, and he'd better leave a good tip, too.

"So, Samuel." Marty's voice causes my grin to fade. "Tell us a little about yourself. Like—oh, for starters, you mind if we call you 'Sam'?"

I feel my lip curl. I won't be calling him anything but "worthless". Worthless stammers out a reply. "Y-yeah. That's fine. I don't mind Sam."

Marty smiles, offering the skinnie far too much grace. "Okay, Sam, tell us about yourself."

"Uhh, well, I dunno what there really is to tell. I'm a loading dock—" He stops before his cheeks flush. Disgusting. "O-oh. I mean, I w-was—well, you know. You guys were—"

"Relax, buddy. You don't gotta be so nervous. We're

gonna be coworkers after all. How long were you workin' at Sal's before Charles hired ya?"

I lean back in my chair and cross my arms, entirely disinterested in the conversation. The skinnie answers Marty. "Almost nine months."

"Hey, that's respectable. I bet Sal was pretty shocked that you flew the coop so suddenly?"

The lump of flesh called a nose on that creature's face scrunches and his brow furrows. "Actually, since you mention it, he wasn't surprised at all. I told him this morning and he said he was *aware*. Wished me luck and signed my time card for my last paycheck before shaking my hand and sending me off to—well, to the Herdsters office."

Marty nods. "Ah, sure. Makes sense. I bet Charles called him and let him know. Remember, Sal's a member of our union, too. I'm sure he'll be a bit sad to lose a hard worker, but you're movin' up in the world now, kid!" I do my best to keep from retching as a smile tugs at the skinnie's face. "So what else with you? Got a wife or kids?"

"No. No kids. An ex-wife, but that's ancient history. I, uh—" He scratches the back of his neck. "I did start seein' this gal. Hoping things work with her." Another troglodyte like himself, no doubt. "What about you?"

Marty grins. "Got myself a beautiful wife of two years, and our firstborn is on the way. Less than a month out from her due date, and lemme tell ya, they only get more beautiful when they're pregnant. O'course, she's got a bit of a mood on her some mornings, but I get that she's carrying quite a hefty burden inside of her!" The two share a nauseating grin. "Pierce here knows. He's got a wife and two ki—"

My palm slams into the table, causing the dinnerware to clatter and Marty's words to cut short. His eyes widen at me in bewilderment, but I communicate everything I need to with the glare I fire at him.

The silence I command is interrupted by the waiter as

he proffers a plate adorned with various salads to each of us. The one laid before me is heaping and exquisite, each exotic leaf and frond perfectly washed and sparkling with delectable oils and seasoning. It's the crown jewel of this establishment, and well worth the hefty price it commands. Marty's selection looks delicious as well, and even the meager plate set before the human, though about half the size of mine and Marty's, is likely going to be the best salad that lump of flesh has ever eaten.

I savor each bite, basking in the richness of both texture and flavor. I love Bianca's cooking to death, but even she couldn't pull off a dish this complex. The ginkgo truly brings the artistry of it all together, forming taste combinations that—

"I've got a dog. Big fluffy white fella named Saxon. He's a sheepdog and about as smart as a box of rocks, but he's a lovable guy."

I stop mid-chew and shift my smile of appreciation for this luxurious meal into a grimace of annoyance and disgust. He wasn't speaking to me, of course, but the skinnie's words grate in my ears all the same. I can't even have one nice thing without a fucking human ruining it.

Marty smiles at the skinnie, finishing his own mouthful of salad before replying. "Is that so? Tina's super allergic to most of those furry creatures so we never had any pets. It'll make things awkward when our little boy or girl gets to the age when they end up wantin' a puppy for Christmas!"

The two chuckle and carry on with their meals and small talk. I finish my lunch in silence and repulsion, opting to continue not humoring the fleshbag who interrupted my culinary delight. As the other two place the last bites of their own food into their mouths, the waiter returns with a slender black check presenter adorned with a golden inlay of the restaurant's name. He sets it on the table, bows and departs again. I glance down at it, then at the skinnie whose smile has fallen away as he flips it open to review the damage.

Well, that's enough fun for me. The check's his problem now. I rise from the table, rolling my shoulders and cracking my back in the process. "Thanks for lunch, skinnie, even though it's Charles's money paying for it. Hopefully you can do some simple math to figure out the tip our waiter is owed." I shoot the human a grin, letting him know where he stands on this totem pole. He gives a shaky nod before fishing out his wallet; Marty only frowns at me.

I stroll back toward the car, the doorman once again opening the colossal threshold to the scorching outdoors. This heat wave is gonna cause problems, I can just tell. It's already an air conditioner repairman's wet dream with how hard those units are having to work. The valet brings my car around and I plop fifty cents in his palm. Fun as it'd be to make the skinnie pay for this, too, I just don't feel like interacting with him anymore. I know I'll have to, but I'd prefer to keep as much distance between myself and the little scab as possible.

Truthfully, I'd prefer he be dead, but we can't always get what we want in this life.

A minute or so later, Marty and the skinnie emerge from the restaurant and we all pile into my Cadillac. The next several hours are business as usual: rolling from union partner to union partner, exchanging pleasantries, chatting about the weather and the damn good season the Yankees have been having, and collecting union dues. Marty seems a little more on edge today than he normally would be, and a little less friendly with the clients we visit. The skinnie stays in the car.

Around four thirty in the afternoon, Marty and I step out of a jewelry store and back onto the frying pan sidewalk. The owner had offered me a silver necklace with a small half-moon pendant to give to my wife, free of charge. I told him that Bianca's got plenty of neck adornments already, but volunteered Marty's wife for the gift. The jeweler obliged, throwing in a clasp extender to accommodate the diplodocus woman's thicker appendage.

I glance toward my car, parked about two blocks away; parking in this part of the neighborhood is always rough, so we're lucky we even got that. Marty holds the small box in his hand, looking down at it vacantly. I give him a tap on the arm and a smile. "I'm sure Tina is gonna love that."

His eyes snap up to me. "What the hell is your problem?"

I step back. "Whoah, where is this coming from all of a sudden? What did I say?"

He jabs a finger in the direction of my car. "You've been nothing but cruel to Sam today, same as you were with Eggsy."

My confusion shifts to irritation. "What's your point?"

"My point is, Pierce, that he is our *coworker*. What was that bullshit with lunch, huh?"

I shrug. "Charles paid for it—"

"The bill came to almost *forty dollars*. Charles gave him enough money to buy *ten* reasonable lunches, but you decided to haul us to one of the fanciest herbi-restaurants in the entire city."

"So? The skinnie had sign-on money to cover the rest."

Marty shakes his head. "That was a shitty thing for you to do and you know it. And as far as I'm concerned, you owe me for the remaining part of that bill that I covered for you."

"You—*why* would you do that?"

"Because I'm not interested in being Sam's enemy. Like it or not, he's gonna be working with us for a while. You sticking him with huge lunch checks that *you* ran up and leaving him sitting in your back seat sweating his ass off is only gonna earn you an enemy."

I click my tongue. "Truthfully, I'd prefer he was in a ditch instead of my back seat."

Marty's arms go up in a show of flabbergast. "That's

exactly what I'm fuckin' talking about! You're not even treating Sam like he's alive! When is it gonna get through your skull that he's a *person* just like you or me?"

My lip curls into a scowl. "He *isn't* like you or me. He is a *skinnie*. He is rotten to his core, intrinsically and genetically. Hell, why do you think crime rates are so high with—"

"Pierce, I love you like a brother, but you need to shut the fuck up with this. I don't give a shit about statistics or what happened in your past. We're treating Sam like a coworker until he proves otherwise. Everything I'm seeing from him so far leads me to believe he's a good guy and he's gonna be a hard worker, *if* we give him a chance."

I laugh. "Sure! He'll be innocent and charming until we turn our backs for one second, at which point he'll dart down the road with a briefcase full of cash, just like Eggsy did!"

Both of our voices have been raising incrementally. Marty's is practically a shout at this point. "He *ain't* Eggsy! Eggsy fucked up, and got did in for it! You're accusing Sam of guilt before he's even done anything wrong!"

My eyes flare. "What about the money in the alley, huh?! That little prick admitted himself that he woulda ran off with it if I hadn't caught him!"

"Oh, for crying out loud! Put yourself in his shoes, why don't you? If you were a human, piss broke, working a shit job *and* trying to woo a gal, you wouldn't take an opportunity like that if it was presented to you?"

I straighten my back. "Unlike skinnies, I have honor and integrity."

Marty's eyes roll. "Yeah, sure. You'd fork over that fortune to some organization you don't even know, that has employees like *you* that hate every fuckin' human they see, pointin' guns at 'em and talkin' about how much they want 'em *dead.*" He jabs an accusatory finger at me to emphasize his point. "You want Sam to turn out to be a thieving, backstabbing son of a bitch like you've already got him figured to be? Keep treating him like you are. See how that goes for you. Maybe after he cuts your throat with his caveman knife made of bone he'll spare me, seeing as I actually think he might be worth the fuckin' air he breathes."

Before I can respond, he spins on his heel and storms down the sidewalk toward the car. I see his head shaking and catch glimpses of his lips moving, but whatever he's muttering is carried off in the other direction by the scalding breeze.

A moment goes by before I follow after him, mind awash with annoyance and disdain. He still doesn't get it. His heart is too soft. He knows what I did, what I *had* to do, even *why* I did it—but he still sympathizes. His hand ain't been bit by the striped cat hard enough yet to know you never put your hand near a striped cat. Mine has.

We take our seats in the front of the car again; I jam the key in the ignition and begin rolling toward our next destination. The skinnie looks to Marty and I with a weak smile, dabbing at the sweat on his brow with a handkerchief. "How'd everything go?"

Marty tosses the envelope with the jewelry store's dues into the glove compartment before slamming it shut. I know he's upset, but I'd still prefer he didn't damage my car. "It was fine." He pauses, glancing down at the small rectangular box still in his hand before twisting toward the back seat. "Hey. You said you were datin' a gal, right?"

The skinnie blinks. "Uh—yeah. I'm supposed to see her again tomorrow night."

Marty grins. "That's swell. Here. I think she'll like this." He tosses the package back to the human who catches it in surprise. My eyes shoot toward Marty; he just shrugs at me. "Tina's got enough of that shit, too. Plus she was never much of a fan of stuff like suns and moons on her jewelry."

The skinnie's eyes widen at the contents of the box. He

withdraws the thin silver chain, staring at the small, sparkling crescent moon that dangles from it. "H-holy *shit*. This is really nice! Are you sure I can have this?"

A wink from Marty betrays the tone of his words. "Well, that's gonna cost you, actually." The skinnie shifts and sheepishly reaches for his wallet. Marty chuckles and waves a hand. "Not your money, you rube! You're gonna come in with us during our next stop." He glances at his wristwatch. "Probably our *last* stop of the day. I'm spent."

My fingers tighten on the steering wheel. The skinnie stammers. "You w-want me to come *with* you? What do you need me to do?"

Even though his posture has straightened in his seat again, Marty still faces the human with the aid of his lengthy and pliable neck. "Just watch what we do. If someone addresses you, be polite, but don't get rattled. We mostly service dinosaur-owned businesses, but they shouldn't give you any trouble. If they do, they'll have to answer to us. Isn't that right, Pierce?"

I don't reply.

It only takes a few more minutes to arrive at the last location on today's checklist, Murphy's 8-Ball Lounge. The place is a bit of a dive near the edge of a rough neighborhood and tends to draw in an even rougher crowd. We'll see if the skinnie can keep his head. If not, hey, it wasn't my fault. Charles would have nothing on me.

Cheap black paint chips and flakes off of the front door, with clumpy strands being flitted by the wind as I pull it open. Inside, the stagnant souls of cigarettes burned by the tens of thousands are caked into every surface. Six pool tables rest underneath six sets of light fixtures with many of their bulbs burned out and ignored. A dingy bar at the back with a poorly stocked shelf of dusty liquor bottles is helmed by a twitchy deinonychus, nervously glancing at the three of us as we walk down the center aisle of pool tables toward him. I've seen him before, but he isn't Murphy. He's just the bartender, and I never caught his name.

The telltale *clack* of pool balls draws my attention to the fella who appears to be the only patron in the establishment at this time, a rotund tyrannosaurus who struggles with the pool cue given his stubby arms made even stubbier by his stomach. He shoots me a toothy grin before shifting around the table to line up another shot.

There's no sign of the owner, only these two gentlemen. I lean against the bar before addressing the feather-laden deinonychus. "Is Murphy around?"

The bartender's eyes skitter from me to my partner. Marty withdraws and lights a cigarette, adding one more spirit to the ghosts of nicotine past that clog every pore of this establishment. The skinnie lags behind by several paces, glancing around at the varied but sparse pop culture decorations adorning the walls. Before the deinonychus can answer, a voice calls out from the opening door that leads to the back office.

"Yeah, I'm here. How you doin', Pierce?"

"Not too bad, Murphy. Slow night tonight?" I glance around to emphasize my words.

Murphy nods, scratching the bottom of his baryonyx chin. "Yeah, well. We've been havin' more of those lately." Another clatter of pool balls.

"Sorry to hear it, buddy. Hope things pick up for you."

He doesn't respond to me, instead looking past me to the skinnie standing aimlessly in the center of the pool hall. "What about you, pal? You lookin' for some pool? Buy a couple drinks, you get a few games on the house."

Before our extra baggage can reply, Marty clues Murphy in. "He's actually with us. Guess you could say he's getting some on the job training as we do our rounds." His smile isn't returned by the baryonyx.

"Izzat so? Huh. Guess weak species stick together."

I lift an eyebrow. "Come again, pal?"

He shrugs. "Nothin'. It's nice that the Herdsters is embracing diversity. Wouldn't want the best choices for the job handling the hardest work, after all." Murphy glances at the talons on his fingertips.

I rub my forehead in annoyance. He's made off-handed remarks like this before, and it's taken a lot of self-control for me to keep from punching him in the throat for it. Skinnies? Yes, they are a subservient and inferior species. But claiming that carnivores are better than herbivores? Go three rounds in a ring with me and see who comes out on top, buddy.

Marty tries to rein the conversation back in. "Murphy, you know why we're here, and we've had a long day. You mind if we handle your membership dues so we can get outta your hair?"

"Well, I been meaning to talk to you fellas about that. About my *membership.*" I frown, already knowing where Murphy is going with this. "Y'see, times are pretty tough right now. As you can see, we've been having a lot of 'slow nights'. Enough that I'm a bit short."

Clack. "How short, Murphy?"

He flexes his lower jaw from side to side, eliciting a loud pop from the joint while revealing his razor sharp teeth. "All the way short. In fact, I think I'm gonna withdraw from the Herdsters. Don't seem to be much point in membership for a little establishment like mine, what with times bein' so tough and all."

I sigh. "Murphy, if you want to withdraw from the union, you gotta take that up with the Local 237. I don't have the paperwork for that in my back pocket." I shake my head. "It also woulda been nice to get a heads up on your plan to back out so that we didn't waste a trip out here."

The baryonyx's yellow eyes narrow. "Nah, it's not a wasted trip. I was actually hoping you fellas might help me with some back dues. Y'know, seein' as we really ain't been gettin' our money's worth." I straighten up, as does Marty. We both realize the situation that is developing. "You two have a lucrative day today?"

I speak through gritted teeth. "Half day, actually. You chose a bad one to make a play like this, Murphy."

He shrugs. "What can ya do? Guess we'll just have to ma—"

"Pierce, look out!"

The skinnie's shout causes me to spin around, narrowly dodging away from the colossal jaws that just snapped in my direction. The god damn tyrannosaurus is with them, too, and he just about took my fucking head off. He stumbles forward, his momentum having anticipated making contact with me. He rights his balance before spinning around and dashing toward me again.

I hear Marty yell something but his voice quickly turns to a choked gargle as the deinonychus leaps onto the bar and wraps his feathered arms around my partner's neck, squeezing as hard as he can and leaning back to leverage his weight into the choke hold. Marty grasps at the deinonychus and flails his head around, gasping for air and knocking several glasses to the floor in a loud crash.

I duck away from the tyrannosaurus's second bite, avoiding that one just as narrowly as the first. If he catches me in those teeth, I'm done for; no living dinosaur can overpower a t-rex's jaws. He doesn't lose his balance this time, quickly resetting before attempting a third lunge, turning his head sideways to grasp at my midsection. His teeth catch the bare edge of my suit jacket as I leap back, loudly ripping the fabric. He glances at the bit of non-flesh in his maw before spitting it on the ground and charging once more.

I have to do something. His teeth are killer, but the rest of him—

Before he can make contact, my tail cracks out from

behind me, one of its spiked tips tagging him in the back of his knee mid-lunge. The puncturing impact makes him stumble uncontrollably; he lifts his head and rotates his stubby arms to try to regain balance. Just the opening I need.

I duck down, planting my feet firmly as he topples toward me. I jam one hand into his stomach and the other into the large portion of scales where his lower jaw meets his neck, using his momentum to heave him overhead. He lets out a holler as he flips over in the air, aided by my grip before slamming back-first into the felt of a pool table. His tail slaps the overhead light free of its fixture, spewing shattered glass in all directions. The table snaps in two, crashing into the floor and launching pool balls straight up into the air. The tyrannosaurus gasps; I assist him by raining several kicks into the top of his head until he goes limp.

My attention shoots back to Marty. He lurches forward and manages to loosen the bartender's grip around his neck by slamming the clinging deinonychus into the bar. Both dinosaurs stumble and gasp for breath; I take several steps toward them and withdraw my pistol only in time for the claws of a baryonyx to rend across my hand, sending both the weapon and my blood sliding down the walkway behind me.

Murphy roars as he lashes out repeatedly with his talons. I do my best to deflect his attacks but more gashes open on my arms and more of my blood spatters across the ground. I try to strike at him with my tail but he anticipates the attack, slapping it away harmlessly with his own before lunging again.

As he brings his deadly claws down again, I see a brief opening. I push my left arm into his grip, feeling the searing heat of my flesh being ripped open, but force his stance wide before bringing my right fist thundering into the bottom of his jaw. Murphy's teeth loudly clatter together in response to my uppercut and his eyes gloss over. He rocks back on his feet before crumpling.

I breathe heavily, staring down at the incapacitated baryonyx before turning back to Marty. He's regained his composure in time to clobber the bartender in the face with his stocky fists. After a solid couple hits, he hoists the smaller dino upward and launches him over the bar, the ear-splitting crash of a half dozen liquor bottles filling the room. My partner stumbles, catching one of the bar stools with his arms as he gasps. Aside from our mutual labored breathing, the room is silent.

I step toward him, clutching the worst of the ribbons of scales that dangle from my forearms, trying to prevent as much further blood from escaping as possible. "I told you... that you gotta quit smoking."

His neck lifts with an effort and he offers me a weak smile. *"Haah... haah...* shut up..."

I try to return the smile but a rustling of glass shards causes me to shout. "Marty!"

Too late. The deinonychus rears up with a full liquor bottle in hand and clubs Marty over the head. The sickening *crack* of unbroken glass on bone portents the colossal thud of his body hitting the ground. His neck topples like a loosed rope before his head collides with the carpet. Whether he's dead or not, I don't know.

The bartender's furious gaze fires in my direction, half-blinded by glass shards jutting from his forehead and cheek. He screeches past the oozing blood as he leaps onto the bar and hurls himself toward me.

My tail was already wound up before his feet left the bar.

Within an arm's reach of me, the sides of the thick spikes on my tail tip collide with his head like a couple of baseball bats, causing his neck to bend violently and abruptly. The combination of his momentum and the whip-crack of my tail brings his shriek to an unceremonious, gurgling end as his limp body crashes into the floor. His visible eye drains of color and his mouth hangs open, offering only a soundless, horrified scream.

My attention turns back to Marty. He's still lying motionless. Don't be dead, Marty. I can't lose another—

Scorching pain fires through my spine as teeth clamp into my back between two of my plates. I try to spin around but dual sets of talons rip down my shoulder, causing me to stumble and fall to a knee. My tail instinctively plants itself flat behind me, keeping me upright as best it can as Murphy looms overhead, my blood dripping from his jaws and hands.

"You just *had* to make this difficult, didn't you? You couldn't just hand over the fuckin' money? Now I gotta clean all this up, *and* dispose of two—" He glances over at the lifeless deinonychus before shaking his head. "—*three* dead bodies."

I clutch at my shoulder. My fingers do little to stymie the bleeding. Exhaustion catches up to me quickly. "The Herdsters are gonna... find out about this..."

"I'm not worried about the Herdsters. I'll be long gone by the time they figure anythin' out. And so will you and your pal. Just in a different manner of speakin'." He laughs. "I never did like you, Pierce. An herbivore actin' tough is embarrassing. Sure, you get a lucky shot in every now and again—" He wipes a fist underneath his snout to emphasize the point. "—but at the end of the day, the food chain remains the same. It's simple genetics."

My vision starts to blur. It's getting awfully difficult to hold my head up. Not that it'll be a concern for much longer.

He rolls his shoulder and pops his jaw again. "Enough yacking. It's the end of the line for—"

Crack!

Murphy stumbles forward, eyes wide in surprise. The splintered top half of a pool cue slides across the floor. Murphy slowly turns around to lock gazes with... the skinnie. He holds the other broken half of the pool cue, staring at it as though it's the last thing he'll ever see. Truthfully, it probably will be, along with Murphy's jaws closing around his head. He looks back up at the baryonyx.

Murphy roars and lunges. *"You little fuck!"*

The human hunches down and rams the broken end of his makeshift spear into Murphy's leg just above the joint, the now sharpened wood piercing straight through his scales. The baryonyx howls as he falls to his knees, clutching at the cue that stands upright out of his leg, blood beginning to trickle from its sides to the floor.

Fueled by nothing but adrenaline and rage, I lurch forward, wrapping both hands around Murphy's head. He screams and grasps at my forearms, but not in time. With a loud snap, I rotate his neck much farther than it can naturally go. His arms fall slack at his side; as I release my grip, his body collapses to the ground, half of a pool cue still jutting from his leg.

I consider following him down, but choose to slump back on my laurels and attempt to remain conscious instead. I took a pounding and lost a lot of blood. I also don't know if that tyrannosaurus is down for the count. If not, he could easily finish me off if I do decide to take a nap on this comfortable looking carpet.

My hazy eyes find the human again. He stares down at Murphy's now lifeless body with a look of shock. He stumbles backward, nearly tripping over the maw of the still unconscious t-rex before the back of his shoe clatters into something small and metallic. He glances at it before stooping down to retrieve...

My revolver.

He stares at the device, holding it before him like a treasure hunter who just found a golden goblet. He brings his hands to the proper resting position to wield the weapon, finger on the trigger, spinning toward the tyrannosaurus and aiming it at his unconscious form. He remains like this for several seconds, but he doesn't shoot and the beast doesn't stir. He then focuses on Murphy, aiming the gun at his body while sliding his feet cautiously. Finally, he looks at me.

His breathing is erratic. His eyes are wide and his pupils are dilated. He's even more pale than when I ordered that fifteen dollar salad for lunch. The barrel of the gun slowly rises.

So this is how it happens. Done in by the skinnie I was so close to executing not even twenty four hours ago. I was right. Of course I was right. Marty's bleeding heart is gonna end with both of us bleeding out in this dingy pool hall. Well, at least I'll die knowing I was—

The revolver rests inches away from me, but it faces the wrong way. The human holds its barrel, extending the grip to me. "We gotta get out of here. I think Marty is in bad shape, and I'm not gonna be able to get him back to the car by myself."

I blink. In response, the human gives the revolver a small shake, beckoning me to accept it. I oblige, now taking my turn to gaze at it as though it's a long-lost relic. The human moves past me and over to Marty, glancing at the dead deinonychus before bending over to Marty's head and clapping a gentle hand to his cheek. He tries to beckon Marty back to consciousness, and it seems to work, albeit very slowly. With labored movements, Marty's neck begins shifting and his arms draw inward. He mutters something incoherent.

"Pierce, please. I need your help to get Marty up."

I'm not exactly in tip-top shape myself here, human, but let me get right on that request. I struggle to bring one knee up, planting a palm on it and sucking in air before hoisting myself upward. My legs buckle, but my tail works overtime and keeps me upright as my other shoe flattens itself on the carpet beneath me. I shake away the dizziness and turn toward the two of them. Marty's at least gotten his arms underneath himself and his neck halfway airborne again, but his head still rests on the ground.

"P... Pierce... wh... did we..." His words are slurred and broken. Whether he's concussed or not, I don't know.

"C'mon, buddy. Save that energy for walkin'."I use the little remaining strength I have to toss one of Marty's arms over my shoulder. The human does his best with Marty's other arm, but nearly crumbles underneath the diplodocus's weight. His assistance is not a complete waste. Together the three of us take small steps toward the door, Marty's neck still dangling loosely, his head very nearly dragging on the ground despite his body being mostly upright.

The setting sun is still high enough in the sky to dazzle me as we push the door open. No pedestrians are nearby, so there's no one to take account of the two battered dinosaurs and one unscathed human that exit a pool hall and bar that's now host to at least two dead bodies. With a struggle, we get to my car. I decide to help Marty into the back seat so he can lay down, though given his size it's not a very comfortable bed. He still graciously accepts, immediately closing his eyes and breathing heavily.

We're gonna have to get ourselves to a hospital. I fish out my keys and begin stumbling over to the driver's seat, but the human's hand stops me. "Look. I know you don't like me, but you're not in any condition to drive. Let me handle it, I'll get you guys to a doctor."

My eyes flare in his direction, but that's about all I can do in protest. I don't like it, but he's right. I'm barely staying on my feet as it is. I'd probably wrap my Cadillac around a light pole before we make it two blocks down the road. The keys land in his open palm. He nods before moving around the vehicle to the driver's side door. I slide into the passenger seat and shut my eyes. The only sensations I feel are the quiet rumble of the engine and the gentle hum of the pavement beneath our wheels.

"Pierce?"

I just wanna sleep, but I'm too tired to tell him off. "Yeah?"

"Was that—uhh—was that an average day at the office?"

I smile. "No, Samuel. No, it was not."

Chapter Ten: Samuel

The incandescent bulbs high above my head spread soft light across the skin on my folded hands. They rest on my lap, intertwined together and entirely unmoving. At this point, I've intimately learned every crevice, layer and recess of the flesh overlapping my muscle and bone, because my eyes haven't gone anywhere but my folded hands for nearly half an hour.

I killed a man.

I mean, I didn't break his neck myself, but I stabbed that baryonyx in the leg, and that gave Pierce the opening to…

My hands finally release themselves, rising to my forehead. My fingers run through my hair, upheaving glistening droplets of sweat that seem endless. Even this medical clinic waiting room is a damned oven in this days-long heat wave. I shudder involuntarily, suppressing the urge to scream as the words keep repeating themselves in my head.

I killed a man. I killed a man. I killed—

"Hey, kiddo. How ya holdin' up?"

The sudden voice and clap on my back from a colossal, firm palm cause me to jump. I spin toward my assailant, raising my arms reflexively to protect against a lethal assault, but instead I'm greeted by the warm smile of Charles Rossi. He isn't offended by my skittish and defensive gesture in the slightest.

"It's alright, Samuel. Everything's gonna be fine. Just take a breath, okay?"

I do as he asks, releasing my posture and drawing in slow, steady breaths to calm my heartbeat. My shock quickly shifts to embarrassment and fear; I didn't even notice the triceratops sit next to me. If he had been an enemy, perhaps that t-rex that we left out cold or some friend of Murphy's who came across the carnage we caused, I could be dead right now.

As dead as that bartender. As dead as Murphy.

Except for the two of us, the small waiting area is empty. The last thing Pierce said to me before he passed out in the car was the address of this clinic. I would have taken the two of them to the Metropolitan Hospital, but I assumed he had a good reason for wanting to come here. My best guess was that they knew the folks who ran this clinic, and maybe those folks wouldn't ask questions. Sure enough, as they unloaded his unconscious body from the car, there were no questions.

Charles clears his throat. "I spoke with the doctor. Pierce is still under. He lost a good amount of blood, but he's stitched and bandaged up. Martin is awake, and the doctor is convinced that he doesn't have a concussion. However, the nasty lump on his head seems to be preventing him from recalling most of what transpired." He takes a slow breath. "Samuel. What, exactly, happened today?"

He wears an expression of stern authority. I can't tell if there's concern behind those purple orbs, but there's no doubt in my mind that he wants me to answer, and answer truthfully.

I oblige his request, proffering every detail I remember from the moment we walked into Murphy's 8-Ball Lounge until our conversation here. I recall the dingy lighting, smoke-caked surfaces and surly demeanors of all three dinosaurs that were... handled. The bartender's erratic movements, the tyrannosaurus's constant glances at Pierce before he crept forward to attack, and Murphy's lackadaisical attitude leading up to their assault.

I told Charles that I called out to warn Pierce of the t-rex's lunge, but after that, I hid. I was terrified. Creatures twice my size were pummeling and lacerating one another not even twenty feet away. I didn't have a gun, and it was literally my first day on this job. Hell, it still *is* my first day. What was I supposed to do against power and fury like what I witnessed?

It wasn't until the fighting was nearly done that I was able to find my feet. The tyrannosaurus was unconscious. So was Marty, though I worried that he might have been more than unconscious given how hard that bottle smacked into his skull. The deinonychus bartender's neck had been broken mid-flight toward Pierce. But Murphy, who had been briefly knocked out, was back on his feet and tore into Pierce's exposed back, bringing him to his knees. The baryonyx was gloating over Pierce when I stepped out from behind one of the unbroken pool tables.

I lower my head in shame before speaking honestly to my boss of exactly one day. "I ran toward the door. Murphy was so distracted with Pierce that he didn't see or hear me. My hand was on it, ready to push it open and sprint down the street in any direction, to end up any place but there. I was scared, Charles. I knew that if I tried to intervene, I'd end up dead."

He looks at me without emotion; neither sympathy nor scorn reside in his eyes. "I shall guess by the fact that the three of you are still alive that you did not run."

"No. I didn't. And for the life of me, I can't tell you why." Going against every fiber of my survival instinct, I speak candidly. "Pierce hates my guts. He doesn't view me as anything but an inferior species. He spent all day making snide remarks and instilling a sense of worthlessness in me. Marty's actually respectful and even showed me a kind gesture, but he clearly takes his marching orders from Pierce and from you."

My conscience screams at me to dash toward the exit of this clinic, to escape from this place like I so desperately wanted to escape the pool hall, but I clench my fists and press on. "And you, Charles… you offered me a job and more money than I'd ever made before, when refusing the offer would mean my death. What choice did I have? And now that I'm your employee, you've saddled me with the man who was holding a gun to my head just last night and talking about how much he wanted my brains on the gravel beneath my knees. So why the hell did I grab a pool cue, break it over Murphy's back and skewer him in the leg? Why'd I save Pierce and Marty's lives when my own life is of so little value to them, and to you?"

Charles crosses his arms and lowers his eyelids. I watch the gears turn in his head. His breathing is steady, giving the illusion of a monk deep in meditative thought. After a moment, his eyes reopen and refocus on me. "I have risen to the rank I presently hold within the Herdsters for one reason, and one reason alone: I am a good judge of character. Those who report to me, those who respect me, those with whom I break bread and share drinks—they are all people who I value and respect in return. I do not offer respect to just anyone, and you are someone with whom I am still *very* unacquainted. But there's a reason I offered you this job. It wasn't to keep you quiet, or keep you on a leash. It's because I could tell that you are a good man, and someone capable of loyalty and respect."

I glance at the floor, pondering his words. Is that all true? I mean, I think I'm a good person, but… "I killed Murphy. How does that make me a good man?"

He purses his lips and lowers his brow. The upward-curved horn on the tip of his snout glistens in the soft illumination of the room. "You acted in self defense. You protected the lives of Pierce and Martin. It was a regrettable situation, and I am sorry you were put into that spot, but the nature of the world we live in is that sometimes we must defend ourselves against wickedness."

I fidget in my chair before he continues. "The Herdsters offer a valuable service to many organizations all around not just this city, but the entire country. We are an organization of justice that fights for the rights of those who have no voice by themselves. We stand against the tyranny of employers who would underpay, overwork and abuse their labor force. Because of that, we make enemies. There are people who do not want us to succeed, and we must occasionally defend ourselves from those attacks."

I think back to Murphy and his reasoning for attacking us. It seemed like he just wanted the money we had collected, but was there more to it than that? And more importantly... "Is that what happened with that human in the alley? Eggsy?"

Charles's expression almost imperceptibly sours. He lets out a sigh. "What happened with Egbert was regrettable, and Pierce acted out of line. Egbert should have been brought in and questioned, not handled in such an inelegant manner on the street. We are not murderers or criminals. But to answer your question more directly: yes. Egbert was an enemy of the Herdsters. He tried to steal money not from us, but from those that we serve. That was money from people like Sal Fontana, dues they contribute so that we can help them when they need our help. Whatever demons Egbert was wrestling with, he chose the wrong path to address it."

I bite my lip, feeling my hands tremble in my lap. "I just don't know if I can do this. After today, after what I did, I don't know if I've got it in me."

He places a gentle hand on my shoulder and offers a warm smile. "Despite what you may think, you aren't being forced to work for me. I want you to be my employee. You aren't a prisoner here."

"But you've got my address. My social security number. What would stop you from—"

He lowers his snout, peering at me as though over the top of glasses he does not wear. "Are you someone who's trying to bring harm to the Herdsters or our clients?"

"N-no, of course not."

"Then there's nothing for you to be worried about." He rustles my shoulder with the hand that still rests on it before withdrawing his arm. "I'd ask that you take a few days to think it over, at least. If you're still convinced that this isn't the path for you, I'll call Sal and get you your old job back. I'll even talk to him about getting you a raise, though I doubt you'll make the same money there as you would here, even with a pay bump."

I do my best to return his smile. "Thank you, Charles. I'll... think it over."

He places his hands on his knees, hoisting himself up to his feet. With a few steps he crosses the waiting area, peering around the corner into one of the two small exam rooms. He gives who I presume to be the nurse in Pierce's room a nod of acknowledgment before turning my way once more. "Regardless of what you might think of your character or your actions tonight, you saved the lives of these two men. You had the choice to run away in that pool hall, but you chose goodness and justice. That more than proves I was right in my assessment of you, Samuel. Have a good night." With that, he pushes through the clinic's exit toward the sunset-soaked street, the bell suspended above the door emitting a brassy jingle in his wake.

I resume peering at my clasped hands; they still tremble, but at least they've come somewhat under my control. After a few minutes, I rise from my seat, cautiously moving toward the same room Charles had poked his head into.

Pierce lies on an examination bed properly sized for his gargantuan form, close to eight feet long and about half as wide. His tail dangles off the side and the spikes on its tip rest on the linoleum floor. If it weren't for the steady thrumming of the heart rate monitor attached to him, I'd mistake his motionless sleep for rigor mortis. Numerous sutures and bandages cover his arms and shoulders, discoloring themselves with the further leakage they prevent.

A compsognathus turns toward me, brushing the bangs that poke from beneath her nurse's cap away from her cheek. "He's still unconscious and likely will be for some time. We're keeping Mr. De Luca here for the evening, too, as a precaution. You're free to leave, though, Mr. Lawson."

Before I can leave the building, another voice catches my attention. It's quieter and more labored than normal. "Hey, Sam."

I take a few more steps down the hall and peek into a second exam room. Marty lies on his side on another impressively sized bed, holding an enormous ice pack to the top of his head. The way he cradles his own face between his arms gives him the appearance of a curled-up cat.

I offer a weak wave. "Hey, Marty. How you feelin'?"

He smiles with some effort. "Like I got hit over the fuckin' head with a bottle of booze. At least, that's what I think happened. I can barely remember a damn thing."

I step into the room. No nurse or doctor is present. "Yeah, that's what happened. I thought bartenders were supposed to pour the drinks into glasses for ya, not clobber ya with the merchandise."

He chuckles, though the action clearly causes him discomfort. "Needless to say, I won't be offering my patronage to that particular establishment no more." He shifts the ice pack, briefly exposing the enormous lump underneath it. "Doctor said I ain't concussed, but I sure as shit got a nasty headache."

"Well, why don't I let you get some rest? I—"

"Sam, listen. C'mere." He releases the ice pack with one of his hands to beckon me over. I oblige, taking a few steps deeper into the room. "I heard what you said to Charles. This place ain't exactly big, or sound proof." My eyes widen, but he quickly waves a comforting hand. "Don't worry about the staff here, they're friends of the Herdsters. That's why Pierce had you bring us to this clinic."

He takes a deep breath before focusing his gaze intently on me. "What you did today was a *good thing*. I was out cold for most of that fight, so I didn't see you get the upper hand on Murphy, but if you hadn't done what you did, I wouldn't be here talkin' to you right now. He'd have killed Pierce, then me." He glances down at the floor between us regretfully. "I'm sorry that we put you in that spot. I knew Murphy was an asshole, but I didn't in a million years think he'd be capable of trying to pull what he did, and if I *had* known, I wouldn't have put you at risk like that." His eyes focus on me again. "But now, with all things considered, I'm thankful you were there. If you weren't, my little boy or girl would be growin' up without a father."

I try to offer him a smile but my lip quivers. Marty sighs before continuing. "I know this was a hell of a first day. And please believe me when I say, this is not the norm. We can get rough with folks, but only sometimes, and only when it's absolutely necessary. Like Charles said to you, we'll defend ourselves when it needs doing, but we aren't thugs." He shakes his head. "It'll take some convincing to make you believe that after the way Pierce treated you, I know. And I'm sorry that he's been so cruel to you. It's just—" He purses his lips. "I don't know that it's my place to tell you this, but I don't think he'll ever tell you of his own accord. I'd ask that you keep this between us."

He gestures with his head toward the open door behind me. Understanding his meaning, I reach behind myself and gently push it shut. Marty sighs again. "Pierce had a brother. His younger brother, Francisco. Called him 'Franky'. Franky worked for the Herdsters, too. Pierce had gotten him a job doin' mostly the same thing we do, collecting dues and helping out with pickets and functions as needed." He frowns and his eyes go out of focus, looking beyond me to a memory. "He was a good guy—reckless, and loud, sure—but he was a good guy. Always had a joke to crack, no matter the situation. And you could tell Pierce really loved him."

The pieces slowly fall into place in my head before Marty clarifies. "His brother was killed. And the man who killed him was a human."

Now my eyes go out of focus as I process what he just said. Before I get too far into my own head, Marty raises his free hand again. "I know that this isn't a good excuse for him being the way he is. I don't agree with his philosophy that humans are inferior to dinosaurs. I know things were different between our species not that many years ago, but if I needed any sort of convincing that humans are just as capable and worthwhile as us dinosaurs, you provided it today. And I really hope that Pierce sees that, too. I'm only telling you this because I believe that you're a good man, and deep down, past all that bitterness and resentment he still harbors, I believe Pierce is a good man, too."

I scratch the back of my neck as I consider his words. As quickly as I want to discard the excuse, can I say that I would be any different? If my younger brother was killed by a dinosaur—if I had one, that is—would I be forgiving and understanding, especially after how I've been treated by so many dinosaurs over the years?

Marty shifts the ice pack on his head again, snapping me

out of my introspection. "Like I said, I don't tell you any of this expecting you to give Pierce a pass for his shitty behavior. I just want you to know that his attitude is his own, and it doesn't reflect how anyone else views you, myself included. I know people out there can be assholes, and I'm sure you've gotten burned your share of times. But I hope that the two of us can be friends, at least." He smiles genuinely and extends his free hand toward me.

I accept his handshake. "Thank you, Marty. I'd like that very much."

His teeth become visible past his grin. "Alright, my ploy worked! Now that we're friends, you gotta get me and Tina a present for our baby shower!" I blink in momentary confusion until his raspy chuckle clues me into the joke. I give him a light smack on the arm, earning another laugh followed by a whine. "Hey, no fair beatin' up the injured guy!"

I shake my head and chuckle as I take a step back. "Speaking of, did your wife get told you're here yet? Or Pierce's—you did say he's married, too, right?"

"Charles said he's gonna give them a call for us. I told him to tell Tina not to worry, I'm just gonna spend the night here for observation, should be good to go by tomorrow. As for Pierce... well, Bianca might be comin' by to visit him."

I guess Bianca is Pierce's wife. I nod to Marty. "Alright, bud. Is there anything else I can do for you before I head home?"

He rotates onto his back with a heave and a groan. "Could you ask the nurse to get me some more ice on your way out?"

"You got it." I pull open the door to the room, fulfilling my new friend's request with the nurse before heading toward the exit. Passing by the chairs in the waiting room, I notice a small rectangular package resting atop one. I scoop it up, recognition rapidly coming to me as I pull off its lid to reveal the crescent moon pendant that Marty had given me.

I put two and two together; Charles must have retrieved the day's money from Pierce's car and found this in the back seat while doing so. He didn't know which of us it belonged to, so he just left it on the waiting room chair.

I hold the small silver moon in my hand, running a thumb over its smooth surface. A smile forms on my lips as I think about Aubrey for the first time in several hours. I remember the date I have with her tomorrow night, imagining the look on her face when I give this to her. Though... is it too soon to be giving her gifts like this? It'll only be our second date, after all. My smile fades away as my conscience begins wrestling with itself as to the proper timetable of appropriate gift-giving during the courtship process.

My feet carry me outside the clinic as I continue battling my id. I'm getting swept away with thoughts of Aubrey, even after everything that happened today. The words of both Charles and Marty ring in my head, but I still fight against the reality of my actions. You can make arguments that I acted in self defense or that I'm a "good man" until you run out of breath, but the fact remains—I helped kill a guy. Was his life worth less than Pierce and Marty's? What about the bartender?

Several blocks down the sidewalk, I stop and stare at my reflection in a shop window. The man who looks back at me is the same one as before, the same one I see every morning in my bathroom mirror. But somehow, he looks different. More hardened. Like some piece of him was removed that can't be given back. He tries his hardest to smile. It doesn't look genuine.

Is Aubrey going to want to be with a man like this?

My mind swirls with contradiction and confusion. On the one hand, Charles treated me with dignity and kindness and Marty offered me his friendship. On the other, I know that these men are capable of dealing in death, even witnessing it firsthand today. They claim to not be mobsters or murderers, that they only defend themselves and their clients. If that's so, what about Eggsy? Sure, he was stealing money, but did that mean he deserved to be shot dead in an alley? Why not report him to the police?

On top of that, Charles told me that I'm free to leave the Herdsters, but is that actually true? After what I've seen, would I ever truly be safe? If I decided to quit and go back to Sal's, would I have to look over my shoulder, constantly dreading the bullet that would bring my story to a rapid close? Could I even flee the city to somewhere safe, or would I always be in danger? I mean, I don't think their organization's reach is quite Gorewellian, but Charles did say they operate in every major city. I might just be a loose end that's easier to tie up with a tap to the back of my head.

And even if I could run away, getting safely to some backwater town where they couldn't find me, that would mean giving up Aubrey, wouldn't it? Why would she follow some guy she just met to another town? And wouldn't I just be putting her at as much risk as myself?

I stare at the box in my hand again, imagining the crescent-moon pendant resting against her collar. A vision fills my mind of her devastated eyes staring at me as I tell her about my plans to run away, confused and questioning. Her hand wraps around the necklace before tearing it off, casting it on the ground as she curses at me for wasting her time and breaking her heart. I can only sit with my head hung, unable to tell her anything due to the danger it would put her in. She'd abandon me just like I'd be abandoning this God-forsaken city and the rotten mess I've gotten myself into.

It seems that I'm damned if I do, and I'm damned if I don't. At the very least, I still have a date with her tomorrow night, and despite the scrape at that pool hall today I don't have a mark on me. It'd make things a lot harder if I had to explain a black eye or broken nose to her on our date, and it'd be infinitely more awkward if I was dead.

Raptor Christ... I need a drink.

—

The next morning I find myself standing in the front lobby of the Herdsters building again. It was a restless night with a lot of things blasting around in my mind as I tried to sleep. Even the glass of rum I stopped for on the way home didn't seem to alleviate my anxiety. The only notion that helped me find slumber was that I'd get to speak with Aubrey during our date. I coulda called her last night, but I figured it would be better to discuss things in person. I'm also uncertain as to how much I can reasonably tell her, but having someone to talk to about this stuff is better than nobody at all. As much as I love Saxon, the walking carpet isn't exactly a conversationalist.

I aimlessly mill about for a few minutes before Marty's face pokes around a corner. If he still has a lump on his head, it's concealed by the flat cap he wears. "Hey, Sam. Come on over here, will ya?" I oblige, trotting over to the diplodocus. "Pierce and I usually muster at the parking garage entrance in the morning. You're welcome to meet us there instead of standin' around the lobby lookin' lost."

I scratch the back of my neck. "Yeah, sure. Sorry about that. I'm still getting used to how things work."

He gives me a clap on the back, his immense strength nearly toppling me. "You'll catch on! I'm just glad you came back after all that excitement from yesterday." His words make me flinch; he doesn't notice. "Don't you worry, today's gonna be a real treat. You get to witness the finest feature of the International Brotherhood of Herdsters in full swing: *bureaucracy!*"

I cock my head, unsure of his meaning until he leads me

farther down the hall toward two signs adorned with large letters: "Roscoe Truckers Association Voters Here" and "Stegen Island Cab Company Voters Here". The signs flank two doors leading to separate rooms; within each, folding tables blanketed with paper, pencils and ballot boxes are tended to by dutiful Herdster employees. The smell of freshly brewed coffee permeates the space between the rooms, affording the otherwise sterile environment a welcoming feeling.

Marty gives me a nudge to pull me out of my enraptured state. "Pretty exciting stuff, I know. We usually don't do two-fers like this, but it just worked out this way. The fellas from both companies should start rolling in around nine and will probably keep trickling through until four or five."

I half-register his words, distracted by my attempt to locate the origin of the delicious scent of caffeinated goodness. He seems to catch on to my distraction, stepping through the door to our left. He has to lower his neck so his head doesn't collide with the top of the threshold. His large fingers find the handle of the object I was unconsciously searching for a moment ago, a coffee pot brimming with freshly brewed alertness. He pours some into a thick paper cup and hands it to me. I glance at the coffee in my hands, then back up to him. "So what are we gonna be doing today, then?"

He pours a second cup for himself, speaking after he takes a swig. "We're gonna be glorified hall monitors. Keep an eye on things, point folks in the right direction, make sure nothing gets out of hand."

I wince. "Out of h-hand?"

"Oh, no. It won't be anything like that. In fact, I imagine the worst that might happen is there'll be a few fellas poking around outside trying to snipe some of our members. Basically, an organization can only switch unions with a vote, so competing unions will try to entice people with promises of better rates or bigger benefits." He scoffs. "They can't even come close to the Herdsters, but they still try to sucker 'em. Today's vote ain't about that, though. These two companies are newer to our union, so they're voting on their own internal leadership. Pretty big companies, too, so we'll have a lot of guys comin' through here today!"

I cautiously blow on my coffee as he explains, waiting for it to cool down so I don't scald my tongue with roasted bean water. Before yesterday, I'd hardly known a thing about the Herdsters or other unions for that matter, let alone how they operated. As I filled out my new hire paperwork, Charles explained a fair amount of what they do and what my role would be, though most of it went over my head. Contracts, work conditions, fair compensation, pickets, collective bargaining; they were a myriad of phrases that made some sense on their own but much less sense on a grand scale.

Marty and I spend a little more time chatting with one another. I ask about Pierce; Marty tells me that he's conscious as of this morning but still in pretty rough shape, so he'll likely be at the clinic through the weekend resting up. I don't necessarily wish ill upon the guy, but I am glad to have a little time away from the stegosaurus and his unending hatred toward me. Marty's words from yesterday echo in my mind, about the circumstances surrounding Pierce's brother and his untimely end, but also his hinting about Pierce potentially coming around to me. If it's possible, it'd definitely make things a hell of a lot easier on this new career path I'm still uncertain about.

After a few minutes, some dinosaurs begin wandering into the building, looking for their appropriate voting area. Marty leads me outside the front entrance so we can keep an eye on the primary ingress point; according to him, that would be the most likely place for competing union representatives to loiter and try sweet talking our members. However, the only use of our vigilance is to point voters toward where they need to go; we see neither hide nor hair of any honey-tongued competitors all day. Marty eventually backpedals, saying that it'd be pretty ballsy for those jokers to come 'round our turf and try to stir up trouble.

In a futile gesture, I wipe the completely drenched handkerchief across my forehead and silently curse Marty for the bright idea of having us stand in this horrific heat all day. It certainly put extra pep in the step of our visitors as they hustled to retreat indoors and into properly conditioned air. One fella mentioned that the weatherman suggested it might make it to the triple digits today, and I believed him. Heat like this might be common further west in the dusty deserts, but our fair city with all its conductive steel and paved walkways is quickly becoming a pressure cooker.

As the work day draws to a close, with the last of the voters trickling out and the signage being brought down, Marty gives me a clap on the shoulder. "Ya did good today, bud. Like I said, a nice, easy day that hopefully helped settle you in a bit better." He begins turning away before pausing and shooting me a sly grin. "I just remembered. You said you got a date with that gal tonight, didn't ya?"

I blink, not recalling having brought it up to him today. It takes a moment for me to remember mentioning it in the car yesterday when he gave me that necklace. "Y-yeah. Supposed to meet up with her at seven."

His grin widens and he winks. "Good luck, champ! Not that you'll need it, I bet you're a smooth one when it comes to the ladies." I can't help but chuckle, knowing all too well that I am certainly *not* smooth. "I'll expect a full breakdown on everything come Monday. You can't keep being mysterious, not after I've prattled on about my Tina and our little incoming bundle of joy. You gotta return the favor and give me a little juicy detail on the love life of Mr. Lawson!"

I offer a polite smile and wave before heading out. "Have a good night, Marty."

Truthfully, his penchant for chatting was quite helpful today. It kept me distracted from the anxiety of my second date with Aubrey, though I still felt twinges in my gut whenever the thought of her crossed my mind. I could tell Marty was doing a little probing of his own, attempting to get me to share a bit more about my pursued relationship, but I held my tongue and managed to sidestep the conversation. As glad as I am that he considers me a friend, I have no clue how the bombshell of me dating a velociraptor gal would go over with him, or anyone else within the Herdsters.

Or Pierce, for that matter. Hell, he might just kill me on the spot if he found out that I was pursuing a dinosaur with my caveman impurity.

The trip home takes me a bit longer than it did back when I was working for Sal. I have to take a couple buses to get to and from the Local 237, unlike simply being able to walk to work. Not that I'd mind a change of pace like this for a job that'd get me some more money, but I'm still not sold on the Herdsters. Yeah, today was peaceful and quiet, and maybe Marty's right that most days aren't bloody. But I never had to stab a guy in the leg and watch my coworker break his neck at any of my previous places of employment, either.

There's nothin' for it right now. I'll just have to talk to Aubrey about it.

But how much am I gonna tell her? The aspiring cop who went charging headfirst toward gunfire with a bad knee—what is she gonna think if I tell her I helped kill a baryonyx? Despite not being an actual police officer, she'd probably arrest me on the spot. If I do get into a serious relationship with her, would I ever be able to tell her something like this? And what if more violence goes down in the future? What if I get hurt, or come home covered in blood? Is it worth the secrecy and dishonesty just to make enough money to provide for us? Can I even get out anymore without putting myself or her at risk in doing so?

The bus lurches to a halt at the nearest stop to my home. I climb out, dejected and disheartened by my current fucking mess of a situation. My watch informs me that it's a little past six. Considering the place I invited Aubrey isn't too far from my apartment, I should have enough time to freshen up, take Saxon out and then walk myself over to the restaurant.

Dinner and a movie. A classic combo for an aspiring couple. I've got no clue what's playing at the theater, but they usually run movies until the wee hours of the morning on the weekends, so we shouldn't have a problem getting a ticket to something. Whether it'll be any good, who knows? But I'll be spending that time with Aubrey.

After attending to Saxon, I take care of my personal hygiene, washing my face and dabbing a bit more cologne on my neck and wrists. I wanna look sharp, but not too sharp, so I go with a checkered button-up shirt and some black slacks. Not as snazzy as the jazz club, but not lookin' like a beatnik either. I hesitate at my hat rack, considering tossing on a familiar flat cap before I decide against it. I'd rather let the top of my head cool itself as much as possible against this wicked heat, so I give my tangled mane a quick pass with the comb before heading out.

The scorching rays fail to relent in their merciless onslaught upon the poor citizens of Old York City even as the sun begins its slow retreat into the west. It's easy to tell that everybody is sick and tired of the heat at this point, with sweat-covered brows and annoyed scowls adorning both the humans and dinosaurs I pass on my way to the chosen date spot. While I can certainly sympathize as I dab away the moisture with a handkerchief, I can't help but wear a smile as I stroll, the fluster of my work situation being temporarily silenced by the prospect of this evening.

I'm gonna do everything I can to make this work. I might have been dealt a tough hand with this Herdsters business, but I'm not gonna let it discourage me. Aubrey is too special of a woman to let slip away.

Just as the mental image of her form fills my mind for probably the seven hundredth time today, the real deal comes into view on the horizon, appearing like a shimmering mirage from the reflected heat on the concrete. She stands outside the entrance of my chosen dinner location, Lucky Louie's Malt Shoppe. I put a little hustle into my step, getting within about fifty feet before she turns my direction and notices me.

Her mouth instantly widens into a smile, making my heart skip a beat. She lifts a greeting hand. "Hey, Sammy!"

"Heya, Aubrey! I hope I didn't keep you waiting too long, especially in this damned heat."

She shakes her head, her smile not faltering in the slightest. "Not at all, I only got here a couple minutes ago." Her eyes fall upon my outfit. "You look sharp as always!"

She puts me to complete shame, being draped in a jaw-dropping single-piece dress the color of dark peaches. A row of evenly spaced buttons travel all the way from her collar down to the hem that rests just at her knees. A thin, similarly colored belt hugs her narrow waist and contours her subtle but seductive curves. Her arms are free of sleeves, granting vantage to her slender blue arms that just a few nights ago held me close as we danced and, later, as we kissed. Her hand raises, brushing aside some of the short blue hair that intrudes on her line of vision, further unveiling her sparkling citrine eyes to me.

She is beautiful.

Only now does her smile falter, her face reddening as she glances to the side nervously. "W-well?"

I snap out of my daze. "Oh my God. I've been sittin' here

staring like a freak! I—aw, geez. I'm sorry. Y-you look really nice!"

Her smile returns and her cheeks flush more deeply. "Thank you. I hoped you'd like it."

I dart forward to draw open the door to Lucky Louie's. She bobs me a polite little curtsy before stepping into the diner. Several booths with red lining span the windowed wall, and a bar with red-topped circular stools faces the kitchen. The smells of sizzling beef patties and bubbling oil fryers permeate the quaint restaurant. Some decade-old swing music echoing from a jukebox tucked against the far wall competes with the sound of an enormous metallic contraption that churns ice cream and flavored powder into delicious concoctions. It seems that particular juggernaut is working overtime today as the majority of the shop's patrons crowd around the bar, either slurping down tasty malts or awaiting delivery of one from the frazzled teenager fulfilling their orders.

We scoot ourselves across from one another in a booth, the squeak of the faux leather recalling the unpleasant memory of my first meeting with Charles. However, I can't linger on the sour memory as Aubrey extends me another beautiful smile. "This restaurant seems nice, I've never been here before."

"I've only been a few times myself, but the food's always good so I thought it'd be a nice place for us to try." I glance around the establishment, coming to the realization that there are zero dinosaurs in the vicinity save for the velociraptor seated across from me. The entirely human clientèle peer over their shoulders toward us in between sips of their malts.

Aubrey doesn't size up the location as I do, instead resting her snout atop her palms and batting her eyelashes at me. "I'm not boring you already, am I?"

I catch a small glimpse of the feathers at the end of her

tail swaying under the table, but before I can defend myself a waitress wanders over to us. The bags under her aged eyes communicate a lack of desire to work here, or anywhere for that matter, and her sour expression clashes with the cheerful pink and white stripes of her aproned dress. She scans me, then Aubrey for a long moment before arching her eyebrows. Her several-pack-a-day smoker's rasp rolls past a curled lip. "What can I get for ya?"

My cheeks redden in embarrassment and I glance down. However, Aubrey smiles at the woman. "A cheeseburger and fries would be great, thank you!"

The waitress scribbles on a pad of white paper before turning to me. "And you?" Her tone is curt, and her eyes seem accusatory, as though I should be ashamed for bringing one of *them* into a fine human establishment like this.

"Uh... I-I'll have the same. No tomatoes, please."

With a click of her tongue, the waitress saunters back to the kitchen. I feel like a total idiot, not having considered the implications of bringing Aubrey to a place like this, especially after—

"No tomatoes?" Her playful voice brings my eyes back to hers. "Am I gonna have to be worried about a picky eater around my cooking?"

It takes a second for my brain to catch up. "N-no. I'm not really picky about much. Just don't like raw tomatoes—look, Aubrey. I'm really sorry. I didn't—"

She lifts a finger to stop me and closes her eyes for a moment as she takes a deep breath. When she reopens them, her gaze meets mine with warmth and comfort, her gentle smile putting me at ease. "Don't apologize. I did a lot of thinking over the past couple days, and what you told me outside of Birdland really stuck with me. Do you remember what you said?"

I don't have to search my memory for very long before a small smile creeps onto my lips. "Fuck 'em."

"That's right. I already had my conniption in that jazz club and I was worried I'd ruined the whole night for both of us, but you were a true gentleman and saw past my foolishness. So from now on, I'm not gonna let the looks or sneers bother me." She reaches a hand across the table and places it on mine. "A fella like you is worth a little discomfort from strangers. You better believe I'm a tough woman, so it'll take more than that to discourage me from you."

I know she's sayin' words at me, and they're really nice words, but hot damn my heart is going a mile a minute and I got a lot of blood rushing somewhere it don't belong right now. I opt to stare at her hand on top of mine, trying desperately to contain the thoughts of what I want to do with her.

A dry spell really does things to a guy, y'know?

Literally shaking away the lustful notions, I turn my hand over to accept hers. Her fingers squeeze between mine and her yellow eyes narrow ever so slightly, bringing a rapid end to the tenuous, momentary armistice that I had formed with my libido.

Either my expression is way too telling or Aubrey is practicing to be a mind reader; she lets out a giggle. "This is gonna be fun."

I scrunch up my face, but can't help but smile. "Oh, is that so? You're just doin' this to torment me, huh?"

She gives a playfully wicked grin. "Mmhmm! And you'd better believe I'm gonna *revel* in it!"

We both share a laugh, earning a few more over-the-shoulder glances from the other patrons, but neither Aubrey nor I pay them any mind. Tonight is for us.

Aubrey suggests we play a fun little dating game she had been suggested by one of her book club acquaintances where we take turns asking each other questions. No matter the question, you had to answer it, and you only got to ask one question before the other person got a turn. You also weren't allowed to just say "Same question for you", you had to switch it up and then maybe come back to that earlier one later if you really wanted to ask it.

We pass the imaginary baton back and forth as we learn more about one another, with questions ranging from "Where did you go to high school?" to "If you were a sea creature, what would you be and why?" I got to learn a lot about Aubrey from the game, including that she's an only child like me, and that her favorite jazz song is "Walkin'" by Miles Cratis but her favorite jazz album is *Moanin'* by Art Drakey and the Jazz Couriers. I also learn that she'd be an octopus because they're "majestic" and also they "can dump a bunch of ink out of their asses to run away—when necessary, of course."

Our laughter is briefly interrupted when the waitress returns with our food, two cheeseburgers, one sans tomatoes. Aubrey's eyes light up at the display before meeting mine again. "You ain't asked me what my favorite food is yet."

I chuckle. "I feel like this is a leading question, but why not? What's your fav—"

"Hamburgers! I will never say no to a juicy burger."

"Oh, so you're saying I made a good call with picking this place?"

She nods excitedly as she takes a bite of the burger, but switches to feigned indignance as she speaks past her mouthful. "Hey, you already asked your question, it's my turn!"

I raise an eyebrow. "Isn't it un-lady-like to talk with your mouth full?"

She washes down the meat patty with a swig of water before shaking her head. "I refuse to answer any more questions until I get to ask one." A contemplative talon scratches at the bottom of her snout as I munch on a few of my fries. "Tell me more about this sudden change of career choice. You're working for the Herdsters now, right?"

The question catches me off guard, causing me to sputter on the fried potato in my throat. I paw at my own glass of water and gulp some down to allow me to breathe again. Aubrey doesn't seem to find any deeper meaning in my choke, merely expanding upon her question. "You mentioned it when you called me on Wednesday night, but we didn't really get to talk that much."

She's right about that. I was so frazzled that night that all I could manage was to tell her about my new job and then ask her out. I told her I'd explain more on our date; I'm surprised she waited this long to ask me about it. Maybe she was waiting for me to volunteer the info myself and got impatient. She watches me attentively as she takes another bite of her dinner.

"Not much to tell about it, really." I scratch the back of my neck. "Had a bit of a *fortuitous* meeting, I guess. Ran into a fella who works for the Herdsters. He was impressed by my quality of character and offered me a job."

Aubrey cocks her head. "Well, you're certainly a character, but what did you do that impressed him so much?"

I smirk. "I thought we only got one question." She silently sets her burger down and folds her hands on the table to await my answer. Guess that rule only applies for her. "I returned some lost money to them."

This causes her eyes to widen. "You what?"

I really hate having to do this. I don't like being dishonest, but I can't tell her everything. I gotta give her a *version* of the truth. "I came across an envelope that had money that belonged to them on my way home from work. It was misplaced, musta been lost by the fella who collected it. I returned it and got offered a job for my trouble."

She blinks and shakes her head, trying to piece together the story. "How would you have known the money belonged to the Herdsters?"

"Coincidentally, it was the same envelope Sal Fontana—

the owner of Sal's Butcher and Grocery—had me hand the Herdsters rep earlier. I could tell it was the same one because of his handwriting on it."

She blinks again. "That certainly *is* a mighty coincidence. How much money was in this envelope?"

I shrug. "Dunno exactly, but it was quite a bit. In fact, Charles Rossi gave me a bit of cash out of it as a 'thank you' along with the job offer."

Aubrey's eyes narrow for a moment and go out of focus before they widen toward me. "Did you say 'Rossi'?"

"Y-yeah? You know him?"

She crosses her arms and looks down, a finger tapping on her forearm as she thinks. "Not exactly. I spoke with a cab driver about the Herdsters. He seemed to be a somewhat simple fella, but he had nothing but good things to say about the organization. Mentioned the name 'Rossi'." I breathe a sigh of relief which she quickly cuts off by looking back up at me. "I also did some digging over the past couple days, about the Herdsters. Did you know they're being criminally investigated in several states by the government?"

"No, I didn't." There's no half-truth here, I legitimately didn't know that. I mean, maybe it isn't that surprising given what I know now, but how far in over my head am I?

"No major convictions have stuck yet, but there have been numerous cases tying the Herdsters to organized crime around the country." She reaches past our plates of food to place her hands on top of mine, her face awash with concern. "Are you in trouble with them? Are they making you do anything *illegal?*"

The whispered word sends a chill down my spine but I quickly shake my head. "N-no! I wouldn't do anything like that! I'm an honest guy!"

Her eyes remain on mine, seemingly peering into my soul. After a moment, she smiles and nods. "I know you are, Sammy. That's one of the reasons I like you." She lets the sentiment linger and returns to her meal, glancing out the window next to us with a dreamy expression as she nibbles on her remaining fries.

My heart practically tears in half. On the one hand, she just said she likes me which makes me want to jump out of my chair and cheer. On the other, I just told her I'm an honest guy right after lying to her about my entanglement with the Herdsters. Is this what my life is gonna become? One where I have to talk out both sides of my mouth to not make this woman suspicious of my dealings? How long will that last before I fuck up or, more likely, she catches on? She's not a stupid woman—far from it. She might even sniff out my bullshit before we're even done with dinner.

She turns back to me, a new expression crossing her face. I'm not exactly sure what she's thinking, but she seems to open her mouth to begin speaking before closing it again and reconsidering several times. Finally, she takes a deep breath and gets out what she wanted to ask. "This might seem like a strange request. And please know, I'm not trying to get you into any sort of trouble, not with you being so new to the Herdsters... but if I asked you to do me a favor involving your work, could you do it?"

I blink, somewhat vexed by this sudden question. "I mean, yeah, I'd be happy to. What is it you need me to do?"

She purses her lips. "When I went into the station on Tuesday night, after everything that happened at Birdland, I found out that one of those officers that arrested Miles Cratis is involved with the Herdsters. I'm not exactly sure how, or in what capacity, but I know he was advocating for the Herdsters with some of the other officers. He had pamphlets in his locker." She taps one of her talons on the tabletop as she thinks. "A lot about it doesn't make sense. First off, he's an asshole cop who hurt Miles Cratis and ruined our first date. Second, the police already have a union, one they've used for a lot of years. It doesn't make sense that one fresh-faced recruit would be trying to stir up trouble or get the police to swap unions, especially with all the scrutiny that the Herdsters are under these days."

She looks back up at me and she speaks earnestly. "I'm sorry to ask it of you since you're so new, but could you keep your eyes open for anything suspicious? Anything regarding the police being involved in some way with the Herdsters... could you let me know?" She fidgets. "I'm not a cop, but I still want to do my best and if there's something dirty going on, I need to let Captain Aaron know."

I nod to her. "Yeah, I can do that. I'll be sure to bring you any news of suspicious goings-on I come across."

She smiles and takes my hand again. "Thank you. This means a lot to me."

I return her smile, but realize her request has sealed my fate with the Herdsters. Now I've got no choice but to keep working for them, otherwise she'll figure out something is up. She returns to her nearly finished dinner, polishing off the last bite of her burger and the few remaining bits of potato from her plate.

At this point, there'd only be one clean way out of my arrangement, and that'd be to get the hell out of dodge. I try to put on a playful tone. "Hey, since you got to ask me like ten questions in a row, that means I get a few, right?" She smiles and shrugs, still chewing the last bit of her food. "Would you ever consider not living in Old York City?" She cocks a perplexed eyebrow at me past her glass of water. "Y'know, moving somewhere less crowded, less bustling? A small town."

She shakes her head. "I've already finished with that part of my life. I grew up in a small town, and it was boring. Something about this place makes me feel more fulfilled."

"But what about your dream of becoming a police officer?"

This makes her expression tighten. "What about it?"

"I mean—don't you think you might have a better shot of becoming a cop for a smaller town? It'd be less of a risk to—"

"What, so I can track down Farmer Bill's escaped pigs and maybe break up a bar fight once every two months? What kind of life would that be? I'd be better off not doing it at all if I'm not gonna do anything useful." Though I sense some bitterness in her words, she seems to try to rein herself in. "Part of the reason I moved to Old York in the first place was to be somewhere where I could make a real difference. That just won't happen over in Podunk."

"I didn't mean any offense, it was just—"

"I know. You were trying to offer an alternative to accommodate my situation. It's something a lot of people have done for me since…" She trails off, her expression becoming more sullen as her head sinks. Just as I'm about to reach across the table and put a reassuring hand on hers, she lifts her eyes again. They are filled with sorrow. "Do you think I can be a cop?"

My hand completes its journey, coming to rest on hers. She immediately accepts it, tightening her fingers around mine. "Of course I do, Aubrey. You're one of the strongest women I've ever met. You charged into battle like you were gettin' off one of those landing crafts on D-Day, and that was literally the first time I met you. The amount of passion and zeal you showed when Miles Cratis was bein' arrested was, frankly, intimidating." This earns a small giggle past her clouded eyes. "But that's the kind of woman you are. You're one of a kind, and I think the police force would be foolish to not let you help protect this city."

She bites her lip. "Thank you, Sammy. You're one of a kind, too."

I want to lean forward and kiss her, but the clatter of our plates being removed by the annoyed waitress breaks both of us out of the moment. She glares down at us like she caught two teenagers trying to sneak out late at night before letting out a huff. "Anythin' else for ya?"

I glance at Aubrey who dabs at her eyes with a napkin. "A couple chocolate malts?" She nods at me. "A couple chocolate malts." My repeated request sends the waitress back toward the kitchen with a roll of her eyes. I shrug and speak quietly. "The staff usually aren't this rude. Must be the heat."

Aubrey giggles. "Must be!" She balls up the soiled napkin, damp with a few loosed tears and some makeup smudges. Though the moment for a comforting kiss has passed, she pulls my hands into hers again, beaming her beautiful smile at me from across the table.

I meant what I said about her being a terrific cop, if she was given the opportunity, but there's still the one thing. Her physical impairment that kept her from being able to dance with me to the more upbeat song at the jazz club. And if her knee is bad enough that it can't handle that sorta exertion…

"Hey, Aubrey. If you don't mind, could I ask about your—"

My question is cut short by the sudden dousing of lights in the restaurant. Aubrey and I both glance above us at the darkened light fixture, then around the rest of the establishment. The music comes to a slow end, the record needle murmuring out the dying breath of some poor swing record that won't complete its rotation. The hums of the busy malt mixers fade out, earning surprised gasps and annoyed moans from the waiting patrons.

I look back to Aubrey. "Did—did the power just go out?"

She stares out the window. "Uhh, I think so, and then some." I follow her pointing finger out to the street and the surrounding structures. Not a single electric light can be seen performing its duty. The towering building across the road stands black and ominous, only lit by the waning sun and its reflection offered by the early moon. Several windows of apartments above are thrown open, and confused heads poke out, surveying the road and the building in which our currently darkened restaurant resides.

I scratch the back of my neck. "Well, this is a new one. Can't say I've ever had a blackout happen during a date!"

Aubrey turns back to me with a smile. "Let's hope it's not a sign of bad luck. You'd let me know if you were a walking jinx, right?"

"Well, my uncle is a black cat and I frequently spend my weekends walking underneath ladders."

"You goofball." Aubrey looks past me toward the entrance. A few customers have wandered out of the restaurant, while others sit around remarking about the occurrence. "Well, does this mean we aren't gonna get those malts?"

"I imagine that fella still knows how to stir with a spoon, right? We might as well enjoy the ice cream and wait for everything to come back on."

It turns out, the panicked teenager was *not* up to the task of hand-stirring chocolate malts, and the fry cook, presently without power or light in his kitchen, stormed out into the store front to handle the ice cream orders while sentencing the teen to mopping duty. The bad temper of our waitress is now on full display as she loudly curses after banging her shin on a chair leg in the lackluster lighting. She mutters further obscenities as she limps into the back of the restaurant.

After several minutes, the irritated fry cook extends Aubrey and I the best smile he can as he presents us with two hand-stirred chocolate malts and our check. I quickly scoop up the slip of paper and fetch a few bucks out of my wallet to cover the bill and a tip. Aubrey smiles at me and bats her eyelashes as she takes the first sip of her chocolate treat, speaking up when I sample my own malted delight.

"You know, I *am* gonna pay for some of our dates. I

appreciate you being a gentleman and all, but you'd better not spoil me."

"Hey, I just got this new job and all. I want to spoil you a *bit*."

Her eyes playfully narrow as she takes another sip, but the cold provided by my own malt pales in comparison to the chill that fires up my spine as her ankle brushes against my leg underneath the table. Just as quickly as it made its presence known, it disappears again, the only sign of the wayward appendage being the sassy smile on Aubrey's lips.

Language has forsaken me. "I—uhh, I was—umm. I was gonna ask—uhh—"

I cannot remember what I was going to ask. There's really just one thought rolling through my head at this moment, and it ain't the head on top of my shoulders.

Another fifteen minutes go by as we finish our malts, the delicious chilled beverage doing well to soothe my heated *everything*. A few more questions pass between the two of us, but our interest in the conversation is frequently sidelined by the world of darkness. The power still hasn't come back on, and most of the other patrons have left. The waitress finally makes her way back out to the front, collecting the check and my payment and offering a smile when I tell her to keep the change. However, she also lets us know that they're going to lock up in the next few minutes.

Aubrey and I oblige the suggestion, making our way out to the blackened street. The only lights visible are those of the headlamps of passing cars, and it seems even the vehicles are making themselves scarce in this strange occurrence. The skyline is haunting, a distressing level of shadow that I've only seen a handful of times. Sure, blackouts have occurred before, but this one seems to stretch on forever. Usually a blackout is a single building or, at worst, a city block or two. But save for the straggling vehicles on the road, everything is just *off*.

I offer a hand to Aubrey which she accepts readily. "The theater is only a couple blocks away. You okay walkin' over there?"

She lifts an eyebrow. "I doubt a theater is gonna do us much good now, what with them needing, ya know, *electricity* to play the movie and all."

"Hey, smarty. I figure the power might be back on by the time we get there, or maybe we wait around for a few minutes."

"And if it isn't?"

"I guess we call it a night and get you a cab back home?"

She ponders for a moment before nodding. "Alright. Let's do that."

We make our way down the sidewalk, strolling together hand in hand like a young married couple. We pass by several people who mill around, perplexed and impressed by the marvel of such a catastrophic failure of our city's infrastructure. Guess they weren't lying when they said folks shouldn't leave their refrigerators open. Maybe one too many grannies without an air conditioner did that and blew the whole fuckin' city's power grid.

Still, the darkened skyline affords a strange, otherworldly beauty to the space above and around us. If I was out here by myself I might be a bit freaked out, but with Aubrey by my side it almost comes across as romantic. The passing cars and chatter of people offer a familiar aural backdrop, but the absence of the constant thrum of electricity is noticeable. It offers a certain level of calmness you don't normally feel unless you're far away from the skyscraper-laden landscape, surrounded by trees and flowers instead of light poles and buried electrical wires.

We arrive at the theater with nothing but a further darkened sky above us. At this point the sun has fully set, leaving us only with the moonlight and the somehow still hot air around us. I step up to the box office, glancing through the glass to find absolutely nobody manning it. Aubrey raises an eyebrow at me as I turn back to her. "So? How long we wanna wait?"

I feign indignance. "Geez, am I that miserable to be around that you wanna ditch me so fast?"

She giggles before stepping closer to me and planting a quick kiss on my cheek. "You know that's not what I meant. I'm just a little worried that the power might not come back on and that I won't be able to get a cab back home." I glance up and down the street, noticing a significant lack of typical traffic for this hour. Even with the setting sun, taxis are normally numerous, but it seems they are going into hiding this evening.

I notice a bench beneath a couple movie posters leading up to the theater's entrance. I lead Aubrey over to it and offer her a seat which she accepts. The slight overhang of the theater marquee, normally covered with dazzling lights, instead offers even more darkness in the continued outage. With a sigh, I take a seat next to Aubrey.

She glances at me with concern. "Everything okay?"

I shrug. "Well. I'm not sure what to do now. I was planning to give this to you with, you know, *light* so you could actually see it, but that might not be possible tonight."

Her mouth hangs open for a moment. "G-give? Give me what?"

I withdraw the slender rectangular box from my pocket, having been careful to keep it concealed from Aubrey during our date. "Just something I thought you'd like. But if you can't even see it—"

Her eyes dart from the box back up to my face. "U-um! I can actually still see pretty well! Velociraptors have good low-light vision, y'know! Not as good as *some* species of dinosaurs, but it's pretty good! And—well—and—" Her fingers fidget on her lap and her tail quivers in anticipation.

I offer her a smile. "Okay. I still think it looks a lot nicer in the light, but it'll look nice on you no matter what." I slowly lift the lid of the box and present the crescent moon necklace to Aubrey.

Her hands fly up to her mouth as she gasps, the trace amounts of moonlight glinting from her saucepan eyes. *"Oh! Oh, Sammy!"* Her trembling fingers lift the pendant from its velvet-lined resting place, her thumb sliding across its smooth silver face. "It's beautiful. I love it!"

"May I?" Her eyes find mine again as I lift the necklace out of the box and unclasp it. Reaching forward gently, I bring the two ends together at the back of her neck, our faces coming within inches of one another. With the clasp reconnected, the pendant rests just above the collar of her dress, shimmering in the increasingly limited light of the actual moon high above us. I smile at her. "It looks really nice on—"

She doesn't let me finish the sentence, bringing her lips to mine and wrapping her arms around my shoulders. The gesture, while a little surprising in its suddenness, is entirely welcomed as I return her kiss, resting my hands on the flat of her back as I beckon her toward myself. She scoots closer, exploring my tongue with hers, drawing in breaths between each kiss. Her eyes close in bliss as we share the passionate exchange, heat radiated amidst the still sweltering night air around us.

She eventually withdraws, placing her forehead against mine as she lightly pants. Her eyes reopen, focusing on mine with desire and adoration. "Sammy..."

My heart leaps at the potential words that might follow her utterance of my name. I wonder if she's about to say the same thing I want to say to her, that I've *wanted* to say to her. Is the second date too soon to say it? Because to hell with the rules, I know what I feel in my heart.

"I—"

"We're *closed!*"

The shrill voice causes both Aubrey and I to jump and spin toward its source. The theater's door is held ajar and a grouchy ankylosaurus pokes his large flat-topped head through the opening. I sputter in response. "Uhh! S-sorry! We were—that is, are you—"

"We're *closed*. Can't you see that the power's out everywhere? No power, no movies. Now *beat it!*" With a puff of air from his slitted nostrils, he slams the door. The sound of its lock latching into place offers additional finality where it wasn't needed.

Of all the rotten timing. I slowly turn back to Aubrey whose look is far off. I expected to get a giggle out of her, but she seems to be in another world altogether. "Geez. Sorry about that."

Her eyes focus on me, but her gaze still seems distracted. "I-it's okay. Let's get a cab. I should get home."

I nod to her and rise from the bench; she follows suit. I offer her my hand which she quickly accepts, the redness of her cheeks clearly visible even in the limited light.

We begin making our way down the street back in the direction from which we came. I glance around for any sign of the telltale yellow and black checkers, but see no symmetrical patterned shapes on vehicles for several blocks. Very few cars are on the road at all, and none of them seem to be taxis.

Aubrey appears to be looking as well, but her expression shifts between far off distraction and some sort of flustered annoyance. Her tail that had been happily swaying behind her all night has wrapped itself around her midsection; she cradles its feathered end with her free hand. I consider asking her if everything's okay, but I can only guess how that would go or if she'd even give me a straight answer. Did I do something to upset her? I don't think I did; she seemed to really like the necklace that's still hanging around her neck.

For a moment her eyes meet mine, then quickly dart away as her cheeks deepens another shade.

Is that it? Is she—

Aw, geez. That *would* be going awfully fast, even for two divorcees on a dry spell. I mean, *I'm* on a dry spell. Guess I don't know about her. But is she getting nervous about... that? The possibility of us—I mean, we're both adults, right? We can decide when it's right to—

"I don't see any cabs." She stops in place, still holding my hand and cradling her tail.

I turn to face her. "Me neither. This is a really weird night." Her eyes don't wander away from mine. "How far away do you live?"

"A ways. Too far to walk, at least at night."

I gulp. The stagnant heat doesn't relent in the slightest, causing my brow to pummel me with sweat. My heart attempts to burst its way out of my chest and crawl down the sidewalk in search of less stressful pastures. Meanwhile, Aubrey continues gazing at me with her twinkling yellow eyes, diamond pupils shimmering and full of vulnerability.

I barely hear myself say the words as they roll past my lips.

"Do you want to come up to my place?"

Chapter Eleven: Aubrey

Oh my God.

He asked me.

He really asked me to—

You'll just let him down.

But he asked me to come up to his place. That means—exactly what I think it means. We're both adults, after all. We're both familiar with what comes next. We both *want* this.

No, you don't. This is way too fast for you, isn't it?

It's a little fast, yeah. But—

You just got done telling yourself how you wanted to slow things down, and now you're gonna have sex with the guy? You're a walking contradiction, ain't ya?

I am not, I know what I'm doing.

I glance back up at Sammy. His eyes are wide and his posture rigid. "Uhh! I-I didn't mean it like th-that! If you're—ya know, I mean—if that's—"

I squeeze his hand, bringing his stuttered backpedaling to a swift halt. "I'd like that."

His mouth hangs open in shock. "O-okay. I'm j-just a couple blocks away." He spins on his heel and begins marching toward our destination like a drill sergeant just gave him a direct order. His nervousness is actually pretty cute.

Slut.

I shake my head, feeling my feathers bristle in my hand. I don't know when the tip of my tail climbed into my grasp, but every time I try to will it away it just shudders in defiance and stays where it is.

It's telling you this is a mistake.

Shut up.

Sammy nervously glances over his shoulder at me a few times, perhaps worried that I'll suddenly have a change of heart, but I follow along down the darkened sidewalks. Truthfully, my own mind is swimming with emotions. I was so close to saying something to him back underneath the marquee, after he gave me this beautiful necklace and shared a passionate kiss with me. I felt safer in his arms than I have in months, maybe years. I felt for him—I *feel* for him something I haven't experienced in longer than I can remember.

You don't love him.

I... might. I wanted to say it. I wanted to whisper it to him and continue exploring him. I think—

You don't love him. You don't deserve him. You're worthless.

Shut up. I'm not going through this tonight. Not when he's so close to me. Not when I want to be with him.

You'll only disappoint him. He'll want nothing to do with you.

Please, shut up. I don't want to hear it.

Why would anyone want anything to do with you, after what you did?

Shut—

"This is the place." Sammy's voice distracts me as he brings us to a stop in front of a five story apartment building sandwiched between two much more impressive looking structures. It's clearly in need of some upkeep because it sticks out like a sore thumb, with several vestiges of wood and brick dangling limply from its surface. Sammy scratches the back of his neck. "S-sorry, it's not much to look at."

I smile, drawing myself closer to him—

Neither are you, Aubie.

"I-I don't mind." My words stutter from my mouth, but Sammy smiles at me.

"Okay. Uhh, I think I got a flashlight in my apartment, but I'm up on the fourth floor. Want me to go get it?"

Ha! Not even in his home yet and he's already trying to abandon you!

Shut up!

"N-no, I'll come along."

He glances down at my leg. "I'm sorry it's so high up. Will your knee be alright?"

Worthless limb on a worthless woman.

"Yeah. I'll just take it slow and careful."

He nods and smiles. "Okay." As we step toward the door, he abruptly stops. "Oh, one other thing. I have a neighbor who's—well, for lack of a nicer way to put it, he's a real piece of shit. Not that I'm trying to sneak you in or anything, but for both our sake, it'd probably be better if he didn't swing open his door and start shit with us. He'd definitely be the kind to do that."

Already ashamed of you around his neighbors, what a catch this guy is, indeed!

I swear to God.

"Th-that's okay." I offer him a smile, though I know my expression is all sorts of fucked right now. Of any night for me to get a little reprieve from this bullshit, I wish it'd be tonight.

We travel up the small stoop leading to the front door;

Sammy pulls it open and gestures for me to enter, ever the gentleman.

A gentleman you don't deserve.

Sammy silently closes the door behind himself before nodding toward the stairs leading up to the second floor landing. I take his hand again, feeling his warmth through our connected limbs. He offers me the side nearest the banister, but I slowly ascend without its aid, continuing to cradle my damned tail. I try shoving it aside but it snaps back into place like it's spring-loaded.

At the second floor, we turn to wrap back around and find the first stair leading up to the third story. However, the wood boards beneath our feet squeak and groan loudly with our steps, another sign of the building's age. As we nearly pass the door of this level, it clicks open, a trace amount of light escaping through the crack.

Oh no.

Busted!

"Izzat you, Samuel?" A raspy, elderly voice emanates from the opening.

Sammy turns toward the voice, giving my hand a little squeeze as he does so. "Oh, good evening, Mr. Garbowitz. I'm sorry, did I wake you?"

The door widens further, revealing a gallimimus gentleman who appears to be in his twilight years. He stares at Sammy past enormous, thick-rimmed glasses that rest tenuously at the end of his snout. "Ohh, no, you didn't wake me. I'd usually still be watching my shows, but this electrical outage has put a damper on my TrawlNet enjoyment." His head quivers as he slowly turns in my direction. A moment goes by before his eyes widen and a sly smile crosses his weathered lips. "What's this? A lady caller this evening?"

Sammy nervously replies. "Uhh—well, y'see—I was on a date with—"

The elderly neighbor chuckles playfully. "Well? Are you going to introduce me or are you just going to stammer?"

I take the initiative away from my incapacitated date, extending a hand. "I'm Aubrey Carter. It's a pleasure to meet you, sir."

Another grin crosses his face. "Please, call me Harold. I've been trying to get Samuel to call me Harold for months now but he just won't do it!" He accepts my hand, but rather than shaking it plants a quivering kiss on my fingers.

I can't help but smile at the show of courtesy, but Samuel places his hands on his hips. "What's this about? Are you trying to steal Aubrey away from me, Mr. Garbowitz?"

Harold chuckles again, but doesn't answer. Instead he turns his slow neck back into his apartment. "This power outage might not be ending for a while. If the boys downtown haven't fixed it by now, they probably won't fix it 'til morning at the earliest. Come on in, let me get you two some candles." He doesn't wait for us to accept his invitation before wandering deeper into his own home, leaving the door wide open in his wake.

Sammy turns to me with a shrug and a whisper. "This isn't the neighbor I was warning you about, by the way. That'd be Roger up on three who's an asshole."

I giggle. "I figured this wasn't the bad one, unless you're actually worried about Harold stealing me away." I stick out my tongue before stepping into the apartment, earning a speechless look from my date.

Some date. Now you're wasting time with an old codger. How pathetic.

I distract myself from the ceaseless intrusions by glancing around the dimly lit room. A myriad of candles are sprinkled throughout the home, shedding enough light to give the space a feeling of nostalgic comfort. However, the coziness is betrayed by the mountains of newspaper that adorn almost every surface, with numerous towers of the folded parchments piled in each discernible corner of the room. The only clearly visible furniture is a recliner parked in front of a small television screen and the twin-sized mattress against the far wall.

Harold slowly hobbles over to a small kitchen cupboard, expending a bit of effort to bend over and rummage through its contents. I peek over my shoulder and gasp, quickly snatching up a few candles and knocking the newspapers they were sitting on top of to the floor. Before Harold can complete his slow rotation to glance at the racket, I've put the candles back down on the non-fire-hazard bookshelf surface and face him with an innocent grin.

He grins in return. "Ahh, don't mind the clutter. Years of reading the paper tends to accumulate, I'm afraid." He turns back to the cupboard; Samuel merely shrugs at me. I guess he's aware of his neighbor's hoarding habit. I'd just prefer to not burn to death tonight is all.

Spending all night here? Yeah fuckin' right. You'll be on your ass in the street before—

Shut up!

With a half dozen small candles grasped between his knobbly fingers, Harold begins the slow trek back to Sammy and I. He grins again, peering at me past his enormous spectacles. "So... erm, Aubrey, was it?"

"Yes, sir."

"Aubrey. How did you meet this fine young gentleman?"

Pure, stupid coincidence.

"H-he recognized a jazz song I was humming at a bus stop and struck up a conversation about it."

His grin widens and his journey is half-completed. "A jazz enthusiast, are you? I know Samuel enjoys that music, but I've always been more fond of ragtime myself. Don't listen to it so much anymore, but Greta and I used to love dancing to it."

I perk up. "Greta is your wife?"

He nods, though looks a bit sorrowful. "She was. Died about six years ago."

"Oh, I'm sorry, sir."

He shakes his head, replacing the solemn look with a warm smile. "That's life. But enough about me. This Samuel you bagged is quite a fella. Did you know, he brings my morning paper up to my door every day!"

Through my peripheral vision, I notice Sammy scratch the back of his neck. "It's no trouble."

Harold shakes his head again, still a few shuffled paces away. "No, no. Don't sell yourself short, son. You're the only neighbor I have who would do that for me." His eyes take on a weary look of self-realization. "It's only getting harder for me to get up and down those stairs, so that little gesture means a lot to an old man like me."

He's finally arrived close enough for Sammy to accept his gift. "Thank you, Mr. Garbowitz. For the nice words, and for the candles, too."

A shaky hand finds its way to Sammy's arm; Harold gazes at my date with a warm smile. "Greta and I were never able to have any children of our own, but if I had a son, I'd have hoped he'd be a kind man like you." He blinks. "Ah, do you have a lighter in your home? I could find one for—"

Sammy cuts him off. "I should have some matches, it's alright. Thank you though!"

Harold slowly turns my way, extending a hand. "It was a pleasure meeting you, Aubrey!"

My hand reflexively finds his to complete the parting gesture, but I say nothing. I can't say anything. Not past—

You're trying not to think about it, ain't ya? You're not pulling one over on me. That ain't how this game works and you know it.

Shut up.

I do everything in my power to not look rude as I make my way back into the hall with Sammy. He doesn't seem to notice my contorted expression in the near pitch-black hall, simply offering his free hand to me again as we continue the journey upward.

See, I know what you know. I'm in here just as much as you are. I ain't even real, just a voice in your fuckin' head. So who's really the bad guy here, huh? Is it me? Or is it the daffy bitch who can't get over—

Shut up.

We arrive at the third floor, Sammy doing everything in his power to move cautiously and quietly past this door. I tiptoe along with him, trying—

Watch your step. You wouldn't want—

Shut. Up.

Sammy glances back at me before nodding upward. He said he's on the fourth floor. One more to go.

You don't belong here. You don't belong with any man. Not after what you did.

Please stop. Please. Not tonight.

"This is the place."

Sammy glances at me nervously before fishing around in a pocket for his key. Inserting it into the lock, a soft click grant us admittance to his—

"Boof!"

What looks to be a throw rug on legs dances in place within the darkened apartment, tail wagging and tongue flopping freely from its owner's mouth. Beady black eyes gaze up at Sammy, but the creature's excitement doubles when it notices my presence.

"Heya, Saxon. How ya doin', buddy? But what did I tell you about that barkin'?" The dog gives an acknowledging rumble as it accepts Sammy's affection. "Aubrey, this is Saxon. Saxon, Aubrey."

I step into the home, momentarily distracted from my internal tormentor by the adorable shaggy hound that prances over to me. His tail wags happily as I pet the furry beast. "Oh, my. Hello there, Saxon. Even more handsome than your owner, I see!"

Nice one. Why not just tell the skinnie he's ugly to his face?

I stop scratching Saxon's head and straighten up, my face contorting further in a furious grimace. Already bored of me, the dog spins back toward his owner as Sammy rummages in a kitchen drawer. "Here we go. Let's get these candles lit." He sets the wax cylinders on a tiny dining room table before striking a match and bringing it to wick, allowing a moment for the flame to pass to each candle.

With a flick of his wrist, the match extinguishes and Sammy puts his hands on his hips. "Better. At least we can see *somethin'* now!" His eyes meet mine; with effort, I've reset my expression back to a neutral one. "Hey, uhh—sorry to do this, but I gotta take this big lunk out to potty. If I don't, he's gonna make a stinky mess in here. Will you be alright for a minute while I run downstairs?" I nod, and with a snap of his fingers the sheepdog falls in tow behind him. Sammy gives me a smile before the patter of feet belonging to both dog and human descend outside the now closed door.

As the subtle illumination continues to brighten the room, I take in the spartan furnishings and near complete lack of decoration. Though the space is clean, there's hardly anything here. Not even a couch or television reside in the apartment, only a single wooden chair next to the minuscule dining room table.

Wow, you sure picked a winner, didn't you?

I cautiously step across the room, my eyes coming to rest on the small bed tucked into the opposite corner. Next to it, a shoddy end table holds—

Wait. Is that a clock radio? I move closer, bending down to examine it.

It's the same kind that I have.

Guess that's all this skinnie can afford in this dump.

I straighten up, balling my fists. Shut up. I mean it.

What? I'm just tellin' ya what you already know! What you're too afraid to say out loud. This skinnie is a broke chump.

My eyes close and my lip curls. That's not true. He got a new job, and besides that, why would I give a shit how much money he has? He makes me happy.

Pfft. Yeah, that's gonna solve your problems. How's he gonna provide for you, huh?

I don't *need* him to provide for me. I can do that for myself. Hell, I could provide for *both* of us!

Some modern woman you are! What next, you'll have him puttin' on an apron and washing the dishes? Get real.

Shut up! Why can't you just leave me alone?!

Leave you alone? You dumb bitch, I AM you! I ain't a fuckin' ghost, though I might as well be with how quick you betrayed me—

"Shut up!"

"Whoah, Aubrey? Is everything okay?!" I spin around to watch as the door latches shut behind the man whose home I'm standing in.

The realization of my verbalized outburst causes me to stammer. "I-I'm fine! Everything's okay! I was just lookin' at your—at your clock radio here! It's the same one I got at home!"

Real smooth. He knows you're a fuckin' nutcase now. Pack it up, you blew it, just like I knew you would.

My voice shakes. "U-umm—th-this is a good brand! I picked this one cuz it's got a great speaker and really carries the depth of bass notes well. M-most speakers sound too tinny or washed out!"

What are you babbling about now? Look at him! He's getting annoyed with you!

Sammy cautiously steps forward, momentarily glancing

at the clock radio before bringing his eyes back to me. "You look pale. Are you sure you're alright?"

My legs start shaking. "I-I remember hearing 'So What' on it for th-the first time. Did you know that even th-though the written key signature of 'So What' has no sh-sharps or flats, it has a tonic chord of D and uses the Dorian scale? This m-makes the tonal center change and—and—"

This is pathetic. Just throw yourself out the fuckin' window already and be done with it.

"Aubrey, you're freakin' me out. What's going on?"

It wouldn't be the first time you cast yourself down and ruined a man's life, would it? Would it?!

I try to blink the tears back. "I... I..."

My knees give out. I crumple, my tail coiling so tightly around me that it threatens to cut off its own circulation. My hands clap over my face, covering the shame of my muffled sobs.

In an instant, Sammy is on his knees next to me, placing gentle but confused hands on my shoulders. His touch only makes me shrink further inward. "Aubrey..."

You can't do anything right. You're a disgrace. You won't even tell him what's got you so upset, will you, Aubie?

My stomach churns, the hollow pit within screaming out in silent agony.

Because if you do tell him, he won't want you anymore.

I grit my teeth, trying to suppress my weeping.

What man would?

With all of my might, I lower my hands and open my eyes. Past the tear-clouded haze, I see Sammy. He is inches away, face awash with worry and fear. He says nothing but keeps his hands on my shoulders, gently rubbing his thumbs up and down my scales to try and calm me. He watches intently as I do everything in my power to compose myself.

What man would want a broken woman like you?

If any man would, it would be Sammy. Please, God. Let it be Sammy.

I draw in a shaky breath and step toward oblivion.

"Eight months ago... I was in the hospital..."

—

The first thing I remembered was a rhythmic electronic thrum. I recalled hearing it and immediately superimposing the furtive piano intro of Art Drakey's "Moanin'" on top of it. The beat didn't quite line up, but the ivory in my mind slowed itself adequately to keep time.

Despite the steady beeping belonging to a heart monitor, I didn't know where I was. I couldn't open my eyes and my head hurt like a son of a bitch. The pain came in waves, starting off localized and manageable before spreading out across my body. First was my arms. Even attempting to lift them off of the bed beneath me was a herculean effort, and the moment I tried the bruises and lacerations made themselves aggressively known. Dull throbs and stings fired through my scales and elbow feathers until I stopped trying.

Next was my back. Any effort to sit up was only met with agonized soreness, my vertebrae entirely uncooperative. I wasn't sure if my tail was still attached to my body since I couldn't see or feel it at all. In reality, it hung next to me in a separate ceiling-suspended sling, but I wouldn't know that for a while yet.

Around the time I began trying to unsuccessfully test my neck's range of motion, a set of footsteps made their way past Art Drakey's everlasting piano solo. Some murmured voices later, the footsteps vanished again. After a few more minutes of trying and failing to turn my head, a voice appeared.

"Aubrey, are you awake?"

I thought I replied "Yes, I'm awake," but in reality my

teeth didn't move and my tongue didn't flex. All I provided was an affirmative moan.

"Good. I'm Dr. Weber. Do you know where you are right now?"

"No, I don't," I grumbled past my still half-paralyzed mouth with a single guttural syllable.

"You're at the Metropolitan Hospital. Do you have any memory of what happened?"

To this, I responded with neither grunt nor gurgle. Instead, I racked my brain, trying to decrypt the riddle of what would cause me to end up in a hospital, and in a state like this.

I heard a chair slide forward and felt a set of fingers lightly come to rest on my own. "I'm terribly sorry to say this... but you had an accident."

An accident? What sort of—

"Your neighbors called us. Said that they heard a loud crash in your home. When they went to investigate, the front door was open. And you were inside, unconscious."

I tried to shake my head, convinced this was just an elaborate dream involving sleep paralysis. I was probably just aching because of—

"You fell down the stairs." He sighs. "You've been here for two weeks. And..."

No. Oh my God, no.

"You had a miscarriage. We couldn't save the child. I'm sorry."

This isn't real. This isn't real. This isn't rea—

All at once, agonizing pain fired through my right knee. It felt as though someone was prying my knee cap off of my body with a pair of rusty tongs, wrenching the cartilage and tearing the tendons loose. I screamed, opening my mouth as wide as I could, forcing any air that had found its way into my broken body out in a single, sustained shriek. At once, the doctor scrambled upward, barking orders to someone else. I didn't even feel the needle pierce my arm. Slowly, the pain in my knee subsided and my consciousness slipped away once more.

My baby. I lost my baby.

When I regained consciousness, the pain returned immediately, but this time I did not scream. I wanted to. I wanted so desperately to wail and gnash my teeth, I wanted to fly from the bed and destroy everything around me. I wanted to draw razor blades across my wrists.

Instead, I ran away. Deep in the recesses of my mind, buried in the alcoves and twisting hallways, I came across a small lounge. Within, a single record player with a mountain of records stacked next to it greeted me. All of my favorites were here: John Coalmane, Miles Cratis, Art Drakey, Horace Bronze; album after album after album, all excitedly waiting to find their way to the record spindle to dazzle and enthrall me with their joyous, energetic highs and their solemn, soulful lows.

The doctors would come and go, asking me how I was feeling, testing my appendages, administering more medicine. I barely responded to them. I had no interest. I was too enraptured by the music, hidden away in the one place where pain couldn't find me. Slowly, the splints and bandages were removed as the scrapes and bruises healed.

Of course, the worst of it was my knee. The doctors explained that my leg had essentially twisted itself around a hundred and eighty degrees during my descent. Even after setting it back into place with surgery, the likelihood of the appendage being completely paralyzed was so high it was practically a guarantee. Even if I did miraculously retain feeling in my lower leg, the knee would never be the same.

Their words rolled over me inconsequentially, drowned out by blissful brass and playful percussion. Even as they poked and prodded the cartilage, searing pain blasting through the appendage and the rest of my body, I didn't flinch or groan. I was too enraptured by Miles Cratis, playing songs he'd never played for anyone else, just for me in my own personal sanctuary. I knew the records well enough to remember most without flaw, but after expending my internal catalog several times my imagination started forming improv sessions, combinations of sounds and styles that sometimes worked and sometimes didn't. That's the true joy of jazz—many times artists just throw things at the wall and see what sticks. Despite my broken body, within my mind I had found paradise.

However, it was short-lived. The first time I registered any sort of outward emotion after my initial outburst was when they switched me to a new bed, one that would support me sitting up. Until then I'd been content to merely stare at the ceiling whenever my eyes weren't closed, pissing into a bag and caring about no one and nothing around me. I'd shut everything out in favor of my music. But when they situated me on the new mattress, my eyes were able to lower themselves for the first time to...

My stomach. My smooth, hollow form and the now vacant womb it concealed. The pronounced bulge that had once hidden an infant no more than a month away from breathing its first breath, letting out its first cry, opening its eyes for the first time was absent. In its place... nothing. Emptiness. A void filled only with "what could have been".

All at once, the music stopped. The only sound was that of the retching sobs that leaked past my gritted teeth. Tears streamed down my cheeks and I went into a panic. The nurses who had just transported me had to restrain my arms as I began grasping at my midsection, convinced it was an optical illusion and that my baby was still there, obscured by the hospital gown or the odd angle. My baby was so close to being born. They were going to fill my life with joy and love. I wanted them so badly.

I only calmed down when they jammed another needle

into my arm and fired more chemicals into my body. As sleep overtook me, the vision of my little miracle smiling up at me as I cradled them in my arms faded away forever.

It was the last time I cried in the hospital.

My first visitor didn't arrive until a week after I initially woke up. The tall pterodactyl stepped through the doorway holding a small vase stuffed full of flowers. He set it on the vacant table next to my bed before peering down at me. My eyes were open, focusing on nothing in particular as another rip-roaring solo blasted through my internal record player's immaculate speaker. Hiding in my lounge had transitioned to less of an escape from the physical pain since most of my bruises had healed and my knee, still bound in a sling, had reduced its presence to a dull throbbing. Now the music had become an escape from my emotions.

He offered a gentle, sad smile. "How are you holding up, Carter?"

I didn't respond.

"The others from the station send their well-wishes and sympathies. Believe it or not, Ruth was asking about you. Was worried because she hadn't seen you for a few weeks."

The name barely meant anything to me.

The captain pulled over a chair and sat next to the bedside. He folded his hands in his lap, staring at the space between his feet for a moment before he raised his eyes to me again. "Do you remember what happened?"

My only response was to turn my head and meet his gaze. My expression was apathetic. I did not smile, nor did I frown. I just looked at the being seated next to me before turning away from him again to stare at nothing.

I remembered what happened. I didn't at first, but it returned to me. The late-night carefree whistling. The lackadaisical attitude. The smell of bourbon on his breath. The shouting match. My pleas with him to change his ways, to go back to being the man that I had married instead of the drunken oaf he had become.

I remembered his yell, and the shove that sent me into the air. I remembered seeing his eyes for the last time, hazy, incoherent, and utterly loveless as they rose into the sky.

I remembered the blame. The blame on my husband for being in such a drunken stupor that he would do that to me, but even more than that, the blame on myself. Blame for putting myself in that position, for having married a man capable of doing something like this. Blame for not catching the railing of the stairs and preventing my fall. Blame for being so careless with such a precious life inside of me that was now lost forever.

I had convinced myself that my child's death was my fault.

I spoke none of this aloud, content to return to my music, but the captain placed a hand on mine as though in reply. "I'm terribly sorry this happened to you, Aubrey. Truly sorry. I can't even imagine."

Captain Aaron was the only visitor I received.

—

The candles atop the dining room table are about halfway consumed. At some point during my rambling, Sammy had helped me to my feet and set me on the edge of his bed before quickly retrieving the solitary dining room chair and sliding it over to sit across from me. Though I didn't see his face for most of my story, my focus too far off as I recalled that horrific time, his attention never strayed from me. He didn't interrupt, merely listening to the words that tumbled past my lips. Even Saxon was patient and attentive, lounging on a nearby folded blanket on the floor, peering at me past the strands of shaggy white hair that hung over his eyes.

I stare at my shoes, my eyes dry and weary. A faint smile tugs at my lips as I gently shift my right knee. It feels tense after the several flights of stairs and my topple to the floor, but it still moves. "Frankly, it's a blessing that my knee still works. It took a lot of physical therapy, and it's still not perfect, but I'm glad I don't have to use a cane or a wheelchair. Now, it's a reminder, I guess. One I'll probably always have, for the rest of my life."

I bring my eyes up to Sammy's. He meets them attentively, his face awash with sympathy. I try to smile, but my lip quivers. "That's everything. That's all of me. I wanted to tell you all of this sooner—I *needed* to be honest with you about everything—but I just couldn't until it boiled over." I fight back the tears that begin churning up again. "I'm a broken woman, Sammy. I was going to be a mother and I lost my baby. And I just don't know if you want to be with a woman as broken as I am."

In response, Sammy gingerly rises from his seat and closes the gap between us. He bends down and gently wraps his arms around me. Though his actions are slow and deliberate, I still can't help but gasp in response. In his embrace, he whispers to me. "I'm so sorry, Aubrey. I'm sorry for everything that happened to you. But none of this changes how I feel about you. Not in the slightest."

I shudder at his words, clenching my teeth to suppress the sob as I grip the back of his shirt. I cling to him, terrified that he might slip away from me. He pulls me closer, caressing my hair as I bury my face in his shoulder. Makeup and tears stain his handsome shirt, but he doesn't complain.

Sammy. Please. Please don't reject me. I'm sorry for being so broken. I want to be with you. I...

I...

With a delicate motion, he shifts backward, bringing his gaze to meet mine. I hold my breath as I stare into his deep blue eyes, twin swirling galaxies of compassion and kindness that etch themselves upon my heart. His lips part; as if in slow motion I watch them form the words before he speaks them.

"I love you."

At once, the veil of darkness around me shatters. I let out a singular cry, one of bliss, relief, solace and triumph. I try to press my lips against his, but I can barely move, sapped of all strength by the deluge of emotions that wash over me. His warm touch comforts me, and his soft kiss causes my heart to swell with affirmation and longing. When my breathing finally steadies itself enough for me to articulate words, I form the ones I so desperately wanted to say earlier tonight, the words I want to repeat over and over again:

"I love you, Sammy."

I melt in his embrace, shuddering away the last vestiges of my sorrow and pain in residual sobs. In their place flows the love and acceptance of this human who stopped to compliment my humming of a jazz tune at a bus stop. I do not know what I did to deserve fate bringing this man into my life, but I am eternally thankful for it.

The light begins to dim as one of the smaller candles expends the last of its energy and gives up its spirit in a sprig of extinguished smoke. My trembling has subsided and my stuttered sobs have been replaced with gentle breaths as Sammy takes a seat next to me on the bed. I rest my head against his chest, hearing his heartbeat. It drums out a rhythm filled with love for me; mine taps out its own steady solo of reciprocation. He runs his comforting hands across my back, reassuring me, wordlessly accepting me, flaws and all.

With a sigh, I lift my eyes to meet his. "I'm sorry about all this. I didn't want to ruin our night, but I couldn't keep it bottled up any longer. I had to tell you. I had to be sure you wouldn't reject me."

He smiles and runs a soft hand against the side of my

face. "You didn't ruin anything. I'm glad you trusted me enough to tell me this, but I meant what I said before. Everything that happened to you—none of it changes a thing about how I feel. If anything, it only convinces me of how strong you are."

I lower my head. "I was a mess for a really long time. It all hurt so much, I just couldn't escape the prison I made for myself in my head. It took a long time for me to even be able to get out of bed, let alone function like a normal person." The end of my tail quivers in my lap. Pins and needles communicate how long it's been stationed in its defensive posture.

Sammy glances down at it before placing his hands gently on the appendage. It twitches in surprise at his touch, but quickly relaxes as he strokes its feathers. "I can't imagine. I've never been in a position like that. My ex-wife and I never had any kids, thank God. It would have made the divorce so much worse if we did. But if she had gotten pregnant while we were together, and we lost the baby, I'd have been devastated."

My hands come to rest atop his, but he releases my tail and balls his fingers into fists. A scowl forms on his lips. "I'd have been devastated... but I'd have been there for her. And I sure as fuck wouldn't have been the *reason* for it happening." His eyes snap up to meet mine. "Is your ex-husband still around? Because if he is, I'd very much like to have some choice words with him."

I gently wrap my fingers around his fists and let out a sigh. "He's not in the picture anymore. Truthfully, that night was the last time I saw him. When I returned home, our car was gone along with most of his belongings. I couldn't afford the mortgage on my own so I had to sell the house." I try to extend a sympathetic smile. "For what it's worth, if I saw him again I'd also have choice words, or more."

Sammy's anger persists for a moment before he finally

relinquishes it, uncurling his fists and accepting my fingers interlacing with his. He shakes his head. "I just can't believe there'd be someone like that in this world. Human or dinosaur. You just don't *do* that. It's despicable." His eyes quickly widen. "I would never hurt you. I promise you that."

I lean forward and kiss him. "I know. You're a gentle, loving person. You're exactly the man I want."

He returns my kiss. "I love you, Aubrey."

I nuzzle into his embrace as he caresses my back. It takes a moment for me to notice, but the familiar feathered appendage that had been barricading itself against my stomach has finally withdrawn, instead wearily resting upon the floor next to the bed. I nudge myself even closer, bringing our bodies into contact. I feel Sammy tense up but he doesn't pull away, instead continuing to offer his comfort and warmth to me.

I want him. I want to be with him. I want to make love to him. I want to feel his arms around me. I want to feel his body against mine. I want to feel him inside of me. I want to share my love with him physically and emotionally. I want... I...

My jaw pops as I let out an enormous yawn. My hands fire up to the sides of my face in embarrassment. "Ouch."

Sammy leans back, first looking at me with concern, then with amusement. "'Ouch' is right, I heard that one. Sheesh!"

I giggle, then let out a weary sigh. "I'm sorry, Sammy. I really did want to... be with you tonight, but I'm exhausted. I feel like I'm about to pass out."

He shakes his head before offering me a gentle smile. "It's okay. There's no rush on that sorta thing." He averts his eyes and blushes. "I-I mean—I want that, too, but I want it to be the right time for both of us. You went through a lot tonight."

I rub my thumb across the crescent moon pendant still

dangling around my neck. "You're a really special guy. I'm happy you fell in love with me."

He draws me closer still, his breath sending a tingle down my spine. "I'm happy you fell in love with me, too." His kiss is soft and tender, full of hope and affirmation. He slowly parts from me and rises from the bed, glancing over toward the closet. "The bed's all yours. I think I got an extra pillow and blanket in there. Saxon and I will have a little slumber party on the floor over—"

My fingers tighten on his shirt sleeve. He glances down at me in confusion. "Sammy. Just because we're not gonna have sex right now doesn't mean you have to sleep on the floor."

He cocks an eyebrow. "A-are you sure? I don't wanna make you uncomfortable."

I gaze up at him, though keeping my eyes open is growing more difficult. "Your arms around me have made me the most comfortable I've been since I got out of the hospital all those months ago."

He stands stock still for a moment, his cheeks brightening another shade of red before he reaches down to unlace his shoes. I bend over to unbuckle the straps on the backs of my own shoes, setting them off to the side before bringing my legs up onto the bed and scooting back. He climbs onto the mattress next to me; my arms immediately encircle him and my tail slinks around to meet the flat of his back. He returns my embrace, gazing at me with comfort and security. I nuzzle myself against his chest, the scent of his cologne filling my nostrils as my breathing steadies. I feel his fingers run through my hair before reality fades away and sleep claims me.

For the first time in eight months, not a single nightmare intrudes my rest.

Chapter Twelve: Pierce

In an instant, my eyes fly open and I lurch upward, gasping for air and clutching at nothing but the tangled bed sheet wrapped around my fingers. It takes a moment for the red to fade from my vision and my breathing to steady. My heart beats loud in my ear canals, its throbs slowly draining into dull sensations of pain across the still freshly sutured gashes peppering my body. I unconsciously place a hand on my bandaged arm only to pull it away as the ache rapidly turns to a sharp sting.

I sigh. What was I dreaming about? Whatever it was, it startled me awake something fierce.

The spot where Bianca would normally be laying is vacant. The lack of bright sun angling itself across my bedroom floor gives me a clue to the riddle of time; my bedside clock quickly solves it. Nearly eleven in the morning. I try to roll my shoulders but the lacerations across my back remind me of their existence, blinding pain causing my jaw to clench and my breathing to hitch.

This is how it's gonna be for a while, I suppose.

I lurch out of bed, the normal aches of a rough night's sleep drowned out by the boiling lava pouring from the bandaged scales and flesh under my arms and back. I grit my teeth and plant my tail on the wood flooring beneath me to keep from slumping into the bed again. After a few moments, the pain subsides enough for me to shuffle over to the bathroom sink, pour a glass of water and uncap the bottle of painkillers my doctor prescribed to me.

Let's see… "Take one every eight hours, as needed." I briefly consider taking eight every one hour, but decide to play it safe and pop only two of the suckers down my throat. I've heard of fellas getting addicted to this stuff, and I'm not about to start collecting vices beyond the few bucks Bianca lets me spend on sports betting each week. I think the Yankees got a real shot this year, especially with all-stars like Yogi Terra and Mickey Mangle leading the—

My hopeful rumination is interrupted by the lacerations on my back jolting me with pain as I straighten up. I hiss through my teeth, letting out a silent curse at the son of a bitch who put me in this sorry state. Even though Murphy is dead, I can't help but continue being angry at him. He could have at least done me the courtesy of keeping his attacks localized. Eviscerated arms I can deal with, but the punctures on my plates and trapezius muscle are especially annoying.

I didn't wake up until halfway into Friday; I barely knew where I was and, allegedly, gave the nurses at the clinic a bit of a fight as I tried to climb out of bed in my medication-induced stupor. It was Bianca who got me to calm down, her firm grip on my shoulders and gentle gaze giving me enough clarity to accept laying back down and allowing the nurses to continue switching over my bandages.

As always, Bianca is the foundation of my otherwise tumultuous life. She was there to comfort me when I received my second strike. She was there to listen to me vent after Charles saddled me with yet another skinnie. And she was there as I lay injured and helpless in a clinic bed. Bianca's sister Martha watched the kids, leaving my wife to keep me company as I healed up, though she did run home to check on them when we had that freak power outage on Friday night. By the time I woke up the next day, the lights were back on and she was by my side again.

 I wasn't discharged from the clinic until late last night. The kids were ecstatic to see me, even though I had only been away for a couple days. Bianca had to ask them to be gentle with the hugs, considering my still fresh bandages and irritable wounds. Angela started crying when she saw my wrappings, asking what had happened through her sobs. I told her I got into a little scrape at work, nothing to be worried about, and that I'd be right as rain before she knew it. Russell, the little smart aleck, asked if I was turning into a mummy. I told *him* that he'd be joining me in the pyramids if he kept up with those wisecracks.

 It was late, though, and past their bedtime, so after we said goodnight to Martha and sent her on her way we shooed the kids up to bed. I wasn't far behind them, making my way upstairs with some difficulty and onto my mattress in a stinging thud. I'm not one to usually sleep for more than about seven hours, but these injuries have been sapping the life out of me. At least they're healing quickly, based on what the doctor said.

 Hoping to feel the effects of the painkillers soon, I take a seat on Bianca's vanity stool and slowly unwrap the bandages encircling my left arm. The dried, sticky discharge painfully pulls at the loosened scales surrounding my sutures; I wince as the last layer comes up and fresh air scrapes against the angry gashes. There are nearly a dozen craters and valleys across both my arms, all excavated by the claws of a now dead baryonyx. I dab at the sparse rivulets of blood that escape from the irritated flesh before wrapping fresh dressing around the appendage.

 Several minutes later, I finish with the other arm,

having performed a similar ceremony to the first. Glancing up at the mirror, I rotate myself a bit to examine the reflection of my shoulder. Just as I consider how best to tackle the project of changing those bandages, the sound of a familiar car pulling into the driveway interrupts me. A few moments later, several sets of various-sized footfalls enter the home, the voices of Russell and Angela on full energetic display. A third voice bids them calm as it ascends the stairs.

"Oh! You're up." Bianca smiles at me as she steps past the bedroom threshold. "Did you sleep well?"

I shrug, feeling the bite of my back injury in doing so. "Well as I could. Sorry I wasn't up for church this morning."

She moves forward, gently placing herself beside me and planting a kiss on my cheek. She exercises caution to not touch any bandaged part of my body, having witnessed exactly how much pain I'm in across the past few days. Thankfully, the painkillers are starting to work their magic. She speaks in a protective, motherly tone while watching my face in the mirror's reflection. "Can I get you anything?"

"Actually, could you give me a hand with changing the dressing on my shoulder?"

She smiles, kisses me again and steps back to the door before calling down to the children. "Russell! Angela! Watch TV for a few minutes, I'll be down to make lunch shortly!" They offer their acknowledgment of their mother's words, though the sound of the television indicates that they're way ahead of her on that particular command. She closes the door and moves toward our closet. "Let me change out of my church clothes, then I'll help."

The dress draped over Bianca's body hugs her curves in a subtle and tasteful manner, but I still find myself staring as she begins disrobing. Noticing my hungry gaze, she offers a coy smile as the silk covering loosens and falls away, exposing her undergarments to me. However, her words take on a matter-of-fact tone. "Do you wanna tell me about what happened?"

I blink. "What do you mean?"

"With your arms and back. With that fella that attacked you and did this to you." Her smile is replaced with a notable frown as she collects more casual Sunday afternoon attire from a hangar.

"You've already got the story. Disgruntled asshole in a pool hall jumped me and Marty with a couple of his goons. We handled 'em, but the baryonyx got a few good hits on me, plus one real dirty one." I jab a thumb at the bandages adorning my back.

"Right, and *why* did this baryonyx and his cronies attack you outta nowhere?"

I click my tongue. I know it's a woman thing to ask questions they already know the answer to, but it's still frustrating, especially given my current pain levels. *"Like I told you,* they were trying to rob us. It was the end of the day, we had a stack of dues in the car, and they thought they'd pull one over on us with a sneak attack and take that money for themselves."

Now dressed, Bianca moves across the bedroom to my back. She gestures for me to turn toward the mirror. "I don't know that I buy that, Pierce."

My reflection's eyebrow arches at her. "Are you calling me a liar?"

"Don't be stupid, of course not. But I don't buy that reason." She begins undoing the bandage on my shoulder, the disturbance causing me to wince despite her soft touch. My reflection stares at her in befuddlement; when she notices, she shakes her head. "Do I have to spell it out for you?"

"Considering you've completely fuckin' lost me, yeah, I could use a little help."

Her lips purse at the utterance of foul language, but she

shrugs and continues pulling the tape from my back. "You just got done telling me about Charles threatening your life, and out of nowhere some nobodies try to kill you. That timing doesn't strike you as odd?"

I shake my head. "Charles gave me a second strike. Why would he try to have me killed if I haven't gotten a third one yet?"

"Maybe you did get a third strike. Maybe his way of telling you was this attempt on your life."

My snout scrunches. "In that case, why wouldn't he have just had me done in at the clinic? The staff are friends of the Herdsters, they'd probably smother me with a pillow for a hundred bucks."

Bianca huffs. "Look, I'm just saying this is an awfully big coincidence. We already know Charles doesn't like you. Why do you think it's impossible that he'd have a hand in this?"

"I never said it was impossible. I don't know for certain that it *was* him and not just some shitty lowlife trying to score some easy dough." I sneer. "Last time Murphy tries to pull that on anyone."

Bianca's expression softens. She knows my meaning, so her next question catches me off guard. "How, exactly, did you get out of this fight in one piece?"

I try to smile, though the last throngs of bandage peeling away from my scabbed wounds causes it to falter. "You shoulda seen the other guy."

She returns the smile, but presses the question. "I'm serious. With how bad of shape you're in, and the fact that Marty got knocked clean out, how did you pull through this? How did you get yourself to the clinic? They said you were out cold by the time you arrived, and I don't think two unconscious dinosaurs can drive a car."

My hands fold in my lap as I consider. I've got no reason to keep anything from her... so why didn't I mention him before? I mean, in regards to what happened. Lord knows I vented relentlessly to her when the skinnie was assigned to me by Charles. But now—

A sharp jolt of pain fires through my shoulder as Bianca applies ointment to the lacerations. I hiss through my teeth, earning a sympathetic look from my darling wife but no uttered apology. Instead, she waits for my response, rubbing the chemicals across my scales and dabbing at the residue with a handful of cotton balls.

Fearing the further torture she might inflict if I keep my silence any longer, I answer her. "It was about the last thing I expected, but Samuel stood up to Murphy. Didn't do much besides piss him off, but it gave me a chance to get the upper hand. We got Marty to the car before things got dark for me, and Samuel drove us to the clinic."

Her hands stop and she stares at my reflection in bewilderment. "Samuel? That human that Charles assigned to you?"

"The very same."

Her eyebrows flit. "You certain he wasn't trying to hit you and missed?" My only response is to look at her with contempt. "Come on, Pierce. Why would the human who you held at gunpoint suddenly *help* you? He probably screwed up and watched his partners die in that pool hall. Figured he had to stay close to you and Marty to survive after a bungled job."

My snout scrunches again. "If that's the case, why wouldn't he have driven Marty and I off a pier? We were both so injured that we wouldn't have raised any fuss as the car sank to the ocean floor."

Another sharp pain in my shoulder indicates Bianca is being a little less gentle than she otherwise might be to emphasize her point. "Look—All I'm telling you is that you're too trusting of people. And I don't think you should trust that human. There's a very real chance he's already in Charles's pocket and is just waiting for the right opportunity to turn over on you."

I mull it over as she begins applying fresh bandages to my back. "I'm not so sure, Bianca. Yeah, I lost a good amount of blood, but I saw what I saw. Samuel wasn't trying to attack me, he distracted Murphy. In fact, after Murphy was taken out, Samuel picked up my gun. I thought for a second that he was gonna do me in right then and there, but instead he handed it to me and asked me to help carry Marty."

Bianca seems to consider my words before shaking her head and sighing. "Well, if you want my opinion, if the skinnie isn't in Charles's pocket, he should be in yours." For some reason, hearing Bianca say the word "skinnie" makes me wince. She doesn't notice. "I know you've got no love for their kind. Neither do I. But it'd be better to have a dog on a leash than for it to be running rampant and biting at your ankles."

All I manage is an acknowledging hum. She works in silence for the next minute or so, letting her advice linger in the air as she finishes wrapping the bandages around my shoulder. She concludes by placing her gentle hands on my arms. "All done. I'll go get started on lunch."

I rotate my head toward her, the pain in my back reduced to a dull throbbing between the medication and redressing. "Thank you, Bianca. I'll think about what you said."

She leans down and kisses me. "I know you'll do the right thing. I didn't marry a pushover, after all." Her tail offers a departing swish as she moves through the door and out of sight, her voice calling to the children on her way downstairs.

I turn back to the mirror, staring at the mangled mess of dark blue scales that stares back at me. If Bianca is right, and Samuel is in Charles's pocket, I'm probably fucked. Any maneuver I try to plan would be fed right back to that triceratops bastard, and I can't just dump the human because that'd be my death sentence.

Is that why Charles was so keen on getting Samuel tied up with me? I mean, it certainly seemed like the two had never met before everything went down on Wednesday, but maybe it was some sort of act to throw me off. And Charles knows my relationship with skinnies, that I'd be distrustful of Samuel, and I was.

I... *was*. After Murphy's pool hall, I'm not so sure anymore. If Samuel was in Charles's pocket, there'd have been no reason for him to save my ass from Murphy. He coulda just left me to bleed out in that damned place. Instead, he got Marty and I to the clinic.

He saved my life.

My eye twitches as conflict pours into my conscience. I suddenly recall the dream I had this morning. What was done to me. What I had to do. What it cost me, and how it changed the man I am today.

Am I really going to forget all of that in favor of one lousy human doing one noble thing for me?

I shake my head. Bianca's right. It'd be better to have the skinnie in my pocket than to let him run loose. And if worse comes to worst and he's already Charles's property, guess I'm fucked anyway.

—

The ceaselessly sweltering sunbeams bounce from glass to concrete, leaving a shimmering layer of heat on the surface of the road. Under advisement of my personal consultant, I've chosen to not operate heavy machinery on this balmy, beautiful Monday morning. Of course, what I mean by that is, Bianca demanded that I not drive while under the influence of my painkillers, so now Marty had to cart his sleep-deprived ass all the way out to the suburbs to pick me up. I asked my darling wife to give me a lift into work, but I guess the life of a housewife with two kids on the tail end of their summer break is far too busy to accommodate such a preposterous request.

Another yawn escapes Marty as he keeps his eyes forward, his '57 Chevrolet Bel Air providing a comfortable transport to the office. I still prefer my DeVille, but beggars can't be choosers. He notices the stale air and fills it. "I'm glad to see you're mending up pretty well. You sure you're ready for a full workload?"

I shrug. "I'll be fine. Spent enough time in bed over the past several days, I'm about ready to stretch my legs." He nods and the uncomfortable silence returns. This time I try to repel it. "Were you back to work on Friday?"

He takes another drag of his lit cigarette, pushing the thin trail of smoke from his lips and out the cracked driver-side window. "Oh, yeah. 'Sides the lump on my noggin, doc said I was right as rain so I didn't need to take a day off."

"Anything interesting happen?"

Marty opens his mouth to reply, but hesitates. After a moment he shakes his head. "Not really, no. Bureaucratic stuff, a vote at the office that we ran security for."

"Mm. And Samuel, how—"

"Pierce, you really oughta—wait. Did you call him by his name?" The indignance that started to spark in his voice was instantly quashed by his realization.

"I did. That is his name, isn't it?"

Marty's eyes dart over to me before refocusing on the road. "You surprised me is all. I was expecting you to call him—well, it don't matter. I'm still gonna make my point. You really oughta give Sam a chance. He's a good guy. He helped us at—"

"I know. I was there."

"Yeah, well, I wasn't. Down for the count and all. And I overheard him talkin' to Charles at the clinic."

I shift forward. "What did he say to Charles?"

Another glance, this time with concern. "Whaddya mean? He told Charles what went down at the pool hall."

"Did he—" I catch myself before I blurt out more. I trust Marty, but I also don't know that I want to divulge all of my distrust of Charles right here and now. Clearing my throat, I rearrange my thoughts. "After you got knocked out, I took care of the bartender, but Murphy got the drop on me. Did a number on my back. He was about to deliver the *coup de grâce* when Samuel popped outta nowhere and skewered the son of a bitch in the leg. Gave me the chance to send him to bed. Is that what Samuel told Charles?"

Marty nods. "Long and the short of it, yeah. I wasn't in the room with them so I didn't catch everything, but I do know that Sam was real torn up about what he did. He ain't never killed anyone before."

I blink. "And he still hasn't. I'm the one that finished Murphy off."

"You know what I mean, Pierce. He's upset because he *helped* kill a guy. I spoke to him afterward, tried to console him and tell him he did the right thing. It was rough what happened to him."

An involuntary scoff escapes my lips. "Rough for him? What about us?"

Marty's eyes flash in my direction. "This is exactly what I'm talkin' about. You keep treatin' Sam like he's less than us. Yeah, he might not have gotten clobbered or slashed up like you or me, but he had to endure a hell of a lot more than most guys at their first day on the job." I sigh, but before I can respond he continues. "My memory's still hazy about how that fight went down, but I remember clear as a bell what I said to you outside the jewelers, about how you were treating Sam that day. It's a god damn miracle that he didn't run outta that pool hall and leave both of us to die. That's the kind of man Samuel is. His species don't matter, he is a *good man* and you'd better start treatin' him like one."

Spent of breath and fury, Marty's fingers tighten on the wheel as the air stales again. After a moment, I reply. "May I speak now?" Marty glances at me warily before nodding. "I was *going* to say that I agree with you. I thought a lot about things while I wasn't sleeping off these injuries, and you're right. Samuel does appear to be a good *person.*" Though I am genuinely coming around, I still find it difficult to form non-scathing words when referring to a... *human.*

Marty's softened tone still carries some edge. "Not 'appears to be', he *is*. He *is* a good person."

"Yes. He *is* a good person. And I'm coming around to him. But I'm sure you understand why I am still wary of his kind, so I'll have to ask for your patience as I reconcile these feelings during my interactions with him. Is that acceptable to you?"

Another wary sideways glance. "So, you're gonna be nicer to him, yeah?"

"I will try."

"Pierce..."

"Fine. Yes. I will be nicer to him."

This earns a smile from my partner. "Good. That's all I wanted to hear. Ya know, when you get to know Sam, he's actually a pretty witty fella."

The air between us finally softens as Marty shares a little about what he and Samuel discussed on Friday. As we roll into the parking garage and exit the car, I make sure to thank him for having gone out of his way to pick me up. He lives clear on the other side of town making it a long hike, but he waves it off before grinning and saying I can pay him back by covering lunch today. That sounds like a fair trade to me.

As I pull open the employee entrance, the familiar shape of a human with shaggy brown hair poking out from beneath a flat cap comes into view. He holds two cups of coffee, one in each hand, and is just about to bring one to his lips as he spots us and flinches, nearly spilling the beverage.

"O-oh! Pierce, you're b-back! I, uhh—" He glances at the two cups, clearly having intended to give one to Marty and keep the other for himself. "I d-didn't drink any of it yet. I mean, I was about to, but I didn't, so you can have this one!"

I wave a palm. "Don't worry about it, Samuel. I'm not much of a coffee drinker."

Marty, on the other hand, quickly accepts the proffered cup from our human companion and quaffs the hot beverage in two gulps. "Whoo, that hit the spot. Thanks, Sam!"

Samuel scratches the back of his neck. "Don't mention it." He turns my way, diverting his eyes before they linger on me for too long. "How are you feeling?"

I shrug and do my best to put on a smile. "Like I got slashed to ribbons by claws and teeth. But I'm still standing, thanks to you." He stares up at me with his mouth agape as though he never expected me to utter such words. Thinking quick, I wink and give him a friendly nudge on the arm with my fist. "Ya did good, kid—"

He yelps and nearly bowls over backward, spilling coffee all over his pants as he barely keeps his feet beneath him. The force of my gentle tap almost sent him sprawling. Marty spins in my direction and balks at me. "Pierce, what the hell, man?"

"Aw, geez. Sorry! I didn't—sorry!" I whip out my handkerchief and bend down to try and clean up the mess but Samuel recoils away from me. I sigh. "I really didn't mean to shove ya that hard. I was—ugh, look, I'm sorry."

The human eyes me warily before turning to Marty. Though the diplodocus beside us doesn't look thrilled at my fumbled attempt to be casual, he relents with a nod. Samuel accepts the handkerchief. "It's alright. You dinosaurs are pretty damn strong, but I also wasn't expecting it. No big deal."

I shake my head. "No, it is a big deal. I was shitty to you last week and now I nearly knocked you on your ass. I'm gonna try to do better." Marty's eyebrow raises at me. I clear my throat. "I'm *gonna* do better. You're a part of the team, right? I should treat you like that, especially after what you did for me and Marty."

Wiping as much coffee away from his pants as he can, Samuel glances up at me suspiciously. After a moment, a small smile tugs at his lips. "I appreciate that. Thank you."

Before I can speak up again, Marty interjects. "Hey, fantastic! We're all friends now! *So,* Sam! How'd that *date* of yours go?" My brow furrows and Samuel's fleshy cheeks redden. "I told you I was gonna get the scoop from you come Monday. You owe me some juicy details, pal!"

As Samuel lets out a nervous chuckle, all I can do is shake my head. As much as I'd like to treat the human a little better, I could not be less interested in his love life. A quick idea allows me retreat. "Let me get you a fresh cup of coffee."

Traversing the corridor of the ground floor level, I pass by several other Herdsters beginning their daily hustle and bustle. The coffee maker in one of the employee lounges is already seeing extensive use, with Cheryl from accounting loading up fresh filters with ground beans and refilling the water basins the moment they're consumed. I don't regret not being a coffee drinker as I bear witness to this coordinated chaos in search of wakefulness.

After chatting with some of the desk jockeys in line as we await a fresh pot to fill our grasped foam cups, I head back toward Marty and Samuel with his replenished coffee. I'll have to do my best to not spill this one all over him, too. What a way to win a friend.

I slow my pace, bringing my free hand to my chin in contemplation. What, exactly, should I do with him? I definitely agree with Bianca that it'd be better to have Samuel on my side than on Charles's, especially given the level of honor he displayed at the pool hall. He might not be strong or smart, but loyalty and integrity are fine traits in a man. I just have to hope that he's not terribly loyal to our boss yet.

I glance to the side of the vacant hallway, catching sight of the door to Charles's makeshift office. He doesn't have another more proper residence in the building, having vacated the comfortable and airy upper level vista in lieu of this windowless dungeon of a conference room. Within, several large filing cabinets contain paperwork pertaining to his station. He is a man of closely guarded secrets, only divulging to you what he deems necessary to divulge.

Though the door is closed, he is assuredly inside his office by now. If he wasn't, the door would be both closed and locked. I step a little further down the hall, noticing the ajar portal leading to the neighboring conference room. This one, though seldom used, has not been converted into an isolated dominion for a methodical and calculating triceratops. I cautiously step toward it, pushing the door open to view its contents.

Within is a large wooden table covered by a thin film of dust. A dozen or so chairs rest around it, musty and purposeless. In the far corner, a collection of filing cabinets yearn to cry out their metallic shriek, but nobody accesses their contents, if they have any to begin with. It's no wonder most folks don't like using this space; its lifeless walls and artificial light lend it a sense of dread and isolation. I crane my head, looking past the table toward the corner of the room. My eyes fall upon a small vent on the wall, near the floor and about a foot and a half wide.

I wonder—

"What's up, Pierce? You got that coffee for Sam?" The voice causes me to start, even though I know its source. I step out of the conference room and turn to face Marty and Samuel. My diplodocus partner's long neck stretches as he peers past me into the vacant space. "What's goin' on in there? Nobody ever uses that room."

I offer an innocent smile. "Nothin'. Thought I saw a mouse. Come on, let's get our work order for today." I hand Samuel the still steaming cup which he graciously accepts and we make our way into Charles's next door quarters.

The morning pleasantries are as hollow as usual. Charles asks me how I'm mending, I tell him that I'm fine. He exchanges the bare minimum of small talk with Samuel and Marty before handing us a list of locations to visit. It's the end of the month, meaning most of our clients have paid up. Now comes the "round up" where we visit those who have asked for more time or have been delinquent on their payments. It can be a little frustrating when excuses turn to belligerence, but a cursory glance at the list doesn't lead me to think that any of these shops will put up too much of a fuss today.

It's by design. Charles wants to put on the front that he cares for Marty and I's well-being. Doesn't want to give us too much of a troublesome workload on our return to duty.

Duplicitous prick.

Well, I'll look at the half-full glass. This'll mean more opportunity to get on Samuel's good side. If I want my plan to work, I'll need to butter him up a little bit. An easy day should make that a pinch.

And just as I had anticipated, the shift soars by in a breeze. Our most problematic client of the morning is one particularly cantankerous quetzacoatlus whose aged, sharpened beak snaps in our direction with each of her titters and complaints. I'm not worried about the old broad legitimately attacking us, but her temper is flared to the point where a finger might get lost if we tried to put hands on her. Marty does his best to defuse her frustration as he politely reminds her that it's our job to collect union dues, and our stop here is because of her delinquency in payment. He assures her that we'll get out of her hair *and* she'll be in good standing with the Herdsters again if she settles up her debt. With a final weary sigh and a visible sink of her wings, the shopkeeper scoops a parcel of bills from the back of the register's till and forks it over.

Stepping out of the store and back under the baking sun, Samuel's eyes squint. Whether due to the bright light or being deep in thought, I can't say. He's been shadowing us during our stops, observing our interactions and only piping up when called upon. During one of our first stops, a small drugstore, he was offered a complimentary root beer by the soda jerk on duty. He graciously accepted, enjoying the cold treat on this scorching day. If an interaction like this occurred last week I probably would have punched him in the back of the head and made him spew soda everywhere. Guess I'm turning over a new leaf.

Marty pipes up first. "Phew! This summer's never gonna end, huh? What say we grab some lunch?"

I shrug before glancing at the human in our party. He still seems a bit far-off in thought, but nods his acknowledgment. I gesture at him. "You're the non-herbivore here. Where do you wanna eat?"

This breaks him out of his sun-soaked trance as he stumbles over his words. "Uhh—oh! I, um—I didn't think about it." His eyes dart between Marty and I. "S-somewhere that can accommodate us all, I guess?"

Marty grins. "That would be nice! Last time I tried to eat a piece of bacon I couldn't stop shitting for three days."

Samuel thinks for a moment. "Well, there's a little place not too far from here that serves a kick-ass baked potato. I get 'em fully loaded, but they've got plenty of herbivore-friendly toppings, too."

I glance at Marty who offers an approving nod. I smile

down at Samuel. "Sounds good. Point us in the right direction."

We pile into the Bel Air and head westbound before arriving at the advertised restaurant. From the outside, the joint is nothing to write home about. A shoddy unlit sign and a dingy door would lead you to cruise right past a place like this without a second thought. However, upon pushing through its entrance, I'm met with the heavenly scent of roasting spuds alongside a myriad of other southern-style vegetables. The fella behind the counter, ostensibly pulling double duty as server and chef, offers a warm welcome to the two ill-sized dinosaurs that hunch over in the small establishment alongside their human companion.

Samuel looks up at our crouched posture in embarrassment. "S-sorry, fellas. I didn't really think about the low ceiling."

I wave a hand. "So long as their chairs won't collapse under me, I don't mind."

We each peruse the menu. As he stated he would, Samuel orders a baked potato fully loaded with bacon, cheese and sour cream. Marty goes for a vegetarian option called an *Especial* that's topped with pico de gallo and guacamole. I go with the classic, sans meat, and toss a side of collard greens onto my order. As promised, I pay for lunch.

We crowd around a table, pretty much having the whole restaurant to ourselves. It's a diminutive place, clearly designed for take-out or street eating more than dine-in, but the air conditioner does the Lord's work in this continued heat wave. We make small talk until our meal arrives; it's as succulent as it smells, delivering a dose of comfort food bliss. Marty and I nod our approval to Samuel as we chew our potatoes and veggies, and the small talk moves aside in favor of contented silence.

As I dab the last remnants of potato from my snout,

Marty slides out of his chair. "Gentlemen, if you'll excuse me, I gotta go pinch a loaf."

Samuel's eyes widen. "Oh, no. There wasn't bacon in your potato, was there?"

Marty chuckles. "Nah, I'm good! I just usually go around lunch break. Be back in a few." His neck winds around near the top of the small restaurant, dodging underneath an oscillating ceiling fan as he scopes out a small alcove near the back that likely houses a restroom. Samuel chews the last bite of his food as Marty disappears. Truthfully, I was expecting this to happen around now. Hoping for it. I wanted a little alone time with Samuel.

I clear my throat, catching his attention. "So. I trust today is going a little better for you than last week?"

He smiles nervously. "Y-yeah. Though the day ain't over yet. There any chance we're gonna get jumped by ninjas on our next stop?"

A puff of air escapes my nostrils. "No, I don't think so." I lean a bit closer. "Say, I wanted to ask you. What are your thoughts on Charles?"

He leans away from me. "Is this a test?"

I shake my head, realizing I must look a bit intimidating as I scrutinize his expression. I do my best to soften my own. "Not at all. It's an honest question."

He thinks for a moment before shrugging. "I guess I don't have a strong opinion about him. He offered me a job, and he said some kind things to me at the clinic when—well, when I brought you and Marty in. But aside from that, he seems to be a typical boss. Friendly enough, but more interested in the work gettin' done than being your friend."

"And what are your thoughts on me?"

Some of the color drains from his face. I do my best to look non-threatening, though I doubt it's much good. He stumbles over his words. "Y-you're—I mean, I don't have— that is—"

"Samuel. It's alright. I'm not interrogating you. I'm trying to get to know you a bit better. I'd prefer for us to be *friends.*" The last word nearly catches in my throat, but I force it out as naturally as I can.

He gulps before turning his eyes downward. "S-sorry. I'm still sorta wrapping my head around all this."

"Listen. I'm—" My teeth clamp into my tongue to focus its efforts. I don't enjoy having to do this, but it must be done. I lower my voice. "I'm only gonna say this once, so listen close. Regarding what I did in that alley, beating you and holding a gun to you—I was doing my job, but I was also pretty upset and took it out on you. Since then, you've proved that you're a stand-up guy. So..." I wince before stepping off the precipice. "I *apologize.*"

Samuel stares into space as though a ghost hovers above my shoulder. I know there's nobody behind me, so I merely wait for him to process everything. After a moment, his eyes refocus. "Th-thank you, Pierce. I don't know what else to say."

I do my best to grin pleasantly. "Great. Let's put all of that behind us. Listen, I need your help with a special job. You up for it?"

His eyebrow arches. "Wh-what kind of special job?"

"It'd be something after our shift, back at the Herdsters building. Once we're done with our rounds, we'll head back and I'll tell you more about it, okay?"

"This isn't a trick or somethin', is it?"

My grin falters. "Aren't we trying to be friends now? Why would I trick you? I legitimately need your help, and I think you'll find it in your best interest to—"

"Heya, fellas! Phew—that bathroom was a tight fit. Glad I was able to get my mitts under the faucet to wash my hands!" Marty playfully tousles the hat on Samuel's head, causing the human to grimace and recoil away, albeit with a grin of his own. "What were you guys gabbin' about?"

I glance at Samuel who still looks apprehensive. "Not much. I was tellin' him that Cheryl in accounting had some paperwork that still needs to be filled out. I forgot to bring it up before we left, so we'll have to swing by later and get it taken care of."

Marty grins at Samuel. "Hey, we could just swing by now. It'd be no trouble—"

"No, let's get the rest of the route banged out and head back afterward. No reason to hike all the way now and waste more gas."

He ponders this for a moment before shrugging. "Don't matter to me either way. Let's get a move on, shall we?"

Samuel does not protest against my improvisation.

The rest of the day goes by even smoother than what came before. Aside from the odd argument or sass, each of our stops conclude with successful retrieval of the establishment's owed payment. By the end of it all, I start to think that maybe this human is a good luck charm. His polite, innocent nature even seems to imbalance a few of the more belligerent visits, leading them to acquiesce a bit quicker than usual.

With the last stop handled and a dashboard compartment stuffed full of envelopes, we make our way back toward headquarters. As we travel, I mull over how I want to approach this, and how best I might get what I need. It's a hell of a gamble, but if Samuel is willing to play ball, I might find some dirt on Charles that'll let me get the upper hand on him.

As we find our usual spot in the employee lot and Marty throws the parking brake, he angles himself to address both Samuel and I. "Home, sweet home. You know which paperwork it was that Sam needed to get done?"

I nod. "Cheryl should still be in, I'll get it from her and have Samuel fill it out in one of the conference rooms." Marty begins to open his door but I interrupt him. "I can take care of it, you don't need to come in."

He glances back at me. "What, you want me to sit out here in Tyranno-Satan's asshole? That potato at lunch was good, but I don't intend to bake myself in this oven."

"Of course not. But I was hoping you might be willing to grab us a few cold sodas, and maybe stop by Zeke's bar. I wanted to pick up some betting slips for the game this week, but couldn't on account of being out of commission all weekend. And I *would* have gone after work, but..." I gesture toward Marty's car.

His lips purse as he considers. "I suppose it wouldn't be a problem."

Withdrawing my wallet, I hand him a twenty. "This should be enough for the sodas and my slips. Get yourself a few, too."

In response to the proffered money, his eyes light up. "Well, shit. Now it ain't a problem at all! Alright, I'll be back in a half hour or so."

I clap his shoulder. "Thanks, Marty. See you soon." After Samuel and I climb out of the car, it pulls out of its spot and turns toward the road, disappearing from sight.

The human looks up at me apprehensively. "You still ain't told me what this is all about."

"In a minute. I need to run upstairs and talk to Cheryl. Wait for me in the empty conference room next to Charles's office, if you'd be so kind."

He walks with me into the building and steps into the disused room as I head upstairs. Cheryl is at her desk, as expected; a homely parasaurolophus with pudgy cheeks and a voice like that black and white cartoon character Snooty Boop. She bats her big eyelashes at me as I approach, once again choosing to conveniently forget that I'm a happily married man. Despite being faithful, I'm not above using an advantage like this, earning a giddy giggle with my compliment of her bangs. She fishes out blank copies of the paperwork I lie about Samuel still needing to fill out.

"If someone asks, I got you the forms and everything's squared away. Can you do that for me, doll?"

Cheryl practically melts at my words, giving me a smile and a wink as I depart.

Sheets in hand, I make my way back downstairs. As I pass the door that leads to Charles's office, I gently test the knob. Locked. I give a soft rap with my knuckles. No answer. I assumed he was already at Santiago's, but now I know for certain.

Within the barren conference room next to Charles's office, Samuel rocks himself in one of the weary chairs. It creaks and groans in discontent with each of his movements. His eyes meet mine as I step through the threshold, nudging the door with my tail to close it behind me. "So what is this all about, Pierce? Why all the cloak and dagger?"

I glance over my shoulder cautiously, despite having just closed the door. No one followed me in. I take a seat across from the human, withdrawing a pen from my jacket pocket and sliding it and the paperwork to him face-down. My hands fold in front of me atop the conference room table, and I take a deep breath. "I want to ask you to do something a little… dishonest."

He blinks. "Dishonest?"

"It is my suspicion that Charles is our enemy. I believe that he is actively working to have me eliminated, and I believe his intention is to use you to achieve that goal, likely sacrificing you in the process." As expected, he freezes, staring at me like a deer caught in headlamps. I knew my words would shock him, but the direction in which his mind goes is vitally important.

I watch him carefully. *Very* carefully. Watching for any sign of duplicity or alternate allegiance. A twitching eye, a throbbing vein, an unusual bead of sweat. Anything that might indicate he serves another master, that my suggestion just threw a wrench into a plan already in motion via opposing forces.

I see no signs of inevitable betrayal; only a stunned, confused human. I try to assuage his discomfort. "If I am wrong and everything's on the up and up, then there'll be no harm in what I ask you to do. But if something is amiss as I expect it to be, we could be saving our lives and uncovering a lot of corruption in the process." I frown. "This is obviously a tremendous request for me to make, but I don't have anyone else to turn to."

Samuel mirrors my frown. "What about Marty? Why not—"

"Marty is like a brother to me, but he's also got a soft heart. He'd do everything in his power to avoid conflict, up to and including going to Charles directly. We just can't afford to go that route."

His nose scrunches and he crosses his arms, staring at the table between us. After a moment, his eyes meet mine again. "I really don't mean any disrespect with this, but *why* would I trust you? I mean, I appreciate your apology back in the restaurant and it's certainly a welcome change of pace to get treated decently, but the fact remains—I just don't know you that well. I thought you were gonna kill me less than a week ago, and now you're asking me for favors that—well, I don't even know what you want me to do yet, but I'm guessing it's risky based on all this deception and closed-door conversing we're doing."

A slow tendril of air passes out of my nostrils. Now it's my turn to cross my arms, leaning back as I consider how best to talk through this. He has a point—I *did* want to kill him. I was very close to doing it, too. He got lucky. However, given what transpired on Thursday, perhaps it was a good thing that his luck held out.

My tongue clicks against my teeth. We've already come

this far. May as well go a little further, for the sake of trust.

"A little over six months ago, my younger brother Francisco was killed. And I know for a fact that it was Charles who ordered the hit." The phantasm of Franky's smile intrudes on my mind's eye and I hear his infectious laugh somewhere off in the distance. I remain steadfast, not letting my emotions get the better of me. "My brother was a flawed man. He had demons with which he was wrestling, and I was helping him fight them off. But Charles decided that Franky ran out of time. He ordered a Herdster enforcer to murder my brother."

Samuel shakes his head in disbelief. "Jesus, Pierce. That's awful. But—if Charles did this, why are you still workin' for him?"

A sigh escapes my lips. "I said that I *know* Charles ordered the hit, but in reality I don't have concrete proof. Orders like this almost never get carried out without getting signed off on by a dozen different high-ranking fellas, so it wasn't a spur of the moment thing. It was planned and accounted for. But I know in my heart that this wouldn't have happened without Charles's involvement. He hated my brother and wanted him gone, like he wants me gone now."

More gears turn inside Samuel's head. "Why does Charles want you gone?"

"I just got a second strike for killing Eggsy. I... got emotional. I shouldn't have done what I did, I shoulda brought him in, but I made a call and it was the wrong call. My guess is either I've earned a third strike somehow that I don't know about, or Charles decided I'm more trouble than I'm worth."

Samuel turns a shade paler at the mention of Eggsy, but presses on. "Y-you said that was a second strike? What was your first?"

"I killed the son of a bitch that killed my brother."

Practically all color has faded from his visage now.

"Fucking hell. How many people have you killed, Pierce?"

"That's not something for us to get into right now. What matters is that I need your help, because if my life's on the line, so is yours." Samuel's eyes widen, and I quickly catch my faux pas. "That *wasn't* a threat. I'm saying that Charles uses pawns, and you're the lowest ranking one he's got. He will happily sacrifice you if it means finding a checkmate."

The human goes back into thought, his leg bouncing restlessly under the table. I'm starting to get a little impatient, considering this plan hinges on happening before Marty gets back, but I have to let Samuel make up his mind. I can't force him into this, he has to join willingly. After a moment, he glances up at me again. "If you killed someone that was working for Charles, why did he let you go with just a strike? Wouldn't that be... I dunno, something they'd punish harder for?"

I shrug. "Hell if I know. Honestly, I was prepared to face the consequences and catch a bullet in the back of the head for what I did." Franky's smile finds its way into my memory again. "I loved my brother dearly, and I avenged him. Charles or whoever else upstairs should have known that I wouldn't let something like that go. I did what I did, and I do not regret it in the slightest."

My gaze steels itself upon the human seated across from me. "That's who I am, Samuel. You might believe me to be a monster or a remorseless killer, but the truth is I am a fiercely loyal and honorable man. I will protect what is dear to me with every fiber of my being. My family and my friends mean more to me than my own life." I straighten my back. "If you'll help me with this, if you'll help me get to the bottom of whatever Charles has been scheming and help figure out a way for us to beat him at his own game, I will call you a friend."

Samuel holds my gaze with a surprising amount of strength. Where before I witnessed a quivering, helpless lump of skin, I now see someone with acuity and resolve. After a moment, his eyes lower and his brow furrows. I give him some time to think it over, though I do hope he makes a decision soo—

"I'll do it."

My eyes widen before I offer a respectful nod. "You've made the right choice."

He scratches the back of his neck. "What, exactly, did you have in mind for this 'dishonest' thing?"

In response, I rise from my seat and step over to the corner of the room, bending down until my knees touch my chest. A quick examination answers my question before I ask it. Herdster labor at its finest, the maintenance fellas who last worked on this ventilation system didn't even bother screwing the panel back on, instead just pushing it into place. I slide a nail between wall and metal, and with a small *shunk* the cover slides free.

I straighten up and turn back to Samuel who watches me with curiosity. "Charles's office is right on the other side of this wall. He always locks his door and he has the only key. There aren't any windows, so this is the only other way in." I gesture at my body. "For *obvious* reasons, I can't fit through this space, but I'm pretty confident that you can."

He tips his cap back a little with a quiet whistle. "Good thing I ain't claustrophobic, I guess."

"It's not a lot of wall, anyway. Your head will probably be poking out the other side before your feet disappear here." I lean down again, peering into the shaft. "I'm guessing the vent cover on the other side will be loose, just like this one. But you'll need to make it quick, I don't know how much time we have left."

"What do you want me to do when I'm over there? Am I swiping something?"

I shake my head. "He'll notice if anything goes missing. Take those forms and that pen with you, and see what you can find near his desk. He has a small leather notebook he keeps in the top drawer of his filing cabinet. It comes out whenever he has an important phone call to make or note to take, and I've never seen the inside of it. I'm willing to bet you could find some info in there."

"And what, exactly—"

"Anything you can. Mention of me, mention of you or Marty, anything regarding Murphy's pool hall, anything relevant."

He blinks in surprise. "Wait, you think Charles had something to do with that fight?"

An impatient huff escapes me. "I don't know. I have a suspicion, but that's why I'm asking you to go, and we're running out of time, so *go.*"

"O-okay!" The human snatches up the blank forms and the pen before approaching the vent. After glancing at me one more time, he drops to his stomach and starts shimmying through the tight space. As I expected, he's able to squeeze in, though his cap falls off his head before he begins the journey. About four and a half feet in, the echo of scraping metal heralds the other vent cover coming free. A moment later, his feet vanish.

I bend to speak through the passage. "Alright. Find whatever you can and jot it down. I'll be right outside keeping watch, but I'll keep my tail through the door. If you hear my spikes knocking, *get out of there.*" I demonstrate the audio cue by bringing up the tip of my tail and tapping it against the wall. "And *don't* forget to put that vent cover back on when you're done! Charles isn't stupid, he'll notice if it's out of place."

"Got it!" I hear the faint sound of Samuel shuffling around in the office, the metallic squeal of a filing cabinet drawer being pulled open giving a clue as to his first stop.

This might just work. I don't know for certain that he'll find anything, but at the very least he's on my side.

I keep a hand on the doorknob behind me, remaining still and straining my ears. It's after normal business hours, so most folks have gone home. Though I hear the odd voice or two coming from somewhere upstairs, it's pretty quiet. My plan is to pretend I'm mid-exit of the conference room should anyone wander past, and to rap my tail spikes against the wall on its way through the door if it's an emergency. Admittedly, I feel a little stupid holding a pose like this, but it's the safest way to give Sam the time he needs if Marty suddenly turns the corner.

I gotta hand it to the human, he's really surpassing my expectations. Of course, I didn't tell him that the fella who killed my brother was a skinnie. I always had an inherent and well-placed distrust of their kind ever since I was a kid. My folks brought me up that way, taught me to stick to my lane and be cautious of those tricky skinbags. Sure, society was moving in a direction of "equality" and "rights", but as far as I was concerned they'd always be a rung lower on the totem pole. It wasn't until I started working for the Herdsters that I softened, even beginning to trust the few humans we had in our employ.

Even Lorenzo. That sallow-eyed, heartless fucker. Even he got me to warm up to him before he stabbed me in the back by killing Franky. "I don't know where your brother is," my ass. I hope the excuse is doing him good in hell.

After I blew his brains all over the concrete, I promised myself I'd never trust another human, not for as long as I live. And I intend to keep that promise. Sam seems alright, for a skinnie, but I don't care how many times he stabs a pissed off baryonyx in the leg with a broken pool cue, I'll never trust the—

Voices. *Two* voices, approaching from the direction of the parking garage. One of them is Marty's, and the other—

Oh, fuck.

My spikes bang against the wall several times and I pray

to God that Samuel doesn't have wax in his ears. As their shadows bend around the corner, I hastily pull my tail out of the doorway and begin the pantomime of having just exited the conference room, clicking the latch shut as two figures come into view.

I glance up as though I didn't hear him coming. "Oh. Evening, Charles. Figured you'd be over at Santiago's by now."

The gray triceratops comes to a halt ten feet away, offering me a disingenuous grin. "Good evening, Pierce. I was, but I realized I forgot something in my office. I needed to have a meeting tonight but—well, my mind's just all over the place." He taps the side of his head in a gesture of forgetfulness. I don't buy it for a second. He doesn't forget anything.

He holds the bundle of envelopes containing today's dues in his hand. I guess he bumped into Marty in the parking garage and Marty handed over the money here instead of Santiago's like we usually would. The convenient timing couldn't be more inconvenient for me. The diplodocus steps forward, offering me a bottled soda and a small stack of betting slips. "Got what ya asked for. Is Sam's paperwork squared away?"

Charles's eyebrow lifts. "Paperwork?"

I stuff the slips into my pocket and grasp the soda, my fingers tightening on it nearly to the point of shattering the glass. "Yeah, I was told there was a form he forgot to fill out when he got hired, so we stopped by after our shift so he could get it squared away. He's in the spare conference room doing it now."

Purple orbs examine me. I'm an honorable man but I'm not above lying. I just wish I was better at it. Charles is a smart guy; I pray to God that he doesn't crack my flimsy shell. After an uncomfortable moment, he gives a shallow shrug. "Well, thank you for getting it sorted out." He steps toward his office, key in hand. "If you—"

"Did you want a soda, Charles? I'm not really in the mood for this one." In my desperation, I fire out the quickest thing I can to distract him, something, anything to give Sam another few seconds.

He pauses, glancing back at Marty. "No, thank you. Martin already offered me his."

His key slides into the lock. I grit my teeth, fearing the inevitable. Sam's still gonna be in that office, practically with his dick in his hand, and we're both gonna be fucked.

Just as Charles turns the knob, the door behind me swings open. Sam steps into the hall, two sheets of paper and a pen gripped in his hands. He extends them in my direction. "H-here you go. All done."

I do everything in my power to keep the vein in my neck from pulsing as I accept the forms. "Thanks, Sam. I'll get these up to accounting right away." The human smiles at me fretfully, scratching the back of his neck. I pray that it's interpreted as his usual nervous behavior. Marty, for his part, wears a far-off smile as he sips his chilled, fizzy beverage.

Charles simply stares at us. Straddling the threshold of his office, his interrogating eyes move from me to Sam, trying to piece things together.

We have to leave, *now*. I just pray that Sam didn't make a mess and that he got that vent cover put back in place like he was supposed to. He threw his cap back on, so that's something. I casually turn to Marty. "Let's get going, bud. We'll swing upstairs and—"

Charles's icy words cut me off. He speaks while staring at the human beside me, a malevolent grin tugging at the sides of his lips.

"Samuel. Can I speak to you in my office, please?"

Chapter Thirteen: Samuel

The gray triceratops's eyes that were just moments ago probing and inquisitive have turned downright menacing. I'm not sure if he already knows Pierce and I were up to no good right before he arrived on the scene, but I can't shake the feeling that we are well and truly fucked.

But how would he know? I mean, dinosaurs got some good senses, especially carnivores, but would an herbivore like him be able to sniff out... I don't even know what? A bit of dust from the vent? I brushed myself down, made sure of it, and everything was put back in its place. He hasn't even been in his office yet. How *could* he know?

It's not just the stupid look on my face, is it? I'm not gonna win any awards for acting, but I've spent enough time at the poker table to know I can stifle my expressions when I need to, and I haven't stopped practicing my neutral face since I heard Pierce's tail spikes clattering against the wall. I scrambled my ass out of that office on the double and made sure to look as calm, cool and collected as possible.

I know Charles isn't an idiot, but I pray to whatever mystical deity will hear me that we aren't completely screwed already.

There's no mirror nearby for me to know how well I'm

playing my part, but Pierce doesn't even look fazed by the request. He merely glances down at me, paperwork scrawled with incriminating evidence squeezed between his fingers. He wisely holds the forms at his side, obstructing their surfaces from Charles's view—it'd be pretty damning for our boss to notice the blank fronts and inked backs of that purportedly "official" paperwork.

The triceratops's terrifying purple orbs practically drill a hole through me. "After you, Samuel."

I look to Marty who stands by wholly uninterested in this cataclysmic development. I know before my mouth opens that it won't work, but I make a play all the same. "M-Marty's my ride. Will I—"

"I'll take care of you, don't you worry about it."

Shit. Could he have phrased that any *more* threatening? Pierce doesn't react, instead working his way toward the staircase leading up to the accounting department.

Marty springs to life, taking a break from his soda-induced stupor to follow his partner. He glances back at me. "See ya at Santiago's in a bit, bud!"

If I even make it that far. I might already be dead.

Resigned to my fate, I slide past Charles into the office with which I had so recently become acquainted. Everything is as I found it, I'm sure of it. I might have flaws, but one of 'em ain't being a klutz. Even though I was rushing to get the hell out of there, I tucked his black notebook into the drawer from which I had plucked it, I nudged the chair partially underneath the table, and I tugged the vent cover back into place where it belonged.

The door latches shut behind me, causing my skin to crawl. A premonition of his triplicate horns puncturing into the back of my skull and exiting the front of my head drizzling with brain matter fires through my still-intact mind. No such death befalls me. Instead, Charles steps to the other side of the conference table and takes a seat, extending a sickly pleasant smile.

"I trust the past few work days have been a bit less stressful for you?"

I fidget, recalling the pool hall. "Yes, sir."

"Good. I'm glad to hear it, and again, I am sorry that you had to go through everything you did last week." The honey sweet words slide past his widening grin. "Pierce has made it back to us in one piece, more or less. He has you to thank for that."

Shit, how much do I tell him? He's obviously probing for information. Several options rocket through my mind before I respond. "Y-yeah. He spoke to me about that. He did thank me."

His eyebrow lifts. "Oh? The two of you becoming friends now?"

God damn it. "U-uh, no, I w-wouldn't go that far—"

"Please, Samuel. You don't need to be nervous around me. I'd hope you would understand that by now."

I take a deep breath to steady myself. "Yeah. You're right. And I'm not. I mean, nervous about you, in particular. It's just—"

"You haven't had a good relationship with dinosaurs. I know."

Wait, how would he—

"I've interacted with humans like you before. Humans that can't keep eye contact, who stutter and mumble and do everything in their power to remain unnoticed. I know your type, Samuel. That's part of the reason I took an interest in you."

All I can do is stare in befuddlement. His saccharine smile does not falter.

"I have a special job for you. It's one that requires a man of your talents. A man who would prefer to be unnoticed, who can do what's asked of him, without question." He waves a dismissive hand. "Nothing intense. Just a little security and cleanup."

"Security?" I gulp. "C-cleanup?"

This elicits a chuckle from the triceratops. "As I said, nothing unbecoming of your station! You really must learn to relax. Can I count on you for this assignment?"

Do I have a choice in the matter? I nod my head, doing my best to not glance in the direction of the corner vent. "Yeah, of course."

"Excellent." Charles leans over, draws out the same black leather-bound notebook I had just perused not minutes ago from its filing cabinet home, and casually flips it open. "I'll need you at Olwark Port, building six-seventeen at ten o'clock PM this Wednesday. Do not be late."

A blood vessel in my eye nearly pops from straining so hard against reacting. I wrote down a lot of stuff from his notebook, but that particular location on that particular day and time is seared into my memory. I made sure to memorize the hell out of that entry, if only for four little letters attached to them that Charles has omitted from his request:

OYPD.

Instead of gasping or blurting out something stupid that would tip my hand and get me strangled to death, I speak matter-of-factly. "Uh, that isn't a problem. Should I take a taxi out that way, or—"

"I did consider that, and I've got an answer for you. But know that I'm not just giving this to you. At least not yet. Do well on the job, and you might be able to keep her." As he speaks, he fishes around in another cabinet drawer, one in which I didn't spend much time, before withdrawing a set of car keys. He slides them across the table to me. "1957 Ford Fairlane. Not the newest top of the line car, but it'll do the trick for you. I apologize beforehand about the color."

"The... color?"

He shakes his head and sighs. "You'll know it when you

see it in the employee lot. I'm not a fan of the color, but it wasn't my choice. Belonged to a former Herdster employee who left it in our care."

I stifle a gulp, realizing what that probably means. "O-okay. Thank you, Charles."

He extends another garish smile, its undertones so drowned in murky subterfuge they're almost imperceptible. "Oh, and one more thing, Samuel. Please don't share this with Pierce."

I almost don't want to ask, but I feel it would be more incriminating to not do so. "Why?"

"This is a sensitive mission, and one I do not think he is well-suited for. I know the two of you are beginning to get along, but there will come times when you'll need to operate autonomously of him, and this is the first of those. So, please, keep it to yourself."

I hesitate before acknowledging. "I understand. What about Marty?"

His smile falters, but only for a split second. "Martin is being included on this job, but I'll be making a similar request of him to keep it from Pierce. I'll inform him of his duties once we get to Santiago's." His palms clap the tabletop as he rises from his seat. "Well! That settles your transportation! Let's head over. You can get a feel for how she drives."

I follow him down the hall to the employee parking garage, within which he points me toward a vehicle tucked into a darkened corner. Its color can only be described as *loud,* the two-tone white and lime green seeming to project their own source of dazzling light.

Sheesh. If I end up keeping this thing, it's gonna need a paint job.

Charles climbs behind the wheel of his silver Buick Roadmaster parked in a convenient reserved space near the entrance, and I follow suit in my new, ostentatious mode of transportation. He waits for me at the exit to the parking garage and, as I pull up behind him, he begins the journey toward Santiago's. To my surprise, the Ford drives like a dream. Its steering is responsive and it manages the few turns we have to make on Old York's packed streets with aplomb. It offers little resistance when accelerating, the disused engine purring happily at being given purpose again. I expected the thing to be a heap of rattling bolts and dislodging rust, but this isn't a bad ride at all.

I briefly consider pawing at the radio to find my favorite jazz station before my mind wanders. What the hell am I gonna do about Wednesday? When I was in Charles's office privately, I scribbled everything I could from his black-bound notebook onto the sheets I handed Pierce. Most of it was comprised of dates tied to either names or abbreviations, neither of which I really understood. I didn't see anything about Murphy or his pool hall, unless it was hidden in one of those cryptic entries. However, one day and location stood out to me. Wednesday, September 2nd. Olwark Port.

And, of course, the initials OYPD. Unmistakably the Old York Police Department. There was no context attached to it. No names, no notes, no further clues as to the purpose behind its inclusion. Whether the initials mean that the police are involved in some way or not isn't clear, but after the conversation Aubrey had with me I get the terrible feeling that there's something fishy going on.

I omitted the OYPD notation from the frantic scrawling I turned over to Pierce. After all, it's the reason I ultimately agreed to help him with his mysterious and sudden request. Aubrey had asked me to keep an eye out for anything regarding the police, and I thought prowling around Charles's office would be an opportunity to get some information. I had no idea that I'd instantly come across the letters, let alone that they'd be attached to a rendezvous to which I've now been assigned.

And what do I do about Pierce? Charles told me outright that I shouldn't tell him about this special assignment. But isn't that what Pierce warned me about? That Charles isn't to be trusted?

Raptor Christ. I just want one easy day. This is a nightmare.

Several minutes on the stoplight-riddled roads of Old York bring us to Santiago's. It's far enough from the bustling portions of the city that parking spots aren't yet a premium, so after Charles pulls into his seemingly reserved spot, I find my new car an opening across the street and not too far down the adjacent sidewalk. The triceratops's tail disappears past the door to the bar as I approach; a moment later, I push my way into the establishment.

The last time I stood in this well-kept bar and restaurant, I was certain my life was going to come to an end. Now, the mood is drastically different as a gaggle of dinosaurs drink and make merry, entertaining one another with anecdotes and gossip. Liquid relaxation pours liberally from the innumerable immaculate bottles that rest along the mirror-backed shelves. I'm already recognizing faces from the Herdsters headquarters, including the woman who processed my paperwork when I first got hired. A few unfamiliar eyebrows raise in my direction, but they quickly fall when Marty waves me over to an open seat at his table.

"Heya, Sam! Glad you could join us!" The diplodocus quaffs a sizable portion of his beer, sending it down his elongated neck like it was a bendy straw. Before I can spend too long trying to imagine the miracle of anatomy occurring inside his extensive throat, Pierce's eyes come to rest on me. He carefully watches me as I cross the room and sit with the two of them, just as analytical as Charles but without the same vibe of underhanded design. Whether that's my imagination or not, I can't be certain. A burp escapes Marty's mouth before he smiles at me. "What'll ya have, bud?"

I hadn't even considered a drink before this moment; too many other things racing through my mind. "Uhh, they got spiced rum?"

"My friend, they got everything from beer and wine to freakin' absinthe, though that shit'll knock you on your ass like *that!*" He snaps his stout fingers to emphasize the point. With a grin, his head raises higher and he calls toward the bar. "Hey, Lou! Spiced rum for my friend Sam!"

The bartender calls out an affirmative, followed closely by the telltale clatter of glassware. Before Marty's head descends to eye level again, a familiar voice catches his attention from across the restaurant. "Martin. May I speak to you for a moment?"

Charles reclines in the corner booth that overlooks the entire establishment. It seems to be his usual residence. Tucked away from prying ears and without blind spot, it's clearly a well-chosen sanctuary for a man of his stature. Offering a quick, apologetic shrug, Marty rises from his seat and traverses the restaurant to sit with our boss. His head lowers so the two can speak quietly; I already know the subject of their conversation.

As I shift in my seat, Pierce's continued gaze startles me. He nurses a glass of brandy and appears to be several rounds behind Marty based on the collection of empty beer mugs in front of the now vacant seat. Pierce doesn't say anything out loud. Instead, the minuscule flare of his diamond-shaped pupils communicates everything I need to know:

We'll talk later.

The bartender, a portly tyrannosaurus gentleman with pock marks peppering his impressive snout, sets a glass in front of me, the amber liquid within swirling with the motion. He gives a polite but almost indiscernible nod as he lumbers back to the other side of the bar, demanding no payment for the drink. Whether it's on the house or I've just opened a tab, I suppose I'll find out later.

I take a quick sip of the rum, the pleasant burn coating my tongue and working its way down my throat. The warm distraction doesn't last long as the discomforting, silent presence of Pierce still lingers. I can't talk to him about anything important, nor can I just leave things as quiet as they've been—it might be even more suspicious if we aren't at least sharing a few meager words.

I clear my throat. "So, Pierce. You, uh—you got a family?" I already half-know the answer to the question after Marty's chided remark back at the fancy salad joint, but I hope—

"Yes." His narrowed eyes punctuate the curt response, followed by more silence.

Welp. Guess that's the end of that line of questioning from Sam the expert conversationalist. I take another awkward sip of my rum as Pierce's eyes finally wander away from my frazzled face. He seems to peer at a horizon of deep thought, but what might be going through that hulking stegosaurus's mind, I have no clue. Is he mulling things over regarding Charles? Trying to deduce where my allegiances lie, or what Charles pulled me aside for? Of course, the fact that I'm even sitting across from him instead of lying dead behind the Herdsters headquarters should be proof enough that Charles doesn't know anything. But I just can't—

Pierce lets out an irritated huff. "A wife. And two kids." His eyes flick to me for a moment before wandering away again. "I don't like talking about family. Not with..." His words trail off. I notice his tail twitching behind his seat, the bone-colored spikes flanking its tip swaying like buoys atop restless waters.

I lower my head. "S-sorry."

He sighs. "I know you're just trying to make conversation. I'd rather it be a different topic." His finger taps the surface between us before his focus returns to me. "How about baseball? You got a team?"

"Uh—well, I don't follow it religiously, but I try to catch games when I can. I'm definitely a Yankees fan."

Almost as though I uttered a magical spell, Pierce's eyes light up and a grin overtakes him. "Is that so? I tell ya, they've had some rough years but I think they really got a shot this time. Especially with hitters like Yogi Terra—can that fella swing or what?"

I can't help but smile along with him. "I think he hides powder kegs in his arms or somethin'!"

To my complete and utter shock, Pierce laughs. The guffaw rumbles forth from his stomach in decompressing waves. The entire mood of the evening brightens; though no one else is presently seated with us, the mirth seems to be infectious as several nearby patrons share their own laugh together.

Pierce raps his knuckles against the table as he recomposes himself. "You can say that again! The game last weekend where he hit that grand slam—I figured the ball was goin' to the fuckin' moon!"

The next several minutes are a dervish of factoids and gushing praise for what is apparently a big-time passion of his. I do my best to be polite and engaging, even though some of the statistics he rattles off go right over my head. It's a welcome change of pace from his usual stoic and reserved demeanor around me, showing a side of himself I didn't even know existed before now.

A few minutes go by before Marty rejoins us. A grin spreads across his face as the topic of discussion becomes clear to him, and he interrupts the first time Pierce stops to take a breath. "Uh oh. You got him started on baseball? Better buckle up for a long night, bud!"

"Shut the fuck up, Marty. So, anyway, like I was sayin', Mickey Mangle's batting average might be a little low, but he's slugging at four-fifty-five *and* he hit six homers this month! I still think he's got a solid shot at MVP!"

The three of us keep at the conversation for quite a while, making predictions and waxing poetic about the fate of players traded away and the prospects of those who have joined the team's ranks. I'm not a huge baseball fan but I realize it's pretty late in the season, and despite having some stellar players it ain't looking like the Yankees are gonna make the World Series this year. Still, I can't help but admire Pierce's boundless optimism and devout allegiance to his favorite team.

I'm uncertain how much time goes by, but eventually the other Herdster employees begin filing out. Given the dwindling light outside the drape-covered storefront windows, I surmise that it's a little past eight. Charles also vacates his position of power, offering a "Have a good evening, gentlemen," with his movement toward the exit. His gaze lingers on me as he passes, wordlessly reiterating his warning from earlier.

The table conversation eludes me as my mind wanders. I still don't know what I'm gonna do about Pierce. I mean, it *seems* like we're getting along well enough now, but what'll happen if I spill the beans on this secret mission Charles lined up for me? There must be a reason Charles asked me *not* to tell him, but what could it be? Plus I still need to tell Aubrey about everything. It'd just add an extra layer of headache if Pierce tries to get involved, too.

Maybe I'll just keep this one to myself and we can reconvene afterward on how to proceed with Charles.

A few minutes go by before I finish off my drink and give the most sincere sleepy stretch that I can. "Well, fellas. It's been a lovely night chattin' with you, but I gotta get home. I'll see you both tomorrow, have a good night."

Marty grins at me, his words slurring. "G'night to you, buckaroo! Get home safe, awlright?"

I give him a serious look. "Double for you, pal." This elicits a hearty chuckle from my inebriated dinosaur friend.

Pierce gives a quick nod and the semblance of a bid farewell via grunt before continuing his in-depth analysis of the failings of every other baseball team in the league.

Withdrawing my wallet, I approach the bar and ask how much I owe. The response given isn't a number, but instead a quick tap of a glass mug stuffed with several bills of varying denominations. The word "Tips" is scrawled in black pen on a cocktail napkin, its taped edges yellowed with time. Shrugging, I stuff a few singles into the mug and wish the restaurant employees a good night. With one last summary glance at the establishment, I push through the front door and into the perpetually muggy air. The sun is almost fully disappeared at this point, its lingering beams painting the clouded sky in fading oranges and reds.

I take a few steps toward the nearest bus stop before pausing. Oh, yeah. New car.

Fishing the keys out of my pocket, I cross the street to the lime green monstrosity. If it weren't for the gaudy color it'd be quite a handsome ride. Can't argue with the price, though, so I suppose this radioactive gradient ain't the end of the world. The cushions come to rest under me as I scoot behind the wheel. I didn't have much time to fiddle with everything's position earlier; I felt downright diminutive on the drive here. Whoever previously owned this car was a much larger creature.

I bring the steering wheel down a few clicks so it doesn't dwarf me. The key slides into the ignition, but before turning it I hesitate. Is it too late to give Aubrey a call? She's probably still up, right? And I'd love to hear her voice again, maybe even—

A sudden *kerchunk* and squeaking hinge cause me to spin toward the passenger seat, recoiling away from the massive intruder that invites himself into my vehicle. The blood pulsing through my eyes keeps me from immediately discerning the shape, but as he pulls the door closed behind him and turns my way, recognition dawns on me.

"P-Pierce? Wh—"

"What did Charles talk to you about?" His stern tone does nothing to alleviate my heart palpitations; his demeanor is a complete reversal of the joviality he demonstrated in the restaurant just a few minutes ago.

I gulp. "It wasn't—that is, I didn't—"

Midnight blue orbs with diamond pupils bore their way through my skull. Words so icy they could cut through this ceaseless heat repeat themselves with deliberate menace. "What did Charles talk to you about?"

Well. There goes the resolve I had about keeping my trap shut. "It w-was a job. A s-special job, I guess. He told me not to tell you about it."

His eyes narrow. "Is that so? And you planned to do what he told you? Keep me in the dark?"

"N-no! I mean, I was gonna—"

"Did you *already* forget what I told you about him? This is *exactly* the way he operates, manipulating people into being at each other's throats." His teeth grit into a scowl. "If you let him worm his way into your head, you'll be his puppet, and I'll have no choice but to—"

"For crying out loud! I'm *not* in Charles's pocket! I don't trust the guy, why would I after everything you told me?!" The stegosaurus stares at me as I catch my breath and try to decelerate my heartbeat. "He told me specifically not to tell you about this meeting. Basically threatened me. Said it's some special job for me, Marty, maybe some other guys, I don't know. He didn't tell me anything about the job aside from it happening on Wednesday night at Olwark Port."

Pierce's eye twitches before he slides a hand into the centerfold of his jacket. I wince, fully anticipating a slender steel barrel pointing in my direction, but instead he withdraws two folded sheets of paper. The ink adorning their surface is immediately recognizable. He peruses the page, flips to the second, and scans it before pausing.

"Six-one-seven. Building six-seventeen at the port, then. At ten PM. It's here, all right." His eyes flick up to me. "Not sure if anything else on this form is of great use, but this is certainly an appointment Charles means to keep."

"I'm sorry, Pierce. I wasn't trying to keep anything from you. I'm just at my wit's end with all these threats and orders." My hand moves up to the side of my head. "Not even one easy day since I started here. Why the hell did I take this job?"

Pierce doesn't answer my question, instead stuffing the pages back into his jacket pocket and looking forward. "Go check out the building. See what we're gonna be dealing with."

I blink. "R-right now?"

"Yes, right now. You have a car, and my guess is security will be pretty minimal. Slip in, check out what's in that building, and report back to me tomorrow."

"What about you? Can't you—"

"I have a wife and two kids, remember?" He tilts his head down, eyeing me past his snout. "You got family waiting on you to get home?"

"N-no, but—" My palms turn upward as I gesture around myself. "Did you see this car? You think I'm gonna sneak anywhere in this Technicolor terror?"

"Park a few blocks away."

A hundred other excuses fly through my head, but I already know none of them will work. Pierce has decided that I have to do this mission. Guess that means I'm doing it. Yet another order.

He seems to read my thoughts and softens his expression. "It's a quick look around. Nothing dangerous, we just need to get a feel for what's going on." His heavy hand comes to rest on my shoulder. "I'll remember these favors you're doing for me, Sam. You and me can go far in this organization if we stick together."

Before I can get another word out, he throws open the passenger door and exits the car. He strolls down the sidewalk half a block before arriving next to Marty's vehicle, the diplodocus's neck demonstrating a jolly and decidedly shit-faced sway next to it. The two exchange a few words before Marty relinquishes the keys to Pierce and they both climb in, the seemingly more sober of the two behind the wheel. A few moments later, its tail lights disappear down the still darkening street.

All I can do is grip the steering wheel attached to a lifeless engine. I barely had any time to process his demand, let alone form an adequate protestation. It's late at night, the job sounds risky, and I'm the one putting my neck on the line by scouting this place. The notion of simply going home crosses my mind but is quickly discarded. Avoiding this unwanted responsibility is out of the question; Pierce would tear me several new holes if I came to him empty-handed tomorrow.

This is just the rest of my life, I guess. Fulfilling the wishes of beings ten times stronger than I am who care more about themselves than about me. The urge to give into the bubbling resentment is quelled by just one thought: the light blue scales and furtive smile of the woman with whom I've fallen in love.

Aubrey.

With a sigh, my hand finds the key and turns it, causing the steel and cylinders a few feet in front of me to work their magic and begin propelling me forward. As much as I want to shirk this task, I need to do it for Aubrey even more so than for Pierce. She wanted to know about any involvement the OYPD might have with the Herdsters, and whatever's in this warehouse might be the key to the police's entanglement with my employers.

It's no short ride to the docks that line the eastern seaboard; the sun completes its journey downward during my drive, leaving only the inky blackness of a still sweltering sky in its wake. I squint to make out the signage pointing toward the appropriate cluster of shipping warehouses. Looks like the six-hundreds are near the southern end of this particular dock, with dozens of buildings lying between me and my destination.

I park the car several structures away from where I perceive building six-seventeen to lie, being sure to douse the headlamps even earlier. Glancing down at my clothes, I utter a silent breath of relief that I didn't wear anything too bright today. The breath turns to a groan as I realize that I'm without a source of illumination. Digging around in the car's glove compartment and glancing under the seats prove fruitless; no flashlight, no lighter, not even a book of matches. I've never been regretful for not having taken up smoking until now.

I slip out of the car, being careful to close the door quietly behind myself. Aside from the throaty frogs and humming bugs, life seems sparse at this time of night. A few dim bulbs that hang from nearby poles offer minimal assistance as my eyes strain against the darkness, trying to make out any shapes that may find my presence here an intrusion. When none make themselves apparent, I begin moving forward.

The concrete hides the sound of my footsteps well enough, but I still do my best to move stealthily, sticking to the shadows as I slink past several warehouses. As I arrive at building six-seventeen, I flatten my back against its exterior, peeking around the corner and through the space between the structures. Nothing. The opposite end of the warehouse faces the ocean with about thirty feet of concrete and wood between the building and the water. From what I saw of the other similar buildings flanking this one, large dock doors are on both ends, some for seafaring supply access and others for anything that may travel in by land.

However, the similarities with its neighbors end there as the decrepit nature of this structure becomes apparent. What little brick still holds its foundation in place crumbles at the faintest touch, and its wooden supports splinter and rot before my eyes. Whatever they're housing inside this ruin must not be very valuable. If it was, they'd certainly hold it somewhere a bit more structurally sound. That said, Charles brought *me* in to run "security and cleanup"...

Yeah, it must not be anything valuable.

I cautiously step over to a door on the side of the building. Its small, cracked window doesn't shed any light from within, though that's no reason to get clumsy now. I test the knob, gently twisting it. Unlocked. With a soft creak, the door swings inward.

It takes a moment for my eyes to adjust to the darkness within. Small slit windows near the top of the two-story high structure offer the faintest trickle of moonlight. I squint, desperately scanning the surrounding area for any signs of a slumbering security guard, but the coast appears clear. I nudge the door closed, peeking through the murky glass once more before beginning my search.

Well, two things are for certain. First, this warehouse isn't any nicer on the inside than it is on the outside, with the heavy musk of mildew and metal hanging in the air like a damp blanket. Second, there's definitely something being stored here. Dozens of large wooden crates are stacked up, claiming much of the building's central space with their presence. I can faintly make out a narrow staircase leading up to an access platform above me, likely affixed with a gantry crane for moving and stacking said boxes.

I slink toward the closest crate without others piled on top of it, squinting to try and make out any discernible writing on its surfaces. With how miserably low the light is, all I perceive is black against shadow. My hands fumble through the darkness, fidgeting with its edges, trying to find a place for my fingers to squeeze between and pry its lid up. Even if I was successful, I doubt I'd be able to make out the crate's contents any better than a deaf man could identify celebrity voice impressions.

Stepping back with a huff, I wipe the moisture from my brow with a sleeve. Between the oppressively arid night air and the stuffy confines of this sauna of a warehouse, I find myself wishing I was anywhere else. Glancing around reveals nothing further of note, and the foolish lack of preparation in having no source of illumination causes me to curse under my breath.

Fuckin' waste of time. I keep getting pushed around and end up with—

Suddenly, a bright beam passes overhead, split into a half dozen smaller columns of light by the boxes separating me and its wielder. I drop down, crouching behind the nearby crate and holding my breath. The splintered rays sweep again in the other direction, followed by a heavy sigh and... footsteps.

Shit. There *was* a security guard. How did I miss him? Stupid, stupid. I make a start toward the back door through which I entered, but realize from the now-available visibility that I'd pass directly through this guy's line of sight. There's nothing around for me to hide under or inside of, except—

A closet, at least what I think is one, pressed into an outcropping of the back wall next to the staircase. Its crumbling wooden planks might offer enough of a barrier for me to avoid notice. Still crouching, I scurry over to it, praying to whichever deity will hear me that it's not locked. It opens outward, and as quietly and cautiously as possible I squeeze myself between the gap before gently pulling it closed.

Not a moment too soon, either, as less than a second after I tuck myself away the source of light sweeps itself across the spot I had crouched just moments ago. All I can make out is a vague silhouette behind the flashlight's single piercing eye as its wielder grumbles. "Probably those fuckin' raccoons again." The scanning beam whisks across the space once more before turning away, my dazzled eyes making out a serpentine tail flicking irritably behind the security guard as he leaves.

The light slowly disappears behind the crates until the sound of an unlatching door echoes across the warehouse. An involuntary gasp escapes as the breath I had been holding expires. Sucking in air does nothing to lower my jacked heart rate. I can't keep doing this, I'll die of a stroke before I hit thirty.

As the panic eventually subsides, I let out a sigh. I'll have to wait in this damned hiding hole for a few minutes, otherwise that guard will charge me down. There's no way I can outrun whatever sort of dinosaur he is, so my only option is to sneak out once he's distracted himself. I really hope he's got a magazine or something. If he's a diligent employee, I might be completely screwed.

A bit of movement from the corner of my eye nearly makes me leap out of my skin. I spin toward its source, meeting a pair—no, several pairs of beady black eyes staring apprehensively at me. The furry shapes cower behind a set of brooms and mops leaning against the edge of the closet, shrinking themselves as small as they can in the darkened corner. I must be blocking their exit. I offer an apologetic smile to the raccoons before peeking back through the door.

A few minutes of quiet go by before I muster up the courage to silently push the door open. Neither hide nor hair of the security guard can be seen, so I hustle over toward the entrance that began this fruitless adventure. Cautious peeks around the crate corners give me the confidence to reach the door, peer through its small window one final time, and gingerly pull it open before retreating into the waiting darkness outside.

Finally feeling a sense of relief in the veil of shadows a good seventy-five feet away from the back entrance of the warehouse, I glance at the structure once more. All I gathered from this excursion is that the place is a dump on the outside and housing something serious inside. Something sealed tight that needs guarding at this hour. Something that's gonna call for police involvement in a few days.

There's no use thinking about it. Not right now, at least. Not by myself. I climb behind the wheel of my loaner and ignite the engine, still being careful to not turn on my headlights too soon and draw unwanted attention.

After exiting the port, I bring the car to a stop several blocks down the road. It's pretty late at night for a random human to be using a payphone on a dark street, but I don't see anyone wandering around who might give me trouble. It should be a quick call, anyway. I just hope it's not too late for me to be calling her. The dime slips from my finger and disappears into the metallic slot before the dial tone comes to life, and I tap out the number I've already memorized. Two rings later, her voice wafts into my ear.

"*Hello?*"

"Hey, Aubrey. It's me."

"*Well, hi, Sammy. Pleasure to hear from you, but—*" She pauses. "*It's almost ten o'clock. What's up?*"

"Yeah, I'm sorry to bug you this late." My hand unconsciously finds its way to the back of my neck.

"*It's no trouble. I mean, I was getting ready to get to bed, but I don't mind. Is everything okay?*"

"Yeah. I mean, I'm okay. Sorta. I—well—" I reflexively look over my shoulders, knowing that nobody would be eavesdropping but feeling nervous all the same. "It's probably something we should discuss in person."

"*Is that so?*" She lets out an almost playful hum. "*I wonder if it's just that you want to see me again.*"

Her flirtatious words make my heart skip a beat. Truthfully, I do want to see her again. I want to see her many more times than that. After she unburdened herself of her traumatic past to me and we confessed our love for one another on Friday night, she was so exhausted that we couldn't act on our carnal desires for one another. However, a solid night's sleep brought resolution to that plight, and I woke up to a ravenous woman staring into my eyes. She brought her lips to mine before I could even finish yawning out a "Good morning," desperately prying away my clothing as I reciprocated her passion.

I'm glad that all happened on a Saturday. I would've had to call in sick if it was during the work week.

"I mean, yeah, of course I want to see you again. But I've got some news regarding what you asked me to look into with the Herdsters."

I hear her sit up. "*You do? What sort of—*" She cuts herself off. "*Right. In person. Why don't you come over? I'm already in my pajamas.*"

"Sure, that'd be fine."

A twinge of concern fills her words. "*Oh. You'll probably have to call the cab company to get one out your way this late—*"

"I've got a car now."

Her concern is replaced by surprise. "*You do? When did that happen?*"

"More to tell you once I get there, I suppose."

Though she sighs, I can hear the smile in her voice. "*Alright, mystery man. You've got lots to tell me when you get here. You have my address, right?*"

One of the many things we did together over the weekend besides making love was to exchange important information with one another, the sort of thing one should know about the person with whom they're romantically involved. I tap the pocket containing my wallet, knowing the sheet of paper with her address is safely tucked between its folds. "Yes I do. See you in about twenty?"

"Okay, Sammy. See you then."

The clatter of my dime into the payphone's guts follows the metallic snap of its receiver. The butterflies in my stomach persist, making me feel like a school kid with a playground crush all over again. I'm really over the moon for this gal, but I have to do my best to keep my head straight. I stare at the parked car next to me, its offensively bright colors standing out in the murky darkness like a glowing beacon. Being "gifted" a car by my potentially maniacal boss, getting assigned to some sort of security detail for a warehouse meet-up involving the police, and the stegosaurus with whom I'm just starting to get chummy demanding I investigate the meet-up location ahead of time; I can't help but feel like a wilted leaf stranded inside of a cyclone.

With a deep breath, I clear my head. I'm not alone. I've got a beautiful, strong, capable woman that I can confide in and try to figure things out. We're gonna get to the bottom of this, and we'll do it together.

I just, uh… have to make sure we talk about things tonight *before* we wear each other out.

Chapter Fourteen: Aubrey

I stare up at the familiar exterior of the police station, feeling a chill run down the back of my neck. Gulping does nothing to dislodge the lump from my throat. Despite trying to psyche myself up all morning for the coming confrontation, I'm still petrified. Not even the vivid image of Sammy smiling at me and reassuring me that everything will go well helps to calm my nerves.

It was a pleasure seeing him last night, even if it was a bit unexpected. We got to spend the entire past weekend together, growing closer mentally, emotionally and physically. Even though I was too tuckered out after our date on Friday to do everything I wanted with him, one of the most refreshing nights of rest I'd gotten in months granted me renewed energy and a ravenous desire for his touch.

I didn't think I would ever be with someone in that way again. I had assumed the part of me that could love someone like that died in that cursed hospital room. The horrible monster I once thought was my soul mate had damned me to that hell, and the child I so desperately wanted to love and raise was removed from my womb because of it. I hardened my heart, believing that I would be content to never love again.

But Sammy proved me wrong. The next morning, I gazed at his peaceful, slumbering form next to me, his gentle breathing nearly lulling me back to sleep alongside him. As his eyes slowly opened and focused on mine, his smile pushed aside the last echoes of my antagonizing subconscious. The part of me that worried he would for some reason change his mind between our confessions to one another the night prior and that morning melted away in his rapid reciprocation of my kiss.

We shared much more than that with one another, too. The thought of his gentle, passionate touch sends another shiver down my spine. Our weekend together was magnificent, and his visit last night held its fair share of intimacy. However, as wonderful as the time I spent with Sammy was, the news he delivered to me was so troubling that I could barely sleep.

The police are in bed with the Herdsters. He wasn't positive exactly *how* involved they are, but he was certain of their involvement. I tried to press Sammy for more information, but all I could get out of him was a hint toward a shady meeting at Olwark Port tomorrow night. He said that he was asked to be there, but that he didn't know anything about the nature of the meeting.

The whole thing seemed to make him pretty upset. He offered smiles and hand waves when I asked him, but I could tell he was nervous about it. I could also tell he wasn't sharing every last detail with me. I don't know what he might be keeping from me, but I'm sure he's got his own reasons. And I can't begrudge him since he fulfilled exactly what I asked him to do; he found out whether the police were involved with the Herdsters, and they are.

With a shake of my head and a tightening of my fists, I march up the concrete stairs to the front entrance of Precinct 63. I didn't stop by Captain Aaron's office yesterday morning as I would have any other Monday to reiterate my desire to become a full-fledged police officer; I was still over the moon mentally about the weekend spent with my new lover. But today, he's being paid a visit, and one that won't involve me begging for entry to the academy.

I'll prove my worth by bringing this corruption to his attention.

Two dozen halcyon faces glide past me as I travel toward the office at the hall's end, leaders of years past, clad in impressive uniforms and emblazoned caps. Their respectful expressions emanate the authority of their prior-held titles within each frame. Most retired, some gave their lives in the line of duty. All are honored. Captain Aaron's stern but caring expression will join them someday, and I hope against hope that I'll wear the same colors as he when that day comes.

Through the glass of his office walls, I can see the pterodactyl seated at his desk, beak pointed downward as his pen-laden hand glides across various forms. The less exciting part of police procedure is the virtually endless paperwork, and the captain has to review and sign practically everything that filters through our precinct. My knuckles rap softly against the sealed door. He doesn't even look up from his task, seeming to sense who I am by aura alone. "Come in, Carter."

I step into his office, pulling the door shut after my bristling tail slides through the opening. I can sense it yearning to curl up in my arms, but I deny its advances, instead putting all of my focus on keeping my voice steady and calm. "Good morning, sir."

The faintest of smiles grace the side of his mouth as he glances at me. "I usually expect your weekly visits before now. Sleep in yesterday?"

"No, sir. And I'm not here about that. I... have information that I need to share with you."

His eyes return to his desk as he flips a form face-down

into a wire basket before pulling another over to take its place. "Go on."

This is it, Aubrey. Prove that you've got what it takes. "I believe the Old York police department, including our precinct, may be involved with the Herdsters and, because of that, also involved in their potentially illegal activities."

His pen stops moving, but he doesn't look up at me. Only a moment goes past before it resumes its dance across the paperwork before him. "Is that so?"

"Yes, sir. I believe—"

"You believe?"

I hesitate. "I *know* that the poli—"

"Oh, you *know* now?" His gaze finally lifts from his desk, settling on me with icy scrutiny. "Pray tell, Carter. How do you *know* this?"

My back straightens and my tail stiffens. "For one, Officer Preston has been handing out pamphlets and trying to persuade other officers to switch unions." I pause, noticing the growing annoyance in the captain's eyes. "I-I know *that* action in and of itself isn't illegal, but I think there's more to it. An inside source told me that there's a meeting planned between someone from the OYPD and the Herdsters."

His expression does not soften. "What sort of meeting?"

"I'm... not entirely certain. I know it's happening tomorrow night at Olwark Port, at ten o'clock. I don't know what sort of legitimate meetings would happen at a place like that after dark."

"And who is this 'insider' you mentioned, exactly?"

I unconsciously bite my lip. "A... friend. I'd prefer not to say more."

Slowly, the captain's hand lifts before coming to rest on the bridge of his beak, pinching the space between his nostrils as a long stream of breath exits the orifices. His eyes close and he holds this position for what feels like an eternity. My heartbeat echoes through my ear canals. He has to listen to me. He has to...

Finally, his hand lowers, plucking the pen from where he laid it to rest a moment ago. He slides open a drawer next to him, withdraws another sheet of paper, and begins scrawling into its blanks. His eyes glide across the form as he speaks. "Aubrey Carter, while I cannot help but admire the gumption you have shown and continue to show, it is apparent to me that the message is not getting through to you." A loud scratch punctuates the final arced line of his signature; his free hand scoops the paper up and extends it toward me. "Take this to your supervisor." I blink as I accept the proffered form. Before I can register its meaning, Captain Aaron fills in the blank for me. "You're suspended. Two weeks, without pay."

My jaw falls open. *"What?!"*

His eyes flare and his commanding voice booms. "Did I stutter, Carter?" I try to protest, but nothing emerges as his fury bores a hole through me. "You come to me with vague accusations about shady meetings and secret informants, all while accusing Officer Preston of corruption. Yes, I'm aware that he's advocating for officers to switch to the Herdsters. So are two dozen other officers across nearly as many neighboring precincts. That's how unions work—they make friends with people who in turn try to get other people to join their union. Most of our boys are happy with the PCA, but they still have a choice as to who they want to affiliate with. It's not *criminal*. It's just a business."

"But, sir! I—"

A wicked claw flashes in my direction and a snarl forms on his beak. "I'm not finished. This 'meeting' at Olwark Port that your sleuthing has uncovered? I'm well aware of it, too. In fact, the police are *often* informed when valuable shipments and merchandise are embarking or disembarking from the docks. Tomorrow evening so happens to be one of those occasions, and the Herdsters, being representatives of a company with such a shipment, asked us to have a presence there to prevent any would-be thieves or gangsters from attempting a robbery. It's standard protocol."

He pauses, taking a moment to let the air hang heavy between us. The weight of his disapproving gaze is crushing, but I somehow find the power to utter meek words. "I'm sorry. I didn't know."

"Of course you didn't." His palms turn upward. "I've told you time and time again that you *aren't* a police officer, yet here you are, striding into my office like you've got a badge pinned to your chest, making claims about 'other' officers as if you are one yourself. If you were, you would know better than to do what you just did. It's unprofessional and unbecoming of you, Carter, and I'm running out of ways to say it: *you're not a cop.*"

He sighs and shakes his head before continuing. "As it stands, you've got a flawless record. You're a hard worker. And I know that you've been through a lot." A minuscule wince escapes his hardened expression. "I don't know how else to communicate this point to you, so I'm suspending you. It will be your first and final official reprimand on the matter. Use the time to reflect on what you really want out of this police department."

Even though there isn't a mirror in his office, I know the color has drained from my face. My tail lies on the ground behind me, a lifeless tangle of cartilage and feathers. Whatever mental capacity might have been utilized to maintain my composure is being spent instead to keep myself from throwing up.

For only a fraction of a second, his steeled gaze softens before it turns back to its previous focus atop his desk. "Go."

Without another word, I exit his office. The same framed faces that glowed with pride and achievement along the wall now glare at me in disappointment and rejection. They harbor contempt for the foolish girl who thought herself capable of being more than a simple pencil pusher, who wanted to make a real difference. Each echoing click of hardened leather against linoleum flooring is a shriek of defeat and anguish as my dream is trampled underfoot.

I barely register my supervisor's words as I hand him my reprimand paperwork, nor do I meet his gaze as he frowns at me. He knows that I've been going over his head to speak with the captain, and he's never been happy about it. I suppose this is some sort of vindication for him; his uncaring attitude toward my aspirations is the reason I went straight to Captain Aaron. The captain is a reasonable man. He… he would want what's best for me.

The morning sun warms my scales as I stand on the precinct's front steps again. My eyes drift to the sky, allowing my vision to blacken as the scorching orb's rays sear my pupils. Several other dinosaurs weave past me as they move up the stairs, almost certainly shooting a backward glance in my direction, wondering what this daffy broad is doing staring at the sun. Could I answer them if they asked? Am I trying to hurt myself? Seeking an excuse for tears to fall beyond the pain of my failure?

Without much understanding of how I got there, a city bus pulls to a stop in front of me. I fish a dime out of my purse and deposit it into the tin slot next to the driver before hazily slumping onto a seat. Brick and concrete become a blur outside the bus windows, interwoven with the bustling populace of men and women who move about with purpose. The fella at the corner stall hands a newspaper to a waiting customer while the teenager working at the pharmacy sweeps dirt off the front stoop. A herd of high powered businessmen stride powerfully, adorned in pressed suits and wielding leather cases. A construction worker waves traffic past a bustling site where steel beams and girders ascend to the heavens, assembling another monolithic testament to this city's achievement.

Meanwhile, a velociraptor woman sits on a bus, purse cradled in her lap, staring at nothing as the world of purpose passes her by.

I don't know how much time passes before my feet find the sidewalk again. The fugue carries me forward. I don't know what my expression looks like, if there even is one, but anyone I come across on the sidewalk offers me a wide berth. My journey concludes with me staring up at an apartment building; the front door is unlocked, allowing me to step into the familiar foyer. I'm unsure how my legs led me here, but I know exactly why.

Three flights of stairs later, with my knee bitterly reminding me of its eternal malignancy on my life, I slide to the ground, my back against his door. I know he's not home. But I want to see him. I need to see him. I need him to tell me everything will be okay, that everything I've done hasn't been a waste. Hell, this relationship with him is still so new, we still have so much to learn about one another... but there's no one else's voice I want to hear.

I need someone to believe in me.

Time passes. My legs grow numb from sitting on the floor for so long. The same knee that is hellbent on preventing me from doing the one thing I wanted to do with my life aches from the awkward positioning. I offer it an olive branch of relief, sliding my foot toward my bottom and slowly extending it back outward several times. It quiets down.

My mind ceaselessly cycles between hopelessness, apathy and rage. One moment I try to rationalize my actions, the next I realize how foolish they were. Anger bubbles forth toward the pterodactyl that I respect so greatly stonewalling me in such brutal fashion, then instantly drains away in understanding of his position. I have been a horrible employee, proving definitively that I don't deserve to be a police officer, bad knee or not. I thought that if I wanted it strongly enough, things would just work out... but they didn't. I'll never be a—

"Aubrey? What're you doing here?" His voice drifts to me through the haze. I can barely raise my head to bring him into focus. It takes every ounce of my remaining strength for the corners of my mouth to lift the fraction I can muster.

"Hi, Sammy. I'm having a bad day."

He quickly ushers me into his apartment and we sit on the edge of his bed. His arms are around me in a tight hug before I utter another word. No tears fall. I shed enough of those when I bore my heart to this man. He accepted me then, flaws and all. Now I have to admit to him again that I'm a worthless, incompetent lump of scales and regrets.

Sammy patiently listens to me unburden my emotions a second time. I tell him everything, from spying in the locker room and gaining my initial suspicion of Officer Preston to the reality check that Captain Aaron bestowed upon me after I brought my findings to his attention. Sammy knew that I wanted to be a police officer, but didn't know what a pestering bother I'd been to the captain in my mission to prove my dedication via weekly visits. It hurts me to do it, but with accepted resignation I manage to speak the truth.

"I'm not cut out to be a police officer. I'm just not. Between my broken knee and my foolish actions, I don't have what it takes."

Sammy's hands had shifted down to my upper arms, his thumbs gently massaging the insides of my elbows. The act was calming and loving, and I was thankful that he was still willing to touch me after being such a burden on him a second time. But his fingers stop moving, and he blurts out his first utterance since bringing me inside his apartment:

"Bullshit."

I smile, having known he'd try to make me feel better

with something like this. "I appreciate you, Sammy, but I've finally realized—"

"Nuh uh. That's bullshit. The Aubrey I fell in love with wouldn't give up this easily." My smile falters, but before I can protest further he presses on. "Do you remember the day we met?"

"Of course I do. But—"

"I watched as a jazz-enjoying velociraptor lady charged straight into an alley toward gunshots. I remember thinking to myself, what sorta nut job of a woman would be dashing *into* danger? And do you remember what you told me?" For a moment, the air holds still between us. I know the answer, but when I hesitate he fills in the blank. "You told me that you're a cop."

My cheeks redden. "But Sammy, I lied to you."

He shakes his head. "No, you didn't. What I saw that day wasn't a fluke. It wasn't a silly girl chasing a far-off dream. You did something very brave and heroic, something that a good police officer would do. And you didn't just rush to the crime scene—you stuck up for me when I got arrested. You followed me down to the station and vouched for me when you didn't have to. You had every opportunity to ignore the gunshots or ignore me, but you didn't. That sounds like a cop to me. Or at the very least, someone who deserves to be one."

His kind words swirl around me like an autumn breeze, but my lingering doubts don't relent. "I screwed up today. All of my suspicions were unfounded."

Sammy's nose scrunches. "Were they?"

"What do you mean?"

"I mean, were your suspicions really unfounded? How do you know that for sure?"

"The captain said so. Officer Preston wasn't breaking any rules by talking about the Herdsters, and the meeting at the dock is standard protocol. Police have a presence there if it's a high value shipment, for safety."

Sammy crosses his arms in thought. His brow furrows and his eyes focus somewhere on the floor. After a moment, he glances up at me, then back down again. He gnaws on his lower lip, and I find myself wishing that I could mimic the fairground magicians who can read your mind for a nickel.

Finally, he takes a deep breath and meets my eyes with resolve. "I don't want this to come off wrong, but... do you trust the police captain?"

I blink in surprise. "Of course I do! He's an honorable, honest man. He was—" I pause before drawing in my own steadying breath. "He was the only person who visited me in the hospital after..."

Sammy's hands find my forearms again as he nudges himself closer on the edge of the bed. "I understand. And I don't want to call the fella's integrity into too much question here. But, looking at it rationally, if he *was* involved in some way, wouldn't what he told you be the exact sort of story a police officer would use to cover it up?"

I want to blurt out that this theory is entirely impossible, that Captain Aaron would *never* do something like that, but... how well do I really know him? I've never been to his home or met his wife and son. All of our interactions have been professional, and brief. He certainly seems clean cut and above the board. But Sammy has a point.

My eyes return to him. "I... guess it isn't out of the question, but I still think it's very unlikely."

He smiles warmly at me. "That's all I'm saying. A little critical thinking and a healthy dose of skepticism got me where I am today!" I glance around his still barren apartment, then back to him with a raised eyebrow. His grin turns to a frown. "Hey! I ain't that bad off! And at least I got you, Aubrey."

I rest my head against his shoulder, allowing a faint smile to tug at my lips. His palms move to my back, gently rubbing the tension away from my muscles. As much as the gesture relaxes me, and as much as I want to forgo the painful topic and simply enjoy his company, I force myself upright again. Sammy's blue eyes watch me, his circular pupils holding focus on my face.

My calm instantly shifts to regret. "I'm so sorry for getting you wrapped up in all this. I shoulda never asked you to look for police involvement. I mighta put you at risk." He tries to hold me steady, craning his head to keep up with my attempts to turn away from him. "It was a terrible thing for me to do. If there is something corrupt going on, you coulda been hurt! God, what if they hurt you?!"

"Hey, I'm okay. Nothin's gonna happen to me."

His reassurances don't slow my heart rate. "Preston was one of the sons of bitches that arrested you and then hurt Miles Cratis, and he's the one I suspect of being dirty! What if he saw you? What if he *recognized* you?!" I suck air past clenched teeth, finally losing the fight with my tear ducts as they begin spilling forth. He tries pulling me into a hug but I coil into myself and away from his warmth. "I'm a horrible person. I put you in danger." His shushes fall on deaf ears.

I can barely squeeze the words past my trembling lips. "That's not what a cop does. That's not what you do to someone you love."

He doesn't allow me to say anything more, bringing me into a tender kiss. I sob through closed eyes, unwilling to pull away from his loving gesture but knowing I don't deserve it. How could I do something so selfish?

We part, and Sammy gazes at me. I expect him to assuage me again, but instead his forehead wrinkles in thought. I use the back of my hand to scoop the lingering moisture away from my eyes. As my breathing steadies, he speaks.

"How about a chance to find out what those cops are up to, and an opportunity to keep me safe?"

"W-what?"

"You could come with me. To the rendezvous tomorrow, that is."

A curt breath escapes me. "I think a velociraptor gal who is neither a cop nor a Herdster would stick out like a sore thumb, don't you?"

"Well, about that... y'see, I sorta did a bit of reconnaissance at the port. Poked around a little bit, got a feel for the joint, y'know?"

"I thought you said you didn't know what the meeting was about."

He shrugs. "I still don't. There were a shitload of crates there, but they were sealed up tighter than a nun's hooha and it was nearly pitch black. I didn't bring a flashlight because I'm an idiot. And I almost got caught by a security guard to boot." My shoulders sag at this last statement which he quickly amends. "I didn't, though! He didn't see me or even know I was there. I, uh—well, I hid in a broom closet."

I cock my head. "A broom closet?"

"Yep. Dusty, dingy, home to a couple wary raccoons... but it was concealed. Tucked behind a staircase, with some rotted boards that give good visibility out but practically none in, especially that late at night. If these guys are doing something illegal, I doubt it'll involve doing any sweeping afterward. And even if it does—" He jabs a thumb toward himself. "—that sorta work would probably be assigned to Mr. Lowest-on-the-Totem-Pole."

"So what exactly are you suggesting?"

He takes a breath. "I gotta be at this thing, and visible, right? But you could be there, too. Just... hidden. I figure if you tuck yourself in that cubby, you can see with your own eyes whether what's going down is on the level or if it stinks of police corruption. If what your captain pal said is true, the cops would just be there to keep an eye on a legitimate business dealing. But if things *are* dirty... you'd have proof. Your proof."

I mull over his suggestion for a moment. "Hiding in a broom closet, huh? That's not very cop-like."

"Hey, your police captain said you're not a cop, didn't he?"

I give him a light swat with the back of my hand, causing him to chuckle indignantly. "Just because you're right doesn't mean you can say it out loud."

"I got you to smile again, though. It was worth it."

This man…

My smile fades into thought. "It's going to be dangerous."

"Maybe, but I'll feel an awful lot better with you there to back me up if things get crazy for some reason." He brings a finger to his chin. "You know what you should bring along? A ca—"

"A gun."

He blinks. "Uh… yeah, that might not be a bad idea, too. But I was gonna say, a camera." He blinks again. "Wait. You have a gun?"

My eyebrow lifts. "Of course I do. You think a woman living in a city like Old York should be unarmed?"

"Guess I never thought about it. I mean, *I* don't have one."

"Are you a woman living in Old York?"

He balks. "Well, *no,* but I am a *human* living in a city full of *dinosaurs.*" A puff of air escapes his nostrils. "I'm gonna get myself a gun."

Another grin tugs at the sides of my mouth. "It's a Christmas gift idea. Right now I think we need to come up with a plan. If I'm gonna be stuffed into a closet… if I'm gonna be keeping an eye on you and seeing if there's any wrongdoings, I need to know as much as possible."

Sammy beams with confidence. "Let's draft up a plan, then!"

—

My thumb and forefinger trace the outline of the small crescent moon hanging from my neck. The motion is a welcome replacement to fidgeting with my tail, but I usually have to consciously pull my hand away when it idly slips to the necklace at inappropriate times. Right now, though, my nerves can use some cooling. I considered leaving the pendant at home, worrying that it might stand out amidst the darker, stealthier choice of attire I wore for this particular mission. Guess the comfort of Sammy's gift outweighed sensibility today.

The setting sun paints the dockside buildings in darkening oranges and reds, their shadows growing visibly longer with each passing minute. I staked out a vacant warehouse several hundred feet away from the building marked "617", where Sammy said this ten o'clock rendezvous was going to take place. While it wasn't difficult getting to the docks themselves—no fence meant walking in went unchallenged—I didn't dare approach the building early. Who knows how much security they've got there already, or if the police are already present? I can't risk getting noticed before I get into position.

Sammy and I worked through the plan last night. I'd get to the dock nice and early, just in case there were any unexpected hiccups. He'd arrive after his regular shift, but not so early that it might raise suspicion. Being punctual is one thing; standing around for five hours could be unfavorably noticed.

Though I was able to spend the night with him again, the morning hit me like a ton of bricks. While he got ready for work, I sat around like a lousy layabout, knowing my suspension meant I didn't have a job to go to. Sure, the meeting at the dock had the potential to be a bombshell, but if it isn't… I'll have nothing to do but tuck my tail between my legs and sit around for two weeks. And once I return to work, if I so much as glance up from my desk in a way that

Captain Aaron doesn't like, I'll get served a lot worse than a suspension.

Instead, I spent the day nervously fretting about the coming night of subterfuge and danger. I mentioned my gun to Sammy, but I don't carry it around with me at all times. Even though a city like Old York can be dangerous, God saw fit to grace me with teeth and talons should the need for sudden and violent self-defense arise. I caught a morning bus back to my apartment and fetched the FN Model 1905 from the small gun safe in my bedroom closet. A purse pistol to be sure, but I've taken it to the range enough times to know how to handle it.

My fingers move to the handbag resting next to me, feeling the outline of the gun along with the spare magazine alongside it. Twelve .25 caliber rounds that I pray I won't need to use put my mind at ease. I crane my neck fruitlessly, trying to peer out the window of the empty warehouse I'm holed up within. Getting here as early as I did was probably unnecessary, but I've always been a firm believer in being safe rather than sorry. If I showed up too late and wasn't able to hunker down anywhere without being noticed, I'd blow this entire operation.

I rely on the tried and true jukebox of my mind to pass the time, sinking into the loving embrace of Miles Cratis's warm trills. One of his hits from a few years ago brings motion to my toes, lightly tapping the concrete beneath me in time with the rhythm. "Solar", perhaps an ironic choice given the evacuation of the sun above Old York, is upbeat and smooth. The trumpet and piano playfully swirl around one another, forming an intricate dance of competitive harmony. Cratis tags out for Dave Schildstout's alto sax, sliding into the routine with practiced rhythm, not missing a beat. Both make way for Horace Bronze's piano solo, tying together a symphonic sizzle reel of some of the greatest living talent in jazz.

The music pauses as a glimmer of reflected waning light catches my attention. Sammy's car, the "7 Up Can", as he jokingly refers to it, rolls down the single paved lane between the buildings. It's about the least stealthy set of wheels one could ask for, its downright gaudy lime green and white paint job screaming "Look in my direction!" However, he has the advantage of being expected, so whoever might be congregated in building six-seventeen shouldn't be too suspicious of its boisterous presence in the area.

I hustle over to the side door of my vacant warehouse hideout, popping it slightly ajar and waiting for him to approach. He rubbernecks for any trace of my whereabouts. We agreed on me hiding somewhere nearby, but didn't have an exact place picked out due to the rapidity of our planning. A quick wave of my arm out the door catches his attention and he comes to a stop before backing his car between my warehouse and the one next to it. He quickly exits and glances around before jogging over to the door I'm behind and slipping in.

"Heya, Aubrey. Sorry about the wait, had to run a quick errand." He clutches a small brown paper bag in his hand.

I give him a quick kiss. "No problem, Sammy." My eyes dart to the satchel. "Was that the errand?"

He smirks. "So perceptive of you! I'm glad you got your detective eyes on for tonight." He reaches into the bag and withdraws something resembling a black brick. The camera isn't exactly designed for being stuffed into your back pocket, what with the myriad of silver knobs spattered across its surface. But given our limited timetable, it should do the trick. "It's an Argus C3. Not a bad camera, a little ugly but it's a top seller for a reason."

"Geez. How much did this thing set you back?"

"Oh, it didn't. I had it tucked away in storage. It was one of the few things I evacuated from my ex's place when things went to shit, but I've never been much of a shutterbug so I didn't really need it until now." He shrugs. "I did pick up a new roll of film, though. Whatever was in there probably involved my ex, so it's right where it belongs now: the garbage."

I let out a soft giggle. "Remind me to never get on your bad side." I turn the hunk of metal and vinyl over in my hands. "So, this knob to wind the film, and this bit over here to focus?"

"You're a natural!" I peek at his toothy grin through one of the camera's two openings. "That's the view finder, the other one's the range finder." He prods at the front of the device with his forefinger. "And that there's the shutter lever." I thumb it down as he speaks. "I did take one test photo to make sure the thing still works, so you should have thirty-five left."

"Make that thirty-four." Before he can register my meaning, I bring the camera up and press the shutter release button. The device lets out a sharp *snap,* capturing his candid grin.

"Hey! I wasn't ready!"

"That means it'll be a keeper." My own smile fades. "That was... really loud."

He purses his lips in thought. "Yeah. It's all I had, but you're not wrong. I'm hoping that things will be busy enough in the warehouse that nobody will notice."

I don't like it, but then again... I may not even need to use the camera at all. If this does turn out to be above board, pictures of legitimate cargo handling won't do us any good.

Seeming to suddenly remember, Sammy thrusts the brown paper sack in my direction. "Oh, I got this for you, too. Figured you might get peckish in there."

With a lifted eyebrow, I peel open the container. "A sandwich? You thoughtful son of a gun."

"I woulda got you some potato chips to go with it but the crunching coming from a broom cupboard might be a bit of a giveaway." We both laugh. This fella is a real piece of work. As we calm ourselves, he peeks out the same window I used as my vantage point, glancing both ways down the lonesome lane. "Okay. Like we discussed, I'll head over real quick to get a feel for the place, grab a headcount and make sure I know where everyone is positioned. If the coast is clear, I'll come back to get you, and we'll sneak you in through the side door."

"Sounds good. See you on the other side, Sammy."

This time, he initiates the kiss. I nearly lose myself in its tenderness before he pulls away, too soon for my liking but understandable all the same. "See you in a few." And with that, he slips through the door and out of sight. I watch him until his form disappears behind the neighboring warehouses, a murky outline in the setting sunlight. It should be dark in about ten minutes, leaving another hour and some change until the ten PM meeting time.

I glance into the bag again, grinning at the kind gesture from the man I love. My stomach reminds me that I did not, in fact, have dinner, and a quick decision forces the sandwich out of the bag and down my gullet. I'd rather not play around with trying to eat while I'm hiding in a dangerous place, and Sammy isn't here to watch me wolf this down. Not very ladylike, but a gal's gotta eat.

As I swallow the last bit of ham and cheddar on toasted bread, Sammy comes into eyesight again. He gives a quick glance over his shoulder before ducking into the building. A little winded, he composes himself before speaking.

"Alright. Looks like there's only two guys there right now, and they're both hanging around the pier side of the building. Looked down their snouts at me for a second but once I name-dropped our boss they knew I was the human fella they were told would be here tonight. No cops yet, either. I think we should be able to get you in, no problem, but we should go now before more guys show up."

Scooping up my purse and the camera, I step forward. "Right behind you."

With a final reaffirming nod, he sucks in a deep breath before sticking his head out the door. With a quick left to right sweep, he pushes into the night air. I follow behind, tucking my tail in close to reduce my profile as much as possible. We hustle across the paved path, past his concealed car and away from the slowly illuminating bulbs of the sparse above-head lamps. Our destination is several warehouses away, making the trek a short but dangerous one. Thankfully, the rest of the buildings surrounding us seem entirely vacant of prying eyes.

Coming up to the rotted wood panels, we slow our pace to reduce the already minimal noise we're generating. I made sure to wear soft shoes along with my darkened slacks and top. We slink toward the side of the building, pressing our backs to the exterior wall. Sammy holds a hand out to halt my movement before peering around the corner. As his head flicks back, he gives me a quick nod. We slip around the building and he gently unlatches the side entrance.

We slip through, pushing the portal behind us closed just as quietly as we opened it. On tiptoes we shift past dozens of enormous crates, most stacked two high, each large enough to hold a sizable kitchen appliance. Some errant light entering through the ceiling-high windows illuminates the space enough to prevent me from clumsily walking into anything.

A few yards into the structure and past an outcropping with some rickety stairs leading up to a second story loading platform of some sort, Sammy gestures toward the enshrouded corner tucked behind it. Just as he said, a lone, nearly crumbling door blocks off a cubbyhole just large enough for a few upright brooms and a velociraptor woman to stand within. I slide past the nearest crates a few feet away from the closet and give my lover one more kiss before gently pulling the small metal ring that serves as a handle and squeezing myself into the broom-laden sarcophagus.

My tail coils around my leg as Sammy pushes the enclosure shut, the barely functional latch letting out a soft click as it falls into place. His eyes linger on me for a moment longer before he retreats through the entrance we used. My vantage point is limited due to the crates, but the night sky is visible beyond, with the salty lick of ocean foam making its way to my nostrils past the open warehouse door. This particular unit is right on the dock, more than likely coming at a premium due to the convenience of loading and unloading almost directly from a cargo vessel. This part of the dock wouldn't facilitate any of the humongous commercial barges, but it gets the job done for smaller shippers.

I can just make out the shape of a hulking dinosaur about eighty feet away, stationed outside the main warehouse opening atop a stool not designed for someone of his size. His head turns and he grunts. "S'you again."

I can't see him, but Sammy responds. "Sorry about that, fellas. I was—"

A third voice interjects. "You ready to get to work or what, *skinnie?*" My feathers stand on end upon hearing the vulgar word used against the man I love, but I remain motionless.

"Y-yeah. Where do you need me?"

"Ship'll be gettin' here in about a half hour. Get over to the dock and make sure the anchoring ropes are prepped. We don't wanna waste their time, after all."

"O-okay! Got it!"

As Sammy jogs over toward the docks, the two men sitting guard chuckle. "I doubt the dumb ape even knows what an anchoring rope looks like, let alone how to tie one off."

I bite my lip, knowing it'd be big trouble for me and

Sammy if I kicked this door off its hinges and broke that fucker's jaw. All the same, my imagination runs wild with the possibilities of making that scumbag wish he was never born. I never liked the casual racism hurled at humans, though the opportunities to step forward and put a stop to it rarely made themselves accessible. But now that I've fallen in love with a man as kind and gentle as Sammy... I want to protect him. I want the world to see him for his innate strengths and his everflowing heart, not just the durability of his carapace.

Miles Cratis and his bandmates soothe my bristling nerves, playing their songs on the spotlight-draped stage of my mind. The calming timbre of Bill Ephans's fingers gliding across the piano keys light a spark inside of me, the opening notes of "Blue in Green" sending a chill down my back. The song that Sammy and I danced to on that night fraught with smiles and tears and laughter and devastation. A promising date turned sour by my horrible attitude, one that the man I came to love plucked me out of and held me in spite of. A night that turned cataclysmic as the wicked officers with a vendetta nearly hospitalized my favorite musician in the world. A whirlwind of conflicted emotion as I tried to rebuff Sammy to spare him the pain that dating someone like me would bring, only for him to overrule my attempts and accept me.

He accepted me despite my outbursts and foolish tantrums. He accepted me despite the traumas of my past that I unburdened to him on his bedroom floor. He accepted me despite being a flawed and broken woman of a different species.

The muted call of Cratis's immaculate trumpet swirls around me like an embrace, one made manifest by the man I love. The plucks of Paul Chainers's bass pepper my lips, echoes of Sammy's tender kisses. Jimmy Dobb's percussive taps match the rhythm of my breath in tandem with that of my lover as we share our bodies with one another.

I draw in a slow breath to calm my nerves, allowing a smile to tug at my lips. I've always been enraptured by Miles Cratis's music, but now… I can't think of anything else I'd rather have his songs call to mind.

Regaining focus on my surroundings, the shape of a vessel comes into view beyond the adorned pallets between my hiding spot and the sea. It eases into position, bumping against the protective buoys that line the wood and steel outcropping of dock. The two guarding dinosaurs join the workers who hop off the boat and begin fastening it in place.

A lightbulb somewhere above the warehouse flicks to life, causing me to shrink back even further. Based on the angle of the overhanging platform, no light makes its way anywhere close to me. All the same, I feel more exposed than ever. If worse comes to worst and I get spotted, I could make a mad dash for the door. So long as my knee doesn't give out, I might be able to slip away before the shock of some velociraptor woman hiding in the broom closet wears off and they give chase.

More voices join the chorus of labor outside the warehouse. I can't hear Sammy's among them, but I can't pick out any distinct words either. There must be two dozen of them, if not more. An engine comes to life, the rumble of its combustive guts growing closer. The forklift it powers rounds the corner, sliding its two powerful prongs underneath a double-stack of crates before lifting them with ease. It spins around, the pilot's deft skills on full display as it rolls onto the dock and deposits its payload. Waiting workers throw several hooks and ropes around the topmost crate and, after a moment, it hoists into the air and out of sight, certainly heading toward the ship's hold.

This process repeats for thirty minutes, the view of the dock and those working it becoming clearer with each row of crates that gets removed. The hectic noise is clear enough disguise for the simple click of a camera, so I get to work taking a few photographs. I don't notice a police presence yet, so any attending officers must be outside watching the work being done. Even so, establishing shots of these crates and their mysterious contents being evacuated onto the boat might be handy.

I twist the knob on top of the camera, causing the numbered wheel adjacent to it to shift down another digit. Peering through the view finder, I press the aperture as close to the cracks in the door as I can and take another photo. The snap of the lens is almost deafening to me, but entirely unnoticed by anyone in the vicinity. Good. So long as I don't do something stupid and take a photo against dead silence I should be fine.

A few minutes later, the containers dwindle to a half dozen or so. The one closest to the broom closet door is only a single crate that stands about waist-high. At this point, I've got an almost perfectly clear line of sight over the warehouse, save for a few blind spots here and there. It appears the forklift driver had been staging them on the dock so rapidly that a surplus built up by the ship. I wind the film again as the forklift charges toward me. I'd be more nervous if I hadn't watched him drive just as quickly with zero errors for the past thirty minutes. However, as the dual lifting plates slide under the pallet, it pushes the crate forward three feet before lifting off the ground, the splintering shriek of wood scraping against wood causing me to grit my teeth and pray to God the door doesn't fall off its hinges.

"Ayo, Paulie! Not dat one, dat one's stayin'."

The forklift driver, ostensibly named Paulie, throws his arm over the seat behind him and twists his upper half to address whoever just addressed him. "Well, which other ones gotta go? They all look the fuckin' same!"

"Not dat one! Get dose two over dere and tha rest stay

behind!" The stubby finger of the one barking orders at Paulie points elsewhere, and Paulie lets out an annoyed groan before turning back toward the forklift's controls and throwing the release lever. The pallet crashes to the ground, the forklift's metal teeth clattering against the concrete. He backs up and spins in the direction of whichever other…

Oh no.

I gently push against the door. It doesn't budge.

I put more force into it. Nothing.

I brace my legs and press my entire body into the wretched wood.

I'm stuck.

The pallet completely blocks the door from opening, being pressed so tightly against the frame that even a professional escape artist couldn't wriggle free. My chest feels as though it'll collapse in on itself as hyperventilation takes over. The knee that's been surprisingly quiet this whole time begins stabbing daggers into the surrounding muscles, doubled protestation of the strain I just inflicted by trying to heave the door free and the impending terror of my imprisonment. I never thought I was claustrophobic, but I've also never been pinned into a broom closet in a place I shouldn't be.

I close my eyes, doing everything in my power to steady my breathing and lower my heart rate. Sammy will help me out of here. Once these guys are done, he'll be able to push the crate from the outside and get me free.

As I reopen my eyes, the man of my dreams comes into sight. The rest of the warehouse seems to be empty of other workers at the moment; Sammy shoots cautious glances over his shoulder and speaks in a fast whisper. *"Aubrey, are you okay?!"*

I whisper back. *"I'm okay, but I'm stuck in here!"*

Another peek over his shoulder, keeping a wary eye out for anyone who would notice his peculiar behavior. *"Alright,*

I'm gonna get you out as soon as I can." He glances again before turning to me sternly. *"You were right."*

"I was... right?"

"The Herdsters are involved in illegal shit. They're shipping guns." My jaw falls open. *"Loads of 'em. I didn't see 'em, but the guys were mentioning it by the boat."*

I can't believe it. I had my suspicions that they were a shady organization, but never in a million years would I have guessed that they were gun-running. My eyes lower to the crate barricading me in. Is this one packed with firearms too? If so, why did they leave it?

Sammy sizes up the crate before trying to push against it, testing its weight. *"Okay, let me—"*

A voice from out of sight cuts him off. "Samuel?"

Sammy spins and darts toward the approaching figures, putting as much distance between himself and my hiding spot as he can before they spot him. His trot ends casually and his tone is relaxed. "Yea, Charles?"

His back is to me as he addresses two dinosaurs near the warehouse opening, a diplodocus wearing a surprisingly warm smile and a stern triceratops that oozes authority. That must be Sammy's boss. Neither of the dinosaurs peer past him; good, he didn't raise suspicion.

The triceratops speaks. "You did good tonight, son. I'm real proud of you."

The diplodocus's thick hand claps Sammy's shoulder. "You're proving yourself to be a team player, bud! I knew you were cut out for this sorta work!"

Though I can't see Sammy's face, I envision his smile as he scratches the back of his neck. "Aw, don't mention it. Happy to help wherever I can!"

A large cigar rolls around lazily in the triceratops's lips. "Good. I'm glad to hear that. We'll have you do one more thing tonight, and then we'll call it square on that nice new car of yours. That sound like a deal to you?"

"Y-yes, sir! More than a deal!"

"Attaboy. Alright, what I need from you—"

A stern voice interrupts them. "Well? No issues tonight, I take it?"

My heart sinks into my stomach. No... please, God, *no*...

"William! Nice of you to stop by! I figured it'd just be your underling with us this evening." The triceratops warmly greets the one man I wish wasn't involved in all this as he strides into view like a waking nightmare. "Yes, everything went fine."

The brown pterodactyl doesn't accept the triceratops's proffered hand, instead jamming his thumbs between his stomach and suspenders. He stands even taller than the already quite tall triceratops and glares down his beak. "This is proving to be a lot more trouble than it's worth, Charles. I've got people asking questions at the station. People I'd prefer not knowing about these arrangements."

The man called Charles lowers his hand and his welcoming smile wanes. "I assure you, William. We've got a secure crew here. If anyone's causing you problems, it's likely unrelated—"

"They knew about the dock. About the shipment going out tonight. How secure can your crew be?"

Another voice joins in, its shrill, cruel tone causing me to stifle a gasp. "Can't be *that* secure if they got fuckin' *skinnies* workin' for 'em."

Preston. Fucking Preston, oh my God. He's the one that attacked Miles Cratis alongside Duffy. He's the one that—

Oh, fuck. *Sammy!*

Charles interjects, all pleasantries in tone having been discarded. "I *said* that I have a good crew. At least, I do with me tonight. There are... others not present that I am more wary of, and given what you've told me I may need to reexamine a few things." At this, the diplodocus's head lowers and he glances away. Sammy has shrunk into as small of a silhouette as possible, having shimmied closer to the diplodocus and farther away from Preston. Charles clears his throat. "All the same, everything is fine here tonight. We had no hitches and the goods are almost done being loaded up. Once we wrap up our final tasks, everything will be squared away."

They pass a few other words back and forth, but I don't register them. The horror of unraveling reality is almost too much for me to bear. Not only is the police captain crooked, but Preston is involved too, and he arrested Sammy the day he and I met! If he recognizes Sammy, everything is gonna fall apart, and I won't be able to do anything to stop it. I can't protect him, not against four armed dinosaurs! All I can do is cower in this stupid hole, watching my world collapse in slow motion.

I blink away the despair. Thankfully, Preston doesn't seem interested in Sammy, instead focusing on the developing transaction. Charles's hand extends toward the captain once more, but this time it isn't empty. A thick white envelope rests between his fingers. I quickly wipe the tears from my cheeks before bringing the camera up again. I hate this. I hate that I know this now, but I have to do what I came here to do.

Captain William Aaron, the man I had come to respect so highly, reaches out and accepts the envelope. I press down on the shutter release button.

Snap.

Simultaneously, five sets of eyes spin in my direction. I instinctively duck down, cowering as far back in the closet as I can without making a sound. My free hand covers my mouth to stifle my breathing; my tail squeezes my midsection in terror. Stupid Aubrey, fucking *stupid*. I'm *fucked*.

The diplodocus withdraws a revolver from his chest holster and cautiously steps in my direction. I quiver uncontrollably, wishing that I could turn back time a few seconds and undo this catastrophic fuck-up.

I'm sorry, Sammy. I'm so sorry—

"I saw some raccoons scampering around back there! Musta knocked something over, the little flea balls." Sammy's voice stops the diplodocus in his tracks. "Dunno what else it'd be, Marty."

The dinosaur Sammy called Marty narrows his eyes, his lengthy neck craning as he peers at the crate and its surroundings. I pray to God that his herbivore eyes aren't as keen as mine and that the shadows still adequately enclose me. There's no other way I'm getting out of this alive.

Only the sound of my heartbeat in my ears persists. For an agonizing moment, I hold my breath and tense every muscle in my body, remaining as still as possible. God, please...

With an annoyed huff, Marty stuffs the revolver back into its home. "Little bastards." He rolls his eyes as he turns to rejoin the others. "Yeah, nothin' over there. Just a pallet up against a closet or somethin'. Nobody gettin' in there without a hand truck or an awful lot of spinach."

Slowly, ever so slowly, I let the air out of my lungs. My chest burns from depriving itself of oxygen for so long, but I reintroduce the element to my body in shallow, silent draws. I make a mental note to cuss myself out for how absolutely fucking brain-dead that move was later. For now, I thank God and, even more so, Sammy for saving my ass.

The captain shakes his head, stuffing the envelope into his pocket. "Just do what you need to do. I'll notify the fire department once you give me the call."

He spins on his heel, ignoring the polite grin offered by Charles, and exits the warehouse. Instead of following him, Preston narrows his eyes toward Sammy. "Don't I know you from somewhere, skinnie?"

Sammy lowers his head, averting his eyes and cleverly using his cap to obscure his face. "N-no, sir."

The spinosaurus's sharp snout twists in thought. "You seem awfully familiar—"

"Preston! Car keys!" Captain Aaron's voice booms from around the corner and out of sight. With a click of his tongue, Preston mutters as he turns to leave.

"Tch. Fuckin' skinnies all look the same."

He fades from view and, shortly thereafter, an engine fires up. Headlights make themselves briefly known before turning away and vanishing into the night.

I had slowly risen back up to a standing position, doing everything in my power to keep from drawing any further attention toward my hiding spot. Now, with my legs straight beneath me again, I peer through the same crack in the door I've made my personal peepshow for the past hour. The last of the crates outside the warehouse lift out of sight and the boatmen begin preparing to cast off. They exchange farewells with the Herdsters, offering to buy drinks for one another the next time they're in town. I can't place any specific accents nor pick anyone in particular out of the crowd. I'm too frazzled.

I just want to get out of here. I just want to be away from this place, somewhere safe with Sammy.

Charles's attention shifts from the dispersing crewmen and departing vessel back to Sammy and Marty. Only the three of them remain now. Though the air is notably less severe than it was with the captain present, it still crackles with tension. "Samuel. I already know the answer to this before I ask it, but it needs to be asked all the same. You are *loyal* to the Herdsters, correct?"

Sammy's back stiffens up. "Y-yes, sir! Absolutely!"

"And you wouldn't do something foolish like going to the police about our dealings?" He waves a hand toward the space that Captain Aaron had occupied just minutes ago. "As you see, we've made arrangements with them. Such traitorous actions on your part would prove entirely fruitless."

"No, sir. I didn't and wouldn't. You guys treat me well, and I'd prefer to keep it that way." To be fair, Sammy isn't lying. Well, not exactly. He did come to *me* with information, but as was made brutally apparent, I'm not a cop.

Charles's eyes narrow for a moment before he grins. "Excellent. I knew you were a good man, and I'm glad I brought you on board." He turns to Marty and gives a commanding nod which the diplodocus answers by stepping outside the warehouse. "We've got one more task for you. Once it's done, you'll be all set. In fact, you can take tomorrow off for your hard work here tonight." He pauses a moment. "You... did park farther away from the warehouse, as I instructed?"

"Y-yes, sir. I did." He shifts. "Wasn't sure why... because you didn't want a human to be seen driving something that nice nearby is what I'm guessin'."

"Not exactly." As Charles mutters this, Marty returns. Grasped by their metal carrying handles, two five-gallon containers wearing coats of chipped and partially eroded red paint cause my throat to clog in panic. They clang against the concrete floor, their contents sloshing about and already filling the enclosed space with acrid fumes.

Charles's hand rests on Sammy's shoulder. His violet eyes are piercing and authoritative. "I want you to burn this building to the ground."

The color drains away from Sammy. He turns and stares directly at me, mouth agape, horrified and speechless. Marty speaks up, seeming to believe that Sammy is looking at the crates and not at his imprisoned girlfriend. "Don't worry about those ones. They're stuffed full of shit we had to get rid of anyway. Documents, mostly. Papers we'd rather not have anyone siftin' through in the dumpsters, if you get my meaning."

Sammy turns back to them, finally reclaiming his voice. "B-but *why?*"

Another cigar makes its way into Charles's lips but he hesitates on firing up his lighter, glancing at the gasoline cans only a few feet away. He reconsiders and pockets the device, leaving the unlit tobacco between his teeth. "Part of the operation. It's what we call a 'two-for-one special' in the business. We get a shipment of goods out of here, then an *accident* happens that removes any traces of our actions while allowing us to claim a respectable insurance policy on the building." He steps over and raps a knuckle against the rotted wood making up one of the warehouse's walls. "As you can see, this building isn't long for the world anyway. Salt spray will do that in a surprisingly short amount of time."

Sammy trembles. I'm terrified myself, but he's the one that's visible to those two. Keep it together, Sammy. We'll figure this out. "U-um, o-okay. So I j-just—"

The comforting triceratops hand returns to Sammy's shoulder. If he weren't being asked to commit arson, it would come across as fatherly. "Douse the crates and baseboards of the walls, and light it up. From a safe distance, of course. Once the flames are going, you're free to leave. Marty and I will take care of calling the police captain just as soon as we're sure the building and its contents are properly *disposed of.*"

Sammy's head lowers. "Y-yes, sir."

Marty chimes in. "Good work, buddy. This'll be a piece of cake for you! Charles and I will be a ways down the dock waiting for the show with that spinosaurus copper. Y'know, plausible deniability and all that!" He chuckles and hands over a box of matches. Sammy's spirits seem to lift, though I know that it's not due to the diplodocus's joviality. He caught the same nugget of information I did.

They're gonna leave. We'll have a chance.

Sammy scoops up one of the two jugs of gasoline while the two dinosaurs make their way out of the warehouse and down the dock. I barely notice the shape of Preston join them; he must have stayed behind to oversee the last step of this plan. Safely away from the ignitable liquids, a spark of ember appears in Charles's hand and raises to his mouth before being extinguished with a flick of his wrist.

As Sammy begins sloshing the gasoline against the walls of the warehouse as far away from me as possible, he stares in my direction. I can read his thoughts, clear as day.

"As soon as they're out of sight, we're getting out of here."

He keeps up the show, glancing over his shoulder occasionally to ensure his boss and coworker haven't changed their minds. As he reaches the corner of the building, the stench of gasoline almost becoming unbearable, he quickly sets the can down and runs the length of the warehouse toward the opposite wall near its opening. He cautiously peers around the corner, staring into the darkness for a few moments, likely trying to gauge their apparent location past the inky night.

With a confident nod, he turns toward me and bolts across the warehouse again, sputtering before he reaches me. "We gotta go, *now!*"

I do my best to fight my own panic. "Just help me get the fuck outta this closet!"

He quickly assesses the situation before spinning around to the side of the crate. Forcing all of his weight into it, he pushes as hard as he can, grunting and straining against the several hundred pounds of paper and other incriminating items the Herdsters wished to incinerate tonight. I join him by pushing against the door, bracing my good leg against the wall behind me and heaving all my force into the obstacle. With our combined exertion, the pallet and its payload begin to slide, a slight budge at first, followed by a groaning shunt.

The wood against wood crackles and squeals, both door and crate complaining about being brought into violent union with one another.

With several more heaves, we push the barrier far enough out of the way that the broom closet door can open, if only a crack. Good enough is good enough. I thank my lucky stars that I'm a slender woman and squeeze through the opening, though I have to turn my head back to fit my protruding snout through the gap. With a gasp, I pop through the fracture and immediately into Sammy's waiting arms. An involuntary sob escapes.

"I'm so sorry. I was fucking stupid with that—" My eyes widen. "The camera!" I spin away from his grasp, dropping to a grouchy knee and reaching back through the opening. I find both the camera and my purse, having silently left them on the ground after my absolute bungle of photography during the quietest part of the night.

"It's okay. We're gonna get out of here. I don't give a shit about the Herdsters. I just want you to be safe."

I rise to my feet, belongings in hand, and turn back to him. "I couldn't agree mo—"

Beyond Sammy, the silhouette of a man stands against the darkness. The poor illumination of the single bulb in the warehouse rafters only seems to throw more shadows upon his visage.

Even with the disadvantage, even with the waning light… I recognize his outline. I recognize his shape.

Oh my God.

Sammy notices my horror and spins around, putting himself between me and the intruder. He stands firm before quickly relenting in relief. "Raptor Jesus, you scared me—wait a minute, what are you doing here, Pierce?"

The hulking stegosaurus steps forward, each stride clearing a significant portion of the warehouse floor. His blackened slacks and track jacket exude equal parts menace and secrecy. His midnight blue scales consume the meager light. Only the glint of steel tucked into the holster under his arm betrays the enveloping shadow. His enraged blue eyes snap from me back to Sammy.

His voice is gravelly and filled with fury. "I'd rather ask you, what are you doing with Aubrey?"

Sammy freezes. His eyes flick back to me for only a split second before he responds. "Wh-what?"

"I said, what the *fuck* are you doing with my brother's *wife?!*"

Chapter Fifteen: Pierce

The ice settled further into the bottom of my glass with a soft clink. The mixture had become more water than bourbon at this point. I wasn't gulping it down. I was barely sipping it, in fact. There were more pressing matters to attend to than being polite and finishing the drink set in front of me.

Marty's normally mirthful attitude had entirely evaporated. "Y-you're not serious, right?"

I didn't respond. He already knew the answer. The radio behind the bar filled the void momentarily, Bing Clawsby's handsome croon about the whippoorwills' call foretelling the return to his "blue heaven" doing little to soften the mood.

"You can't just do that. Look, I know it's a bad situation, but—" My sharp gaze instantly cut his words short. He went rigid, then lowered his head. A mutter escaped his lips. "It ain't right. None of this is right."

Marty was usually a good man to confide in, someone with whom you could share private information. Someone who could lend an ear or even a shoulder when necessary. Someone who was loyal, a good friend. But tonight, he was making me regret having spilled the beans to him.

I rotated on the barstool, glancing over my shoulder in the direction of my prey. It was a quiet night at Santiago's, unusually so due to the nasty cold making its late winter rounds. At least half the guys were out sick, either with the illness or caring for a family member with it. But I wasn't sick in the slightest, and neither was Lorenzo.

Adorned in his usual charcoal leather jacket and cow-licked mop of greasy hair, he laughed about God-knows-what with a handful of other Herdsters on the opposite end of the restaurant. The liquor was flowing liberally that evening—Charles's absence meant no one needed to keep up pretenses or act too professional.

Hypocrites. Fucking hypocrites, the lot of 'em.

Marty's head hovered above the bar table between us, speaking in the hushed tone we'd been maintaining for the past several minutes. "Pierce, listen to me." I didn't face him. "You're just now starting to make some progress in the business, movin' up the ladder. How long have you been a Herdster? Nine years and some change? And now you're gonna throw it away on account of—"

I whipped around and growled. "Who's gonna tell 'em?"

He shook his head. "Come on. Charles would have to be a moron to not put two and two together."

I resumed my reconnaissance. Charles could have his suspicions. He wouldn't have proof. That was good enough for me.

"Please don't do it." His beseeching whimper fell on deaf ears. "We can figure something else out."

The last time Marty sounded so broken up was when I told him what happened to Franky's wife. I didn't tell him everything, but given his family's close proximity to mine he deserved to know. Marty had to choke back tears; he and his wife had just started working on one of their own, after all, and he was looking forward to our families having similarly aged kids. He was gonna make a good father.

Franky... woulda made a good father, too.

My little brother had showed up at my front step in the piss-early morning almost two months prior, banging on the door and sobbing uncontrollably. He reeked of booze and I couldn't get a coherent word out of him. I bunked him down in the guest room so he could sober up.

In the morning proper, a couple boys in blue showed up, asking questions about Franky's whereabouts. I lied, telling them I had seen neither hide nor hair of my brother for a few days. The pair wandered off with a tip of their caps. They knew not to give Herdsters too much trouble, so that was the end of it. However, I still had to deal with Franky and figure out what happened to stir him up so badly.

He nursed his cup of afternoon coffee, hands trembling so badly that the warm liquid sloshed over his fingers. "I fucked up," he kept muttering. "I didn't mean to do it, I was just so *angry.*" The tears fell in waves, accompanied by more muttered apologies and excuses but no clear answers. Bianca rubbed his back to comfort him while giving me one of her looks. This was bad; we just didn't know how bad yet.

Things didn't start making sense until I drove to his place later that evening. It was a handsome little two-story home, the perfect starter house for a newlywed couple. My knock went unanswered. His wife worked, despite being *very* pregnant. It was a minor point of contention between Franky and I, never serious enough to turn into a full-blown argument but a disagreement in philosophy nonetheless. I knew that a woman's place was in the home, caring for the kids and keeping things running smoothly. Franky acquiesced to his petite little velociraptor gal's aspirations of becoming a *police officer.* A foolish pipe dream.

I knocked again, listening for any rustling footsteps or calls of "Just a minute" from the other side. None came.

Franky was over the moon for Aubrey when they met. He would speak to me with wide eyes and a beaming grin, telling me all the wonderful traits of this sharp-toothed broad. It was a little unusual, an herbivore getting with a carnivore, but my brother was always a romantic at heart. He wasted no time putting that baby in her after their wedding, either. Us Signorelli's had always been good shots, as my father liked to put it on account of his seven children.

However, it seemed like Franky's infatuation gave way rapidly as time went on. He sang her praises less and less, replacing it with grumbles about her nagging or prodding him. I tried to assuage his concerns, letting him know that the hormones go a bit crazy when a lady's pregnant; hell, Bianca ground my nerves to dust on more than one occasion while she was lugging Russell around in her belly. But he didn't seem to get the point. He'd toss back a shot and call Aubrey a bitch as he poured another.

Tired of waiting, I tested the doorknob. It wasn't locked. I cautiously called out my presence as I pushed the door open; the scene waiting for me on the other side rapidly solved the mystery.

I quickly stepped over the blood that had soaked into the carpet and ascended the stairs without putting any weight on the splintered banister. An assortment of Franky's clothes flew into a luggage trunk along with the piece I knew he kept tucked in the top shelf of his closet. We'd sort out the rest later. I hustled back downstairs, careful not to plant a shoe print at the scene, and tossed what I salvaged into the back seat. My car vanished around the corner before any neighbors started getting curious.

God damn it, Franky. You fool. You drunk fucking fool.

"I'm gonna get better. I'm gonna fix myself up, and I'm gonna do better for her." The lament of an alcoholic was always full of remorse and promises to do right, but I knew my brother better than that. His sober spell lasted all of twenty-four hours before he started sneaking swigs from our liquor cabinet. I tolerated it, being an even bigger fool than Franky for it. But why wouldn't I? He had just lost a kid.

I didn't understand why he never went to the hospital to see his wife. Then again, he never went to see mom, either.

I kept going to work while he sat around my house and drank my booze. It was a month before Bianca finally put her foot down and said he had to go. She didn't have the endless patience that I did for my kid brother. I got him situated in a one-bedroom apartment halfway between my place and the Local 237. Told him he needed to get his shit together and start coming to work again, or else there wouldn't be a work to come back to.

He did start coming to work again. Even seemed to be cutting back on the drinking. Wasn't getting blind-stupid drunk every night, at least. Just his usual brand of tipsy, bringing laughter-filled anecdotes to the other guys at Santiago's after our shifts.

And then he disappeared.

No... he didn't just disappear. He was killed. My brother wouldn't vanish out of the blue.

Another bout of chuckles from the jacket-bound skinnie and his company jostled me from the burning memories. The fury bubbled, causing me to gnaw on my tongue to suppress a scowl. I rose from my stool with a shove and beelined toward the door. I could feel Marty's pleading eyes trail me out of the restaurant. The biting evening cold greeted me with open arms. I tugged at my collar and trudged through the near-ice slush on the frigid sidewalk toward my waiting car.

The engine churned. I revved it a few times to help warm it up before cracking open the dashboard vents. I flicked on my headlights, slid into the sleepy road and turned the nearby corner. A block down, another turn, then two blocks further, another. I doused my headlights, pulling to a stop a block and a half away from Santiago's front visage. The dimmed bulbs of its namesake sign threw enough light at the stoop below it so that I could identify folks as they left.

At least, I'd be able to easily identify the outline of a fucking skinnie.

A half hour passed before I watched Marty hunch through the door, lowering his elongated neck so as to not clobber his skull on the frame. It was a usual move for him, but one that carried a new motion as he craned his head around to look for my car. It wasn't where I had parked it on our arrival. He seemed to breathe a sigh of relief before turning down the nearby alley to his own means home. Its tail lights disappeared down the street and I returned my focus to the present mission.

Lorenzo. The sleaze ball wormed his way into the organization with toothy grins and honeyed words. He fancied himself a cool customer who was often tasked to handle wet work for the Herdsters. Those of us who had previously taken such heavy work knew the gravitas it required, the respect and civility needed even when you were putting a bullet in the forehead of a thief or traitor. It wasn't something in which you reveled, something you gloated about openly. Lorenzo was a fool who earned a spot at the table through tenacity and vile spirit.

Of course, I knew why he was being assigned such jobs recently. It wasn't because of his skill, or his professionalism. It was because he was a skinnie. And that meant he was more disposable than anyone else. Hell, had this not happened, I was on the verge of speaking to Charles about moving him up in the organization. Lorenzo's charm had even started to endear him to me; it was hard to dislike the guy despite being a spear-chucker. He got along with Franky, too; the pair of them could banter back and forth endlessly.

My fingers tightened around the steering wheel, squeezing the racing blood back down my arms. This fucking skinnie probably walked right up to my brother on the street with the greeting of an old friend before murdering him. He's gonna pay. The slimy little fuck will pay with his life.

I'm gonna avenge you, Franky. You had your problems, but I owe you that much.

An hour of churning hatred later, several figures exited Santiago's. The interior lights doused but the sign remained illuminated long enough for me to watch the skinnie turncoat tuck his greasy hair under a flat cap and stuff his hands into his pockets. He sauntered across the road and slid behind the steering wheel of the handsome 1957 Ford Fairlane he'd been gifted by the Herdsters, its dual green and white tones making it an easy vehicle to trail. Meanwhile, my jet black DeVille would blend right in with the other sparse late-night traffic. At least long enough for it to matter.

It was a short journey, coming to a close in a cramped parking lot behind a pair of dilapidated apartment structures. The stench of rotting garbage that forced its way through my closed windows told me all I needed to know about what sort of creatures took up residence here. They wouldn't be any trouble.

Cracked asphalt met the bottoms of my shoes as I rapidly closed the distance between myself and the still parking Ford. Lorenzo had only just shut his driver's side door when I arrived. My delivery was already in hand.

He glanced from me to it, then back to me with a charming grin. "Evenin', Pierce. Thought you already went home for the night. What's the occasio—"

"Shut the fuck up, skinnie. You know why I'm here."

He played at innocence. "I don't. You just saw me at Santiago's, didn't ya? You and your buddy Marty were sulking in the opposite corner from me and the boys. I was gonna get you a drink, but you seemed to always have one in hand."

My thumb massaged the hammer of my vengeance. "Admit to me that you did it."

His hands indignantly found his hips. "Admit *what?*"

"Your bullshit games aren't gonna make this end any better, skinnie. Tell me what you did to Franky."

He balked, bringing a hand to his chest. I tensed up, in case he made a play for his piece, but instead he simply tapped his sternum. "Buddy, I'm just as confused as you are as to why he hasn't been showing up to work recently."

I could no longer keep the barrel from pointing anywhere but his head. I spoke through gritted teeth. "I'm not bluffing. *Tell me.*"

He sighed. "Pierce, Pierce, Pierce... You gotta take a breather. I don't know if it's the booze or that nasty bug that's been circling around that's got you not thinkin' straight, but we gotta handle this more professional-like. What sorta info do you think you'd get from me while pointing that iron at my skull?"

"The truth, if you're interested in keeping your brains inside of it."

He shook his head, holding his hands at his sides in a show of placation. "I don't know where your brother is. I didn't do anything to him, and if someone else did, they didn't tell me about it." His eyes softened and he offered a warm smile. "He probably just ran off for a while. Needed a break from everything, from his lousy apartment and the stresses of—"

The thunderclap of steel striking brass rattled the nearby windowpanes. A crescent of crimson painted the muddied slush behind him as he rocked backward. His stiffened body almost held an angelic pose, arms stretched to his sides and gentle smile gracing his lips. The illusion dissolved instantly as his body rolled against the side of his car's hood, crumpling in a tangled heap next to its front tire. I took two steps closer, aiming the pistol center mass before squeezing out the other four rounds in rapid succession. Each puncture released more encased oxygen and once-vital fluid. They were unnecessary, but cathartic.

I gazed at my handiwork for a moment, taking in every detail, searing it into my memory for eternity. I needed to remember this for as long as I lived.

It wasn't until the nearby lights concealed by curtains began flicking on that I hustled to my car, tucking my revolver into my pocket. I'd dispose of it shortly thereafter in my usual memorial graveyard. As I fired up the engine and rapidly reversed out of the parking lot, I let out a deep, shuddering sigh. It was neither one of relief, nor of contentment. It was a promise. A promise that I would never allow anyone else in my life to be hurt by someone like Lorenzo again.

Never again. I'll never trust a fucking skinnie again.

—

Three seconds is all it takes to cross the warehouse; my stride is long, and my blood is boiling. He can't eke out a protestation before the back of my fist collides with the side of his head, sending the skinnie sprawling across the floor. His limbs bend and contort beneath him, coming to rest in a tangled mass. He doesn't move. Whether dead or unconscious, I don't fucking care. I'll do more—

A flash of movement from my peripheral causes me to instinctively lurch backward, barbed tail swinging around to sweep across my traversed path of retreat. The talons come within an inch of my snout; the velociraptor they're attached to leaps back and away from my defenses. Her pupils are pinpricks, her maw flashing in primal fury. She crouches over the misshapen mound of flesh, claws scrabbling against the concrete and feathers standing on end.

She hisses. "Don't you *dare* come any closer! I'll rip your fucking throat out!"

My pulse remains heightened and my awareness is honed; after all, a predator is feet away baring its teeth at me. My tail swoops about in unpredictable arcs, ready to soar toward my opponent with a spin of my hips. However, I manage to raise an eyebrow at Aubrey. "What is this skinnie to you?"

"Don't call him that! He's *mine!*"

I pause. "What? Don't tell me you're going back to the barbaric days of *eating* the fucking things?"

Her lips curl further upward and she spits. "Shut the fuck up and get away from us! I swear to God, I will kill you, Pierce!"

Out of an overabundance of caution, I take a single step back, hands held to my sides and tail defensively positioned. I consider drawing iron on her, but I don't think that the situation has come to such measures quite yet. It'll be a safety valve.

At the sign of my slight retreat, she seems to regain a modicum of sanity, quickly dropping to her knees behind the skinnie and scooping his motionless body into her arms. She cradles his neck and shoulders, quickly assessing the damage. He's still breathing, although through a tepid snore. A knot is already swelling through his cheek and eye socket, slowly discoloring the disgusting, spongy skin surrounding it.

Her growl has become a whimper. "Sammy, talk to me. Come on, Sammy, *wake up...*"

She's calling him 'Sammy', huh? The implication sends a wave of queasiness through my gut. I turn my attention to the purse and camera laying nearby, then to the half-opened closet door nestled underneath the pulley platform above. "You're working with Samuel, then. A spy. I knew he was a dishonest little *rat,* just like every other skinnie."

Her eyes flare up and her teeth bare again as she gently sets the human down. "I told you *not* to call him that!"

I grin and shake my head dismissively. "I've got no clue how you got tangled up in this mess, but you'd better leave. I need to handle this traitor properly—"

In a dizzying burst of speed, she lunges forward, lashing out with her talons. My sharpened tail makes contact with her arm but she spins in response, deftly negating its inertia and avoiding its spines while resuming her attack. The pause gives me the opportunity to unholster my .38, but not enough time to bring it to bear as her fist makes contact with my forearm. I try to close my fingers around the weapon before it soars away; its smooth wooden grip slips past my nails and it glides through the air. Before it clatters to the pavement, my other palm extends outward, catching Aubrey square in the chest and repelling her back. She stumbles, gasping for air that I forced out of her sternum with the blow.

My eyes snap to the snub-nose revolver that came to rest about ten feet away. Using the moment of opportunity, I dash toward it, but before I can bend down and scoop it up the telltale sound of a racking slide pulling a bullet into the chamber freezes me in place.

"Don't... fucking... *move*..." She labors the words past heaves for air. I slowly, very slowly straighten my back and bring my hands up in a show of surrender, turning just enough to see the small pistol in her hands, pointed square at my head. I see. That handbag wasn't just a fashion accessory, after all.

"You don't want to do this, Aubrey. You shouldn't be here."

"Neither should you." She sidesteps closer to Samuel, bringing herself further into my line of sight. Her breathing grows more composed, and the pistol sways less. "I never wanted to see you or your piece of shit brother again, for as long as I lived."

I bare my own unsharpened teeth in a scowl. "Don't say that about Franky."

"Do you have any idea what that *monster* did to me? To my *baby?!*"

My lips uncurl with a sigh. "I do. I'm... sorry that happened." My words momentarily give her pause. "He was a flawed man. I can't excuse what he did to you, but he was dealing with his own demons, too."

Her eyes go out of focus for a moment, then return to me. *"Was?"*

Before I can reply, the heap on the ground stirs. It mutters in barely more than a whisper. *"Aubrey...?"*

Her attention jolts to the human and the firearm she wields lowers ever so slightly. The momentary lapse is all I need, instantly closing the gap before swirling around and bashing the side of my tail into her gut. She gasps, having barely avoided its spikes because of her slender frame. The concussive force still hurls her several feet across the warehouse; she crashes into the side of a large wooden crate on top of a pallet. Her feet keep beneath her, but she reels.

The gun isn't in her hands anymore. I have to press the advantage while there's one to press. I dash toward her, catching her in the side with a fierce right hook. She cries out, bringing her arms up to defend herself; a left fist into her shoulder knocks her off balance and sends her to her ass. I don't enjoy hurting a woman, but when said woman is a predator who's held you at gunpoint and still has razor sharp teeth in her maw, there's little choice in the matter.

I follow her down, planting a hand on the side of her head and smothering her into the concrete. My other arm wrestles her wrists together, pinning and disarming the most lethal parts of her. She shrieks and flails, gnashing fruitlessly at my side and grasping for anything. Her legs kick and her tail thrashes.

I bark the command as I hunch over her. "Stop fighting, or I'll make this a lot worse."

She doesn't listen, struggling like a lunatic against a straight jacket. So be it.

I lift a foot and bring it down on her right knee.

Her scream is deafening. It accompanies her complete surrender, the energy that was being spent on trying to free herself suddenly converting to squeezing herself into a helpless ball. Her leg spasms; she clutches at it while sobbing uncontrollably. I watch the reaction with some surprise. I didn't think I used enough force to break or dislocate anything. The same tactic on other resisting dinosaurs usually straightens 'em up but doesn't lead to much more than a limp that lasts a couple days.

I blink away the musing. "Are you gonna settle down now? I don't want to hurt you any more than tha—"

A loud clap is accompanied by a spray of splinters breaking off the corner of the nearby crate only a few feet away from my face. I jolt upright, releasing the velociraptor by my feet who responds by curling up further and cradling her leg. The source of the interruption wavers and sways, the human holding it struggling to keep his eyes open. He uses his free hand to wipe away some of the mist of unconsciousness from his face.

"Get... get away from her... I mean it..."

I oblige, taking two long steps away from Aubrey and closer to my resting revolver. I doubt he noticed it; he just grabbed that little semi-automatic that Aubrey had dropped next to him and started blasting. I growl. "Why are you shooting at me, Samuel? I'm your *partner.*"

He takes shallow, rapid breaths. He hasn't gotten to his feet yet; instead, he supports himself on an elbow while keeping the pistol in his other hand aimed in my general direction. "Why are you here? You... weren't supposed to do this job tonight..."

I shake my head. "You told me about this job, remember? I asked you for the details and you told me. Why *wouldn't* I be here? I needed to know what was going on. I needed to see what Charles was sneaking around to do, and whether it was something we could leverage against him."

The cogs in Samuel's head turn, albeit slowly. "He... wanted me to burn this place..."

I need to keep him talking, I've got an advantage now. "Samuel, what was being shipped out of here? What was Charles so invested in that he needed so many guys here, but not me?"

He pauses. The pistol remains trained on me, but he strains his eyes as he digs through his seemingly clouded short-term memory. I probably shouldn't have clocked him in the head, but it is what it is. After a moment, he regains focus on me.

"Guns."

"Are you certain?"

He nods. "A fuckload of guns. Crates and crates. I never saw inside 'em, but overheard some of the crewmen muttering about their big haul of weapons."

I bring one of my surrendering hands to my forehead. Raptor Christ... Charles is involved in *gun running* now? It's one thing for the Herdsters to skirt the law and dance with danger, but this is an entire different fucking league.

I push aside the bubbling fury. "You said he told you to burn this warehouse?" The smell of gasoline was evident from the moment I stepped foot near the loading door, and the red cans nearby further pointed to the truth.

He gestures toward the few crates lingering in the building. "Documents. He said—" His eyes widen suddenly. "Don't fuckin' move, Pierce. I swear to God, I will put the rest of these bullets through your skull if you move an inch."

Looks like the haze has finally passed. He clambers to his feet, legs still swaying underneath him. However, the gun in his hand aims steadier than ever. He stumbles across the warehouse toward Aubrey, not taking his eyes off me until he arrives at her side. He crouches next to her, placing a hand on her shoulder.

"Aubrey... are you okay?"

She responds in a sob. "I'm just glad you're alright."

"It's okay, honey. We need to get out of here. Can you walk?"

She starts to push herself up onto her elbows, her knee violently quaking with each movement. I steal a glance toward my waiting pistol; in response, Samuel's arm tightens.

"I said don't move, mother fucker. You can sucker punch me all day, but you do *not* lay a finger on my woman. I oughta blast you in half right here."

I nearly gag at the words. "*Your* woman? Aubrey is married to *my* brother."

His eyes widen and his back goes rigid. "You mean to tell me... your brother is the piece of shit that hurt her? The vile fucking filth that shoved a pregnant woman down the *stairs?!*"

My chin lifts in defiance. "If you're going to kill me for the sins of my brother, so be it. You skinnies are all the same, anyway."

Samuel's breathing is labored. Fire burns in his gaze. It's a look I know all too well; he's preparing himself for what he's about to do. I stand tall, my thoughts drifting to my beautiful wife and my two loving children. I know they'll be okay, even if I don't come home.

A claw clutches at Samuel's arm. He gasps and briefly averts his stare. Aubrey quivers as she tries to pull herself to her feet.

"Don't. Don't do it, Sammy. You're better than this."

In response, he throws his free arm around her waist, helping to hoist her up slowly. He never once releases the trained sights from my body. Impressive technique for a skinnie who's never shot a man before. Even so, I consider making a dive for the revolver. If things turn for worse, it's an option.

Aubrey winces in pain, sucking air past clenched teeth as she hobbles with her weight almost entirely on her left leg. The two of them shimmy toward the side door of the warehouse, business end of the small pistol squared on me the whole way. They reach the exit; Samuel quickly removes his free hand from Aubrey before twisting the handle and pulling the door open.

I turn my akimbo hands upward in a shrug. "I guess this is it, then. It was a *pleasure* workin' with ya."

He doesn't reply. They slip through the door, tugging it closed behind them. I finally lower my arms, letting out a sigh. While I could scoop up my revolver and chase 'em down, what's the fuckin' point? They didn't shoot me. Hell, they barely laid a finger on me. And now I don't have to see either of them again, traitorous skinnie *or* velociraptor whore.

I assess my surroundings, stepping over to one of the near half dozen crates near the back wall. It's nailed shut pretty tight, save for the hole Samuel's stray bullet planted in it; I line myself up before sending a spike from my tail into the same corner. The force dislodges the lid enough for my fingers to slip between and pry it up.

Papers. Thousands upon thousands of papers, dumped into it like a garbage bin. I fish one out randomly and scan its surface. Something about a zoning permit application dated two years ago. A quick rummage reveals more similar ink; nothing incriminating to my uneducated eyes, but a prosecuting lawyer's wet dream, I'd imagine.

It's not worth taking any of this with me. I should go; hell, I probably already overstayed my welcome. I turn toward my still abandoned revolver, moving with swiftness and—

The unfamiliar roar was sudden and surprising. And, it seems, somewhat disarming, having entirely halted my forward momentum. I stand stock still, almost as though I was involuntarily playing at being one of those street performers who imitate statues and collect nickels. My heart beat quickens, pumping adrenaline to every corner of my body. Strangely enough, there is no pain. Only an odd, spreading feeling of wetness near my stomach.

I turn to face the calamity. A gray triceratops I know all too well stands at the opened seaside loading doors, the gentle lap of ocean waves at his back. Next to him, a smirking spinosaurus in a police uniform who also holds a pistol, though he seems to be aiming it at both me and the third onlooker.

Marty. He holds his empty hands toward me, a frozen gasp upon his normally friendly face. He spins in Charles's direction. *"Why?!"*

The lit cigar between his lips rolls lazily to and fro. He holds a revolver in his palm, grip and trigger draped in a handkerchief that shields his scales from its surfaces. Its muzzle emits a wisp of smoke, an echo of its war cry. Without looking down, I know where the bullet landed.

It still doesn't hurt.

Charles takes a step into the warehouse, aims the revolver in my direction, then fires it four more times. Each reverberation jostles the rotted wood around us, dislodging ancient dust from the rafters high above. I wince in realization that my final thoughts aren't of my family but instead of god damn dusty beams, but the wince is quickly supplanted by confusion. I'm still upright, and nothing further seems to be wrong with my scales or guts. I'm fairly certain my brains are still inside my head, too.

With a grin, Charles tosses the revolver at Marty's feet. Marty stares at it for a moment, then at our boss in utter bewilderment. "Charles, what are—"

"In due time, Martin. In due time. I'm setting the stage, you see." His seemingly jovial words carry venom.

Marty gazes at me with remorse. "God, Pierce. I'm so sorry. I don't know—"

"Shut up, you pencil-necked prick." The spinosaurus takes immense pleasure in his turn of phrase.

Marty turns to the cop, only to jump back at the realization that a gun is trained on him. His hands lift in surrender and he protests. "What the fuck is this?!"

"As I said, Martin. We have some matters that need addressing." The triceratops saunters, as though on a leisurely Sunday stroll through Central Park. His hands are clasped behind his back, still gripping the white handkerchief. "Where do we begin? I suppose the most pressing matter is the one of an uninvited guest in attendance at our evening rendezvous."

His menacing purple eyes stare me down. I don't respond, instead doing my best to perform a slow check of my remaining function and mobility given my current predicament. I flex my fingers; those still work. I shift my feet; good there, too. My tail twitches, uncooperative of the direction I just gave it. That part might be out. I can still fight my way out of this, as soon as I get the opening.

"Somehow, despite not being informed of this non-publicized Herdsters task, you have managed to find yourself in our midst. A startling coincidence, if I do say so myself." He frowns. "Perhaps you were on a late night seaside jog? Your attire suggests such."

I grimace. The fucker is toying with me. "Yeah. That's exactly it. A coincidence."

He smiles. "Of course, seeing that this particular pier is about thirty miles away from your home, that must have been some trek!" I don't respond, and his smile fades. "So, it… wasn't a jog. In that case, someone must have told you about the meet-up?" At this, he turns an accusatory eyebrow toward Marty.

"I-I didn't! I didn't tell Pierce anything! I didn't want him getting wrapped up in this, why would I?!"

A sigh escapes Charles. "That is the question. Why would Pierce get himself wrapped up in this?" He lazily turns to face further into the warehouse before casually striding toward the back of the space. "I had my doubts about his loyalty in the past, considering the foolish and short-sighted actions he seemed frequently prone to taking, but—"

He stoops down and plucks a black and silver brick from the concrete. "This seems damning." His icy gaze returns to me. "Wouldn't you say?"

My fingers tighten into fists. My breathing is becoming more labored. He's wasting time on purpose. I have to do something, but I can't risk Marty getting hurt. "That camera isn't mine. There was another—"

"Another what?" Charles's free hand sweeps across the empty warehouse. "There's no one else here. Not even Samuel! Though I'm guessing you scared him off, given the gun shot we heard a few minutes ago. And here I thought you two were becoming friends. No loyalty among the wicked, I suppose."

I grit my teeth. "Samuel didn't do anything wrong."

Charles shrugs. "I'm inclined to agree with you. After all, he was in sight the entire time as we got the supplies loaded on the ship, and he *was* going to burn this building to ashes." His falsely pleasant grin turns wicked. "He's expendable. I'm not worried about it."

Despite my hatred toward skinnies and the animosity I held toward Samuel because of his involvement with Aubrey, I can't help but growl. "Whatever you do to me, leave him out of it."

My words are dismissed with a hand-wave. "No matter. What *does* matter, right now, is what you just brought up. Sneaking around draped in black, spying on our operations... hiding in *broom closets* to collect incriminating photographs?" He gestures toward the closet door partially pinned by a crate. "This just won't do. It's not becoming of you, Pierce, a man of your *integrity.*" He taps a finger to the bottom of his snout in fake thought. "So what *are* we going to do with you?"

I know Charles. He's planned this. He knew I'd find out about his scheme and show up here. I fell right into his trap. "Just kill me and be done with it. Save me the theatrics."

His grin widens. "You're right. I know exactly what I'm doing, and we've almost got everything ready. There's only one more detail." Filled with a sense of superiority, he closes the gap between himself and my waiting revolver. I lurch forward, only to stop as the spinosaurus's arm tightens. He only has to turn a few degrees to put me in his sights. I'm probably a dead man anyway, but…

Marty. I gotta get Marty out of this. My friend stands petrified, his elongated neck quivering in terror. I only hope that he's still got his piece on him and can find an opportunity to draw. He's never been a fast shot, but he's always been dependable. He's always had my back when I needed him, when it mattered most.

Charles stoops, sets the camera down and retrieves my revolver, laying the handkerchief on its grip before lifting it from its resting place. "You know, all of this could have been avoided if you simply knew to leave well enough alone. You had to go and kill one of my best enforcers, all because of your good-for-nothing brother. A worthless drunk who brought shame on the Herdsters with his reckless lifestyle choices and abysmal work ethic. Top it off with what he did to his unborn child…" He clicks his tongue. "Honestly, I did the world a favor."

My eyes widen. The warehouse is starting to spin, but I bite down on my tongue to regain balance. "What did you just say?"

His gaze offers sarcastic understanding. "I said, I did the world a—"

"No. About his child. How did you know about that?"

Puzzlement crosses his face, followed by rapid understanding embellished by a wicked grin. "Oh dear. This only makes things more *delightful.*"

I turn to Marty. The color has drained from his face. He stares at me, mouth ajar, tears threatening to fall from his eyes. "I didn't know."

There were only a handful of people in the world who knew what happened to Aubrey. Me, the doctors, my brother, Bianca, Aubrey herself, and…

"Marty."

"I swear to God, Pierce. I didn't know what he was gonna do. I didn't mean for—"

He's interrupted by a thunderous guffaw. Charles laughs so hard he has to brace himself with his free hand against his knee. The spinosaurus ignorantly joins in with a chuckle of his own, unaware of why his ally is so amused.

"I *planned* for much of this to happen, but this could *not* have been more perfect. Even *I* didn't account for this. Oh, mercy!" He wipes a laughter-induced tear away from his face before regaining his composure. "Yes, Pierce. Your friend betrayed you. He told me all about what Franky had done to his wife and about his new living situation."

Marty is frenetic. "On Raptor Christ and Mother Mary, I swear to you that I didn't mean for that to happen! I wanted Charles to *help* Franky! I wanted to get him help for his drinking!"

Lorenzo mentioned Franky's apartment. In the frigid lot where I confronted him, the skinnie tipped his hand and removed any shadow of a doubt that lingered as to his involvement. I never thought to consider how he could have learned where Franky was staying. We were careful, and nobody knew about the arrangement. Nobody except…

My head hangs in resignation. It's betrayal on all sides. This is how I die, not by a bullet, but with a separate knife planted in my back from every person I thought I could trust in this cursed city.

A hand claps to my shoulder. I struggle to lift my neck. Charles stares at me, a strange amount of compassion in his eyes. "I understand what you're feeling. I really do. And that's why I'm going to do what I'm about to do." He lifts the revolver, sweeping its barrel across my face. I don't flinch. I'm ready for this to be over.

He takes a deep breath. "As much as I want to kill you, Pierce... I can't. Trust me, I would if I could. You've been a thorn in my side for far too long. Hell, Eggsy would still be with us if you didn't have the connections you do. But here we are. It took an awful lot of planning, but you know me. That was never a problem. *You* are the problem. One I'm going to solve."

My eyes go out of focus. I will myself to bring a fist to the bottom of his jaw, but all my arm does is twitch uselessly. Charles glances at the blood pooling at my foot, then back at me. "You won't die. The ambulances will be here in a few minutes, and you'll get stitched up, and then you'll go to prison for life. You'll be out of my hair, and you'll still be alive."

Marty's shaking voice cracks. "Prison? For w-what?"

Only now do I notice the empty shoulder holster underneath Marty's raised arms. I glance down at the spent revolver by his feet. Five shots. One bullet in me, the other four in the crates and wall behind me.

Charles's eyes find Marty. They are apologetic. Repentant. Almost remorseful.

"Murder."

The handkerchief tightens on the trigger of my gun. Everything goes silent. Marty's elongated neck snaps backward, shuddering in response to the errant signals the remnants of his brain are sending to the rest of his body. His arms stiffen. His legs buckle. Only muscle memory and raw, wasted adrenaline keep his feet underneath him, balancing in a grisly throe. The spinosaurus steps back, both fascinated by the sight and cautious of which direction the body is going to eventually tumble.

It settles on falling backward. My friend's expressionless, lifeless face vanishes behind his stomach as his neck drops to the concrete like a cut rope. Blood pours from the splayed scales on the back of his skull.

Three more shots rip through the night air, the bullets soaring harmlessly over the foaming ocean. I try to fall to my knees, but Charles catches me, hoisting me up. He drops the revolver at my feet and stuffs the handkerchief into his breast pocket before shoving his fingers into my jacket. He fishes out my spare ammunition, rattling it around in his grip before stepping back and letting me continue down to the concrete.

His words are icy. "This is your fault. And now you'll have to live with that. No one will believe you when you say that I caused this. The police belong to the Herdsters—well, the ones that matter, anyway." With this, he throws a sideways grin to the waiting spinosaurus. "Officer Preston here will be among the first responders, and he'll help the detectives piece together exactly what happened. Two disloyal Herdsters, disgruntled with one another, get into a gun fight in a warehouse they planned to burn down. One died, the other was injured, but it's clear as day that they were the only two here."

Almost in response to a passing thought, he strides across the warehouse and scoops up the camera he left where my revolver was lying. "Well, as soon as we dispose of this, it'll be clear as day." He turns to the one he called Preston. "Let's go make a phone call and get you in position. Once he's in custody, make sure the warehouse still goes up in flames.

It's awfully easy for gasoline-soaked boards to accidentally catch fire."

"You got it, Mr. Rossi." The spinosaurus displays his teeth gleefully as the two wander out of the warehouse. I fruitlessly clutch my side, trying to apply pressure to the bubbling wound that only now begins aching, as though someone is slowly plunging a butcher knife between my ribs. I force the pain into the recesses of my mind and stare helplessly at the shape of my friend.

Marty. I'm so sorry. You deserved better than this.

My teeth nearly crack from the force applied to them. I can't waste energy on tears. Not right now. I have to get out of here. I have to avenge Marty. He deserves it. His wife and his unborn child deserve it. I heave and grunt as I attempt to swing a knee beneath me. The leg doesn't cooperate. My tail, normally so adept at helping keep balance, is a worthless sandbag stapled to my back.

I turn the sorrow into fury. Get up, Pierce. Get the fuck *up*. You're not gonna go to prison on account of this son of a bitch. You're gonna get *up*—

"Pierce...?"

The meek voice behind me is immediately recognizable, and the last one I wanted to hear. As much as my body yearns for a bullet to the back of the head, my conscience won't abide it. I manage to rotate enough to bring Samuel into view. His arms hang limp at his sides. He still clutches Aubrey's pistol, but doesn't bring it upon me. Instead, he stares at Marty's lifeless form. His lip trembles.

I don't bother making excuses. It looks how it looks. He'll solve the puzzle a toddler could solve and bring an end to my miserable—

"How could he do this? How... how could Charles *do this?!*"

I struggle to speak. "You... saw?"

He nods. "I was at the side door. I heard the gunshots and saw everything after that."

"And you... heard, too?"

"Most of it, yeah..."

"Then you know... this isn't gonna end well... for either of us..."

"Yeah. I know."

He steps closer to me and kneels down. My hand instinctively finds the revolver in front of me and tightens. I plant my other blood-soaked hand on his shoulder, causing him to stumble with my weight before he steels his legs. With a heave and a grunt, I manage to get my feet beneath me again. If a second wind won't come to me naturally, I'll force one upon myself. I can die once the work is done.

"We have to... stop him..."

Samuel stares up at me. "How? He's already leaving."

"You got that... Fairlane, don't ya?"

"Y-yeah."

"Then *drive*."

Chapter Sixteen: Samuel

I'm honestly a little impressed that my hand didn't start shaking until now.

Of course, now that it *is,* a doctor could easily diagnose me as having developed sudden onset Parkinson's. I struggle to keep a grip on the pistol clattering in my grip as the overflowing wellspring of adrenaline threatens to launch the object over my shoulder. However, steadying my hand plays second fiddle to keeping Aubrey on her feet and getting us both as far away from this nightmarish place as possible.

She winces with each step, sucking air past clenched teeth. I didn't see what that son of a bitch did to her, but I heard her scream clear as day. Her cry of pain ripped the fog of unconsciousness away from my addled head and lit a fire in me to protect her.

Pierce. That mother fucker hurt my girl. After all his sweet-talk of trust, he dared to lay a finger on my Aubrey. I shoulda emptied this entire magazine into him when I had the chance.

The sour face I unconsciously make catches Aubrey's attention. She offers a pained smile. "It's okay, Sammy. Let's just get out of here. We're almost to the car."

I nod, continuing to point the shaky pistol behind us just

in case my once-trusted partner decides to make a play at chasing us down. The small roadway between the warehouses bathes in darkness, the few flickering light poles doing little to combat the night. We move as quickly as Aubrey's hobble allows, keeping close to the next row of buildings in case gunfire rings out and we have to duck for cover in their alcoves.

With effort, we arrive at my stashed Fairlane. Despite its bombastic palette, the car is tucked far enough between structures that we should be able to get loaded up and moving before alerting anyone. Not that there's anyone to alert... this entire dock is practically a ghost town.

I yank open the passenger door and gingerly assist Aubrey as she sits. Her grimace breaks my heart; I respond by bringing a gentle hand to the side of her face. "We'll get you fixed up. I'm here for you, sweetheart."

Her hand covers mine and she gazes at me, yellow eyes scintillating with both pain and relief. "I'm just glad we're both okay. Let's get the hell out of here, this was a... a stupid..." Her focus fades, then suddenly snaps to me in horrid realization. "Oh *fuck,* Sammy. The *camera!*"

I blink before fruitlessly slapping my hands against my pockets, as if I could have stuffed that two pound brick into my pants. "Shit. *Shit.*"

Aubrey shakes her head, breathlessly failing to offer an alternative. She steels herself in bitter resignation. "Fuck it. It's not worth it, we just need to leave."

I scowl. "But that's the whole god damn reason we did this! What was the point of putting us both in danger if we don't even have the proof you need?"

"Sammy, we can't! It's too dangerous, we've already gotten hurt! My knee is fucked! Loo—" She bites her lip before spitting it out. "Look at your face!"

I bring a hand to the swelling mass under my eye socket. "Hey, I was already ugly. This won't make things much worse." She balks at my attempted humor. "I understand it's risky, but we both took a big risk doing this in the first place. If we run off now, that'll all have been a waste." My eyes dart away, then back to her. "That captain of yours was there, accepting money. If you don't bring in *proof* of that, the proof that's on that camera, then he's gonna keep being corrupt. A good cop can't turn a blind eye to that sorta thing."

She opens her mouth to protest, but stops short. She thinks for a moment, cautiously peering past me to the passage from which we came. With a sigh, she scoots forward and attempts to rise. "Okay, let's go—"

I halt her. "You're in no condition. Lemme go get it. I can be in and out in a jiffy." I smile and extend the pistol out to her, its grip quivering in my tenuous grasp.

She glances down at it, then softly pushes it away. "You take it. I'll be fine here. Just hurry back, and if anything goes wrong—if anything even *feels* a little wrong, you get the hell out of there." She leans forward; her breath intermingles with mine. "You're more important to me than some lousy camera."

Her lips push forward, instantly melting away my apprehension in a singular motion. That electric spark that first ignited between us outside of Birdland sizzles and burns anew, white-hot tendrils of arcing energy soaring between our tongues. She proves to me with tender, caressing movements that she's worth it all.

Aubrey pulls away, gaze full of love and worry. Her hand comes to rest on mine, pistol nestled between us. "You got five left. There's another magazine in my purse in the warehouse…"

"I won't need 'em. Everything will be fine." I plant a quick, parting kiss on her cheek. "I love you. Be back before ya even miss me."

"I love you too, Sammy." Her words swell my chest with confidence and fervor. I straighten up, glancing around to ensure nobody snuck up on us. Seeing that the coast is clear, I give my gal one more smile before I hustle back toward the warehouse we just escaped a few minutes prior.

There's not a soul around, but I still stick to the shadows as best I can before pushing across the single-lane drive between the buildings. The silence is eerie; we're far enough away from the city proper and any of its night life to make things uncomfortably quiet. The faint ocean waves and the occasional sound of a bustling rodent are all that accompany my hushed footsteps. That is, until I come closer to the familiar warehouse.

I only just arrive at the side door when a gunshot penetrates the hushed night air, rattling the nearby windows. I instinctively drop down, covering my head as if my arms are made of lead and could deflect further bullets. My heart races, but I don't feel like I got hit. From the other side of the door, I hear a muffled voice that almost sounds like Marty crying out, then four more shots in quick succession.

Christ, did someone just get killed?! I can't fight back the foolish notion of sticking my head up and peeking through the dirt-caked window to find out. The visibility is God-awful, but I can barely make out a few shapes. Marty's still standing, and the spinosaurus bastard is next to him. A little further in, Charles is pacing and speaking quietly to...

Pierce. It must be Pierce. I can't see him from my angle, but who else would it be?

Is he already dead?

Marty starts to shout again, but that cop named Preston cuts him off. He's... holding a gun to Marty.

What the fuck is happening?!

Charles mutters something, addressing neither Preston nor Marty. Either he's monologuing to Pierce's corpse, or somehow that tough son of a bitch is still alive. Didn't he just take five rounds? I know dinosaurs are tough, but they aren't bullet-proof. I strain, trying as hard as possible to hear what they're saying, but the voices are too muffled through the glass and wood.

I quickly duck down, noticing Charles turn partially in my direction. When I get the bravery to slowly stick my head up again, he's—

Oh, fuck. The *camera*. He's got the god damn camera in his hands, smiling and gloating toward Pierce. Does he... think that Pierce was spying? Is Pierce gonna rat Aubrey out?!

Going against every self-preserving instinct in my body, I make the absurdly stupid decision to crack the door open, just enough so I can hear. The thing shouldn't go wildly swinging inward—at least it didn't when I operated it before—but just to be safe I keep a death grip on its knob, turning it as gently as humanly possible before pushing it open a sliver of an inch.

No one turns toward the change in scenery, and the voices come through just enough for me to register them.

"—no loyalty among the wicked, I suppose."

A pause, then I hear Pierce's reply. "Samuel didn't do anything wrong."

"I'm inclined to agree with you. After all, he was in sight the entire time we got the supplies loaded on the ship, and he *was* going to burn this building to ashes." I can't get a good look at his expression, but his words drop a stone into my gut. "He's expendable. I'm not worried about it."

I have to stop myself from stumbling backward from the blow. That son of a bitch. Here he was, treating me like a member of the team, consoling me in the hospital waiting room after the run-in at the pool hall, bringing me on for this job. He lubed me up with kind words and a fuckin' car, and now he says I'm *expendable*.

Pierce was right about him. Of course he was.

Almost in reply to my thoughts, Pierce's voice carries

through the crack again. "Whatever you do to me, leave him out of it." I blink in surprise. Why the hell would he stick up for me, especially after what just went down between us? I don't even know how the big bastard is still alive given all those shots. Were they just—

I nearly leap out of my own skin when a hand comes to rest on my back. It takes every ounce of effort to keep from making a sound or jostling the door as I swivel my neck to meet Aubrey's gaze. Her eyes are wide with fear and pain. I keep the knob twisted as I pull the door shut as quietly as possible, gently releasing the mechanism to prevent it from emitting its telltale click. It makes no noise. A moment later, both Aubrey and I are on the backside of the warehouse, out of sight and earshot so long as we don't risk anything more than whisper.

"Aubrey, the hell?! You scared me half to death!"

She whispers back angrily. *"I heard gunshots! I thought you were—"*

"I'm okay. I think Pierce got shot, but he's still alive. Charles is giving him the business."

"Sammy, we have to go! This is too dangerous!" She continues favoring her left leg; I feel awful that she had to hobble back here on her own, especially since...

"I don't have the camera yet. Charles has got it."

As though in reply, Charles's laugh booms out. It's distinct—I recall it from the alleyway where I thought Pierce was gonna lay my brains on the gravel and brick, when they interrogated me about the envelope full of money. We both flinch away from it, but realize it isn't directed toward us.

Aubrey raises her arms in defeat. *"Then what are we still doing here? The camera's gone."*

"There might still be a chance. We've got this." I wiggle the pistol in my hand.

She doesn't like this notion one bit. *"Are you out of your fucking mind?! You can't take on three dinosaurs, one of which is a cop!"* Her anger turns to pleading. *"You're not that kind of man, Sammy! You're not a killer!"*

I stare at my shoes. She's right, of course. What am I gonna do, gun them down for a fuckin' camera? Besides, all it's got on it is...

My heart stops. Aubrey's eyes widen in response to my horror.

"I'm on that film."

Her cheek twitches and her pupils dart around as she tries to decipher my meaning. *"What do you—"* Her hands stifle her gasp. *"Oh. Oh no. Oh my God."*

She took my photo. Before we did this whole operation, she took my god damn photo. If Charles takes that camera and develops the footage... I'm fucked.

Aubrey grabs at my sleeve. *"Sammy, I'm so sorry. I'm so sorry! I didn't—"*

I pull her quivering, terrified form into my embrace. *"It's okay. We both screwed up. We gotta make it right now."*

After letting her go, I peek around the corner before sidling next to the door again, letting out a sigh. She didn't know. Neither did I. But holy shit, that was a god damn stupid thing to do, taking my picture with a camera we planned to use in a *sting operation.* There's nothing for it now. We'll just have to get the camera back, or—

The echoing boom of another gunshot scatters to the winds surrounding the warehouse, rapidly consumed by the lapping waves against the docks. My mouth opens in a horrified cry I dare not act upon.

Marty. The gentle, charismatic diplodocus who treated me better than nearly any other dinosaur in my life stiffens, then tilts backward. The elongated neck that was so strange to witness in action crumples to the ground with him, a worthless tangle of scales and muscle with no further purpose. His final expression is one of shock, betrayal and... sadness.

Why? *Why?!*

I tighten my squeeze on the gun, preparing to kick the door down and bring swift justice to the wicked son of a bitch that just murdered my friend. Another three shots ring out from the revolver in Charles's hands before he drops it in a clatter at his feet. He mutters something else to Pierce; the blood pounding in my ears deafens me to the discussion. I suck air past clenched teeth and put a hand on the doorknob—

Aubrey's tap of my shoulder causes me to spin. She recoils back from my fury before steadying herself and shaking her head at me. *"Preston."*

I turn back to the small window. The spinosaurus is still there, and still armed. The smug grin on his face further enrages me; I can gun him down first, then deal with Charles.

"Sammy, don't!"

She stands strong against my glare. I love her, but right now I'm too fucking pissed off to listen to reason. I'll die, but I'll die avenging an innocent man who was murdered in cold blood.

A friend…

But what about Pierce?

Is he still alive? If he is, he's probably hurt.

Can I help him?

Should I help him?

I bring my distracted gaze to the muddied glass again, only to flinch and quickly flatten myself to the wall next to me. My free arm swings over, squashing Aubrey to the same plane as I. She gasps but quickly follows suit, turning her head and drawing her tail as close to her body as she can. We still hold a profile, but at least it's lessened and partially obscured by the shadows.

Charles and Preston come into sight for a brief moment in the open, then vanish behind the next warehouse over.

Neither of them stop or turn our direction. Thankfully, the side entrance is far enough from the main loading doors that we were able to remain concealed. Even so, Aubrey and I stay perfectly still for another sixty seconds, breathing lightly and praying neither of the villains double back and investigate the alcove between buildings.

They don't.

Pushing the air slowly through pursed lips, I release my arm from Aubrey's body. I turn to her, expecting her to whisper another command, to demand we leave this instant. Instead, she says nothing. She merely looks to me expectantly. At a loss for words.

At least that makes two of us.

I take a deep breath before nudging open the side door. My pistol's at the ready, just in case someone unexpected jumps out, but after taking a few cautious steps into the warehouse my arm sags to my side.

Marty's body is only a few yards away. I want to run over, shake him awake, yell for him to get up so we can get out of here, but I know it would be a useless effort. The bullet sank right into his skull and flew out the other side. The gentle fella who had a kid on the way with a wife I was hoping to meet someday is nothing but a pool of red in a crumbling building on some God-forsaken dock.

I bite my lip, trying not to let the tears start falling when motion in my peripheral causes me to turn. He grunts as he struggles to stand, clasping a hand to his side. Blood oozes from between his fingers.

"Pierce...?"

In response, he brings up his dark blue eyes to meet mine. They're weary, like those of a man who's gone days without sleep. He says nothing, instead merely lowering his head and letting out a surrendering sigh.

I turn back to Marty's lifeless body. "How could he do this? How... how could Charles *do this?!*"

Pierce's voice is raspy and broken. "You... saw?"

"I was at the side door. I heard the gunshots and saw everything after that."

"And you... heard, too?"

"Most of it, yeah..."

He grits his teeth. "Then you know... this isn't gonna end well... for either of us..."

"Yeah. I know."

Seeing the stegosaurus's addled body, I don't even know if he's gonna make it another ten minutes. The blood pooled by his feet nearly rivals how much is currently soaking into the concrete underneath Marty. Pierce might be tough, but I don't think he's immortal.

All the same, I can't help but step toward him. His breathing is labored and he heaves himself upward, using me as a brace to get to his feet. His weight nearly topples me, but I lock my legs in place to keep from sprawling over. He scoops up the revolver below him as we both straighten up. I steady him as best I can when he rocks back, keeping him upright for the time being.

His hazy eyes meet mine. "We have to... stop him..."

"How? He's already leaving."

"You got that... Fairlane, don't ya?"

"Y-yeah."

"Then *drive.*"

I stare at him in disbelief. "Pierce, you're about ready to collapse. We need to get you to a hosp—"

In a flash, his exhaustion is overtaken by rage. "Did you not hear a fuckin' word I just said?! Marty is lying *dead* over there, and you and I will be next to him at the pearly fuckin' gates in real short order unless we handle Charles *now!*" He half-shoves me toward the side door as he stumbles forward. "Get your spear-chucking ass to the car and *drive!*"

Further protest is impossible. Now that he's got his feet under him, I glance over to the corner by the broom closet.

Aubrey's purse, and that spare magazine. I dart over and snatch it off the concrete. As I turn toward the exit, my breath hitches.

Aubrey and Pierce stare each other down, her sizing him up, and him glaring in half-consciousness. Their tails flit back and forth aggressively, like they were two cats who came face to face in an alley. Neither speaks; the air hangs heavy. I gulp, frantically searching for some magic words to utter and make this rancid mess blow over and not result in further bloodshed.

After an agonizing moment, Aubrey releases a sigh through clenched teeth and hobbles toward Pierce. "Take off your jacket." He grunts a rejection, and her tone turns authoritative. "Take it off."

Pierce grimaces before acquiescing, hissing as his arm moves away from the red splotch on his undershirt. Aubrey swipes the jacket from his hands, briefly evaluates it, then sinks her teeth into the fabric before tearing it nearly in two. Pierce doesn't protest, apparently getting the hint. He lifts his arms, wincing as Aubrey wraps the makeshift bandage around his torso. The wince becomes a rumble of pain as she tightens it around his wound before pulling the ends of the soaking fabric into a knot.

She steps back. "I don't know what sorta good this will do. You're about ready to pass out, or worse."

He tucks his revolver into the now exposed shoulder holster. "It'll do for now. Thank you."

Aubrey's eyes harden. "Things aren't over between us. Not by a fucking long shot."

Pierce's returned gaze is much softer. "I know."

I cross the warehouse and hand Aubrey her pistol and purse. "We have to go. The clock is ticking."

The three of us move as quickly as we can, me with a bruised face and rattled mind, Aubrey with a bad knee battered even worse, and Pierce leaking his guts out. We're a far cry from the action heroes of those serialized radio shows I listened to growing up. We might not even make it to the damn car without one of us toppling over, let alone chase down and overtake a murdering crime boss and his crooked cop sidekick.

We better come up with a plan, quick.

I jam the key in the ignition as two more car doors slam shut. Aubrey strains to pull her leg into a half-tolerable position in the passenger seat as Pierce slumps in the back. I try not to think about how much blood is gonna be caked into the upholstery, instead focusing on wrenching the parking brake loose and jamming on the accelerator. Aubrey looses a yelp as I peel out, twisting around the corner of the warehouse and down the narrow corridor between buildings.

"What the hell are we gonna do, Sammy?!" She grips the side of her chair with her free hand, pistol squeezed in the other and purse on her lap.

"I have absolutely no idea." I glance in the rearview mirror for only a moment, trying to focus on keeping the car steady and not slamming into the structures whizzing by on both sides. "Pierce?"

He doesn't reply; from the looks of his limp neck movements and half-open mouth, he's opted to fall asleep. Aubrey spins her head toward the rear of the car, then back to me. "I don't even know if he's still *alive.*"

"Shit. *Shit.*" I crank the wheel, tires squealing underneath us as the Fairlane skids onto the larger tarmac that grants primary entry to and exit from the docks. It's a short stretch that weaves past a few industrial buildings before merging with the Old York roadways proper beyond an unmanned front gate. We're already behind, and I don't even know where—

Ahead, a silver Buick Roadmaster slows to a stop, the glow of its brake lights dimly illuminating the swath of makeshift roadway between us and them.

"Sammy, what are you—"

Its headlights give shape to the outline of a phone booth several feet in front of the vehicle.

I crush the pedal against the floor of the car, inertia pressing me into the seat.

"Sammy!"

The Roadmaster's passenger door begins to open.

I angle my front bumper toward their rear.

"Oh my God, Sammy!"

I don't know what else to do, so I pray.

It's a quick prayer.

"Sa—"

The thunderous crunch of steel colliding with steel rocks all three of us forward. Aubrey screams; Pierce's head bounces off the shoulder rest of the front seats. The occupants of the Roadmaster jolt as well, the momentum forcing the passenger door closed as their vehicle is thrust away from the collision. The driver, who I can tell to be Preston now that I'm only a few feet of glass and partially crumpled steel away from him, attempts to spin the steering wheel away from the phone booth, but his reflexes aren't quick enough. Their front bumper slams into the enclosure, spraying glass from all four sides and ripping the massive fastening bolts out of the concrete beneath it.

The toppled phone booth becomes a makeshift partial ramp for the car, its front right wheel propelling the vehicle to an upward angle before wedging into the hollow gap that was occupied by glass only moments ago. Curses ring out from the car's two occupants as Preston slams on the gas, the wheels screaming furiously in an attempt to dislodge one of their brothers from its imprisonment. The phone booth buckles and shakes with the vehicle's weight before it releases its catch, sparks accompanying the car frame's descent from the mangled metal. A loud hiss escapes the previously entrapped tire as it collides with the pavement.

Aubrey shouts. *"Sammy, what the fuck are you doing?!"*

My only reply is to slam on the gas again, forcing my Fairlane's crumpled bumper further into the rear end of the damaged Roadmaster. Preston must be laying on the brake; my car's wheels impotently squeal as they spin in place, plumes of smoke billowing from the friction-burned rubber. The engine shudders, and with a lurch both vehicles begin to move. Instead of simply pushing the Roadmaster forward, its front wheel alignment causes it to begin a slow spin, rotating counter-clockwise as we try to forcefully occupy the space within which they currently reside.

More screeching, more scraping as my front bumper shifts to their driver's side wheel well. Two pairs of furious eyes fall upon me as they complete their one hundred and eighty degree rotation; the silver bulk slaps indignantly against the driver's side of my car. I slam the brake pedal down; the lack of momentum stops my car from moving more than a few feet forward. Something shifts in my side mirror: Preston throws open his door and begins climbing out of the Roadmaster, obscenities on his tongue and pistol in hand.

I rip the gear stick into reverse and floor it. Preston dives back into his seat, narrowly pulling his legs and tail out of the way as my rear bumper crashes into his door, ripping it off its hinges. Both cars come to a halt with the collision.

Preston spits more curses as he rights his balance and tries to jump out again. To my surprise, the back door of my Fairlane suddenly bursts open, knocking Preston backward with a howl of pain. The spinosaurus sprawls against Charles inside the Roadmaster; the two shout and shove as they struggle to straighten themselves in their seats. I spin around, seeing that Pierce had unlatched the back door and lunged his legs into it to temporarily incapacitate Preston with the makeshift battering ram. He wheezes and coughs, pulling it shut as blood spatters from his mouth.

Glad to see he's still with us, even if it's only for a few more minutes by the look of him.

Preston doesn't try to exit the Roadmaster a third time. Instead, the barrel of his pistol levels in our direction.

Oh, *fuck*.

Glass explodes above my head, showering the window's entrails across my back and neck. The revolver roars again and again, the crunches of lead lodging itself in steel causing me to nearly black out from adrenaline-induced panic. Aubrey screams; I can only pray she isn't hit as we both cower for our lives.

The shooting stops. My ears ring, but I can make out Preston's voice. "—pieces of shit, I'll fuckin' kill ya—"

Aubrey's arms swing up and past my shoulder, her closed hands steadying her leaden reply.

Charles howls. "Preston, *go!*"

Tires squeal in tandem with five shots that Aubrey quickly squeezes off. I ignore the back of my head being peppered with spent bullet casings as I thrust the gear stick forward and mash the pedal, cranking the wheel as hard left as I can. Our car misses the crumpled phone booth by inches, swinging around and fish-tailing with my attempt to straighten out and give chase. The industrial buildings around us begin moving in the opposite direction.

Though my heart feels like it's about to rupture, I perform a cursory assessment of whether I got hit or not. I don't think so. A glance at Aubrey doesn't reveal any immediately noticeable wounds, but her pupils are as thin as razor blades and her teeth are bared. She flings the spent magazine away from the bottom of her pistol and jams her hand into her purse to withdraw the other. It clicks into place, and with a pinch of her thumb and forefinger and a quick pull, the slide thrusts forward with a fresh payload.

The rotation I forced upon the silver Buick pointed it straight back into the port and its familiar surrounding warehouses. Preston doesn't seem to be aiming for any evasive maneuvers, though Charles's car shudders and jerks every second or two. Sparks fly off the front end of the escaping vehicle accompanied by the sound of metal grinding against pavement.

"Their front tire is flatted." I jump, startled by the unexpected proclamation from behind me. Pierce breathes heavily, having hoisted himself upright to peer over Aubrey and I's shoulders. He's clearly still hurting, but it doesn't seem like he got tagged by any other rounds. Either that, or the bastard is indestructible.

The fleeing car jerks again, its driver struggling against the peeling rubber of the maligned tire. The spinosaurus rummages for something, keeping between one and zero hands on the steering wheel in the process. If I was a betting man, I'd wager he's reloading that revolver.

I respond the only way I know how: by flooring it and kissing their rear bumper again. The frenetic gesticulations of the car's occupants convey their fury as Preston tries to maintain control past the crunch of steel against steel.

"Raptor Jesus, what are we *doing?!*" Aubrey's frenzied words go unanswered. I'm sorry. I don't *know* what I'm doing. I'm trying to stop them. What the fuck we're gonna do when or even *if* we stop them... I haven't the faintest clue. But this is all I have right now.

We soar under the signage and past the gating that marks the entrance to the warehouse block. The ocean grows before us; screaming tires accompany both vehicles skidding around the corner and down the narrow road that runs parallel to structures and sea.

Pierce rumbles from the backseat. "We need to stop them, or we won't get another chance."

He's right, of course. The Roadmaster is smashed up, but so is my Fairlane. Even with their handicap of a damaged tire, with some luck and enough room to breathe their top-of-the-line engine could very easily grant them an escape.

It's now or never, Sam.

Ahead, several stacks of pallets piled next to a warehouse approach rapidly. I jerk the steering wheel quickly to shunt my car to the left and jam the accelerator down. This time, as my bumper makes contact with theirs and shoves further, it knocks their straightened course awry and their traction begins slipping. The angle of their front is forced toward the warehouses and the waiting collision.

The passenger door flies open, and Charles tumbles out of the vehicle, rolling gracelessly away from the impending disaster. Brakes screech in impotent futility.

The Roadmaster slams into the pallets, buckling the planks against one another. They warp and contort for a fraction of a second, creaking and groaning as they are smashed between an unstoppable car and an immovable wall. The pallets spring back against the pressure, firing splintered wooden flechettes in all directions as the front of the car is hurdled up and away, rotating in a manner cars are not meant to rotate. If Charles's bulky form was still in the passenger seat, the counterbalance may have prevented a full-on flip. Without him, Preston is left to cover his head and scream as he inverts.

With a earsplitting crash, its driver's side slams into the paved road. It slides forward as it continues tipping before landing belly-up like a submitting dog. Glass explodes out of every window that still held intact. The momentum forces the upturned car away from the broken pallet ramp and toward the ocean. It spins as it grinds against the pavement, finally slowing and coming to rest so precariously close to the paved lip that a wayward gust of wind could topple the vehicle into the lapping waves below.

My own car lurches to a halt, its engine sputtering and coughing in annoyance with the repeated injuries I've been inflicting upon it. My whitened knuckles don't release the steering wheel, even though we aren't moving forward anymore. The only sound I hear is Pierce rustling in the back seat; from the rearview mirror, I can see him craning his neck in the opposite direction of the upturned Roadmaster. With a grunt, he shoves open the back door and clambers out before limping around the car and toward the nearby warehouses.

I assess our position... the sign on the nearest warehouse reads "620". We're only a few structures away from where all this foolishness started, and by Pierce's trajectory it looks as though that's where he's headed. My frazzled brain catching up, I also frantically look around. Charles is nowhere to be seen.

It might make sense for... but why wouldn't he—

A hand coming to rest on my shoulder causes me to audibly yelp. Aubrey only tightens her grip in response. Her eyes are bloodshot and worry-stricken, and her voice is hoarse. "What do we do now?"

I shudder. "We h-have to go help P-Pierce..."

She gulps, then looks down at the pistol still gripped in her other hand. With a deep breath, she nods. We both throw open our respective doors and—

A burst of fire scores across the side of my face, forcing a hiss of pain past my teeth and causing my knees to buckle underneath me. I try to hold onto the car door's frame to prevent crumpling, but my fingers slip and my legs give out. My elbow painfully bangs against the pavement, doing little to gracefully break my fall.

Aubrey shrieks something. It sounds like my name, but the ringing in my ears is too loud to make it out. My eyes are working just fine, however, and they relay the form of a spinosaurus roughly ten yards away, awkwardly contorted against the crumpled roof of the upturned vehicle. A tremendous amount of his own weight is pressed against his bent neck. He's bleeding and breathing heavily, but his hands are wrapped around his revolver, and it's leveling itself in my direction again, just as upside-down as he is. He squints, gnashes his teeth, and prepares to exact his revenge.

I can only cower behind my arms.

The dull thump of exploding gunpowder makes its way past the incessant tinnitus. I flinch before realizing the direction of the sound wasn't quite what I expected. Another five explosions join their brother, each one further puncturing the now bullet-addled spinosaurus. The first shot struck true, passing through the creature's eye socket and expelling bone and gray matter into the remnants of the Roadmaster. The other five merely reiterate the point Aubrey was making. Preston's wrists go limp, the revolver emitting a soft clatter as it touches down on the mangled car roof.

His loosening muscles cause his body to shift, ever so slowly tipping the precarious balance of the silver Buick. In slow motion, Preston rises up and out of sight, the back end of the car acquiescing to gravity as it plunges the rest of the vessel into the sea. A loud splash heralds its arrival; from my perspective, I cannot witness anything further. All I can do is imagine its descent into the briny depths, pulling with it the corpse of one son of a bitch of a cop.

The dim port-side lamp above me darkens as a shape soars around the car. Aubrey crouches, screaming in panic as she grasps at my head. *"Sammy! Oh my God, Sammy! Talk to me!"*

I do my best to smile, though the movement causes my face to light on fire all over again. "I'm okay. Just... grazed, I think."

"Raptor Jesus, your *face!*"

There's no mirror down on the ground with me, so I settle for bringing a hand up to my cheek. I wince, feeling the loose flaps of skin giving far too much leeway to my fingers.

The blood that had been pooling inside of the nasty welt Pierce gave me now freely pulses from the fresh wound that traces down my cheek bone to the top of my neck.

I weakly grin with the side of my mouth not housed behind mangled flesh. "It's only a scratch."

"A *scratch?!* We need to get you to the *hospital!*" Aubrey plays medic for a second time, deftly tearing a sizable strip away from the bottom of her shirt with her talons before pressing the cloth to my cheek. It instantly fills with blood; I place my hand atop hers that holds the makeshift sponge. Her citrine eyes are aghast, her slender lip quivers.

"Thank you."

She blinks. "F-for what?"

For treating my injury. For saving my life. For being an incredible, beautiful, loving woman who accepted a guy like me. My frazzled mind can't settle on an option beyond the simplest: "For everything. I don't deserve a gal like you."

She glances away, then over her shoulder toward where the Roadmaster rested only moments ago. When she turns back to me, tears well under her eyes. "I… I killed him. I shot a *police officer.*"

My arms move on their own, wrapping her in the best hug I can manage from my prone position. I press the side of my face that isn't eviscerated to her waist and shush her. She trembles, returning the embrace as she sobs. "It's okay, honey. You didn't do anything wrong. You were protecting us. If you didn't… I wouldn't still be here."

My words make her lurch out another anguished cry and she grips me even tighter. "Sammy, I love you."

"I love you too, Aubrey."

I love her… but we're not done yet.

Leaning back from the embrace, I use my non-bloodied hand to wipe her tears away. "I need to help Pierce. If he's not already—well, if he has or hasn't found Charles, I need to get that camera back and I gotta help him."

Her eyes widen. "Let's just go! You're already hurt, we have to get you to a doctor!"

A grunt unconsciously looses from my throat as I get to my feet; she swiftly follows me up, favoring her good leg as she stands. "Not without Pierce. He needs our help."

Aubrey's mouth hangs open, searching for further protest, but none are uttered. Instead, she steels her resolve with a nod. The two of us make for warehouse six-seventeen, me with a blood-soaked scrap of shirt held to my mangled face and Aubrey with her pistol gripped tightly.

I glance from it to her. "How many shots you got left?"

She shakes her head. "I'm empty. But that triceratops doesn't know that."

"Let's hope it doesn't come down to it."

The familiar structure approaches, its large bay doors still latched open. The scent of gasoline reaches my nostrils before I turn the corner, remnants of the partial task I had completed before freeing Aubrey from her imprisonment. Marty's body still lays where it fell inside the structure, dimly lit by the solitary flickering bulb above the enclosure.

Another step inward reveals a second shape, that of a midnight blue stegosaurus in a heap.

"Sam—" A nauseating metallic crunch rings out as a large red cylinder collides with the side of Aubrey's head. She twists and sprawls, tongue hanging loosely from her teeth and eyes glazed in immediate dreamless sleep. Her body falls in a limp pile, followed by the clatter of the gas can turned makeshift bludgeon against the concrete floor.

Her attacker's eyes fire to me from their hiding place around the darkened corner. I can barely take a step before he lunges out of the shadows. A cannonball of a fist collides with my sternum, the sickening thud and splintering cracks ceasing all forward momentum and sprawling me upright like a flipped turtle. My lungs expel all of their stored air, shriveling and refusing to operate further. I claw at my chest, gasping in a vain attempt to restore function to the apparatuses trapped behind my likely broken ribs.

The gray triceratops stands over me, fists clenched and brow lowered. He stares down his snout at me in disbelief and disgust, the horn at its tip quivering with rage. "What the *fuck* was any of this, huh? What the *fuck* did you think, pulling some shit like this?" He gestures toward Pierce who still remains motionless. "Him? You're in cahoots with *him?* The worthless piece of shit who would just as soon shoot you in the back of the head as help you unload your groceries from your car? The car *I* gave you, remember?"

I can't respond. I can't even breathe. My eyes bulge as I try to suck air into my compressed chest. In my writhing, my eyes fall upon Aubrey. There's no movement, save for a small darkening patch of red that slowly blemishes her beautiful blue hair.

Charles's fury continues to spill forth. "And I don't even know who the *fuck* she's supposed to be! What the hell is this, a whole sting operation?" He pauses before jamming a hand into his pants pocket. The bulky camera that wouldn't even begin to fit in my trousers slides easily from his much larger clothes. "You trying to get evidence? You three, all conniving and scheming against me, for what? Who would you show this to? You ain't with the *police,* because *I'm* with the fuckin' police!"

With a grunt, his hand closes around the device, crushing it to pieces with a single squeeze. The roll of film springs from its home and unravels into a useless and ruined mound beneath him.

He shakes his head. "This is a colossal failure. Everything I planned, *everything* I needed to happen tonight... you three sons of bitches have screwed it all up." His eyes fall on the overturned red can that he used as a weapon against Aubrey; gasoline dribbles from its mouth. He scoops it up before turning toward the wall and thrusting the liquid out of its enclosure. Splashes of sickening chemical douse the wood as he works his way further into the warehouse, emptying its contents.

He throws the expended container aside and turns back to me. "No matter. I'll make it right. It'll be a lot harder to explain two more bodies in this burnt wreck, but William will spin it." His eyes drift past me toward the opening. "As for explaining a dead cop…" He shrugs. "Not my problem. If the captain wants that money to keep flowing his way, he'll come up with—"

A cough catches his attention. I also turn toward the source, still wheezing but at least partially managing to draw in breath again. Pierce stirs, the blood pooling beneath his body acting as an adhesive between his shirt and the concrete; it lets out a thin, tapered snap as the fabric and floor disconnect from one another. He slides a slow knee out from underneath himself before planting his foot. His arms quiver as he attempts to stand and his tail hangs motionless behind him.

Charles places his hands on his hips like an annoyed housewife. "You just don't know when to quit, do you? You worthless piece of shit."

Pierce doesn't respond, merely continuing his glacial ascent.

Charles jabs an accusatory finger at him and spits. "All you've ever been is a thorn in my fucking side. None of my enterprising ventures ever panned out when your thick, short-sighted skull was within a mile of them. You did in Lorenzo, one of my best enforcers, because you were pissy that your good-for-nothing brother went missing. You killed Egbert, a brilliant man with an incredible mind for numbers who was gonna do tremendous work for our organization. How many other loyal Herdsters were you gonna kill because of your hatred-fueled vendetta against humans?"

Egbert… Eggsy, that guy from the alley. How all this

insanity started. The vivid recollection of his bottlecap glasses and the look of shock and fear as he bled out is seared into my mind, offering only a brief respite from the burning in my chest. My lungs slowly churn back to life and begin pumping oxygen throughout my body as they're supposed to, though I can still barely move.

Even though it appears that every ounce of his concentration is dedicated to the herculean effort of straightening his back and not losing consciousness permanently, Pierce manages to form some stilted words. "Eggsy... was a traitor."

Charles's eyes go out of focus. "Egbert got in with the wrong crowd. Owed money to some guys you shouldn't owe money to. I knew about his debt, and I was gonna help him along in the Herdsters so he could make money legitimately to pay it off. He'd work for me, we'd see a lot more success in our own books, and he'd get out of debt along the way." He scowls. "Apparently my timetable didn't work for him. That said, he didn't deserve to die for making a panic-induced mistake. A stern talking-to, or a punch to the gut, maybe. Not a bullet."

Pierce's feet rock, but he stays upright. "Murphy... and his cronies... that was your doing."

A raised brow punctuates Charles's annoyance. "Why would you think I had anything to do with that? Murphy was a lowlife who made a stupid play. The timing was merely coincidental." He shrugs. "Admittedly, he'd have done me a favor if he finished the job, but..."

The triceratops's attention shoots to me. "This human saved your life. I knew there was potential in Samuel from the moment he admitted his knowledge of Egbert's stash. Blunt honesty like that isn't a trait you can force into a person, and it's something that can be shaped into true loyalty." A frown sours his snout. "At least, I thought so.

Instead, he tossed his lot in with the human-hating stegosaurus."

His eyes swirl with disappointment. "You could have gone far, Samuel. I would have brought you into the enterprise. Money, cars, women... you could've had it all. And all it would have cost you was your loyalty. A real shame to—"

Movement causes his focus to dart back to Pierce. He instantly bolts across the space before backhanding the revolver out of Pierce's hand with his left and slamming his right fist into the stegosaurus's gut. Pierce's teeth crunch together and blood spurts from his mouth as he collapses backward again, arms falling akimbo. The thud of his body times itself with the clatter of the revolver that slides within arm's reach of me.

Charles holds his pose for a moment, breathing deeply before letting out a bellowing laugh. The once mirthful laugh from the alleyway is nothing short of petrifying now. "You imbecile! Why would you pick that piece of junk up again? It's got no shots left! I made sure of it!" To illustrate his point, he withdraws a handful of bullets from his own jacket pocket before letting the lead and brass cascade to the ground. "What were you gonna do, throw the thing at me?"

His laughter stops as I climb to my feet, Pierce's revolver in my hands and pointed squarely at Charles's head. He doesn't lunge at me, instead opting to roll his eyes. "Samuel, Samuel, Samuel... I know you're not the brightest crayon in the box, but to make it in this city you have to learn to count the shots. That's a five-shooter, and all five of its shots are gone. See, count with me—one in poor Marty over there—" He gestures toward my friend's body to illustrate his point. "—three to empty the chamber and render that piece no more dangerous than a toy, and *one* in that crate right over there." His finger jabs toward the splintered wooden corner of the nearby box. He shrugs, a confident grin painting his face. "I heard the gunshot from down the dock—that's why Preston and I came back. I have no clue why the two of you were having a fight, but I heard the gunshot, and I know how to count. Five-shooter, five shots."

A cough. Or, at least what I think is a cough. Then another. Then a hollow, gurgling rhythm.

It isn't coughing. Pierce is *laughing*. Past the blood filling his throat, he lets out a pained chuckle.

I already know why.

Charles's eyes shoot to the toppled stegosaurus, then to me. His grin vanishes. Slowly, his head turns toward Aubrey. Or, more specifically, to the empty pistol that lies next to her hand.

I thumb back the hammer of the five-shooter that's still got one shot left in it.

His eyes fly open and lock onto me, beaded pinpricks of fury. He lets out a blood-curdling roar as he charges.

The small hole that appears squarely in his forehead halts the sound. The leg that was mid-stride completes its motion, but the other doesn't succeed in bringing itself forward to continue his upright propulsion. Instead, his torso lurches forward, arms spasming uselessly at his sides and incapable of breaking his descent. Besides his folding knee, his teeth are the first thing to make contact with the pavement; their hollow crack echoes throughout the warehouse. His neck twists underneath his body, the inertia nearly but not entirely somersaulting his legs and tail above him. He slides to a halt, horn grinding against concrete, scales peeling away from his road-rashed face. The much larger hole on the back of his frill pours forth its liquefied wickedness, the sundered brain matter quickly retreating into any porous home it can find underneath its previous housing.

I stand motionless for what feels like an eternity. A wisp of smoke furtively dances at the tip of the revolver's barrel, captivating me with its insubstantial grace. It vanishes, but I keep my eyes forward. I can't bear to comprehend what I just did. My arm quakes and my grip loosens. The expended piece topples from my hand, coming to rest next to the lifeless body of Charles Rossi.

I... I can't... I didn't...

At once, a wave of panic washes over me and I spin toward Aubrey. My legs barely get me there, nearly giving out as I stumble the few feet it takes me to arrive at her side. I lower myself, pleading with God or anyone who will answer that she's still alive. Pressing my ear to her mouth, I listen.

Breath. She's breathing. It's soft and steady, the same as when she sleeps curled up in my arms. I quickly assess the damage to her head. There's blood, but it appears to be from a small cut underneath her hair. It doesn't even seem to be bleeding anymore. That's my girl. Just please, be okay. You got knocked out, that's all.

Another cough. I turn toward Pierce who once again begins the arduous task of getting to his feet, even more labored than before. I'm awe-struck that he's still operational; even so, he isn't running on anything but fumes. I need to get both of them to a hospital.

I thrust my arms underneath Aubrey, being careful to support her neck as I hoist her up. My own breathing is still in rough shape; my chest is on fire and searing pain flows through my cheek. All the same, I do what needs doing and get my feet underneath me, cradling the unconscious form of my lover. The tip of her bristled tail drags against the ground, just as limp as her other limbs.

A waddle is all I can manage toward the car; Aubrey is a slender woman, but she's still a dinosaur. I curse myself for not spending more time in the gym as I awkwardly shuffle forward, trying desperately not to rip any feathers from her appendage with a clumsy stomp.

A minute later, I arrive next to the Fairlane. Its front

end is abysmal. Both headlights are demolished, the bumper dangles impotently on one side, and the hood is bowed into the shape of a tent. Here's hoping it still runs. I gently slide Aubrey into the passenger seat, taking care to hoist and tuck her tail onto her lap so I don't slam the door on it. With her situated, I circle the car, utter a quick prayer as I take my position, and test the ignition.

It gurgles, churning out a series of annoyed whirs before reluctantly coaxing the engine to life. A sigh of relief escapes me. Disengaging the parking brake, I shift it into first and slowly crawl down the pathway. The front bumper growls, unhappy about its angled arrangement against the road. I can't worry about it right now. We need to get out of here.

Pulling up next to the terminus of our fateful night, I engage the parking brake, daring not to cut the engine at the risk of being unable to bring it to life it again. Pierce is mostly upright, moving slower than ever, but he's shifted to a position directly above Charles's body. He bends over painfully, gritting his teeth as he rummages around in Charles's pockets.

I climb out of the car. "Pierce, we have to go. Come on."

His only response is a quick, annoyed glance before he continues his search.

With a huff, I circle the car. "The cops could be here any minute. There's no way they ain't been called with all the commotion we caused!"

"We have to... do one more thing..." His words are incredibly labored, barely more than a whisper.

"What do we—" He ascends slowly, having found his prize. With a flick of his thumb, Charles's lighter flips open, and with another flick in the opposite direction, its flint ignites the oil-soaked wick housed within. The small flame dances at its tip.

"There's... evidence of us... everywhere. This is... the only way..." His eyelids attempt to close, but he shakes his head, fending off unconsciousness again. He turns remorsefully toward Marty. "I'm sorry. You... deserved better than this..."

I bite my lip. As much as I want to stop him and pull Marty out of here for a proper burial, there's no way in hell that I could manage that. If Pierce goes down before getting into the car, he isn't moving from his spot either.

I'm sorry too, buddy. You were a good man.

Pierce looses the lighter from his fingers. It glides through the air, remaining alight as it travels. Upon landing next to the gasoline-soaked ground, the flame instantly spreads, climbs and grows. It furiously rolls outward and upward, hungrily engulfing the fuel and beginning to chew on the wood.

Pierce steps back, nearly tripping on his own lifeless tail. I dart forward to catch him, keeping him upright with a considerable amount of effort. We both continue until we are clear of the building, free of its lapping flames.

He stares ahead at the unfolding spectacle of destruction. "Marty's gone... Charles is gone..." His breathing is stilted, but he presses on. "It's just... you and me, now..."

I don't reply. Pierce turns away from the inferno and toward me. His dark blue eyes struggle to maintain focus; he clings to consciousness by a thread. However, he asks his question earnestly.

"So are you in... or are you out?"

A wall collapses, bursting glass offering a comparatively pathetic pop against the growling fire. The tin roof peels and buckles, strands of the worthless stuff falling deeper into the belly of the beast. Black smoke rolls upward, melting into the midnight sky above. The entire dock is coated in brilliant orange and red, the roiling flames casting living outlines against the backdrop of street lights and skyscrapers. Even the ocean waves fall silent in obeisance to the majesty of fire, its roar proclaiming victory over man's hubris.

I watch helplessly, next to the only man in the city I can rely on. A man who would have sooner painted the alley walls with my blood than given me a chance only a week ago. Someone who I'm still reluctant to call a friend, but who's offering me an opportunity.

Me... a killer... I've got blood on my hands now, too. Almost in reply to the thought, the wail of sirens in the distance make themselves known. What chance will I have if I try to strike out on my own? If I run away with Aubrey? A life on the run from the cops is no life at all. I can't do that to her, or to us.

I want a chance at life. It isn't gonna be easy, but it's all I've got for now.

"I'm in."

Epilogue: Samuel

"—around the corner, but with how hot summer was you shouldn't be expecting snow anytime soon. That's all for this crisp and cool morning weather report. It's 6 AM and time for another Miles Cratis instant classic, 'Blue in Green'."

A lot of folks say that the sense most closely tied with memory is smell, but I disagree; it's always been sound for me. My dreams give way to bleary consciousness before melting into the memory of that evening at Birdland Nightclub, where a very special, very beautiful woman and I had our first date. We got to hear Miles play this exact song, but more importantly, I got to dance with her, and kiss her for the first time, too. As much as I love this music, I love her even more.

Almost in response to my wordless proclamation, Aubrey tightens her grip on me, arms wrapping around my chest and feathered tail pressing into the flat of my back. She stretches, then nuzzles her snout into the crook of my neck. Her breath dances across my skin. "Mmm… just a few more minutes…" I'm in no rush to turn off the clock radio or deny her request, opting to run my fingers through her hair. She murmurs her approval, squeezing even closer to me.

As the blue strands dance across my fingertips, I recall

that horrid night when I fled from a roaring inferno with two knocked out dinosaurs in my battered Fairlane. Pierce had barely opened the back door before he tipped inward, fully unconscious. I struggled to push his legs and tail in as the sirens grew closer, only just managing to close the door behind him. We peeled out, forcing the angry and tired engine on one last jaunt for the night. I made a beeline for the clinic to which I had previously taken Pierce and Marty, the one under Herdsters jurisdiction. The staff recognized me and didn't ask any questions, quickly wheeling both Pierce and Aubrey into the facility.

As I had surmised, Aubrey was mostly unhurt. She stayed the night at the clinic, just to be sure she didn't have a concussion, and the cut on her head only required a few sutures. Aside from a nasty bruise and some swelling, her knee was okay too. I recall the horror I had felt when I saw the blood seeping into her beautiful blue hair, terrified that I had lost the woman I loved. My fingers trace the now invisible scar and I thank God for not taking her away from me.

As for me, a few of my ribs were indeed cracked. Nothing to do about those but rest and take a shit load of aspirins. The bullet's kiss to my face needed more help. A total of eighteen stitches were required to seal the line drawn from my cheek bone to the top of my neck. The doctor was amazed that I survived it; had the bullet angled inward by another quarter inch, it woulda popped my jugular. God's protection or blind stinking luck, I wasn't gonna complain either way.

Pierce, on the other hand, was in a very bad spot. By the time they got the blood bag attached to him, he was practically flat-lining. The bullet was lodged in his gut something fierce, and the amount of exertion he had expended during our escapades didn't help it any. The doctors pulled the slug out of him, but he didn't wake up for two weeks.

Aubrey's eyes finally open up, clouded by drowsiness but slowly finding their focus. The diamond-shaped pupils resize, surrounded by brilliant yellow irises within which I could lose myself for an eternity. She smiles, then brings her lips to mine. I reciprocate the tender gesture.

A moment later, we part and I speak up. "I'd stay like this with you all morning if I could. But today's the big day."

Her smile fades. "Ah. He's coming back to work, then?"

"Yep, and I'm his ride."

She already knew this, of course. We had agreed to be more transparent with one another after everything that happened. With the hell that occurred on those docks, the bombshell of Aubrey having been married to Pierce's brother seemed like nothing more than a leaf in a windstorm. After she made it home and we were able to move past the initial shock and dread of what had transpired, the topic was bound to come up.

She wasn't keeping anything from me purposefully. The only thing for which I could fault her was saying that she was divorced, when in truth she had filed the paperwork with only one signature on it. Her husband, Francisco Signorelli, had disappeared without a trace. Whether he moved halfway across the country or lay dead in a gutter, Aubrey only knew that she was rid of him, and that was enough for her.

For my part, the mistake I made was not being more forward about my work dealings. I kept myself tight-lipped about what I was doing for the Herdsters, including which branch I worked out of and with whom I was associated. I justified it as keeping Aubrey safe, considering what I knew the Herdsters to be capable of. Her ex-husband also didn't share much about his dealings with her, not even that he was working for the Herdsters to begin with. He was always vague, saying he was doing jobs with his older brother. When Aubrey asked what sort of jobs, he'd hand-wave it, saying she shouldn't question where the money's coming from that's buying nice clothes for her and paying for their mortgage.

She didn't know he worked for the Herdsters, but she knew his brother's name was Pierce. They weren't close, but they had met at the wedding. If I had even done something as simple as telling her Pierce's name, it could have been a massive headache avoided. Sure, he isn't the only fella named Pierce in the city, but there's probably a lot less dark blue stegosaurus Pierce's, so it wouldn't have been a difficult puzzle to piece together.

Neither of us were angry with one another about it, but we agreed that transparency would be best from then on. After all, I was still working for a dangerous and likely criminal operation, and she was nested in a corrupt police department. We'd both need each other, and as much information as we could possibly get, if we had any hopes of making this work.

Aubrey remains thoughtfully still for a moment before she replies. "He isn't still angry about anything, is he?"

I perform the best shrug I can manage from my prone position on a bed with a velociraptor lady laying on top of me. "Truthfully, I didn't talk to him about anything regarding you and me. We got our story straight for those fellas questioning us, and that was it."

She finally releases her grip, allowing both of us to sit up. She massages her knee, a morning ritual with which I'm well acquainted at this point. "Well, go ahead and hop in the shower first. You'll need to head out before me."

I climb off the bed, stretching my back and working my way across the more furnished apartment. Aubrey demanded that I fill in a few missing pieces—a living room set, a television, and her record player, of course—if she was gonna move in. There were no complaints from me, or from my roommate. The walking carpet shimmies up to his feet as he stares past the white fur that overhangs his eyes. He doesn't bark, instead panting happily in my direction.

A quick scratch behind his ears elicits some furious tail wagging. "Good morning, champ. I'll get your breakfast and take you out to potty in a few minutes."

Aubrey speaks up. "I can take care of him while you get your shower, it's no problem."

I turn to her and raise an eyebrow. "You sure? He can be a little stubborn with people who ain't me."

She grins, then claps a hand to her hip. "C'mere, Saxon!"

He bolts across the apartment, skidding to a stop in front of her, tongue joyously flopping from his mouth. I cross my arms. "Yeah, that's all well and good, but—"

She extends a hand, palm facing the floor, and speaks with authority. "Saxon, *sit.*"

He immediately does so.

"Lay down."

He does that too...

"Roll over."

What the actual hell—*when* did she teach him to do all this?! I behold the circus spectacle of animal taming with an agape jaw. The shaggy white dope murmurs out pleased grunts as Aubrey scratches his exposed belly. All I can do is sigh and acquiesce that this woman has done a better job in training my dog in a week than I had in several years.

The grin she shoots me drips with pride. "I did some work with him during that time off I had. Not like I had anything better to do just sitting around here." She pauses. "At least, after... well."

She doesn't have to finish the thought. Neither of us are going to forget that night for a long time. We both stare into space for a moment before I try to break the awkwardness with a smile. "I'll get that shower now. Thanks for taking care of Saxon for me."

I make my way to the bathroom and turn the levers for

the faucet, letting the water heat up since that wretched heat wave had finally broken as of a couple weeks ago. As the shower water gets to an agreeable temperature and I step under its calming downpour, my mind drifts again to that night. The three of us all made it out of there alive... but for two of us, something was taken away that can't be given back. Pierce is a killer; he's done in at least four people, and those are only the ones I know about.

Aubrey and I had never taken a life before.

After she was released from the clinic, I stayed with her at her apartment. Her first night back home was horrible. She couldn't stop shaking; hyperventilation overtook her at the drop of a pin. She kept apologizing, and all I could do was hold her and reassure her that she hadn't done anything wrong. After all, she'd acted in self-defense. She saved my life. If she hadn't done what she did, I wouldn't be there with her.

A few times, the tears gave way to anger. She'd push me away, staring at me as though I was an intruder in her apartment before shouting accusations at me. Blaming me for the entire mess, blaming me for being the worst thing to ever happen to her. Unable to create a reasonable reply, I'd merely apologize and head for the door, only for her to dart across the room and stop me, weeping apologies of her own and begging me to stay.

It was hard... but so was everything that had happened. And she wasn't wrong. She didn't deserve such a burden as the one I'd caused to befall her.

Things didn't start to even out until I admitted to her what I had done. I didn't wait long; I had no intentions of hiding anything from her. When I told her that I was the one who killed Charles, she didn't react at first. Her eyes analyzed my features as she processed the words. I also told her about the pool hall and how the regret I felt for my actions there paled in comparison to this. Back then, it could have been argued that I was defending Pierce, and that it wasn't my hand that killed that baryonyx. At the warehouse, however, nothing stopped me from scooping Aubrey up and dashing away from that place. Charles was strong, but he wasn't fast. Even with Aubrey in my arms I likely could have outran him and left Pierce to his own fate.

But I didn't. I scooped up that revolver and ended a man's life. When I admitted all of this to Aubrey, it was my turn to break down, trembling uncontrollably and trying in vain to push back the tears. She didn't waste another moment before throwing her arms around me and comforting me. She shushed my sobs and apologized for reacting coldly, admitting that she already knew what I had done despite being unconscious during the act. She saw in me the pain she was feeling, even though I didn't say it out loud until then.

We were both changed irrevocably on that horrific night, but as we held each other and unburdened our guilt and sorrow in its aftermath, we knew that we still had each other.

I conclude my shower, toweling off and dressing myself as Aubrey reenters my apartment with a relieved Saxon in tow. He trots across the space and plonks down on his new favorite resting spot, the oval-shaped throw rug resting between the couch and television. Aubrey approaches me. "I got Mr. Garbowitz's paper for him, too."

I place my hands on her hips. "He asked us to call him 'Harold', remember?"

Her arms weave around my back. "You haven't started, why should I?"

I can't mumble out a reply before her lips find mine, tender and serene in their dance. It brings back those same swirling memories from the sidewalk down the street of Birdland Nightclub's front canopy. In the wake of travesty and conflict, under the starlit city sky, she accepted my kiss. Now, after everything we've been through together, I accept hers.

We still have each other.

—

The roadways offer a lot of time to think, doubly so when the trip is extended by a detour out to the suburbs. I've had a lot to think about over the past several weeks. I think about the narrative I have weaved, repeating it over and over in my head to ensure there's not a single loose thread upon which someone could tug to unravel the entire tapestry of half-truths. I'm perfectly open and honest with Aubrey now; as for the Herdsters, they're an entirely different beast.

As I laid in the hospital bed on that horrid night, the doctor passing his needle and thread through the flesh on my face over and over, I was already mentally preparing the story I'd need to tell when I was inevitably asked. Even before Pierce woke up, the questions started rolling in. An awful lot of representatives from an awful lot of different branches in the Herdsters were very interested in my retelling of events.

All I could do was turn Charles's machinations in on themselves, crafting the scenario into one where Pierce, Marty and I were suspicious of the Herdster boss's foul play. When we discovered his scheme to torch the warehouse and a bunch of evidence of his misdeeds, we chased him down, colliding with the squad car at the nearby phone booth. The story played out mostly the same as what actually happened, save for replacing Aubrey with Marty in the passenger seat and giving him credit for gunning down both Preston and Charles before succumbing to his own wounds. We didn't have time to stop the fire that Charles had started, or to pull Marty's body from the burning building.

It's a sad replacement for a proper funeral, but at least the fiction gave Marty a more honorable end than he really got.

The inquisitors seemed content with this story. Of course, I had to retell it about a half dozen times to a half dozen different pairs of investigating officials. None of them were police, only higher ranking Herdsters who needed the full story. They were incredibly tight-lipped about most things when I tried to ask them questions, but I did gather that the notion of Charles being dirty wasn't a massive surprise to them, nor was his gun-running or involvement with the Old York Police Department.

As for Aubrey, I had a cover story for her, too. Hand-waved her as being a private investigator that I hired to monitor Charles, and who was going to gather photographic evidence of his wrongdoings to back us up. Of course, the camera was lost in the fire, and her injury was due to being discovered and attacked by Charles. She had come to and was discharged from the clinic before the investigators started turning up.

There was only one loose thread left. I scoured the newspapers, finding a brief article about the warehouse fire in Friday's morning edition, but absolutely nothing about the dead cop or two dead Herdsters. It seemed that the police captain was pulling double duty to cover everything up. By the time Aubrey returned to work, everyone acted like it was business as usual, as though Officer Preston never worked for them at all. Hell, from what she told me, Duffy even got himself a new partner and carried on like nothing changed.

If the corruption flows that deep... I don't know that anything can be done to salvage it.

I just hope Aubrey can stay safe. She's in the dragon's den again, keeping her head low and doing her paperwork without ruffling any scales. I tried to talk her out of going back, but she refused. I knew she would—that's the kind of woman she is. She believes that it's right to stay where she is and try to make a difference. She insists that there still might be some way to expose the captain, but that her chances of finding anything incriminating will reduce to zero if she quits.

Even so, there's no getting around the fact that she went to the captain with information about that event at the warehouse, an event that went completely tits-up for whatever criminal enterprising he was doing. Even if he doesn't know that Aubrey was directly involved, he might connect the dots and try to come after her for something if he suspects her in some way.

We'll cross that bridge when we get there, I guess. No matter what, I'm gonna stay by her side.

I pull to a stop in front of a home upon which I'd never laid eyes before today. I check the address scrawled in my untidy handwriting again, glancing up at the house to ensure it's the right place. With a self-reassuring nod, I shut off the engine and exit my car. The two-story structure is extravagant in comparison to what I'm used to. Massive bay windows overlook its handsome yard, and the front door is well over nine feet tall. I take a breath before knocking on the wooden obelisk.

A moment later, it swings open. The stegosaurus woman on the other side greets me. "Good morning, Samuel. Please, come in."

"Thank you, ma'am." I remove my cap as I step through the threshold.

"Oh, stop that. I told you to call me Bianca." Her welcoming smile puts me at ease. "Besides, I'm not *that* much older than you."

"Y-yeah. Sorry about that. Force of habit." I feel my cheeks redden.

She titters. "Go ahead and have a seat in the living room. Pierce should be ready in a few minutes." She makes her way toward the kitchen. "Did you want a cup of coffee while you wait?"

"Sure, that'd be nice. Thank you." I do as she asks and

gingerly place myself on the living room couch, gazing around like a paleontologist in a museum of antiquity. I knew Pierce was doing well for himself, but this feels like a damn mansion. The gargantuan 21 inch television presents my reflection back to me via its darkened screen. The decorations on the walls and end tables offer a portrait of a modern upper-middle-class family, one in which the matriarch clearly has exceptional tastes.

I got to meet Pierce's wife and both of their kids when I came to visit him at the hospital one day. Russell and Angela were a hoot, friendly and energetic and excited for their dad to wake up. They were practically bouncing off the walls with the idea of going to the beach "again"... I could only assume they had gone recently. And it certainly wasn't Bianca who put the idea in their heads; she tried to talk them down from the notion, but they wouldn't relent. With a sigh, she gave up and let them enjoy their flights of fancy. The oppressive late August heat had finally died down and given way to cooler September skies, but there might still be a few weeks of good beach weather left for them.

Bianca was pleasant with me, but very direct. The moment her children weren't within earshot, she demanded to know what happened. For consistency's sake, I gave her the same story I had given the Herdsters. As it painted her bed-ridden husband in an honorable light, she didn't protest, but I had the feeling she could tell that I wasn't being entirely truthful. However, having another person at the ready to coach Pierce on what to tell any investigating officials upon his awakening was a good thing in my book.

Truthfully, that was the reason I was visiting as often as I was. If Pierce made a full recovery or if he remained comatose for years, neither would have made a tremendous difference to me. I still had my doubts as to whether he was someone that could be fully trusted. Sure, he proved himself a mostly honest man, but his seething hatred for humans wasn't about to go away overnight. The two of us endured a hell of a tribulation together; even so, I felt like I'd still have to walk on eggshells around him if I didn't want to risk being disposed of.

Bianca circles the couch, placing a saucer and cup on the rustic table between us. The tendril of steam that rises from it relaxes me. "It smells delicious. Thank you."

She smiles, settling into the armchair across from me with her own cup in hand. "I'm not a bad cook, but coffee isn't my specialty. Pierce never cared much for it, so I'm afraid it's just the canned stuff."

"That's okay with me." I take up the gift and enjoy the aroma before sipping at it. Canned or not, that's a damn good cup of joe.

The air is silent between us for only a moment before she speaks again. "Thank you for offering to drive Pierce. It's been a tough recovery period, but he's anxious to get back to work." She fidgets. "I just… didn't want him driving himself with the painkillers the doctors have him on."

"Hey, it's no problem. I'm happy he's in working shape again." I bite my lip, stopping myself from making a comment about how I didn't even expect him to still be alive, let alone having recovered enough to be coming back to the office in only a month. Instead, I offer a shrug. "Things have been a bit slow. They got me pulling routes with a floater, some fella named Barry. He's okay."

Bianca smiles politely, but she casts her eyes down. Neither of us bring up Marty. He was my friend, but he was an even closer friend with Pierce and Bianca. His wife had their baby three weeks ago, a boy who will grow up never knowing his father.

The brief awkward air is cut by two sets of rapidly descending footsteps, fast enough to be mistaken for machine gun fire. Bianca turns toward the commotion. "Slow down on those stairs, you'll break your necks!"

"Sorry, mom!"

"Okay."

The sources of the young voices pause for only a moment to size me up before darting past and toward the kitchen.

"Be ready for school in ten minutes!" Another set of muffled affirmatives past the clatter of cereal falling into bowls acknowledges Bianca's command. She sighs. "Sorry about them."

"Hey, no problem! I ain't a parent but I get that they can be a handful sometimes."

"Oh? Well, are you married?" She asks past the rim of her coffee cup.

"No—well, I *was,* but right now I just got a girlfriend."

Her only reply is a muted "Hmm." I take another sip of my own caffeinated delight, puzzling over whether Pierce had said anything about Aubrey or not to her. If he has, Bianca's keeping a tight leash on that knowledge. If not... it makes me wonder *why* he wouldn't have.

Before I can ponder it too deeply, a slower, heavier set of footsteps descend. I glance at the stairwell, watching a familiar pin-stripe suit containing a familiar midnight blue stegosaurus find the landing. He slowly ducks his head underneath the rim of the second floor before glancing in our direction. All things considered, he looks good, even if his movements are more rigid than normal. His gaze turns from his wife to me, offering only a small grunt and a nod in acknowledgment of my presence.

Bianca sets her cup and saucer down as she stands. "Do you have everything you need, honey?"

Another grunt.

"You have all your medication, your keys, your—"

"Yes, yes. I have everything. Don't treat me like a child." Even though there's a veneer of annoyance, I sense no actual anger in his voice. He turns to me. "Let's go."

As I pull myself away from the comfortable couch,

Bianca crosses the room and embraces Pierce. She plants a kiss on his snout; I avert my gaze, not wanting to be an awkward human staring at a stegosaurus wife wishing her husband a good day. A moment later, we both traverse the scenic pathway extending to the short drive that holds my restored Fairlane and its fresh coat of blue paint.

He pauses for a moment, revering the sight. "Is this the same car?"

I grin. "Yep. Took almost a hundred bucks to get it fixed up and repainted, but it looks good as new, don't you think?"

He frowns in response. "I woulda dumped it into the sea, myself. It could have incriminated both of us."

"O-oh..." My smile fades rapidly, and I climb behind the wheel without another prideful word. Pierce lowers himself into the passenger seat, moving slowly and deliberately, letting out a wince as he straightens his back. I fire up the engine and pull out of the driveway before asking, "How are you getting along? Y'know... are things healing up okay?"

He doesn't look at me. "I'm in a tremendous amount of pain."

I gulp. Maybe I expected a bit too much in thinking that us surviving an ordeal like we did would lend to easier conversation.

The majority of the drive is silent and awkward. I consider turning on the radio, but think better of it. Instead, I watch the peppered buildings slowly grow wider, taller and more industrial as we approach the city. The bustle of street cars and well-dressed individuals going about their Monday morning fare breathe life into the stoic structures that surround us. Traffic thickens, not becoming unbearable but forcing a few unexpected slowdowns. If the newspapers are right, continued growth like Old York is experiencing will mean practically unusable streets in twenty years instead of the occasional rush hour traffic jam.

But that's a problem for down the road. For now, I enjoy the relative peace and ease of the journey.

A few minutes away from work, Pierce finally clears his throat. He turns my way before lackadaisically gesturing toward my cheek. "Looks like that isn't going away."

Without thought, I trace the line with my hand. The groove in my flesh is healed, the stitches long gone, but the mark remains, and probably always will. "Some of those serials I listen to have a fella with a scar on his face. It either makes him cooler, or more intimidating." I glance at Pierce. "I dunno if it does either for me."

He shrugs. "You're asking the wrong guy. It just makes you even uglier than you were."

I blink, unsure if that was an attempt at a joke or just a nasty jab. I clumsily fill the void. "Aubrey hasn't complained about it, I guess."

At this, Pierce merely turns away, gazing out the same window with which he entertained himself for the past fifteen minutes. That was probably a stupid move on my part. He and I haven't discussed Aubrey whatsoever, not since the two of them fought one another. We formed a tenuous peace in the mutual goal of trying to stop Charles, but I've got no clue how to proceed now.

Aubrey, Pierce, and me... an awkward trinity of crossed soul threads. I find myself wishing yet again that things were just a little simpler. A beautiful woman in my arms, a normal job that affords us a home, and a life that isn't filled with danger, duplicity and death. Why is that so much to ask?

The front of my Fairlane rocks upward as the wheels ascend the slanted curb granting us entry to the employee parking lot. It loops behind the building and travels underneath the structure; I find my usual parking spot and settle the car in for at least a temporary rest before taking it out again to do my rounds.

As we climb out of the vehicle, Pierce speaks up. "How have things been here in my absence?"

"Not too bad, I guess. They paired me up with Barry since you were out."

He scoffs. "Barry's a moron." I don't reply, but I'm not inclined to disagree. Barry is friendly, but also comes across as being a few grapes short of a bushel. "Anything else eventful?"

We make our way toward the door, passing through the employee entrance and down the familiar hallway. "Not too much. A new person transferred in to... to take *Charles's* place." I lower my voice when saying his name. "She seems nice so far."

"Oh?" We turn the corner.

"Yeah, she's a stegosaurus like—"

Pierce freezes. His eyes widen and his hands ball into fists. I cock an eyebrow at his sudden halt before following his gaze. At the end of the hall, a greenish-blue stegosaurus woman in a form-fitting turquoise dress-suit hands a paper to one of our secretaries. She smiles and bids the other woman a fond good morning before turning our way. Her dark blue eyes light up and her lipstick parts in a wide grin.

"Ah, good morning, Sammy!"

She strides across the hall, planting one high-heeled foot in front of the other in a graceful display of balance and elegance.

It isn't until the two of them are in close proximity that my foolish human eyes recognize the resemblance.

Pierce grits his teeth and growls. "Aurora... what are you—"

Her disarming smile does not falter, but her eyes flash at him. Her emphasis oozes with saccharine insincerity.

"And good morning to you, too, *big brother.*"

Acknowledgment

A little over two years ago, I got my start by writing fanfiction for a game that meant a lot to me. Even though it was my first effort, it was incredibly well received and gave me the motivation to try my hand at a more serious stand-alone story. This book wouldn't be in your hands if it weren't for the support of my friends and family:

My dad for offering a bunch of information about police procedure and firearms.

My beta readers for offering constructive criticism and helping me improve the final draft, including Rachel W., Andy M., Zach D., Daisii B., Jude K., Tracy and Chad G., and Rachel A.

My friends Albert "Mike" M. and Rachel M. for being very supportive and encouraging through the entire process.

All of my friends in the Snoot space, too many to list but your support has been incredible. Thank you!